KERI ARTHUR

D0042156

*Darkness hides the
most delicious pleasures—
and the deadliest dangers....*

EMBRACED
BY DARKNESS

AUTHOR OF *DANGEROUS GAMES*

READ ALL OF THE STEAMY, ACTION-PACKED RILEY JENSON ROMANCES FROM MASTER STORYTELLER KERI ARTHUR!

FULL MOON RISING
January 2007

KISSING SIN
February 2007

TEMPTING EVIL
March 2007

Dell

DANGEROUS GAMES
April 2007

And coming in spring 2008

DESTINY KILLS

9 780553 589610

ISBN 978-0-553-58961-0

US $6.99/ $8.99 CAN

50699

From Dell

From one of the hottest new voices in paranormal romance comes a provocative new series that will plunge readers into a world where vampires stalk the night and werewolves succumb to the tides of their desires with every full moon.

Meet Riley Jenson, a heroine unlike any other: a gorgeous werewolf with a touch of vampire in her blood. Each book will bring Riley face-to-face with some of the sexiest men in recent fiction—and launch her into a world of peril and pleasure that will leave readers panting for the next installment!

EMBRACED BY DARKNESS

races from a secluded island of white beaches and hot-blooded newlyweds to an erotic dance club in the darkest corner of a city. On the hunt for a ruthless serial killer, Riley Jenson must choose: between Kellen, a perfect lover whose only fault is that he wants her full-time, and the kind of freedom that quickens Riley's blood—or might get her killed....

hunter....Fans of Anita Blake and Charlaine Harris' Sookie Stackhouse vampire series will be rewarded."
—*Publishers Weekly*

"Fun and feisty...[An] effective crossbreeding of romance and urban fantasy that should please fans of either genre." —*Kirkus Reviews*

"Well-done and entertaining." —*Sunday Oklahoman*

"A sexy and fast-paced novel aimed at the mature reader...The author excels at showing not just characters, but how they interact as a society....This is not a novel where characters have sex and that's that; there are consequences and drawbacks to being a member of a race that simply can't deny sexual urges at certain times of the month. It may sound like great fun, but Arthur doesn't shy from the logical result of such behavior."
—*Davis Enterprise*

"Sexy and exhilarating, with characters that revel in their sexuality and take it any time and any way they can get it...Provocative and edgy, with enough heat to scorch the paper it's written on. It's a pleasure to see that within a genre that is getting crowded with uninspired and repetitive stories, it is still possible for this author to create a unique and very strong heroine. For those who like Anita and Elena, the kick-ass and sensual Riley is worth a loud and satisfied howl....A series to keep its readers hooked emotionally and sexually." —ARomanceReview.com

"Arthur creates a shadowy and believable world where werewolves, vampires and other supernatural creatures co-exist with humans, and where Riley and her kind are held hostage by the monthly lunar cycles....Arthur also cooks up a nicely paced *cloning* plot that Riley has barely begun to unravel by story's end—leaving the door wide open for all kinds of possibilities. *Full Moon Rising* definitely grabs the attention and Keri Arthur is an author to watch." —BookLoons.com

"Unbridled lust and kick-ass action are the hallmarks of this first novel in a brand-new paranormal series.... 'Sizzling' is the only word to describe this heated, action-filled, suspenseful romantic drama [which] keeps readers on their toes in constant suspense....Breathtakingly scorching, *Full Moon Rising* sets a high bar for what is now a much-anticipated new series." —CurledUp.com

"Keri Arthur has done a wonderful job with *Full Moon Rising*. It's a great story that's suspenseful, has hot were-wolves, sexy vampires, a huge amount of butt kickin', and no-holds-barred sex. If you like a twist to your paranormal romance, you'll love this book" —FreshFiction.com

"An enjoyable paranormal with romantic elements and an exciting, action-packed plot. *Full Moon Rising* is a gripping tale which grabbed my attention from the very beginning and didn't let up until the very end....I highly recommend *Full Moon Rising* to paranormal readers." —ParaNormalRomanceReviews.com

"Grade A, desert island keeper...I wanted to read this book in one sitting, and was terribly offended that the real world intruded on my reading time!...Inevitable comparisons can be made to Anita Blake, Kim Harrison, and Kelley Armstrong's books, but I think Ms. Arthur has a clear voice of her own and her characters speak for themselves....I am hooked!" —AllAboutRomance.com

Embraced by Darkness

KERI ARTHUR

A DELL BOOK

EMBRACED BY DARKNESS
A Dell Spectra Book / August 2007

Published by
Bantam Dell
A Division of Random House, Inc.
New York, New York

This is a work of fiction. Names, characters, places, and incidents either
are the product of the author's imagination or are used fictitiously.
Any resemblance to actual persons, living or dead, events, or locales
is entirely coincidental.

Dell, the colophon, Spectra, and the portrayal of a boxed "s"
are trademarks of Random House, Inc.

ISBN 978-0-553-58961-0

Printed in the United States of America
Published simultaneously in Canada

www.bantamdell.com

OPM 10 9 8 7 6 5 4 3 2 1

I'd like to thank :

everyone at Bantam who made this book look so
good—most especially my editor, Anne,
her assistant Josh, Jae Song, the wonderful artist
responsible for my last few covers, and
finally my line editors, who make sense
of all my Aussie-English.

A special thanks to my agent Miriam,
and my ever-supportive family.

Embraced by Darkness

Chapter 1

The only trouble with getting away from it all was actually getting away from it all.

Six weeks of lazing around on secluded and luxurious Monitor Island, with nothing to do except eat, drink, and lust after the occasional hot-bod sounded like heaven itself. And it was.

For the first three weeks.

But now, with the fifth week done and dusted, the wolf within hungered for the company of my own kind. Werewolves are not, by nature, solitary souls. We tend to live in packs just as much as our animal counterparts.

My pack might now only consist of my twin brother Rhoan, his lover Liander, and my lover Kellen, but I was missing them all something fierce.

Especially Kellen. He'd been here for the first three weeks, and the result had been a deepening and strengthening of our relationship. I might be totally capable of looking after myself, but it was an absolutely delicious sensation to have such a big strong wolf wanting to take care of me. In some ways, he reminded me of an ex. Talon might have been as crazy as a March hare, but he'd also been a wolf who knew what he wanted, and who went to great lengths to get it. Kellen was built in that mode, but he was far more caring than Talon ever could have been. Add to that the fact he was a great lover, and you had an overall package that was nigh on irresistible. At least to *this* wolf.

Even so, I hadn't really expected to miss him *this* much. Not after only a couple of months of being together—and especially considering we'd probably spent more time apart than together in those months. Of course, I knew now that a lot of that separation was due to Quinn, the enigmatic vampire who swore his feelings for me ran deep—even as he used me to achieve his aims of killing the people who had destroyed his lifelong friend and creator. Even now, despite the feelings I had for Kellen, part of me still hungered to be with Quinn. Would probably *always* hunger to be with him.

Because I had a connection with Quinn that I'd never found with any other man. Not even Kellen.

But Quinn was out of my life for the moment—maybe even permanently—and I couldn't really regret that. I'd never condoned force in *any* relationship, and that's basically what Quinn had done when he'd used his vampire wiles to curb my nature. His methods might have been psychic rather than physical, but in the end, it was the same thing. *Anything* that forced someone down a path they would not otherwise have taken was abuse, no matter how prettily the situation was wrapped.

What I needed to do was forget him. Just get on with my life, and stop remembering he was ever part of it. Even if the very thought made my soul weep.

But the last two weeks alone had left me with nothing to do except think about the people in my life and the events of the last ten months. In fact, all that I was supposedly here to forget.

I rubbed a hand across tired eyes, then leaned my forearms on the balustrade of the small patio lining the front of my pretty little villa unit.

The breeze coming off the sea was cool, teasing my short hair and sending goose bumps fleeing across my bare flesh. I briefly thought about going inside to grab a shirt, but in the end, I couldn't be bothered.

I let my gaze roam across the waves, watching the foam hiss over the white sand. It was a peaceful sound, as peaceful as the night itself, which made me wonder what the hell had woken me in the first place.

Certainly there was little noise coming from any of the other villas that lined this half-moon section of beach. Not even the newlyweds were stirring, and they'd been at it nonstop since their arrival five days ago.

And they thought *werewolves* had stamina.

I smiled and plucked a leaf from the nearby eucalyptus branch that draped over the railing, then flicked the leaf skyward from the stem, watching it twirl all the way to the ground.

What I wanted was to go home. To get on with my life and my job. To spend more time with Kellen. But I had just under a week of vacation left, and while I might be going slowly insane with boredom, I couldn't just pack up and leave. Rhoan and Liander had given me this holiday as a gift to help me rest and recuperate, and I couldn't—wouldn't—hurt their feelings by returning before my time was up.

"Riley."

My name whispered across the wind—a demand rather than a mere attempt to get my attention.

I straightened quickly, my gaze searching the moonlit night for some sign of the caller. Some hint of where the voice had come from.

A difficult task when it seemed to come from everywhere and yet nowhere at once.

"Riley."

Again the voice rode the night, stronger than before, and clearly male in its resonance.

It wasn't a voice that belonged to any of the men who inhabited the five other villas in this small cove. Nor did it belong to any of the staff members who looked after the villas or who worked in the main resort complex one beach over.

But there were three other accommodations scattered across the island, and I hadn't really had much to do with their guests or employees. But even if it *had* been one of them, why would they know my name? And why would they be calling me in the dead of the night?

It was odd—and the mere thought of something odd occurring had excitement racing through my veins.

Which was a rather sad statement about just how bored I was. Or perhaps how addicted I'd become to the adrenaline rush of being a guardian. Hell, I'd give away the killing any day, but not the thrill of the chase. The hunt was everything to a wolf, and no matter how long I might have denied it, I was a hunter—every bit as much as my brother.

I studied the night for a moment longer. The wind whispered through the trees, void of any voice but its own. I could sense nothing and no one near, and yet something *was*. The electric charge of awareness raced across my skin, making the small hairs on my arms stand on end.

I spun on my heel and walked back into my room. I didn't mind walking around sans clothes, but most of the guests currently on the island were human, and humans tended to get a little antsy about the whole naked thing.

Though up here in Queensland, that attitude was a whole lot less noticeable than down in Victoria. Of course, the weather in my home state often precluded the desire to strip down, simply because the weather was about as predictable as a tiger snake during mating season.

I pulled on a low-cut T-shirt and a baggy pair of shorts, then returned to the patio.

"Riley, come."

The voice swirled around me, rich and arrogant. A man who used—and probably abused—power. And my wolf soul reacted to the command in that voice, but not in the way I expected. Not fiercely, with anger, but meekly. As if she wanted to do nothing more than tuck her tail between her legs and cower.

And there could be only one reason for *that*.

The voice belonged to a pack member. And not just any pack member, but the alpha. The wolf who ruled the pack as a whole.

Only the voice didn't belong to *my* alpha, the man who had ruled the pack for as long as anyone could remember. I would have recognized the voice of my own grandfather.

So what the hell was going on?

Frowning, I walked down the steps then strode through the trees and out onto the moonlit sand. The wind was sharper out from under the cover of the eucalyptus, and filled with the scent of the sea.

And nothing else. No musky male scent, no hint of wolf. Nothing to suggest there was another soul awake and aware out here on the beach.

A shiver ran down my spine. Maybe I was imagining it. Maybe this was nothing more than a dream, and any minute now I'd wake up and laugh at my own stupidity.

After all, our pack had threatened to kill us both if we ever contacted—let alone went near—any pack members. And not even our mother had dared to contradict that particular order.

Not that I thought she'd tried. Though I had no doubt she loved us, she'd always seemed as relieved as the rest of the pack to see the back of us.

"Riley, come."

Again the order ran across the night, stronger than before. I closed my eyes, concentrating on the sound, and tried to define just where the voice was coming from.

After a moment, I turned around and padded up the beach. The villas gave way to thicker strands of eucalyptus and acacia trees, the strong scents filling the night.

It didn't matter. I wasn't relying on my olfactory senses to track this particular trail, but rather my "other" senses. The senses that were new and somewhat unreliable.

The part of me that could see souls rise.

Of course, seeing—and hearing—the souls of dead

people wasn't a gift I particularly wanted. Hell, I had enough trouble dealing with the *living* dead without having to worry about the actual dead popping along anytime they pleased.

But as was often the case in my life of late, it seemed I had little choice in the matter. The experimental fertility drug I'd been forcibly given by Talon had not only kick-started some latent psychic abilities, but had given them a little twist, just for the fun of it. Clairvoyance had been one of those latent skills—until recently, anyway. Seeing dead people walk through the shadows was the not-so-tempting twist.

And I was hoping like hell it was the *only* twist the drug caused. I didn't want to be like the other half-breeds who'd taken the drug. I didn't want to gain the ability to shift into any animal or bird form I chose, simply because while such an ability might be a buzz, it came at a price. Every one of the others had lost their ability to retake human form. I might love being a wolf, but I didn't want to spend the rest of my life in that shape. Or any other shape, for that matter.

Seeing dead people wasn't *that* bad by comparison. And until tonight, the dead hadn't contacted me long range. I'd only seen them close to their bodies. Well, mostly, I thought, shivering as I remembered the lingering, insubstantial wisps in Starr's bloody arena.

Not that I was entirely sure I was hearing the dead now, but it just seemed odd I couldn't see or smell anyone else. My senses were wolf-sharp. If someone had been close, I would have known.

I padded along the white sand until I reached the peninsula rocks. The wind here was sharper, the sea rougher, slapping across those rocks and sending white foam flicking skyward. The tide was up, so I'd be getting wet if the voice wanted me to clamber around to the next cove.

I stopped and scanned the horizon. This section of the main island was closest to Lighthouse Island, the larger of the two small islands that sat within swimming distance of Monitor. It housed the Monitor Island Research Center, a joint government and private concern that was investigating the sea life and the reefs. I'd done the tour last week, and had been bored to tears. Sure, reefs were pretty. So were the myriad of fish that lived amongst them. And we surely had to know why they were all disappearing. But hey, I just couldn't get all worked up about the science. Wolves are hunters by nature, not conservationists. We usually haven't the patience for occupations that involve long hours of inactivity.

Awareness tingled across my skin, as sharp as needle stings. Whoever the voice belonged to, he was close.

"Riley, turn around."

For the first time, memories stirred. I'd known that voice in the past. I turned and studied the trees.

A man stood amongst them. Though at first glance he appeared solid, a more careful study revealed an almost gossamer look to his hands and feet. As if, by the time he got to his extremities, he didn't have the strength to maintain the illusion of substance.

He was a tall man, rangy in build, with strong arms and blunt features. Not attractive, not ugly, but somewhere in between. But even if he'd been the ugliest spud on the planet, it wouldn't have mattered, because the sense of authority and power that shone from his gray eyes was all that would ever matter to a wolf.

And *this* wolf wanted to hunker down before it.

But I wasn't just wolf, and the other half of my

soul bared its teeth and got ready for a fight. I locked my knees and skimmed my gaze up to his hair. Thick and red. Definitely red pack. Definitely *my* red pack. But who?

As I dropped my gaze to his, recognition stirred again. I knew those eyes, knew the cold superiority behind them. But I'd be damned if I could dredge up a name.

"Why are you calling me?"

Though the question was soft, my voice seemed to echo across the silent night. A tremor ran down my spine, and I wasn't sure whether it was due to the chill wind hitting my bare arms and legs or the sudden sense of trepidation creeping through my soul.

Amusement sparked briefly in the translucent gray depths. "You do not remember me?"

"Should I have any reason to remember you?"

This time, the amusement reached his thin lips. "I would think you'd remember the wolf who threw you off a mountainside."

Shock rolled through me. Oh my God . . .

Blake.

My grandfather's second-in-command, and the wolf who would have killed both Rhoan and me if he could. The wolf who almost *had* when he'd thrown me off that cliff. Ostensibly to teach Rhoan a lesson about never back-talking the pack second.

Hate followed the shock, swirling thick and sharp. I clenched my fists, and found myself fighting the sudden urge to punch the cold amusement from his lips. But he wasn't here, he wasn't real, and I'd only look like a fool. So I simply said, voice low and venomous, "What right have *you* got to call *me*?"

"My right is pack-given."

"The Jenson pack ceded its rights over me and Rhoan when they kicked us out."

"Pack rights are never surrendered, no matter what the situation. Once a pack member, always a pack member."

"*You* threatened to kill us if you ever saw us again."

"A statement that still stands."

"So why the *hell* are you contacting me? Fuck off and leave me alone. Trust me, I want as little to do with you as you with me."

I turned on my heel and began to walk back down the beach. Part of me might have been curious as to why he was contacting me, but curiosity didn't have a hope against old anger and hurt. None of which I wanted to relive in *any* way.

"You will listen to what I have to say, Riley."

"Fuck off," I said, without looking at him. Even as my wolf cowered deep within at my audacity.

"You *will* stop and listen, young wolf."

His voice was sharp and powerful, seeming to echo through the trees. I stopped. I couldn't help it. My very DNA was patterned with the need to obey my alpha. It would take a great deal of strength to disobey and, right now, it seemed I had none.

Even so, I didn't turn around. Didn't look at him. "Why the hell should I listen?"

"Because I demand it."

I snorted softly. "I was never one to listen to demands. You of all people should know that."

"So very true. And it *was* one of the reasons you and your brother were ostracized." Amusement laced his harsh tones. "Your grandfather feared one of you would challenge him."

Surprise rippled through me and I swung around.

He was still in the trees, still in the shadows. Maybe afraid that the wind from the beach would blow him away. "Why would my grandfather fear that? Neither Rhoan nor I was allowed the illusion we were anything more than an inconvenience to our mother and the pack. And inconveniences don't rule." Especially if they were female. Or gay.

"You have a long pattern of doing the unexpected, Riley."

"Yeah, and I have the scars to prove the foolishness of that."

He chuckled softly. "You never did learn your place."

Oh, I learned it all right. I just didn't always cower down like I was supposed to. I thrust my hands on my hips and said impatiently, "As much as I adore reliving old times, it's fucking cold out. Tell me what you want, or piss off."

He studied me for a minute, gray eyes abnormally bright in the darkness, his form waving slightly as the wind swirled through the trees.

"The pack needs your help."

"*My* help?" My sudden, unbelieving laugh had a cold, ugly sound. "That has to be the joke of the century."

"There is nothing amusing about the situation, believe me."

"So why me? There have to be hundreds of other people you could ask."

Which *wasn't* an overstatement. The Jenson pack might be one of the smaller red packs, and it might be the poorer cousin when it came to wealth and land status, but Jenson pack members were to be found in all avenues of government and throughout much of the legal system. I had no doubt those pack members could muster up something—someone—far more influential than me.

Unless, of course, the crisis was of a more personal nature. Despite everything, anxiety pulsed, and I added quickly, "Is Mother all right?"

Blake's smile was thin. "Yes. She sends her love."

Like hell she did. We were her firstborn and her love for us was unquestioned, but once we'd left the pack, contact ceased. Blake might have had pack approval to contact me, but I very much doubted she would have asked for any message to be delivered. She knew how we felt about him. She wouldn't hurt us that way.

"You can't sucker me with that sort of shit, Blake. Just get to the point."

Amusement flared briefly in his eyes. "We have need of your guardian skills."

Again, surprise rippled through me. "How would you know I was a guardian? And why would you bother keeping track of two outcast and useless pups?"

"We didn't. It came to my attention during our investigations."

"Investigations into what?"

He shifted his weight and his form wavered briefly, becoming as insubstantial as a ghost. Which he wasn't, so how in the hell was he projecting himself?

"One of my granddaughters disappeared four days ago."

He had granddaughters? Good Lord, that made me feel old. Though in wolf terms, I was still very much a youngster. "Which of your sons was careless enough to lose a daughter?"

It was a cruel thing to say, but I just couldn't help

myself. Blake and his sons had been the banes of our existence growing up—and the reason behind many of the scars Rhoan and I now bore. Of course, if I'd just shut my mouth and bowed down like I was supposed to, things might have been different.

Though I very much doubt it.

His gaze narrowed to thin slits of dangerous gray. "Adrienne is Patrin's oldest."

The image of a red wolf with black points came to mind, and my lip curled in response. Patrin was the youngest of Blake's get—only a few years older than Rhoan and me. To say he delighted in following the family tradition of hassling the half-breeds would be the understatement of the century.

"How old is the daughter?"

"Twenty-three."

Twenty-three? Meaning he'd been fifteen when he'd sired his first? Randy bastard. I bet Daddy had been *so* proud—especially given the pack's inherent fertility problems.

"If she's missing, contact the police. The Directorate doesn't do missing."

"You do if there appears to be a pattern to the disappearances. And three others have disappeared the same way as Adrienne, Riley."

I crossed my arms and tried to ignore the pulse of interest. I didn't want to get involved with Blake or our pack, because it could only end badly—for me, if not for them. "Still no reason for the Directorate to get involved. There are special police units for such things. I'm sure you've got contacts that could give you special consideration."

"Something *bad* has happened to her. Patrin's desperate to find her."

It was on my lips to say something smart—something along the lines of *like I'm supposed to care?*—but I held back. I understood such desperation, knew it could force you to do anything—including contact an outcast. I'd felt it whenever Rhoan got into trouble, and I wouldn't wish it on anyone. Not even someone I hated.

"Then contact the Directorate. Give them the information. There's nothing I can do without the official go-ahead anyway."

Which was only a teensy lie. If I was so inclined, I could investigate just about anything. Guardians were the super-cops—the hunter-killers—of the nonhuman world, and we had free rein to investigate whatever we wanted. Though if I *did* investigate, and *did* find something, I'd have to report it back to my boss. And full investigation could only go ahead with his official approval.

"All I'm asking you to do is an initial investigation. If you feel there's nothing the Directorate can do, then I'll try other sources."

He sounded altogether too reasonable, and my hackles rose. Blake and reason just didn't go together—at least according to my memories of the man. "You were ordering me a few moments ago."

"Perhaps I'm seeing the error of my ways."

"And perhaps tomorrow they'll put a woman on Mars." I shifted from one foot to the other. I wasn't trusting this new and improved Blake any more than the last one, but it couldn't hurt to play along. "Why do you think her disappearance is a Directorate matter?"

"Besides Patrin's feeling she's in mortal danger, you mean?"

"Yes."

"There's a pattern, as I said."

Annoyance swirled through me. "So tell me the pattern."

"For a start, they all vacationed at Monitor Island."

Is that why he'd contacted me? He'd been investigating the island and discovered my presence? It'd be my luck, that was for sure. "And?"

"And they all disappeared within a week of returning home from the island."

"Meaning the island might not be the connector."

"Then there's the man."

"Human or nonhuman man?"

"Human. He works on the island, apparently."

Which wasn't much of a clue, considering over half the people working on the island were males of the human variety. "What as?"

Blake shrugged, and the movement made his image shimmer. "Adrienne said he worked as a bartender."

"Blake, there's at least five bars in this cove alone. It'd be nice if you could pin it down a little."

"I believe his name might be Jim Denton."

"So she danced with this Jim Denton?"

He hesitated and annoyance flashed in his eyes. "I believe so."

I restrained a sudden smile. So Adrienne wasn't telling Daddy and Granddaddy everything. Good for her. Though I *was* surprised she'd gone against pack law and danced with a human. But maybe that was the whole point. "And the others?"

"I've talked to one other family. They also mentioned their daughter meeting a man who worked on the island."

"Meeting? What about bedding?"

"That I can't say. But probably."

"And the women were all wolves?"

He nodded.

Well, we werewolves did tend to get around—although I did find it surprising they'd bed the human males over the nonhuman. There were too many inherent risks in that sort of choice—although the mere fact that wolf-human half-breeds existed suggested there were plenty who didn't agree with my point of view.

"That doesn't mean they bedded the same man," I said. "As I've already said, there's more than one male working on this island."

"His description matches the one I have from Adrienne."

So, Adrienne wouldn't give her grandfather a name, but she did give a description? Somehow, I doubted it. There was more going on here than what Blake was saying. "If you've only talked to one other family, how do you know there are three women missing?"

"I know." His voice was grim. "Clairvoyance is a pack inheritance, remember?"

"I don't believe anyone bothered mentioning *that* to the half-breeds." Though it did at least explain where my no-longer-latent clairvoyance skills came from.

Amusement twinkled briefly in his cold gray eyes. "An oversight, I'm sure."

Hate swelled up, its bitter taste just about making me gag. "This *isn't* a Directorate problem, Blake. Go haunt someone else, because I'm not interested in helping you or your get."

I turned and walked away, as fast as I could. That prickle of awareness told me Blake hadn't moved, and yet his voice reached out across the distance as easily as if he were standing right beside me.

"You will help us, Riley."

"That impolite response I cast your way earlier still stands."

"Riley, stop."

My muscles twitched with the need to obey, but my vampire half was having none of that. It was all I could do not to break into a run to get away from his presence—though if I thought it would do any good, I probably would have.

"Riley, I'm ordering you to stop right now, or face the consequences."

"There's nothing you can do to me, Blake. Not anymore."

I should have known better than to tempt fate like that. I really should have.

"If you do not stop this instant," he said softly, "I will kill your mother."

Chapter 2

I stopped.

How could I not? I might not have seen my mother since we'd been thrown out of the pack at sixteen, but that didn't mean I didn't love her. Didn't mean I wanted her dead.

She was my *mother,* for Christ's sake.

I swung around. "Trust me, Blake. You do not want to go this route. It's a *very* bad thing to do."

His smile was arrogant. Confident. "There's nothing the Directorate can do to me. I'm well within the law to chastise my pack as I see fit. If a pack member dies during meted justice?" He shrugged. "The law will not intervene unless the event is reported as something more than fair punishment. And no one in this pack will report it."

"*I* can report it. *I* can investigate it. And trust me, you would *not* want me or Rhoan anywhere near that pack. We're no longer the helpless cubs you booted out."

"And *we* are no longer the dying pack you remember. We've grown stronger, richer. More influential."

Yeah, and I knew exactly *how*. My ability to shadow had provided a means of learning more than a few pack secrets. And if the pack was now rich, it certainly hadn't been via hard work and good money management.

I shook my head. "You really have no idea who you're dealing with, Blake." No idea *what* he was dealing with.

"I want this problem dealt with. Then I will leave you, your half-breed brother, *and* your mother alone."

I shifted from one foot to the other, the need to run fighting with the need to wipe that cold look of satisfaction off his face. The twin desires made my muscles twitch. "And Konner? What's he got to say about all this?"

Blake's grin was gloating. "I defeated your grandfather in battle one year after you left. His ashes were scattered across his favorite hunting trail, as he requested."

I stared at him for a moment, not sure what to think. What to feel.

There'd been no love lost between our grandfather and us, and he'd turned his back on much of the trouble we'd had with Blake and his get. Yet he'd housed the three of us, fed us, made sure we never wanted for anything basic, and had never allowed the games to go too far—except for the one time Blake had thrown me off the mountain. And even then, his hands were tied. Pack rules gave the second-in-command the right to punish as he saw fit—at least when it came to matters of insubordination.

And now my grandfather was dead, killed in a battle for leadership. I closed my eyes and tried to fight the bloody images that came to mind. I'd only ever seen one fight for dominance in a pack, and it hadn't been pretty. Such fights were always done in wolf form, and almost always ended in the death of the old leader. Such were the ways of our wild cousins, and they had always been ours, too.

And the law allowed it, because it came under the title of religious beliefs and customs.

Which was just another way of sanctifying murder, if you asked me. Unfortunately, no one was ever likely to do that.

"If you've got a list of names, send them to me tonight," I said. "I can check them against the island's records."

"I've already done that."

"And I intend to redo it, because I may see something that you missed." I crossed my arms and stared at his ethereal form. "I don't want you harassing my every step, Blake, or I *will* have the full force of the Directorate brought down on the pack's head."

"Patrin wants regular reports."

"I don't give a—"

He held up a hand. "Yeah, I know. Tough."

I glowered at him. He stared back. For several seconds neither of us moved, then he sighed and rubbed a hand across his eyes. "What is your phone number? I'll send you the list of names and whatever other information I have."

I gave him my cell phone number, and added, "Have you got any recent pictures of Adrienne?"

"Yes. I'll send a couple."

At least with photos I could ask around, see if anyone remembered her. See if they remembered who she hooked up with. "What about the families of the other victims? Send me their contact details as well, if you have them."

"I will."

"Good. Now fuck off so I can sleep."

His smile was thin. "I will check in tomorrow night for a progress report."

"I wait with bated breath."

His body faded, dissolving into wisps of color that were whisked away by the freshening wind. I shivered and rubbed my arms, my gaze searching the trees to be sure—really sure—he was gone.

Then I turned around and made my way back to my villa. Once inside, I picked up the vid-phone and dialed my brother. It was the middle of the night and he'd more than likely be asleep, but I didn't care. I needed to talk to him.

The phone rang several times before the receiver was picked up and a sleepy voice said, "Hello?"

It wasn't Rhoan's voice, but Liander's. He didn't have the screen on, either—for which I should probably have been glad. Neither Liander nor Rhoan was a pretty sight when woken in the wee hours of the morning.

"Hey, makeup man, how you doing?"

There was a long silence, then he said, in a voice that was a mix of tiredness and annoyance, "Do you know what time it is?"

"Yep. I need to talk to Rhoan."

"He's under the weather."

"I don't care what he is or how he's feeling." The loving sister, that was me. "I need to talk to him."

Rhoan muttered something in the background. It didn't take a whole lot of imagination to guess what, but Liander told me anyway. "He's right. You can be a bitch at times."

"Totally. Now stop protecting him and put him on."

He did. "You're a pain in the ass, Riley," Rhoan said, voice croaky and words slightly slurred. "Why the hell are you ringing at this hour?"

"Thought you might like to know about the visitor I just had."

He paused, then said, "Have you been drinking again?"

"Not since last night."

"Then why the hell would you be ringing *me* in the middle of the night about a visitor? If you're that damn lonely, come home."

"The visitor's name was Blake."

"So?"

"As in, Blake Jenson. Former second-in-command, now leader, of the Jenson red pack."

He paused, then said, "Fuck."

I dropped down on a chair and draped a leg over the padded arm. "Something I said more than once."

"What the hell was Blake doing on Monitor Island?"

"He wasn't here in body, just in spirit."

"What?" Bedsheets rustled as Rhoan moved. Liander muttered something about coffee and my brother made a grunt of agreement before adding, "How can he be there in spirit alone?"

"I'm presuming it's some form of astral travel. He said clairvoyance is a pack inheritance, so maybe the traveler bit is an offshoot of that."

"Maybe." He didn't sound convinced. Whether it was the whole traveler bit or my sanity was anyone's guess. "What did this spirit want?"

"My help."

"Okay, now I know you're yanking my chain. Pigs will fly before Blake would ask for our help."

"Better start ducking those flying piggies, then, bro, because I'm totally serious."

He blew out a breath. "What help did he want?"

"Patrin's daughter has gone missing. He reckons it's connected to three other occurrences of missing females. He's even contacted the parents of one. Apparently, the one connection between them all is the fact that they vacationed on Monitor Island for a few days before they disappeared."

"If they've disappeared, let the cops handle it."

"I did mention that we don't do disappearances, but he seemed intent on ignoring that."

"Then ignore him right back. There's not a whole lot he can do about it. We're out of the pack and beyond his control."

"He threatened to kill Mom if we didn't help him."

Rhoan didn't say anything for several long minutes. I got up and walked over to the bar fridge, opening it and retrieving one of the chocolate bars the hotel provided. They were hideously expensive, but then, everything on this island was.

"We have no responsibility for our mother," Rhoan said eventually. "She washed her hands of us when we left."

"She could have washed her hands of us when we were conceived. She didn't. She raised us not only against pack wishes, but against the wishes of her own father. We owe her our existence, Rhoan. If nothing else, we should repay the debt."

He muttered something I couldn't quite catch, then the bedsheets rustled again. Perhaps Liander had come back with the coffee. I tore the chocolate wrapper off with my teeth and bit into the rich treat. It was mint chip—not my favorite, but beggars couldn't be choosers.

"What does Blake want?"

"For us to find Patrin's daughter."

"And the others?"

"I don't think he cares about them, other than the fact they might provide useful leads."

Rhoan snorted. "He hasn't changed any, then."

"He's the leader of the pack now, Rhoan. He has the power he always longed for, and it shows."

"The bastard couldn't possibly get any more arrogant."

"You want to bet?"

"No." He paused, and must have taken a sip of coffee, because the slurp came down the line. "If the cops and missing persons can't find them, what makes him think we can?"

"He knows we're guardians."

"For someone who never wanted to see us again, he seems to know an awful lot about us."

"Because he wants our help, and he intends to get it one way or another."

Rhoan sighed. "So, what are you ringing me to do?"

"He's sending me a picture of Adrienne, as well as the information he has on the other missing girls. I'll pass a copy on to you. I need you to see what you can find about Adrienne's whereabouts over the past week."

"You'll check your end?"

"Yeah. Though I'm not expecting any big revelations. The fact that they all disappeared after they'd returned home suggests there has to be some factor other than this island."

"You'd think so." He yawned. "Is that it?"

"For now. Enjoy the rest of your night, bro."

"Thanks, bitch."

I grinned. "I'm sure Liander will be willing to rock you to sleep."

"I'm sure he won't. I might just puke, the way my stomach is feeling. I'll ring tomorrow if I find anything."

"Good. Night." I'd barely hung up when the phone bleeped to indicate an incoming message. From Blake. He certainly wasn't wasting any time. I forwarded a copy of the entire file to Rhoan, then finished the rest of the chocolate and rose to my feet. The size of the file suggested there was a fair bit of information, and there was no way I was going to scroll through it all on the itty-bitty phone screen. I didn't have a laptop with me, but the hotel had a business center in their main lobby. I grabbed another bar of chocolate from the fridge, then headed over to the next cove.

The lobby was deserted. Though there was a concierge on duty, he was probably in a back room sipping coffee and watching the football replays. I padded across to the business center and swiped my keycard through the slot. The door clicked and I pushed it open. The only light in the room was the pale blue glow coming from the computer monitors, which was fine by me. I could see perfectly well in the dark, and if I turned on the lights, I might attract the attention of

the concierge. And yakking about banalities wasn't in
my plans at three in the morning.

I moved the mouse to get the screen up and running,
then attached the phone to the USB port and opened
the file. I'd been right—it was huge, and filled with
various comments, photos, a sketch of the man
Adrienne had supposedly met on the island, and reports from the various police departments. Obviously,
Blake had some very serious contacts if he was able to
get hold of these.

I flicked through the files, scanning the information.
Not all the women lived in Melbourne—one lived in
Ballarat, a regional city in the heart of Victoria, and the
other lived in Yarrawonga, a city on the border of
Victoria and New South Wales.

And despite what Blake had said, all four women
had actually disappeared at different times *after* their
return home. The first victim had disappeared close to
eight days after, and the other two at day three and day
five. Adrienne had the shortest time gap—she'd van-
ished straightaway. None of the women had been seen
since, and there'd been no credit or banking activity in
any of their accounts.

The other women were remarkably similar in looks,
too. They were all tall and athletic—the sort that
looked as if they could run twenty miles without a drop
of sweat marring their makeup—and all three had
blond hair, and either blue or green eyes. Adrienne was
the odd one out in that her hair was red and her eyes
gray, but it wasn't the classical red of our pack, more a
wispy, dark-strawberry blond.

Which suggested Adrienne's mom wasn't red pack.
Once upon a time, that would not have been possible,
but just before we'd been kicked out of the pack, our

grandfather had overturned the age-old policy that forbade the red pack breeding with anyone other than red pack members—a policy meant to maintain the so-called purity of the pack he and past alphas had prized so much—and had finally allowed the intermingling with other packs and colors. In an effort, of course, to counter the pack's increasingly problematic fertility issues and the declining birthrate. It was a policy Blake had obviously allowed to continue if the pack was now prosperous.

I leaned back in the chair and stared at the screen. Was there something going on here? Or was Blake reading more into the situation than there really was? Okay, the women had seemingly disappeared, but the only thing all four had in common was the fact that they'd spent time on this island. But a lot of single women came through this place, so why would these four be the ones to disappear?

And why would the kidnappers wait rather than doing the deed when the women were on holiday far from family, friends, and their regular schedule?

It made no sense.

I frowned and rechecked the file for dates. One a month for the last three months. Adrienne was again the aberration, disappearing two weeks after the third woman. But that itself meant nothing. People disappeared every day, every hour, the world over, and many of them for reasons other than foul play.

I clicked back to the photos, and again was struck by their similarities. And Adrienne's differences.

I tapped my fingers against the desk, intrigued despite myself. As much as I hated the man, I very much doubted Blake was crying wolf. Not when his own get was involved. Something *had* to be happening, no matter how unlikely it seemed from reading these files.

I needed to question the parents of the other women. Blake might have questioned one lot already, but he had an emotional investment in this whole mess and probably wouldn't have been listening to the responses with a critical ear. He was a tyrant, not an investigator.

I closed the file and unhooked my phone from the USB port. What next? I scrubbed my hand across my eyes, then looked down at the time. Nearly four. I should try to sleep, but adrenaline was still pumping through my veins and the itch to move, to dance, skittered across my skin. And not human-type dancing, either.

While wolf clubs weren't permitted on the island, they did have twenty-four-hour bars, complete with music—which, at this hour, was little more than an old man at a piano. There probably wasn't going to be many people there right now, but going to the bar was a better option than going back to my villa and drinking alone. At the very least, I could talk to the bartender. He might even recognize the picture Blake had sent me.

I shoved my phone into my pocket, then pushed back my chair and rose. My footsteps echoed as I walked across the empty lobby, but the concierge still didn't come out to greet me. Maybe he was asleep in his little back office.

Soft piano music greeted me as I entered the semi-darkness of the bar, but underneath the tinkling rode the murmur of conversation. I stopped on the top step, allowing my eyes to adjust as I looked around. This particular bar was one of the smaller ones, but it was right on the beach and had one whole wall that could be opened up. On nice nights, patrons could spread out into the sand or stroll through the waves. Tonight that wall was closed—probably because the weathermen were predicting storms—but the floor-to-ceiling windows offered little obstruction to the view. Surprisingly, there were at least a dozen people in here. Most of them were couples who cuddled in the cozy booths that ringed the remaining walls, but there were at least five others who sat by themselves and sipped drinks. Probably staff who'd just finished, I thought, as I clattered down the stairs and walked across to the bar. They had that "over-it-all" expression that workers around the world seemed to get after a long shift.

The bartender wandered down from the other end and gave me a somewhat bored-looking smile—his usual expression, from what I'd seen in my time here on the island. "You're up late, Ms. Jenson."

"Got an emergency phone call from a relative's mother," I said, fudging the truth only a little. "Apparently my cousin hasn't reported in for more than a week, and the mother is panicking."

"Mothers tend to do that," he said. "Would you like a drink?"

"Just a beer, thanks." I waited until he poured the drink, then added, "My cousin apparently met a man here. Mom seems to think if I find that man, I'll find her daughter."

"You didn't know she was here?"

I shook my head, then crossed my arms and leaned casually against his bar. With the low cut of my T-shirt, more than a small amount of breast was now on show. His gaze almost instantly wandered down. I might not want to play with him, but I wasn't above using a few tricks to keep his thoughts on my assets rather than making sense of what I was saying.

"He was a tall, blond man with gray eyes and big ears. His name was Jim. Jimmy Denton, I think."

He frowned, and his gaze rose briefly to mine. "That's me."

I looked him up and down. He was portly and middle-aged, and while he seemed like a nice man, I just couldn't imagine someone as young and as vibrant as Adrienne wanting to dance with someone like this. Though stranger things *did* happen when the moon lust was upon us. "Ummm, you're neither blond nor big-eared."

He grinned. It was the first real expression I'd seen. "Thankfully. You sure your friend's mom got the right name?"

Well, no, because I was relying on Blake's report, and who knew how accurate that was? I pressed a button on my phone and retrieved the drawing. "This is a sketch of the man she's looking for."

"No, sorry, I can't remember seeing anyone who looks like that working here." He shrugged, his gaze wandering back down to my boobs. "But I could ask around, see if he was one of the transient workers, if you'd like."

"That would be great." I pressed another button, and retrieved one of the photos of Adrienne. "This is my cousin." I showed him the picture. "Do you remember seeing her at all?"

He studied the photo for a moment, then nodded. "Now, her I remember."

I raised my eyebrows at the amusement in his tone. "Why?"

"She was running around, asking all sorts of questions."

"What sort of questions?"

"About some former guests—several women and a man, if I remember correctly. Some of the staff thought she might have been a private investigator, others a reporter. She was taking notes and stuff."

"No one here saw the notes? Read anything she wrote by accident?"

"Not that I'm aware." He paused, then said, "You know Jared Donovan, don't you?"

I held back my smile. How could I not know Jared? The man had been trying to get into my pants for the last three days. And if ever there was a human who could tempt me to look past ingrained prejudices, then he was it. He was tall, blond and athletic, with long strong fingers and a totally wicked smile.

Had he been wolf, I would have jumped his bones in an instant. As it was, I flirted with him probably more than was wise but, as tempting as he was, I just couldn't get past the whole human thing enough to bed him.

"I know him," I said, after a sip of beer. "Why?"

"Well, he likes to chat up all the pretty girls, so there's a good chance he talked to your friend. He might know more than me. I've got a wife, like."

Meaning, obviously, that he was restricted in the bedding department, but Jared the serial flirt was not. Why did humans bother getting married if they resented the vows that kept them together and exclusive? It was a weird way of doing things. At least us wolves didn't have that worry—once we made a vow to the moon, we were together for life. No ifs, buts, or maybes. Which is why we had to be very, very sure we'd found our soul mate before we committed. "Is Jared on tomorrow at all?"

"I think he's manning the research station boat."

"That service starts up at ten, doesn't it?"

When he nodded, I lowered a shield and reached out psychically, quickly sorting through his thoughts and memories, looking for secrets or lies. There were a couple of odd smudges, as if someone had deliberately blurred certain memories, but it might have been alcohol induced, too. The results tended to look the same.

If someone *had* been in this man's mind, then they were damn good, because I could find no other trace of them. And certainly there was nothing more to add to the information Jim had already told me.

"Anything else I can help you with, Ms. Jenson?" he said, barely skipping a beat as I withdrew from his thoughts.

"No. But thanks for helping." I finished the rest of my beer, then, with nothing—and no one—else to amuse me, I headed back to my villa and tried to get some sleep. It was a long time coming, but I did eventually drift off, dreaming of bodiless faces who forced me off cliff tops.

I woke sweaty and less than rested. After showering, I got dressed, choosing tight shorts and another low-cut T, then grabbed my phone and wallet, and headed up to the hotel for breakfast and a little staff interrogation.

No one, it seemed, could remember seeing a staff member resembling the sketch Blake had sent. Plenty could remember Adrienne and, as the bartender had mentioned last night, they all seemed to think she was some sort of reporter or private investigator.

And she might have been, for all I knew. Occupations had been absent from Blake's report, and I wasn't about to ring him and ask. The less contact I had with that bastard, the better.

One interesting point *did* come out of my questioning, however. Despite Blake's belief that she had danced with someone up here on the island, none of the staff could remember seeing her with anyone at all. She'd simply appeared on the island, stayed for several days questioning everyone who worked here, then left.

Which certainly smacked of reporter-like behavior. So if she was, how did she get onto the disappearances in the first place? The family trait of clairvoyance, perhaps? And had she come to this island investigating the disappearances, only to become a victim herself?

It certainly seemed that way.

But where did the sketch of the man parading as Jim Denton fit in?

There was the possibility that he was the man the other women had met on the island, and therefore the connection between the three disappearances. But if that were true, you'd think at least one of the staff would remember seeing him. But there wasn't a glimmer of recognition anywhere.

I leaned back in my chair and studied the ocean foam as it crawled up the sand only feet from my table. The first thing I had to do when I got home was check whether the man the other women had met here matched the description Blake had given me. If he did, then at least I'd uncovered the connection between the man, the other women, and Adrienne. Although it still didn't explain why no one here could remember him.

I glanced at my watch. It was nearly nine, so I only had an hour to kill before the research center opened to visitors. I ordered another cup of coffee, helped myself to some fruit and Danishes, and watched the cute waiter bustling around the room. My hormones were getting restless. Just as well I was going home to the man I cared about soon.

At ten I rose and wandered across to the little canteen that sold the entry tickets for the research center. Most of the activities on Monitor were included in the overall fees, but the research center and diving trips had to be paid for.

It wasn't until I'd opened my wallet to grab some cash that I realized my driver's license was missing. All my credit cards and cash were still there, but my license was gone. And no matter how much I looked in all the other little pockets or slots, I couldn't see the damn thing.

Either I'd lost it or I'd somehow managed to leave it at home. I rang Rhoan, left a message for him to check the apartment—and to use the Directorate system to report it as missing if it wasn't there—then walked across to the concierge. No licenses had been handed in, he said, but he'd let me know if it did appear.

With little else to do, I went down to the beach to wait for the little boat that would take me to the island. There was already an older couple waiting, and though they gave me a smile of greeting as I strolled up, they didn't actually say anything, too wrapped up in each other's company. Which was nice, I thought. I wondered if I'd ever find anyone to grow old with like that.

Kellen's image suddenly rose in my mind, and I couldn't help smiling. Part of me was already convinced that he was the *one*. The other part—the part that had been hurt before—was fighting to remain distant and take some time.

Of course, I'd always imagined that finding my soul

mate would come like a bolt from the blue—that it would be an instant recognition of fate that blindsided us both—but perhaps that was simply expecting too much. The fact that I loved being with Kellen spoke volumes about the depths of my feelings for him. Hell, even the fact that I not only looked forward to uncovering more of his good points, but his bad as well, suggested I was definitely on the path to love. Whether it was soul-mate-type love, or just a deep and caring relationship was something only time would tell.

I sat down on the little jetty and watched the motorboat gradually growing larger on the horizon. By the time it had docked, other people had joined our little group, most of them couples, which left me feeling decidedly out of place. But then, that was a sensation I'd lived with half my life, thanks to Blake and his damn family.

So why was I helping him now?

It wasn't because of the threat. Not anymore. Truth was, his story intrigued that part of me I'd denied for so long. The hunter hunts—how often had my brother said that? And yet it had taken what amounted to betrayal and repeated attempted kidnappings for me to fully acknowledge the hunter within.

But the wolf was free and there was no stopping her now. And I knew deep down that Blake really hadn't needed the threat to make me follow up on this case. Curiosity would have had me looking, and sooner rather than later.

Curiosity would never make me like him, however, and I was glad he'd come visiting in spiritual form only. I needed to challenge the pack leader as much as I needed a hole in the head, and I had a feeling anger might have led me to do something stupid. The fact that I might have beaten him was irrelevant. I didn't need to get involved with my past any more than I currently was.

Besides, Blake wouldn't have taken a beating lying down. He'd make me pay, as he'd made me pay in the past. And I had a feeling his retribution now would be a whole lot worse than anything he'd done before. After all, I no longer had my grandfather's presence to offer some protection. And Blake was too arrogant to think Rhoan would ever take on the role of protector effectively.

I waited until the others had boarded before approaching the boat myself. Jared gave me a wide smile, his blue gaze sliding appreciatively down my body and sending a pleasant tingle zipping across my skin.

It really was a damn shame he was human.

"Hello, pretty lady," he said, his fingers wrapping around mine, trapping them in heat as he helped me into the boat. "I thought you'd already done this little tour?"

"I have, but I'm bored and needed someone decent to talk to." I met his gaze, a smile teasing my lips. "However, most of the decent men are taken, so you're it."

He laughed, a warm, free sound. "Better to be last choice than no choice, I guess."

"And I'm guessing being last choice isn't much of a problem for you."

His grin was almost wolfish. "Only with a certain reluctant werewolf." He raised my fingers to his lips and kissed them lightly. "But I guess I now have another chance to work on that."

"You can try, but I'm not going to change my mind."

"Half the fun is the chase," he said, then released me and made his way back to the front of the boat.

I have to admit, I enjoyed the view. Human or not, he had good shoulders, a nice ass, and long, strong legs. Legs I could so easily imagine wrapped around my waist as he drove deep inside . . . I thrust away the thought and blew out a breath.

Time to get back home to Kellen and the clubs, before I was tempted to do something stupid.

Jared untied the mooring rope, then backed the boat away from the dock. Once free of the beach, he gunned the engine, and the nose of the boat rose. We surged over the waves, sometimes flying free over the sea before crashing down. I raised my face to the sun and the wind, drawing the freshness into my lungs, and enjoying the sensation of freedom and the thrill of the ride. Dogs, I thought, had it right when they hung their heads out of car windows.

It ended all too soon. I climbed out with the others but didn't follow them as they walked up the jetty toward the research center. Instead, I leaned against one of the pylons and watched Jared as he finished tying off the boat. With that done, he walked over. I had to admit, the front view was as good as the back. The man could definitely work it.

"So," he said, stopping mere inches away from me, leaving the spicy scent and the heat to flow across my senses, teasing and arousing. "What would you like to do for the next hour or so?"

"How about we dangle our feet in the water and talk?"

"Not what I had in mind."

He raised a hand to my cheek, his caress light but sending a flush of heat right through my body. I stepped away, and resisted the urge to fan myself. Human or not, this man was hot.

"But it's all I'm offering," I said, and walked over to the end of the pier.

"You are no fun."

He sat beside me, his legs close enough to touch mine. I had to give him an A for effort. He knew my reasons for not having sex with him—I'd explained them the very first night he'd tried chatting me up—but he still couldn't help trying it on. Maybe it *was* all about the chase for him—and the more I refused, the more determined he became.

"That depends on your definition of fun." I glanced at him. "I've seen what we can do to humans. I'd hate to spoil that pretty body with a few ill-placed scars."

"Scars attract many ladies."

"If you're dead they won't."

He grunted, but the determined flash in his blue eyes suggested he was a long way from giving up just yet. "So what do you want to talk about?"

"Adrienne Jenson."

Something flickered in his eyes. Not recognition, but something else. Something that raised alarms deep inside. He might not have gray eyes or big ears, but he still had to be considered a suspect. He certainly knew more than he was telling. Or was I just being overly suspicious once again?

"I'm gathering by the surname that you're from the same pack?"

"Yeah." I got out my phone and brought up Adrienne's picture. "You seen her around?"

He studied her for a moment, then nodded. "She did the tour here a week or so ago. I remember her hair."

His gaze raised to mine. "It's such a pretty color in the sunlight."

I smiled at the compliment. "Was she with anyone?"

"I don't think so." He hesitated. "Why?"

"Because her mom has been pestering me to find her. She thinks she's run off with a man."

"She looks old enough to make her own decisions about who she wants to bed."

"She is, but this is a human man we're talking about."

He raised an eyebrow, amusement playing around his lips. "So the reluctance is a pack thing more than personal?"

"Both." I switched the phone image to the sketch Blake had sent. "This is the man her mom believes she's with."

Again that something went through his eyes. He knew the man, I was sure of it.

All he said was, "Pretty lousy drawing."

"But you know him, all the same?"

"Didn't say that."

Didn't refute it, either. "He's not in trouble. I just need to know if he's got any idea where Adrienne might be."

He didn't say anything for a moment, then shrugged. "I actually can't tell you much. I've seen him on the island a few times, helping out at the bar and such, but I've never really talked to him."

"Is he here today?"

"Don't know. You could try asking staff-management. They might tell you if he's around."

"Do you know his name?"

He frowned. "I think it's Jim. Jim Denton."

"I talked to Jim Denton last night. He looks nothing like this sketch."

Jared grinned. "Mom's obviously a lousy artist. Or Adrienne was telling lies for reasons of her own." He flung an arm around my shoulder, his fingers draping perilously close to my left breast. "Now that we've discovered I can't help you find your friend, how about we discuss a more interesting topic?"

"Like what?" I said wryly. "You, me, and bed?"

His fingers moved, lightly brushing my nipple, teasing it to life. "That sounds like a good place to start."

"Coffee is a good place to start." I pulled away from his arm and stood up. "I need to be wined and dined before I can get into any sort of sexual discussion."

"A reluctant werewolf," he muttered, his expression a mix of amusement and frustration. "Who'd have thought there was such a beast?"

I linked arms with him as we walked down the pier toward the small coffeehouse. "Just goes to prove you can't believe every rumor about us."

"And isn't it just my luck to find that one exception when I'm feeling as horny as hell."

I grinned. "I never said I didn't want to bed you. It's just the whole human thing that's the sticking point."

"Meaning if I keep trying, I may just wear down your defenses anyway?"

"You might."

"Excellent. Let's get down to coffee and cake, then."

We did. And he did keep trying.

But he didn't get lucky.

*J*ared dropped the tour group back on the main island an hour later, and left me with a promise to continue his seduction attempts during his lunch break. Grinning at his determination, I headed back to my little villa and rang my brother.

"Once again, she rings at an indecent hour," he said, by way of greeting.

I looked at my watch. "It's nearly lunchtime."

"Any hour before noon is an indecent hour after the night I've had."

"Self-inflicted pain garnishes no sympathy from me, bro."

"I'll remember that next time you want sympathy and coffee after a late night carousing."

I grinned. He'd feed me coffee no matter what, because he knew it was the only way to soothe the savage beast. Or at least shut her up. "You had a chance to look at the file yet?"

"No." He paused. "Why?"

"Because I've been asking around about Adrienne and the man she was supposedly seeing, and have hit an odd little wall." I told him about the two Jim Dentons. "It's rather odd to have two people with the same name, and yet no one seems to know or recognize the second man." No one except Jared, that was.

"You done a mind search?"

"Yeah, but without much luck. I found possible evidence of memory tampering on the older Jim, but I'm not yet skilled enough to undo the fudging."

"Memory tampering doesn't indicate foul play. It could just be a vampire not wanting her victim to remember their encounter."

Because drinking from unknowing or unwilling hosts was illegal in most states of Australia. Apparently Tasmania was a little more free and easy, allowing vamps to drink from whomever they pleased as long as they took minimum amounts. Which probably explained why human tourism to Tassie had fallen, and vamp tourism had increased.

"I couldn't see any evidence of bite marks."

"If it happened weeks ago, you wouldn't."

"Trust me, the fudging didn't feel like the work of a vamp."

"Then what did it feel like?"

"I don't know."

"Fat lot of good that'll do the investigation."

"This from the man lazing about in bed feeling sorry for himself." I paused. "Why isn't Liander there pampering you?"

"He had to go to work early. The apprentices are working on the goblin masks today, and he has to supervise."

Because they'd screwed up the goblin masks previously, no doubt. Those two weren't the sharpest pencils in the drawer from what I'd seen of them.

"So what are you going to do next?" he continued.

"I don't know. There's really nothing much more I can do here. I'll need to talk to the parents of the other victims and see if there's some other connector. There's something odd about it all."

"If you add 'I feel it in my bones,' I'm going to come up there and hit you."

I grinned. "There's nothing wrong with that saying—aside from the fact you hate it."

"Mom used to say it," he said. "Usually right before you and I got a beating for something or other."

My smile faded. "I can't remember that."

"I suspect there's a lot you can't remember, Riley."

He was probably right. That time of my life was not

a place where I wanted to linger. "I remember the bad stuff."

"Which just goes to show how screwed our definitions of bad are. There weren't many good times, you know."

"I know." I scrubbed a hand across my eyes and fought the myriad of images that battered at the blocks I'd placed in their path years ago.

"Which is why I can't understand you helping him."

"I'm not. I'm helping Mother."

"I doubt he'd actually——"

"I don't. I think he's capable of any sort of violence imaginable." Especially if it meant getting what he wanted.

He sighed. "So, are you coming home?"

"If you and Liander don't mind me leaving a few days early."

"Mind? We were taking bets on it." I could almost see his grin coming down the line. "I win, by the way. I said the guilt of letting us down would keep you there until the last week."

"So what did you win?"

"A one-night free pass to go anywhere and do anyone."

"You do that anyway."

"Hey," he said, sounding highly offended. "I've been a very good wolf since we had our discussion four weeks ago. I've only had one lover, and that was work related."

So why did he feel the need to break free now? If he was happy with Liander—and I knew he was—why fuck that up by dancing with other wolves? Especially since he'd agreed not to outside of work? "Why did Liander even agree to this bet?"

"Because he was sure you'd miss Kellen so much you'd be following him home two days after he left."

"Well, I *do* miss him."

"Maybe, but the telling point is, you haven't even contacted him."

"Because he wasn't home. He's been off on some business trip again."

"He has a cell phone, Riley."

"Oh, just shut up and stop nagging me," I said, more than a little crossly.

He chuckled. "Want me to meet you at the airport?"

"Someone had better. I can't afford a taxi after all the chocolate I've eaten on this trip."

"Text me the details and I'll be there."

"Will do, bro."

I hung up. The thought of going home had my hormones dancing, and I couldn't help the great big grin that plastered itself on my lips.

Still, before I packed, I headed down to reception and checked if Jim had left me a message. He had, and it was the answer I'd been expecting. No one remembered a man matching the description I'd given him.

Maybe it was just a scam. It wouldn't be the first time a boy had lied about his name to get an easy lay. Although that didn't explain why Blake thought she'd bedded him, when no one up here could even remember seeing him. No one but Jared.

Once back at my villa, I got on with the serious business of packing. Jared appeared from nowhere, and helped carry my luggage to the little plane that would take me back to the mainland. I gave him a polite kiss good-bye, and used the moment to lower a shield and try to read his thoughts—only to hit what felt like a brick wall. Either he was mind-blind, or he had psychic shields as tough as any vampire.

Which raised the question, what might he be hiding? Anything? Or was I just being a suspicious bitch again? Probably, I thought wryly, as I boarded the plane.

Of course, getting a connecting flight back to Melbourne wasn't as easy, so it was a day later when I finally reached the Virgin terminal at Tullamarine airport. Thankfully, Blake's spirit or aura or whatever the hell that was didn't manage to find me during that time. Maybe being on a plane and on the move made me difficult to track.

I collected my bags and walked out of the terminal building, shivering as a blast of cold air hit my skin. I thought about dragging a sweater out of my bag, but honestly couldn't be bothered. I just wanted to get home. I stopped briefly and looked around for either Rhoan's or Liander's car, but found Kellen instead.

Pleasure shot through me, and I dropped my bags and ran into his arms. He laughed softly as he lifted me up and spun me around, then his lips found mine and he kissed me. Thoroughly and deeply, until my head was spinning and desire was pounding through my veins.

I sighed when he finished, then rested my forehead against his and stared into his bright, gold-flecked green eyes. "Missed you."

"And I you." He let my feet touch the ground but didn't release me.

I pressed myself against him and wished there weren't clothes between us. "So how come you're here?"

He smiled and kissed my nose. "Because two weeks

away from you is far too long. I've already informed your brother that you're coming home with me."

A grin touched my lips. "Oh yeah? And why would that be?"

"Because I intend to ravish you senseless."

His words had my pulse skipping about dizzily. I restrained my excitement and tried to remain cool as I raised an eyebrow. "What if I don't want to be ravished?"

He collected my bags, then hooked my arm through his and led the way over to the taxi rank and parking areas. "Too bad. You have no choice in the matter."

"Not even if I'd rather a long and leisurely seduction?"

"Nope. Sorry." His grin was decidedly sexy and not in the least apologetic. "It's been two weeks since I've held you in my arms. Slow and leisurely just aren't possible."

"A man with no self-control." I shook my head in mock sorrow. "Such a shame."

"I've been with you for five minutes and I've only kissed you. How much more control do you want?"

I laughed and squeezed his arm, suddenly fiercely glad he'd come here to meet me. "Where's your Mercedes?"

"Didn't bring it." Mischief twitched his luscious lips. "I thought the returning princess deserved a ride worthy of her status. Hence, the limo."

He waved a hand to the long white limo lining the curb. Excitement began a triple-beat dance through my bloodstream. Making love in the backseat of a limo had always been something of a fantasy for me. In fact, any sort of making out that involved illicit locations was guaranteed to turn me on, but a limo was someplace I didn't get to be all too often. And the few times I *had* been in them had proven a frustrating experience. But then, I'd been with Quinn, and for an old vampire he was amazingly staid in his sexual tastes. Luckily for me, Kellen had proven to be a wolf more than willing to push and explore boundaries.

"And the driver?" I asked, voice several octaves lower than usual, thanks to the force of desire suddenly driving through me.

"Is very discreet. And the modesty screen between us is soundproof and one way. We can see him, but he can't see us."

"And do you plan a ravishment in the backseat of said limo?"

He dragged me closer and dropped a quick, fierce kiss on my lips. "I most certainly do. And with the side windows open so that everyone who passes us can see me taking you."

"Woohoo!"

He laughed, grabbed my hand, and raced me toward the car. The chauffer greeted our rush with politeness, but there was a twinkle in his gray eyes as he shoved my bags into the trunk. He obviously knew what was about to go down.

Me, quite literally.

I grinned as I seated myself comfortably on the plush leather seats. A bottle of Brown Brothers Orange Muscat & Flora—one of my favorite dessert wines—sat in a waiting ice bucket, with chilled glasses beside it.

"You don't have to get me drunk to have your wicked way with me," I said, as Kellen climbed into the car and the driver closed the door behind him.

"Oh, I know." He reached for the glasses and the wine. "But we've officially been an item for a whole six weeks. And as that's something of a record for me, I thought it worth a celebration."

"So all the rumors of you being a ladies' man are true?"

"Alas, yes. But all it took was the right woman to curb my straying ways." He poured the wine and handed me a glass, then raised his own. "To the right woman."

I clicked my glass against his and said teasingly, "I'd love to say 'to the right man,' but hey, I'm not entirely sure you're him yet."

He made a low sound deep in his throat, and pulled me toward him. "I *am* the right man. In fact, I intend to be the *only* man in your life." He kissed me hard, leaving me breathless, then added, "And for the next twelve hours, you are mine, and only mine."

Twelve hours? Oh my.

I took a sip of the wine that did little to curb the heat of excitement. Then, as the limo drove off smoothly, I leaned forward and tasted the same tangy sweetness on his lips.

"You do taste very nice."

"I'd taste even better if you were naked."

I raised an eyebrow, amusement teasing my lips. "And how does me being naked make you taste better?"

"Everything tastes better when there's nakedness involved."

"Such a male response."

"Well, I am a male."

I let my gaze roam down his lean, strong body. Wolves tended not to get muscle-bound—it just wasn't in our makeup—but that didn't mean the male of our species was in any way weedy. Just that they tended to be built like athletes rather than bodybuilders.

"It seems you are," I said, letting my gaze rest briefly, teasingly, on his lap. "However, I refuse to be the only one to get naked in this car."

Amusement touched his lips. "Then shall we remove our clothing?"

"Or remove each other's?"

"An even better idea."

He proceeded to strip me—slowly and deliciously—his fingers sliding so sensually across my skin, teasing and arousing. Then I did the same to him, allowing my hands to roam across the wealth of his chocolate-colored skin, reveling in the heat of it, the steel of muscles rippling underneath it every time he moved.

When we were finally both naked, I settled on his lap, enjoying the tease of closeness as I wrapped my arms around his neck and stared for several seconds into his beautiful green eyes. Then I kissed him, long and lingering.

"I want you," he said after a while, his voice rough, urgent.

"But you can't have me. Not yet."

"Then what can I have?"

"Oh, this and that." I slid my rump down his legs until I was kneeling in front of him. Desire and anticipation swirled around me, so thick, so strong that it sent little droplets of perspiration skittering across my skin. I lightly ran my tongue across the base of his penis. His groan of pleasure was all the encouragement I needed to continue.

I licked my way up and down his shaft, occasionally taking in his balls, enjoying the tremble of pleasure that ran through his body, the way his cock leapt and throbbed with eagerness. I smiled and swirled my lips around the tip of him before taking him fully into my mouth.

Again he groaned—a sound thick with enjoyment—as I drew him deeper, sucking and tasting and teasing him until his movements became desperate and the salty taste of him began seeping into my mouth.

But I didn't let him cross that line. He made a sound thick with frustration when I pulled back, then his hands wrapped around my arms and he was pulling me up, pulling me close, as his mouth claimed mine.

As kisses went, it was pretty much meltdown material.

"Now it's your turn to ache," he whispered, after a while.

And he set about doing that very thing, touching and teasing, making me tremble and ache as I could never remember aching.

"Enough," I said, as he brought me to the edge for what seemed like the umpteenth time, only to back away again.

He laughed softly, his eyes sparking with so much desire and caring that something trembled deep inside. "Then what do you want now?"

"You," I said, and thrust down on him, claiming him in the most basic way possible.

He groaned and slid his hands to my hips, his grip almost bruising as he pressed me down harder. I echoed his groan, loving the way he felt inside.

I began to move and he was right there with me, kissing and caressing, driving me wilder with need. The deep-down ache bloomed, becoming a kaleidoscope of sensations that washed pleasure through every corner of my mind. I thrust my head back, gasping for breath as the need for completion built and built. Only the air itself seemed to burn as fiercely as my skin.

Then the shuddering began and I grabbed his shoulders, pushing him deeper still, wanting to feel every inch of him through every inch of me. Pleasure exploded as his movements became faster, more urgent.

"Look at me," he growled.

I opened my eyes and met his gaze, and again something quivered deep inside. Desire and passion and something else—something that seemed a whole lot like possession—seared those depths, stirring me in ways I didn't think possible.

"You are mine," he said, and his hoarse voice seemed to echo through every fiber of my being.

Yes, I thought. *Oh God, yes.*

And then all thought evaporated as the passion between us exploded and I was quivering, trembling, whimpering, as his warmth spilled into me.

Sated, I collapsed against him, sucking in his spicy, sweaty scent with every intake of breath, feeling it fill me, consume me, as his body had consumed me. Somehow, it seemed so right. He wrapped his arms around me, holding on tight, and for one brief moment, I had that oh so glorious sensation of belonging.

It was in the middle of that one perfect moment that the phone rang.

Chapter 3

*L*eave it," Kellen said, kissing my forehead.

"I can't. It might be urgent." I pushed upright.

"You're still officially on vacation," he said, annoyance edging in his rich tones. "Nothing is so urgent that someone else can't take care of it."

"But it might be Rhoan." Though I doubted it. He obviously knew Kellen was picking me up from the airport, and he also knew about my fantasy involving the limo—a fantasy I hadn't finished with yet. He wouldn't disrupt us, no matter how urgent.

I reached into my handbag and pulled out my vidphone. As I suspected, it wasn't Rhoan. It was Jack. He obviously knew I was back—thanks to the damn tracker permanently implanted in my ear—but it was a little unfair for him to be ringing even before my holidays had finished. Of course, tonight was Halloween, and it was one of the busiest times of the year for the Directorate. Rather like hospitals during the full moon.

If I'd wanted to enjoy the full length of my vacation, I should have stayed on the island where the sheer distance between us made it impossible for Jack to call me in.

But I never actually got the chance to answer the phone and find out what Jack wanted, because Kellen took one look at the number, then plucked the phone neatly from my hand and threw it out one of the open windows. It hit the road hard and disintegrated into dozens of metal bits that went scattering everywhere.

For a moment, shock held me speechless. "What the hell—"

"You're still on holiday," he cut in. "They have no right to be contacting you just yet."

Annoyance rolled through me, but so, too, did desire. Nothing got my hormones scurrying faster than a man taking charge for all the right reasons. Still, I couldn't help adding, "You just destroyed my phone. *And* it might have been important—"

"*This* is important, Riley. Us. Not work." He raised a hand to my cheek, cupping it lightly. "And if it was a matter of true urgency, Rhoan can contact me. He knows where we'll be. He has my number."

I raised my eyebrows, curious despite myself. "So we're not going back to your place?"

"Given your propensity in the past to run off on guardian business, no, we are not. I intend for our night of pleasure to be far away from the madding crowd. And any form of transport."

I wriggled on his lap, feeling his growing readiness, loving the heat of him pressed against me. "I should be very angry with you. And Jack certainly *will* be."

"Jack doesn't scare me. And you, my love, will enjoy every moment I have planned."

"Is that an order?" I murmured, my lips so deliciously close to his that I could taste every breath, every move of his lips.

"It most certainly is," he said, and kissed me.

*O*ur night of pleasure was spent in the Macedon hills, on a property belonging to one of Kellen's friends.

There was just the two of us, a tent, and a huge picnic basket of food on five acres of manicured lawns and lush gardens. We laughed, we played, and we made love—sometimes in full view of the neighbors—and it was absolutely divine. Even the notoriously fickle Melbourne weather dealt us a nice night for a change.

Dawn had barely begun to creep her fiery fingers across the blackness of night when Kellen's phone finally rang. He unwrapped himself from around me and fished out the phone from the tangle of our clothes.

"It's Rhoan," he said, and handed the vid-phone to me.

"So," my brother said, expression wry. "Had a good time?"

"Absolutely wonderful," I said, stretching like a contented cat languishing in the sun.

"I certainly hope so, because Jack isn't happy."

"Jack's never happy." I paused, barely resisting the urge to giggle as Kellen began tickling the underside of my foot. "What does he want me to do?"

"I'll let him tell you himself."

"Rhoan, wait—" He didn't. A second later, Jack's bald head appeared on the vid-screen. And as Rhoan had already noted, he did not look happy.

"I'm not officially on duty for another day," I said, quickly, "so this had better be an emergency."

Which was a pretty dumb thing to say. Just about all the Directorate cases could be classed as urgent, simply because they involved murdering psychos. We very rarely dealt with anything else.

"There is no such thing as vacation for guardians when emergencies happen," he said, voice dark and full of the anger so evident in his expression. "Next time I damn well ring you, answer the phone. Or else."

I didn't ask what he meant by that. I had a feeling I wouldn't want to know. "So what's the problem?"

"Dead people."

"Dead people are a regular occurrence in our line of work, Jack." And if was *just* dead people, he wouldn't be ringing me. Or be so mad.

Jack grimaced, his bald head gleaming under the brightness of the overhead lighting. He had to be upstairs in the main offices—the area the public could enter—not in the underground guardian area. There, the lighting was kept at "dusk" level for the sake of the newer vamps. Not that artificial lighting could hurt them. It was just that some of them tended to get jumpy in bright light. And jumpy guardians were never a good thing.

"This is a nasty one," Jack said, "and I need your talents involved."

Meaning he wanted me there to see if I could pick up anything along psychic lines. Like a soul hanging around with ready information to impart.

I scrubbed a hand across my eyes. While I hoped like hell Kade, Iktar, and the other non-vamps Jack had employed to fill out the daytime division got through training soon, the reality was, their presence in the unit wouldn't have saved me from a situation like this. I was the only one with this particular talent.

And yet, as much as I hated the thought of leaving Kellen and heading off to some gruesome murder scene, I couldn't deny the buzz of excitement that was humming through my system. I was going hunting, and the wolf within couldn't wait.

As Jack had once said, all werewolves were addicted to the thrill of the chase. It was just society that had, to some extent, tamed them. Certainly it was something I'd denied for a long, long time.

"Send me the address, then," I said. "But you'll owe me big-time, Jack."

Amusement flickered briefly through his green eyes. "I'll give you an extra week of vacation next year."

"Yeah, right." We both knew the likelihood of me taking that was slim. "Just send the details to this number."

"Will do."

I hesitated, then asked, "So what did you ring me about earlier?"

"Rogue Vamp," he said, voice all annoyed again. My bad for reminding him. "I took care of it myself."

If Jack was taking care of business, then business *was* bad.

I hung up, but kept hold of the phone. "Seeing you smashed my phone, I'll need to keep this."

He touched a hand to my face, gently trailing his fingers down my cheek to my lips. I kissed his fingertips as they brushed my mouth, saw the flare of desire deep in his bright eyes.

"I figured you might have to leave early, so I arranged for a cab to come back at six."

I glanced at my watch. It was almost that now. I rolled free from his touch and sat up. "I need to go for a quick swim to freshen up."

He caught my hand, stopping me from moving. "I need you to think about something while you're gone."

I raised my eyebrows at the sudden seriousness in his tone. "Sure. What?"

"I want to go solo with you."

I blinked. "What? Now? It's too soon." The reply was almost automatic. As much as I cared for Kellen, as much as I was beginning to think he could be the one, I wasn't ready to go solo with him. Not after the events of the last few months. Not after Quinn. This time, I wasn't rushing into anything, free will or not.

"It's not too soon when it feels so right," he said, and paused, studying me for a moment. "Or are you still playing games with me? Still waiting, just in case something better comes along?"

I sucked in a breath and stared at him. "You really think I'm not serious about us?"

"Honestly? Sometimes I just don't know."

He couldn't have hurt me any more if he'd hit me. How could he honestly think I was playing games? I *wasn't* Rhoan—I had no hunger to fight the restrictions of a relationship and play the field. I wanted a home and a family and one man to call my own—and Kellen *knew* that. "That's a horrible thing to say."

"Perhaps, but it's also the truth. For most of our relationship, I've felt like a third wheel. There was always Quinn, or work, ahead of whatever you and I were doing. I'm not built to stand around and wait, Riley. I never will be."

"But Quinn's gone—"

"Work isn't."

"Dammit, you *know* I can't abandon work. Not when there's so few people in the day division." Hell, we'd discussed my being a guardian—and just what it entailed—up on Monitor Island. We'd even talked about the whole fertility thing, and me being a half-breed. None of it had seemed to be a problem to him.

But maybe he'd had the time to dwell on it since then. If so, I guess I had to be glad my work seemed more of a problem for him than my mixed heritage and inability to carry a child.

He continued, "All I'm asking for is a decision on us going solo. It's not like I'm asking for forever."

No, but if I went solo, it would be because I was sure it would end up with forever. Right now, what I wanted most was time. Time to grow into us. Time to be really sure. I didn't want to go solo only to have it all fall apart. "It's too early—"

"It's *not*." He grasped my shoulders and shook me lightly. "You keep saying you want the white picket fence ideal, and yet you seem totally unwilling to step into the arena and take a chance."

"After being used and abused by a past couple of mates, a certain amount of caution is hardly surprising," I retorted.

"Caution, yes. Feet dragging? No. I won't wait forever, Riley. Patience is *not* one of my virtues."

"It's not one of mine, either. Trust me on that." I reached for my clothes. "I'm going for a swim, then I'll head off to the assignment. And I'll come back to your place as soon as I can."

He studied me for a moment, his green eyes still bright with a mix of annoyance and determination. He wasn't going to give up until he'd gotten what he wanted, and a small part of me couldn't help being thrilled by that knowledge.

"And the commitment I'm asking for?"

I rose. "I want this to work as much as you do,

Kellen, but I won't be pushed into anything. Not again."

"I'm not pushing. I'm just asking you to think about it."

"I will."

"Good." He paused, then added softly, "Just remember, I'm not Liander."

"Well, thank heavens for that. I mean, he's gay."

His grin seemed reluctant, but he rose and drew me into a kiss that was very much a signal of intent. A statement of caring and demand.

In some ways it was scary. In others, exhilarating. I mightn't be sure that I wanted to take that extra step so soon into our relationship, but I *was* sure of one thing. I didn't want it to end.

Which meant I might *have* to take that step, go exclusive, before I was really sure about the true breadth of my feelings for him.

But I didn't say that. Didn't say anything. Just enjoyed his kiss and his closeness while I could.

I had a quick dip in the old dam we'd camped beside, then dressed and hurried over to the cab. Kellen gave me his jacket and another toe-curling kiss, then sent me on my way.

Once we were on the highway and headed for the address Jack had sent me, I retrieved Kellen's phone from my pocket and went through the files.

The information was sketchy, at best.

Apparently, a neighbor had heard strange sounds in a nearby vacant house and, on investigation, had spotted a shadowy figure inside. He'd reported it to police, who'd arrived, found the victim, and called the Directorate.

There were no details of the murder or the victim,

which probably meant the cops had sealed the scene, awaiting our arrival. It also meant the Directorate's forensic team hadn't arrived yet, because otherwise there'd be at least some description of events.

I looked back down at the files. In the past, the strength of my connection with the dead seemed to depend on the freshness of the death. The newer the death, the stronger the connection—and the more likely I'd be able to successfully interpret or understand what they were trying to say. If indeed they had something to say. But part of me was hoping that the soul *wasn't* hanging about. Talking to dead people wasn't on my list of favorite things to do.

We were on the Calder Freeway, heading toward Citylink and Melbourne, when I noticed the driver looking into the rearview mirror, his expression a little worried.

"What's wrong?" I asked, even as I looked around.

"That truck is getting a little too close for comfort."

Which had to be the understatement of the year. All I could see was this huge silver grille—and it was getting huger by the moment.

"Maybe you need to swing into the other lane, and let him pass."

"Tried that. He seems intent on tailgating me."

Just what we needed—a truckie intent on playing chicken. "Can you report his ass?"

"Can't see the license plate."

"Maybe I can." As I looked around, the truck seemed to leap forward, until all I could see were the little bugs caught in the deadly-looking, silver-plated grille. I had a bad feeling those bugs could be us if we weren't very careful. "You might want to step on it—"

The rest of my words got lost in the screech of metal

as the truck rammed into the rear of us, the force of the blow lifting the rear of the cab up for several seconds before sending it lurching forward. The force of the hit flung me about like a rag doll—at least until the seat belt kicked in and just about choked me. How the driver kept control I have no idea.

I looked out the back window again, saw nothing but bug-splattered grille, and twisted back around to brace myself against the front seat. "Floor it!" I yelled. "He's coming at us again."

"Don't you think I'm fucking trying?" the driver yelled back, his face red and his eyes wide with fear.

The cab's engine was just about screaming and, for an instant, the car leapt forward, leaving the growl of the truck momentarily behind.

But all too soon, its thick roar filled the air and I didn't need to look around to know it was closing in fast again.

And then it hit us.

This time, the blow wasn't square-on, because suddenly the car was spinning around and around. Then the truck hit us a third time and the cab seemed to be flying. I was upside down, and the world was tumbling.

I can't remember the cab actually hitting anything, nor can I remember blacking out, but I must have, because suddenly I was hanging upside down, held in place only by the seat belt, the roof of the car underneath me and my hair draping into a small pool of blood. Blood that seemed to be dripping from my forehead.

I groaned, and turned around, trying to see where we were. The driver—far bigger than me—had half-crumpled onto the roof and looked to be unconscious.

His body was covered by bits of glass that sparkled like diamonds in the early-morning light. There were cuts all over his face and his right arm was hanging at an odd angle. Beyond him, the front of the cab had been crushed, the top of the windshield now meeting the bottom. Steam gushed through the bits and pieces of glass that remained.

I couldn't hear the truck, thank God. Just the groaning of wounded metal and the hissing steam. I twisted around and pressed the seat belt release. Nothing happened. I pressed it again, and the thing let go, dumping me onto the roof. Glass sliced into my hands and I cursed softly. I might be a werewolf, and I might be able to heal such wounds easily enough, but it still fucking hurt.

I kicked out the remaining glass in the side window with more force than necessary, then carefully crawled out. The grass and mud felt like heaven under my fingertips, and for a moment I just knelt there, sucking in the cool crisp air and trying to stem the shaking that was beginning to rise from deep inside.

"Hey, you all right in there?" a male voice said from the other side of the car.

"I am," I said, "but the driver's unconscious."

"I've called the cops and the ambulance. You think I should move the driver out?"

"I don't know if he's got internal injuries." Hell, I didn't even know if *I* had internal injuries. Right now, I was feeling kind of numb. Maybe it was shock.

I called to my wolf form, felt the energy of her tingle through me as my limbs reshaped and re-formed, until what stood there was no longer human. I didn't move, sucking in the scents around me, aware of the sharp, rusty scent of the hissing steam, and the piney scent of the man standing on the other side of the crushed cab. But there was no sense of immediate danger. No sound that indicated the truck might be coming back to finish us all off.

I shifted back to human form, the process helping the bleeding to stop and wounds begin to heal, then pushed to my feet. The tree spun briefly around me, then stopped. I blew out a breath, and carefully walked around the crumpled trunk.

The stranger—a small, round man with brown hair—looked me up and down, then said, "You've been bleeding."

"Happens after a car accident." I bent down to look at the driver. His skin tone was normal, and though his breathing was a little rapid, it didn't seem an immediate problem. "The driver has a broken arm. If the ambulance isn't going to be long, I suggest we just keep an eye on him, and keep him calm when he wakes."

The stranger nodded. "Saw the truck that hit you. Got its plate number."

"Really? Could I have it? I know some people who can get right onto tracing it."

"Sure." He pulled a grubby bit of paper out of his pocket and handed it to me. I thanked him, then pulled out my phone and walked away.

Jack answered straightaway. "Riley, you can't be at Richmond yet, so what the hell are you ringing me for?"

"Bad news, boss. Some asshole truck driver ran my cab off the road."

"You're okay?"

"I'm standing here talking to you, aren't I?"

He snorted. "The smart mouth is working, so you've gotta be fine." He hesitated, and in the background, keys clicked. "Another car will be there in ten. It'll take you straight to the murder scene."

"You're all heart."

"I'm a vampire. We don't do tea and sympathy."

Not when there was a crime scene to get to, anyway. "A witness caught the plate number." I raised the bit of paper and read it out. "You want to get a trace done? Oh, and contact the cops. Tell them who I am, so I can leave when the car gets here."

"I'll get straight onto it."

He was a man of his word, and I had no trouble leaving once the new cab arrived. Half an hour later, the driver was dropping me off at the Richmond Street address. The wind whipped off the nearby Yarra River and spun its chill around me. I shivered and hastily zipped up my borrowed jacket, hiding the torn and bloodied state of my shirt in the process.

I slung my purse over my shoulder and turned around. The house was one of those cute, single-fronted Victorian weatherboard homes that Richmond was famous for. Which meant, of course, it was worth a sheer fortune. This one was a little forlorn looking, what with its weatherworn and rickety white picket fence, smashed front window, and a front door that seemed to have more patches than original wood. The "FOR SALE" sign behind the rickety fence had a black and red "SOLD" banner pasted across it, and part of me wondered if the deal would still go through now that someone had been murdered inside. That kind of information tended to turn people off.

Blue-and-white police tape had been strung across the door and windows, and a burly-looking cop stood near the gate, studying me with a somewhat forbidding expression. It was about then I realized I didn't have my ID with me, and that I didn't have a hope of getting inside that building—or past that cop—without it.

I dug my phone out of my jeans pocket and rang Jack again. I got his caramel-haired assistant, Salliane, instead.

Joy. "Sal, it's Riley."

"Ah, so the rumors are true. The bitch returns early."

And Jack wondered why I enjoyed snarking her so much. "It's such a pleasure to hear from you, too, Sal."

She made an unladylike snort. "What do you want, wolf girl?"

"Who's being sent to the Brighton Street cleanup?"

"You."

"Besides me, smart-ass."

Even the small screen of the vid-phone couldn't mask the amusement glinting in her brown eyes. "Cole Reece and his team."

I couldn't help the slight smile that touched my lips. Cole was a wolf-shifter I'd worked with briefly—on a case that had almost led me to being the sixth victim of an ancient god of evil. He was somewhat uptight when it came to the rules, and more than a little judgmental when it came to his opinions on weres, but my wolf soul sure as hell enjoyed teasing him.

"Have you got an ETA on him?"

She paused. In the background, I could hear the sound of typing. Checking the computer tracking system, no doubt. All Directorate personnel—those in the office as well as those in the field—now had small trackers inserted in their ears. Jack had no intention of losing any more staff than necessary. Not after the decimation of the guardian ranks by the madman I'd once called a mate.

"He should be almost on top of you," she said.

I should be so lucky. I shoved the thought aside and looked around at the sound of a car. The black vehicle that approached had Directorate plates. "He is. Thanks."

"You're welcome," she said, voice suddenly polite. Jack had probably just walked into the room. Sal didn't mind throwing crap my way, but she wouldn't do it in Jack's presence. Trying to impress the boss and all that. Why the hell he didn't bed her and be done with it was anyone's guess.

I shoved the phone in my back pocket as the car pulled to a halt. A tall, craggy-faced man of indeterminate age climbed out, his gray hair glinting silver in the cool daylight. His musky, spicy scent swum around me, as refreshing as an evening breeze on a warm summer day.

Which it wasn't, of course, but he did smell as good as that.

"Well, well, if it isn't our only wolf guardian," he said, his deep voice dry but warm. He looked me up and down, then added, "Did they haul you out of a dogfight or something?"

"A wrecked car, actually." And I wasn't the only wolf guardian, of course, but few people knew that. Most seemed to think that Rhoan was a wolf who'd undertaken the blood ceremony and become a vampire. The fact that he could walk in daylight was attributed to age. Few questioned the fact we shared the same last name, simply because that was standard in wolf packs. The same surname always carried down through the generations. "You were expecting someone else?"

"*Hoping* for someone else would be more accurate." He reached inside the car and pulled out a bag. "Someone with less propensity to foul crime scenes."

"Well, I'm afraid it just isn't your day."

"Apparently not." He glanced briefly over his shoulder as the two other men climbed out. One was a cat-shifter, the other a bird-shifter of some kind. I'd seen both of them at a crime scene with Cole previously, but had no idea of their names. Nor did Cole seem inclined to introduce them.

"Get the gear, guys. I'll head inside," he added, then glanced at me. "Are you all right? You actually do look a bit of a mess."

"Let's just say I'd rather be home than here, but Jack's given me no choice."

"Jack's like that. And I'm actually surprised you're not in there already."

"Just got off a plane from holidays and was shunted straight here. Hence, no ID."

"And you're here because Jack's hoping you'll find a little lost soul?"

"That, and the fact we're short on guardians who can investigate day crimes."

"Guardians aren't investigators. They're hunter-killers."

Which was totally true—up to a point. "Let's not get into that argument when there's a victim waiting."

He almost smiled. Almost. "Fair enough. Follow me, then."

I followed. The cop allowed us through after a quick inspection of Cole's ID and a brief explanation. Cole then handed me a set of gloves, donned a pair himself, and lightly pushed the front door open.

Surprisingly, given all the repairs it had undergone,

the door didn't creak as it moved. The long hallway beyond was shadowed, and the silence thick. Even the
whispering wind made little sound as it slid past our
legs and scattered the dust bunnies lying on the worn,
wooden floorboards.

The air escaping from the house was rich with the
scent of blood and death, but there was something else
here, something that had the hairs at the back of my
neck rising.

An evil so vile I had to clench my fists against the
urge to run.

I licked my lips and forced myself to remain calm. If
I could face the god of death, I could surely face whatever remnants of evil lay waiting in this house.

"The death still smells rather fresh," I commented,
glad my voice sounded so normal when I was shivering
inside.

"The neighbors reported it less than two hours ago.
The cops called us straight in."

I nodded, and narrowed my gaze a little. There was
a deeper blob of darkness down at the far end of the
hall, but it didn't look big enough to be a body. It
looked vaguely like a lump of wood, only there didn't
seem to be any missing from the walls or doorframes. I
switched to infrared, and the fading glow of life leapt
into focus.

It wasn't a lump of wood. It was a leg.

A leg that still wore a shoe.

This *was* going to be bad.

Cole pulled a flashlight from his bag and flicked the
switch. The bright beam of light swept across walls
splattered with blood and chunkier bits of God knows
what. Then it caught the limb and stopped.

"Nice shoe," he commented.

"Yeah." It was a silver stiletto, with sparkly bits around the toes. The sort of shoe worn to parties or dances, not abandoned houses.

"I'd better set up a mobile recording unit here."

"I hope you have more than one in that little black bag of yours. I'm thinking we're going to need it."

"I'm thinking you could be right."

He assembled then pressed what looked to be a small black globe against the ceiling, waited until the suction took hold, then hit the record button. The unit whirred to life, and one of the lenses behind the black glass sphere did a circuit of the hall before coming back to rest on the two of us. From here on in, any movement and all conversation would be tracked and recorded.

He handed me a pair of those paper-thin shoe-covers supposedly designed to stop further contamination of the crime scene. Once I'd slipped them over my heels, we moved inside, carefully avoiding the blood and gore. Two bedrooms led off the hallway, but a brief glance through the doorways revealed nothing out of the ordinary. The destruction seemed to have swept past them.

The stink grew richer, stronger, the farther we moved into the house. It wasn't just death, but age, mold, and urine. This house smelled like it had been abandoned for some time—and if the cloying scent of piss was anything to go by, it had been claimed as a squat for the homeless for almost as long.

So what would a woman who wore costly, sparkly shoes be doing here?

The eyewitness report hadn't mentioned anyone being forced into the house. Just a shadow breaking into it.

We stopped near the limb. I stared down at it, seeing the obvious tearing at the end of her leg, in the muscles and flesh. Someone had ripped this leg from her body. Not cut it, not bitten it, but literally pulled it free.

That took incredible strength. Which meant we were definitely dealing with something preternatural.

Cole glanced back to the mobile unit. "Zoom and record all floor elements at current location."

"Scanning." We waited, and after several seconds, the unit beeped. "Area scanned and recorded."

We moved on carefully. Footsteps from behind indicated the two other shifters had entered the house, but Cole didn't acknowledge them and neither did I.

The room beyond the hallway was a living room. Chunks of plaster were missing from the walls, and the grubby window to the right was smashed, allowing the light and the wind to swirl into the room. The smell of urine was stronger, almost masking the scent of death.

Almost.

There were more body parts here. An arm thrown casually on top of the fireplace. A shoeless foot leaning at an angle in a corner. And blood. Lots of blood, splattered in haphazard patterns across the walls and across the ceiling.

Shallow breathing wasn't helping any. The aroma seemed to be seeping into my skin, making my stomach curl.

"Don't move while I place another scanner," Cole said, his voice matter-of-fact.

"How do you manage it?" I asked, my gaze on the kitchen entrance and the shadows and death and thick evil that waited there.

It almost felt as if whatever had caused this destruction was waiting for our reaction. Reveling in it.

I shivered and rubbed my arms. My imagination really needed to be shoved into a box and left there, otherwise I was going to have a whole lot of trouble getting through days like this.

Cole pressed the black globe against the ceiling, then said, "Manage what?"

"The sort of detachment you have. How do you get through day after day of confronting this sort of destruction?"

He shrugged as the scanner whirred to life. "I imagine I cope much the same way you do. You do what you have to, and deal with the consequences later."

No matter how casual he seemed, it had to be a whole lot harder for him. He saw the destruction of good people day after day after day, but he had no hand in the final resolution. Didn't have the satisfaction of seeing yet another murdering psycho removed from society.

I did.

And it was at times like this—when I was confronting such useless devastation—I was fiercely glad that fate had made me a guardian. I mightn't have wanted the job—and I might still be reluctant to kill on order—but if I could help take out the monsters who wreaked this sort of havoc, then hey, I could live with a bit of blood on my hands.

The scanner beeped, confirming that the initial scan of the room had been completed. I moved forward, my gaze on the kitchen. The smell of death and the sense of evil seemed to be concentrated there, and a large part of me didn't want to go anywhere near it. But that wasn't an option. If there was a soul to be found, then that was where I'd find her. With the major parts of her body, not her bits.

My steps slowed as I neared the breakfast counter. The blood was heavier here, huge swaths of color rather than mere splatter.

I licked my lips and forced my feet on through the open doorway between the counter and the wall.

Her torso lay in a corner, huddled between the cabinets and the fridge, as though she'd sought refuge from whatever had come after her.

Her head . . .

Bile rose in my throat, and it was all I could do not to throw up right there and then. Someone had driven a knife through her right eye, into her brain, back out through her skull, and into the plaster. Then they'd shaved her.

And I have no idea why that seemed such a defilement, but somehow, it did.

A hand touched my shoulder and I jumped.

"Jesus, are you all right?" Cole asked. "You're shaking like a leaf."

"I'm fine," I said, voice somewhat restricted as I battled the urge to puke. "I just wasn't expecting . . . *that*." I waved a hand at the woman's bald head.

"No," Cole agreed, then added, "Worse, there doesn't appear to be any hair here. Our killer must have taken it with him."

I looked around and saw that he was right. "Oh, great. A freakazoid with a hair fetish. Just what we need."

He smiled, but there was little amusement visible in his pale blue eyes. "All hunters like their trophies."

I stared at him for a minute, not sure whether to be angry or just let it slide, when energy stirred past me.

I looked away. In the corner near the body, a wisp of thick air moved. It looked to be little more than smoke curling gently upward, barely visible against the darker shadows that clung to the body.

But it was not smoke, and a chill ran through me.

Her soul had come to talk.

"She's here," I whispered.

Cole looked at me, then at the body. "Where?"

The smoke grew stronger, found shape. Became more human in form. "Near her head."

He frowned. "I can't see anything."

"Trust me, she's there." I rubbed my arms, but it did little to ward off the chill. It was almost as if seeing and communicating with these lingering souls brought me altogether too close to the fierce cold of the underworld.

And far too close to that lingering, gloating sense of evil.

Wispy features formed. A mouth opened. *He did it,* she said.

There was an awful lot of anguish in that statement. And a pain that had nothing to do with her dismemberment.

Who? I asked the question telepathically, though I was still unsure as to whether a soul could actually understand or even hear me.

The figure stirred—an insubstantial form with only vague features. *Liam.*

So they *could* hear me, even if some didn't answer directly. *Who is Liam?*

The smoky form became agitated, and the chill got fiercer, until it felt like fingers of ice were creeping into my flesh.

She swirled faster, her movements almost angry. With every turn, energy built in the air, until the small hairs along the nape of my neck were standing on end.

Only then did the words come again. *We were to be married. We were to live here.*

With that statement, the energy fell away, and the soul disintegrated, fleeing to whatever region of after-life it was bound.

And with it went the sense of evil, although that faded a lot more slowly. It was almost as if it wanted to linger but something else was drawing it away.

I shivered again, then met Cole's curious gaze. "She said her fiancé did this."

"Her *fiancé*?" He looked around. "Seems he wanted to get out of that marriage real bad."

"Yeah." I glanced at her remains, and wondered just what her fiancé was. Surely not human. It was doubt-ful, really, that he was even a were or a shifter. As strong as either race was, most didn't have the sheer physical strength to rip someone apart so cleanly. Although there *was* one type of shifter who probably could.

"Would a bear-shifter be capable of doing this?"

Cole frowned. "Maybe, if they were in bear form. But from what I've seen, there don't seem to be any claw marks on any of the limbs."

"No." I looked at her torso and swallowed heavily. "I think I'll get out of your way and go question the neighbors."

This time, the amusement on his lips *did* light his pale eyes. "And you said it wasn't going to be my day."

"If you're not careful, I'll come back especially to mess up your crime scene."

"You probably will anyway."

"Not if you promise to send me a direct report ASAP."

"Done deal."

"Thanks," I said, and got the hell out of there.

Once in the open air—and free of the gloves and the booties—I stopped and sucked in several deep breaths. Death might still cling to my pores, but at least it no longer fouled my lungs.

I looked up and down the street, studying the house numbers. Once I'd spotted the one I wanted, I crossed the road. After shoving open the rickety gate, I bounded up the steps to the front door of the house. There was a small doorbell to the right of the handle, so I pressed it and waited. A dog yapped somewhere in the bowels of the house, then the lace curtains covering the window to the right twitched and a small, sharp face appeared.

"Shut that gate," he said, voice shrill and wavering. "You want the dog getting out?"

I very much doubted the dog would come anywhere near me, but I dutifully turned around and wrestled the gate closed. Only when I'd done that did the old guy open the door. The yappy dog was at his heels, still yapping away. It might be little, but it sure as hell made a lot of noise.

"Yes?" the old guy said. "What do you want?"

"Mr. Hammond?"

"Yes."

"I'm Riley Jenson, a guardian with the Directorate of Other Races. We're investigating the crime you reported this morning."

"Did you catch those buggers? I hate them boys, always breaking into them vacant houses and wrecking things."

I frowned. "Boys? You said in your report you only saw a shadow."

"Well, I did," he said, over the noise of the dog, "but

I know it was probably them boys again. I've run them off a few times since the house was sold."

I shifted slightly, bringing one foot closer to the door. The yappy little dog took a sniff and recognized wolf. The tail dived between its legs and it scampered away as fast as it could. The sudden silence was bliss.

"So you know who bought the house?"

He shook his head. "Seen 'em a few times, that's all."

"Do you know their names?"

"Nah. Just watched them, you know?"

I knew. Every neighborhood seemed to have at least one neighbor who knew all the comings and going, even if they didn't know all the names. "Could you describe them to me?"

"She was a pretty little blonde. He was tall, thin, with dark hair." He shrugged. "They always came in a green BMW, if that's any help."

It wasn't. Green BMWs might not be a dime a dozen, but they weren't exactly scarce, either. "When was the last time you saw the couple arrive at the house?"

"Last night. Three in the damn morning, it was. They were making so much noise Mitzy started barking."

I had a feeling it wouldn't take a whole lot to set that yappy terror off. Still, the question was—why did they come here? Even if they'd just bought the place, it wasn't exactly the most romantic spot for a rendezvous. Hell, the stench of urine alone would be enough to put the most ardent Juliet off her game—though I had no doubt there were Romeos out there who wouldn't have given a damn.

"Did you hear them leave?"

He shook his head. "Not then. Just yelled at them to shut up, then went back to sleep."

Obviously, he was a fun neighbor. I restrained my amusement and asked, "So what were you doing when you saw the shadow?"

"Getting the paper. The bastard paperboy threw it in the bushes again."

Deliberately, I was betting. "And you can't give me a description or anything?"

"It was just a black shadow." He shrugged.

Had he seen a vampire? It was possible—though he'd have to be an older vampire, considering it had been well after seven when Hammond had reported the break-in.

But why would a vampire waste so much blood?

And why would the woman's soul have said her fiancé made the kill if a vampire had been involved? None of this was making any sense.

But then, I guess crimes like this rarely did when the investigation was only just beginning.

"So you didn't see this figure leave, either?"

"No. I watched until the cops came. The boyfriend left not long after I made the report, though. He had all this goo over him. Couldn't make out what it was, but it was red, like blood."

Probably because it *was* blood. "Why didn't you tell the cops about the boyfriend?"

He shrugged. "It's his house, like."

"But didn't you think it odd that he walked out after you'd reported the break-in to the cops?"

"No. Didn't think about it much, really."

I held back my irritation. "Did you notice anything else odd about him, besides the goo?"

He shook his head, then said, "He was barefooted. Odd considering the cold."

Yeah. But at least it meant he'd leave a scent trail, which I might be able to track. "Which way did he go, then?"

"Left." The old man sniffed. "It was strange, really, because his car is still parked up the road."

I stared at him for a moment, not sure I'd heard right. "His car is still here?"

"Yeah. Down there." He waved a hand over my shoulder, indicating the right side of the street.

"Mr. Hammond, you've been extremely helpful."

He beamed. "Always a pleasure to help the boys and girls in blue. Just don't forget to shut the gate properly on your way out."

I left. The beemer was ten cars down from the house, parked in a no-standing zone. There was no one inside and the car was locked.

I dug the phone out of my pocket and dialed the Directorate. "Sal," I said when her not-so-cheery features came online. "I need a plate check."

"Is this official business?"

"Hell, no. I just thought I'd ring you up to piss you off."

"*That* would be no surprise." She sniffed. "What's the plate number?"

I read it out, then peered inside the car while I was waiting. Two warm winter coats had been thrown across the backseat, the vibrant red of one suggesting it belonged to a woman, while the other was definitely male in design. There was also an umbrella and several newspapers.

"Okay," Sal said. "That plate belongs to a green BMW, registered to one Liam Barry."

So it *did* belong to the victim's fiancé. "Could you do a background check on him? I think he might be the boyfriend of our victim, as well as her murderer."

"A lovers' tiff?"

"Trust me, this was more than a tiff."

"It'd have to be, otherwise we wouldn't have been called in."

True. "Can you get that information to me as soon as you have it?"

"I'll think about it, wolf girl."

I didn't bite, just hung up. I set the phone to record then did a slow walk around the car, detailing how I'd found it and who it belonged to. Then I placed the phone on top of a fence post, stripped off my coat, and used it as a shield as I smashed the front passenger window. Though I'm not sure why I bothered—a few more glass cuts surely wouldn't have made much difference to my already impressive array.

Glass sprayed over the seats, glinting brightly in the cold morning light. I shook the coat free of glass, then dumped it on top of the car and opened the passenger-side door.

The car smelled of leather, musk, and the tangy, flowery scent of perfume. The date on the newspaper was yesterday's, and it was the *Age* rather than the *Herald-Sun*. Upmarket rather than mass-market.

I reached for the man's jacket and sniffed it. The scent was musky, entwined in an earthy, piney aroma. Not an upmarket man when it came to cologne, obviously. Either that, or the girlfriend had bought it and he was just wearing it for her sake.

I took another sniff, just to clarify the scent in my mind, then checked the rest of the car. There didn't seem to be anything more than the usual rubbish that collected in cars—CDs, candy wrappers, and dirt.

No indication of drugs or alcohol. Nothing that would explain his sudden, violent outburst.

I closed the door, stopped recording, then called the cow to have the car picked up for closer forensic inspection.

Then I shoved the phone in my pocket, grabbed my coat, and headed back to the house. The bird-shifter was squatting in the doorway, carefully placing a piece of bloodied skin in a bag.

"Could you tell Cole I've just fouled one of his crime scenes?"

"Cole will not be pleased," the shifter said, voice gruff and somewhat harsh. Oddly enough—although perhaps not, given he was a bird-shifter—it reminded me of an eagle's call.

"Yeah, I know," I said, with a grin. "Tell him the green BMW with the smashed side window is the fiancé's. I've already asked for a pickup."

"Will do," he said, still concentrating on whatever was on the floor more than me.

"And keep an eye on this jacket, will you? I need something to change into after the shift."

He grunted, making me wonder if anything I was saying was actually registering. I dumped my jacket over the fence, then called to the wolf within.

Power swept around me, through me, blurring my vision, blurring the pain. Clothing disappeared into the magic as limbs shortened, shifted, and rearranged, until what was standing on the footpath was wolf, not woman.

I nosed around the gateway and, through the many

scents that crowded my olfactory senses, found the one I was hunting for.

With my nose to the ground, I followed. The chill wind ruffled my fur but did little to affect the trail. Liam obviously hadn't run after he'd murdered his girlfriend—not if these spoors were anything to go by. Running steps tended to be longer, the distance between each step—and therefore each scent mark—greater.

Liam had walked. Casually, unhurriedly. As if he hadn't a care in the world, despite all the blood that must have covered him.

I followed the trail into Rose Street, then crossed another road and found myself in a park. Trees lined the rim of the park and seemed to snake through the middle. Liam didn't stay on any of the well-worn tracks, instead heading for a small but thick clump of trees in the middle.

It was there I found him.

Only he was well and truly dead.

Chapter 4

I stopped and shifted back into human form. After tying together the ends of my torn shirt—for some reason, shirts and the more delicate fabrics like lace didn't seem to handle the shifting as well as jeans—I took out my phone, hit record, and made a brief report. Then I set it down and squatted beside the body.

Liam had died with a look of shock and agony on his face. His eyes were wide, his mouth open, and if it were possible for the smell of terror to linger on a body, then it did here.

Blood covered him from head to foot. It saturated his well-pressed pants and drenched his fine-looking cashmere sweater. It also painted the skin across the back of his hands and colored his fingernails. And there were strands of pale hair caught between his fingers, though nowhere near enough to cover the head of his dead girlfriend.

There was absolutely no doubt he was responsible for the girl's murder. But why? And just how did the shadow the old neighbor had reported relate? Did we have a potential witness, or was he—she?—another sick part of this gruesome event?

I scanned him again, wondering briefly how he'd died. There was no obvious cause—no gunshot or knife wounds. It was as if he'd just been strolling through the trees when he'd fallen over backward and died.

Heart attack? It was a possibility. It had certainly taken a heartbreaking amount of strength to do what he'd done—and he didn't smell like a were or a shifter of any kind. But if he *were* human, then his actions were even more extraordinary.

I waited for several more minutes, just squatting there, staring at the body, but nothing registered. Maybe this guy's soul didn't want to come out and talk. Maybe it was too shell-shocked. Or ashamed.

I rose, grabbed my phone and ended the recording, then rang the Directorate again.

"Gee, this *is* my lucky day, isn't it," the cow said dryly.

"I just found our murderer. You'd better send in a second cleanup team."

"You didn't kill him, then?" she said, in her most sarcastic tone. Someone had been reading my file again, and had obviously discovered my reluctance to kill. I'm sure it amused her greatly—though she could hardly talk. Sal wasn't the only one who could break into secure files, and her own such reluctance was the reason she was a liaison rather than a guardian.

"He was already dead when I found him. There's no

apparent reason for the death, so we'll need an autopsy."

"I'll arrange it."

"And tell Jack I'm heading back home to finish my holiday. I'll send him my report tomorrow."

"He won't be pleased."

"Tough."

After all, what was he going to do? Fire me? He'd spent too long getting me into the guardian ranks already.

I hung up, sent the two recordings to Jack, then turned off the phone. The minute the cow told him what I was doing, he'd undoubtedly want to talk to me, and all I wanted to do right now was go back to Kellen's, have a long, hot bath, then curl up in bed beside him.

None of which I could do until the cleanup team got here. So I waited, keeping away the curious and the occasional dog. When the team—three shifters I'd never met before—arrived, I explained events and told them to report their findings back to Cole, so he could include it in his report.

Then I retrieved my coat and got the hell out of there.

I went home long enough to grab my ID, just in case I was called out again, then continued on to Kellen's. He was indeed working when I arrived back at his building. He looked totally scrumptious in black pants and a pale cream shirt, both of which showed off his gleaming chocolate skin to perfection.

He looked up as I entered his office, and did something of a double take. "You look a mess."

"With compliments like that, is it any wonder I'm madly in love with you?" I replied dryly.

"No, seriously," he said, lightly touching the semi-healed cut near my hairline, his fingers so warm against my skin. "What's happened?"

"The cab got shunted off the road by a truck." I shrugged. "I'm okay, the driver's okay, so it doesn't really matter anymore."

"You should have contacted me—"

"So you can do what?" I interrupted, and saw the annoyance flair in his eyes. Not wanting an argument, I quickly added, "I would have rung you if it was anything serious. You want to go out for lunch?"

"Unfortunately, it's crazy here at the moment." He shoved a hand into his trouser pocket and withdrew the keys. "Consider my home your home. I'll be up there as soon as I can."

"Your home might soon *be* my home, so it goes without saying that I'll make myself comfortable there."

"There's no might about that, woman," he said, tone a growl but eyes glinting with amusement.

I grinned, then grabbed his shirt and dragged him to me, kissing him long and hard, right there in his office, in front of everyone. "Don't be long."

I released him and did a sexy walk on out of there. He didn't follow, nor did I expect him to. But I was betting he'd be upstairs sooner rather than later.

I stripped down once I'd reached his apartment, then poured myself a luxurious bath, sprinkling the water with the lemongrass-scented salts I found in the bath cabinet. At least they'd help erase the lingering aroma of death and blood from my skin. I shoved several New Age CDs onto the player, relaxing a little as the ambient beats and melodious singing filled the apartment, then climbed into the rich-smelling hot water. And there I stayed until all the underlying aches from the accident had been washed away and my skin began to resemble a prune.

Once dried and dressed, I wandered out to the kitchen and made myself a coffee. It was two in the afternoon, which meant my earlier assumption about Kellen's appearance had been totally wrong. Work was more problematic than I'd figured, obviously.

But given there wasn't a whole lot I could do about that—other than hope he got up here before nighttime—I made myself a sandwich, then headed over to his computer. I typed up my report and sent it to Jack, then cruised the Net for a while, checking out my favorite music sites to see what was new. Finally, with nothing better to do, I decided to print out the file Blake had sent me and read that again.

Only to discover that Adrienne had shared an apartment with another woman. Blake hadn't said anything about the woman, but it was briefly mentioned in one of the police reports. Yet no one seemed to have interrogated her, which was odd. I placed the file on the desk and went to the white pages to find a phone number. None listed. Either the number was private, or both women used their cell phones rather than having a landline, which was certainly a cheaper option these days. I went back online and signed into the Directorate's database. Nothing major had happened at Adrienne's address beyond a large number of break-ins. But then, while St. Kilda was considered a trendy suburb, it still hadn't shaken its darker past. Prostitutes and druggies still haunted the streets, and break-ins were often a side effect of at least one of those elements. Had to feed the habit somehow.

I drummed my fingers on the desk for several seconds, wondering if I had time enough to go out before Kellen came back up.

Which was unlike me. I'd never run my life to suit a man, and it was stupid to start doing so now. I cared for Kellen, there was no doubting that, but we weren't yet a committed couple. Even if we were, I had no intention of tailoring every moment of my life to someone else's time clock. That just wasn't my idea of married bliss.

And if it was his, then he was in for a huge shock. This was not likely to be the last time I was in his bad books.

So I wrote him a brief note, picked up my purse and his keys, and headed out. I caught a cab and headed to Adrienne's address.

Her apartment was on the Esplanade, one of St. Kilda's main streets and only a stone's throw away from the beach, Luna Park, and the Ackland Street nightlife. The pack's finances had certainly improved more than I'd imagined—either that, or my grandfather had been more of a skinflint than I'd figured. Certainly when we'd been there, a luxury apartment in the middle of a thriving hot spot like St. Kilda was an unlikely acquisition. And the pack *did* own it, not Adrienne or the woman she shared it with.

I paid the driver, then hopped out of the cab and stared up at the building. It was one of those modern structures that really didn't have any distinct style of its own—a slab-sided, low-profiled affair that at least didn't look too incongruous against the more elegant buildings next to it.

I pressed the security buzzer. A thinnish, bored-looking man in his mid-fifties looked at me for several seconds from behind the safety of his desk, then said through the intercom buzzer, "What can I do for you, miss?"

His voice had that it's-all-too-much-effort tone that guaranteed instant annoyance. At least to me.

I pulled out my ID and slapped it against the glass. "I need to talk to the occupants of apartment 303."

"Jodie Carr and Adrienne Jenson? I don't believe either is in at the moment."

"I don't care what you believe. I intend to go up there and discover for myself. Now, let me in."

He did. I strode over to the desk, my heels echoing sharply against the highly polished marble tiles.

"Have you got the master key for the apartment?"

"Have you got a warrant?"

His bored, somewhat condescending tones had my temper rising a little further, but I somehow managed to keep my voice even as I said, "I don't need one. I'm Directorate. Now, am I going to have to throw your ass in jail for being a pain, or are you just going to give me the key?"

"Hey, I was only doing my job, you know?"

"If you were doing your job, this building would not have such a high rate of break-ins." I gave him my sweetest smile. "Someone with a suspicious mind might think there was inside information being sold."

He muttered something under his breath and somewhat sullenly handed me the keys.

When I got up to the apartment, I knocked on the door and waited patiently for an answer. But there was none—and no sign of body heat in the front room under infrared. The apartment itself seemed deathly quiet. I tried again, just in case someone was in the bathroom. Then I slipped the master key into the lock and opened the door.

The thick, flowery scent of perfume hit me almost straightaway, but underneath was a sour aroma I couldn't quite place. I wrinkled my nose and wondered how any wolf could live with a smell like that. It was *awful*.

Trying not to breathe through my nose, I stepped past the door and into a surprisingly large living space. Although perhaps that feeling was enhanced by the white of carpets, walls, and ceiling, and the careful but sparse placement of furniture. All that white could have made the place feel sterile, but there were bold splashes of color in the form of cushions, flowers, and thick, thick rugs that had me wanting to rip off my shoes and run my toes through them. The overall feel of the place was surprisingly warm—though it was a feeling that was undoubtedly helped by the sunshine splashing through the huge wall of windows.

I ripped my gaze away from the million-dollar view and said, "Hello?"

The sound echoed, filling the warm silence. Trepidation tripped across my skin and I shivered a little. Though why I suddenly felt something was out of place, I couldn't really say. My clairvoyance tended not to give out juicy little details like that.

I walked across the living room, my footsteps ringing on the shiny wooden floorboards. The kitchen was small but functional, the fridge filled with fruit, vegetables, meat, and wine. But there wasn't a piece of chocolate or a cookie in sight. How on earth did they cope with the midnight hungers?

I closed the fridge door and headed up the hallway. There was a small laundry area—though it was more a laundry closet than an actual room—a bathroom, and three bedrooms.

Jodie Carr was in the third and largest of the bedrooms.

She was lying atop a queen-sized bed, the blankets tangled around her bare legs and her shirt and skirt darkened by sweat. Her breathing was uneven, her face an unhealthy shade, and there was puke all over her chin and the sheets.

I swore softly and called it in, then walked over to the bed. This close, she smelled of the urine and vomit that stained her and the coverlet—hence the sour smell. It was a wonder she hadn't choked to death.

After carefully pulling her onto her side, I lightly slapped her cheek, trying to get a response. I didn't know if she'd taken drugs or whether this was merely alcohol induced, and I had no idea how to treat either. Still, thank God I hadn't listened to the idiot downstairs and just left.

"Who is this?" a deep voice said from behind me.

I jumped and swung around, my fists clenching automatically.

Blake stood at the end of the bed, his arms crossed. His form seemed more solid than it had been up on the island. Perhaps it was easier to send his psyche into known areas.

"Her name is Jodie Carr," I said, then added, "What the hell are you doing here?"

"Checking up on your progress. Why is this Carr woman in Adrienne's bed?"

"You tell me."

He glanced at me, gray eyes hinting at the anger that wasn't yet showing on his flat features. "Why would I know?"

"Well, she's been sharing the apartment with Adrienne for more than a year, and the pack does own the apartment." I hesitated, but couldn't help adding, "Or does the chief dog not know what goes on in his own kennel?"

His eyes narrowed to slits, and the sense of danger was suddenly very palpable. "Adrienne made no mention of sharing, nor was this person ever here when Patrin or I visited," he said in a tight, edgy voice that suggested he knew—or guessed—a whole lot more than he was willing to say.

Which was an interesting reaction. Why would he hold back *anything* if he was so desperate to find his granddaughter? And if he *didn't* actually know anything about his granddaughter's living arrangements, then why would Adrienne hide Jodie's presence from her father and grandfather? The obvious answer was that she didn't think either would approve.

I glanced down at the woman on the bed, and I realized she was human. That might be one very good reason for the caution. But there could be another.

"Is Adrienne gay?"

His head jerked back so fast anyone would have thought I'd punched him. "No! Why would you even think that? She's my granddaughter."

"And being your granddaughter precludes the possibility of being gay, does it?"

"She is not one of *those*."

Again, his voice held an edge that was almost desperate. So, he mightn't know—or rather, might not *want* to know—the truth, but he guessed it all the same.

The fact that the mighty leader of the Jenson red pack was also homophobic was no great surprise. That had been apparent from his reaction to Rhoan over the years. But it must have been hell growing up in his family, knowing you were the one thing he hated. No wonder Adrienne had kept her sexuality such a closely guarded secret.

"Paramedics," another voice called from the other room.

"In the last bedroom down the hall," I yelled, then stepped around the bed, out of the way. Blake moved with me, his form shimmering, dropping in and out of focus.

A man and a woman came into the bedroom. She looked straight through Blake, not even acknowledging his presence. Which meant it was only me who could see him.

Lucky me.

I flashed my badge and told them how I'd found her.

"Smells like alcohol," one said, as his partner set the bags down. He looked around the room. "You seen any empty pill bottles? Anything to suggest she might have taken something else?"

"To be honest, I haven't really looked."

He grunted and looked at his partner, who immediately began a search. No empty bottles were found in the bedroom, but an empty bottle of sleeping pills was discovered in the bathroom.

"Right-o," the ambulance officer said cheerfully. "At least we know what we're dealing with."

"Will she be all right?"

"Probably. The depressant effects of alcohol can add to the effects of the sleeping pills, and can cause people to go into a coma or die, but I'd say she's puked most of the pills up. It probably saved her life."

Considering she hadn't choked on her own vomit, either, she was one lucky woman. Although she probably wouldn't think so when she finally came to.

"What hospital will you be taking her to?" I asked. "I'll need to question her once she's in the clear."

"The Alfred," the woman said, without looking at me.

"Thanks." I headed out. Blake followed.

"Why are you so interested in her?" he said. "What does she matter?"

"She matters," I said, keeping my voice low and free of anger, "because she may know of Adrienne's last movements. You know, who she was with, and so on."

I walked into the second bedroom and began looking around. This room smelled a little fresher, hinting at lime and citrus. It also had a small balcony attached, with a metal table and two chairs filling up most of the space. An ashtray and lighter sat in the middle of the table. I wondered which of the women smoked. Probably Jodie. It was more a human habit than wolf—there were far too many poisonous scents evident to sensitive noses. And if Adrienne put up with Jodie smoking, they really had to be in love.

There were lots of little bits and pieces scattered about the room that suggested that this room was used more as a dressing room than a bedroom. I opened the closet door to check it out. It was small, and packed with clothes sorted into two different sizes. Adrienne was tall and lanky, if these were anything to go by, because Jodie was on the petite side.

I closed the closet door and went through the tallboy drawers. Underclothing, sweaters, and pajamas, in two distinct sizes. This was looking more and more like a couple's living arrangement rather than two single women sharing.

The paramedics trooped out with the still-unconscious Jodie. I checked the rest of the apartment but didn't really find anything enlightening. I stopped in the middle of the living room and wondered where to go next.

Blake drifted in from the kitchen. "If you'd read my report, you would have already known that there was nothing here."

"Yeah, you searched so thoroughly you completely missed the fact there was another woman in residence."

His expression darkened. Once I would have feared that look, and part of me still did. I was a wolf, and there was no escaping the inherent need to obey my alpha. But even if he'd been real and here, I would have held my ground. I'd faced far worse than the likes of Blake in the last year or so, and much of the fear he still engendered was due more to memories than the man himself.

"Adrienne would have told me if this was a permanent living arrangement."

I snorted. "If so, then she'd probably be the first adult in history to be completely honest with her parents. I never was."

"Yeah, but that was probably more a by-product of your unsavory parentage than any real need to keep secrets."

My fingers curled into my palm, and it took a real effort not to throw that punch. "Make allusions to my mother's line, and I will come down to pack lands and rip your goddamn throat out!"

He studied me for a minute, then a wide, cold smile split his features. "I believe you mean that."

I didn't say anything, just stared at him as the anger pulsed through me.

He shook his head in an almost pitying way, and

added, "You wouldn't get five steps within our boundaries, let alone anywhere near enough to challenge me."

"If you believe that, then your research is not as complete as you think." I paused, then added, "And if you think I'd be coming alone, you're delusional."

"Do you honestly think your brother's presence would make any difference?"

I smiled. A cold, nasty smile. "Learn what we are—and what we can do—before you make rash statements like that, Blake."

He shook his head again, his expression almost amused, and said, "Adrienne had no reason to hide anything from us."

I flexed my hands, but it didn't do much to ease the tension still riding me. "Yeah. You and your sons are so damn tolerant and kind when it comes to homosexuals that she had absolutely no cause to fear your reaction at *all*."

His gaze darkened again. Spectral figure or not, a wise wolf would have shut her mouth.

"I do not wish to hear *that* accusation again." His voice was soft. Deadly. The sort of voice heard just before he threw someone off a mountain.

Despite myself, I shivered.

"If you want answers, you may have to face a whole lot worse than homosexuality."

"Like what?"

I shrugged. "Cases never play out as you expect them to."

"What I expect is Adrienne home safe and sound. Nothing more, nothing less."

"You and the families of the thousands of others who go missing every year. In a case like this, what you want or expect doesn't really matter." I glanced at the time. "I'm off home for some R and R. See you around, Blake."

"Why aren't you going to the hospital to interview this Jodie person?"

"Because she won't be in any real state to talk until at least tomorrow."

I turned my back on him and walked out. Though his gaze felt like it was burning holes in my back, he didn't actually follow, and for that I was grateful.

When I finally got back to Kellen's apartment, he was sitting on the sofa reading Blake's file. He looked up when I entered, his green eyes concerned.

"Your current case involves your pack?"

I wrinkled my nose. "It isn't really an official case. My alpha has asked me to investigate several disappearances."

"Alpha? Don't you mean your grandfather?"

"No. He was challenged and lost."

"Ah."

He put the file down then held out a hand. I weaved my fingers through his and allowed myself to be pulled onto his lap. His arms circled my waist and his scent wrapped around me, until all I could feel was his warm and steady presence. And it was a somewhat delicious sensation, knowing that this big, strong wolf was mine. That he wanted me, and only me.

If I was a cat, I'd pretty much be purring in contentment right now.

"Your pack has no claim on you once another alpha has claimed you as his own," he said. "I can stop him contacting you, if you like."

I raised my eyebrows. "You can?"

He brushed my hair to one side and kissed the nape

of my neck. A tremor of desire rolled through me. "Just say the word, and he is yesterday's news."

"He's a rather nasty piece of work."

"So can I be if someone is hassling my woman."

His woman. I liked the sound of.that. Liked it very much.

"That's so very tempting," I murmured, wriggling closer, enjoying the heat and scent of him as it flowed across my senses. "But I'd better deal with it myself."

"The offer remains if you happen to change your mind." His lips were so close every word felt like a caress against my skin. Desire spread like a wildfire. "Are you finished for the day?"

I draped my arms loosely around his neck and dropped butterfly kisses on his lips, his nose, and his cheeks. "I'm yours to do with whatever you wish."

"Anything?" he said, voice so deep and husky it sent a shiver of delight down my spine.

"Anything at all."

"Even ravish you senseless, until all you want to do is beg for mercy?"

Anticipation sizzled, and I grinned. "It will take a long, long time to get me there, wolf."

"I can be a patient man when I want to be."

"Prove it."

His lips met mine, and from that moment on, there was no more talking, just a whole lot of loving.

And oh, it was good. I might have had many lovers in my short lifetime, but the way Kellen made me feel was somehow totally different from anyone else. There might not be the same sort of connection between us that I'd found—however briefly—with Quinn, but there was a connection all the same. It was deep, it was real, and it was so, so wonderful. He made me feel cherished, safe, like I was the only woman in the universe, the only woman for him. And that was a mighty powerful feeling.

Was it soul deep? I guess more than a part of me believed so, but something within still held back the words he wanted to hear. Maybe it was stupid, given the emotions tumbling through my mind, but I still wanted time to be sure.

Forever was a long time to live with a mistake.

$\mathcal{D}$espite Jack's promises that the Directorate's daytime division would have proper offices by the time I got back from the holidays, it appeared we were still holed up in the old conference room. Which was fine for the moment, but when Kade, Iktar, and whoever else Jack had hauled into the squad finally got through training, it was going to be a mite snug. Not that I minded getting snug with Kade, but Iktar? I shuddered. The featureless spirit lizard was not my idea of a good time.

So why the delay? The night division had more space than they needed—*and* decent coffee dispensers to boot—while we made do with one room, and a coffeemaker that had to be constantly refilled.

Of course, the fact that the night division was basically filled with leashed psychos might have had something to do with it. Wouldn't want the inmates getting restless, and all.

Jack wasn't in sight when I strode in, but down the hall, in the liaison's room, the cow was doing her sultryvoice routine, so it was a fair bet Jack was down there.

Rhoan sat at one of the desks that had been squeezed into our so-called operations room. He glanced up as I entered, and said, "How are you feeling after your brush with the mad trucker yesterday?"

"Other than a healing cut or two, I'm fine. Any word about the driver?"

"Broken arm and a few lacerations is about the extent of his war wounds. The truck was stolen, by the way. Jack said it was found abandoned an hour later."

"Don't suppose anyone saw the driver?"

"Not a soul."

"Typical." I poured us both a coffee, slopped in some milk, then plonked my butt down on the edge of Rhoan's desk and handed him a cup. "I don't suppose you managed to look into Adrienne's movements, did you?"

He wrapped his fingers around the mug and leaned back in his chair. "Did you know she was a reporter?"

"I guessed it was a possibility. She was apparently asking all sorts of questions up on the island."

"Well, if she was working on a story, then she was doing it on her own. According to her boss, she was supposed to be on holiday."

"So she didn't contact him about anything?"

"Nope. Last story she did for him was an entertainment piece on a new nightclub."

"There's a new wolf club? Why didn't anyone tell me?"

He grinned. "If you read the newspapers more, you might have known about it. But it's not strictly a wolf club." He picked up a matchbook off his desk and flicked it toward me. "It's the first mixed-race club allowed in Victoria."

I caught the matchbook one-handed. It was black, with "Mirror Image" written on the front flap in a white, basic font. Underneath this was a phone number and address, and nothing else. I flipped open the lid, and inside sat two neat little rows of matches, their tips black instead of the usual red. There was nothing on the back of the matchbook.

I looked back at my brother. "Mixed-race? As in, open to humans *and* nonhumans?"

"Yep. It operates in the exact same fashion as regular clubs."

I raised an eyebrow. "What happens when the moon is rising?"

"Nothing. They're open all year round."

"Really? Have the laws changed or are the owners just crazy?"

The old rules gave clubs the right to exclude human entry entirely—and this was a good thing, because were loving could sometimes get extremely rough, especially during the full-moon phase. The fact of the matter was, humans just were physically unable to handle it. And I didn't mean sexually. We could shift shape to heal any wounds received during intercourse. They could not. What might be a deep but easily healed wound for a were could be fatal for a human. And the outcry after such a death would be huge, even if the act was consensual.

Of course, the idiots in parliament had been trying to legislate a change for ages, but the Australia-wide protests from both the supernatural community and the saner section of humanity had so far managed to stall them. Or so I'd thought.

"They haven't changed," Rhoan said. "They've just been . . . ignored. This club is operating under a trial license for a year. If everything goes well, the current law forbidding human entry into wolf clubs will be overturned."

"That's just stupid."

"Humans have always wanted what they can't have. It's the whole forbidden-fruit effect."

That was an effect not restricted to humans, but in this case, the laws were there for a very good reason—the protection of humans.

"This club would have to have a hell of an insurance bill." I looked at the matchbook, flipping it over and still seeing nothing of interest. "Did you ferret out the article she wrote?"

"I've requested a copy be sent to us." He paused. "Adrienne is very well liked by her coworkers, you know. That's surprising, considering her family."

"I guess there has to be one good apple in every bad barrel." I took a sip of coffee, then asked, "No whispers of her sexuality, then?"

He raised a pale eyebrow "No. Why?"

"Because she's sharing her apartment with a woman Blake had no idea existed, and I found that woman overdosed in Adrienne's bed yesterday afternoon."

"That doesn't mean there's a relationship. They could be good friends."

"And how many people are willing to off themselves over the disappearance of a good friend?"

"Not many, but then, it wouldn't be the first time someone emotionally unstable has done such a thing."

True. "Nothing else of interest?"

He shook his head. "I haven't had the chance to do anything more. I've been chasing after this damn baby vamp sucking the life out of folk in the Footscray district."

"When will these idiots realize we make the creator pay for the crimes of his young?" The Directorate wasted too much of its time ridding the world of rogue baby vamps when there were often greater evils to worry about.

He snorted. "For some of them, probably never."

"What, their brains go out the door when they become a vampire?"

"Think of it this way. Expecting some vamps to control their urge to create underlings is like handing out free condoms and expecting horny teenagers to actually use them. The excitement of the moment always gets in the way."

Amusement ran through me. "That's the first time I've heard of vampires being compared to horny teenagers."

He shrugged. "It works, though. Most of these babies are created by vamps who are still young themselves and who love the feel of power it gives them."

"So have you caught any trace of his daytime hidey-hole yet?"

"Narrowed it down to a couple of buildings. I'm off hunting once Jack gets here for his daily pep talk."

I grinned. Pep talks weren't exactly Jack's forte, which is exactly why we referred to his morning rundowns that way. And it had the extra bonus of pissing him off—something I liked to do every now and again, just for the hell of it.

I tossed the matchbook in the air and caught it lightly. "I'll check this out once I talk to the girlfriend at the hospital."

"What girl in what hospital?" Jack said, as he strode into the room.

"It's a missing-persons case that may blow up to be a whole lot more."

He walked over to the coffee machine, filled up a cup, then said, "Tell me about it."

I did. He harrumphed. "I don't want it monopolizing your time, but keep me updated on progress all the same."

I nodded. At least I had the go-ahead to pull in Directorate resources if I needed to. "Has Cole handed in his report from the Richmond murder case?"

"It's in the system. Both parties involved tested as human."

"*What*? Impossible."

"Not according to the lab results."

"But he tore that poor woman apart. A human just isn't capable of that sort of strength."

"You mentioned possible vamp involvement in your report."

"Yeah, but if a vamp had been there, we would have smelled him."

He gave me the "look." "Not necessarily. Some of us do wash, you know."

I smiled. "Those of you who do are few and far between." Smelling like the grave seemed to be the "in" thing amongst Jack's lot. Though, admittedly, I did know some very nice-smelling vamps. Jack was one. Quinn was another. Even the cow smelled pleasant, though I was never likely to tell her that. "Besides, if there was someone else involved, wouldn't there have been some indication? Surely Cole and his team would have found something—some hint or clue to suggest this?"

"Not if our vamp was an extremely strong psychic."

"Can even the most powerful psychic push a human to superhuman extremes? I've never heard of a talent that could endow someone with that sort of strength."

"There's a lot of talents out there that we know a whole lot of nothing about," Rhoan commented. "And there are lots of labs playing around with all sorts of enhancing drugs."

"A comforting thought for those of us on the front line," I muttered.

"Give it a few more years and you won't even blink at the sort of crap you see or find."

"Actually, that's a place I'm fighting to stay away from."

Rhoan's gaze met mine, gray eyes serious. "You won't have any other choice but to find that place in yourself. It's either that, or go mad."

"Then going mad is the better option."

I didn't *want* to have the skill to switch my emotions off. Didn't want to ever lose the anger and horror of walking into a crime scene and seeing another useless death. For good or for bad, I was now a guardian, but I'd be damned if I became just another cold-blooded killer.

Which my brother, for all that I loved him, could be. I'd seen it happen. Seen the switch flicked.

It was damn scary stuff.

"Business, people, business," Jack said. "Riley, I want you to go check the boyfriend's current residence. See if there's anything there that hints at supernatural or nonhuman involvement. Then check the girl's apartment and go talk to her parents."

I nodded. "What makes you think the boyfriend may have known this vamp, if indeed there was a vamp?"

"I doubt it was mere coincidence that this vamp and those two young people happened to arrive at that house the same night. Something is going on, and we need to uncover what."

Before it happened again.

And it would happen again.

I shivered and rubbed my arms, wishing my god-damn clairvoyance would be a little more helpful. Like, give me a name, or a location, or something use-ful like that. Weird little premonitions of impending doom weren't going to help anything, least of all my nerves.

"Rhoan, how are you doing with the Footscray killings?"

I jumped off the desk as Rhoan made his report, then dumped my purse on the next desk and sat down, logging into the computer and holding still for the eye scan. Once I'd typed in my password, I entered the sys-tem and pulled up Cole's files. I studied his report but avoided the pictures. I'd seen more than enough blood-shed and human bits up close and personal.

There was nothing that leapt out and waved clue. Nothing that explained the sudden act of violence by a man apparently ready and willing to settle down with the woman he'd so brutally murdered.

Why would he do such a thing? There was no history of violence in Liam Barry's background, no brushes with the law. He'd been a model student through school and university, and had been considered by the law firm he worked for future partner material.

So what had turned him? And how had he managed to tear Callie Harris—the woman he supposedly loved—limb from limb?

I didn't know, but I had every intention of finding out.

I checked both his and his parents' address, then glanced up at Jack, waiting until he and Rhoan had finished discussing the baby vamp case before saying, "I need a car."

"See Salliane."

"Unlike some in this room, that's something I try to do as little as possible."

He gave me his vampire face. The one that said he was annoyed but trying not to show it. "Will you two just quit the crap and get along?"

"Not possible, boss. She's a cow, and I'm a bitch. Two species that will never see eye to eye."

"Just get down there and get that car before I find something nasty for you to do."

I was tempted to ask what could be worse than the murder scene he'd sent me to yesterday, but, knowing Jack, he probably *could* find something worse. So I shut my mouth, collected my purse, and got out of there.

The cow turned around as I entered the liaisons office, and rolled her brown eyes. She always reminded me of a caramel-haired Amazon—she had the height and the strength and the added bonus of big breasts. I pretty much figured she was wet-dream material for most men, which made Jack's reluctance on the involvement front all the more puzzling. I mean, he was a man with needs, and Sal sure as hell was willing to fulfill each and every one of them. Or was it simply the fact that she was also a vamp? Quinn had told me two vamps couldn't actually live together because of the whole territorial thing. And yet we had vamps living downstairs side by side without any real problems, so maybe Quinn had been flinging yet another lie. It wouldn't have been the first time.

"Well, well," she said, voice all sultry. "The mutt in person. Isn't this a pleasure."

I gave her my most pleasant smile. Her eyes narrowed and she stiffened in the seat, as if readying for an attack. Amusement bubbled through me. There might be parts of this job I hated, but God, little moments like this just made it all seem worthwhile.

"Jack sent me in here to show you how the liaison job is really done. He's sick of your crappy mistakes."

Her gaze darkened. "Jack would never say that!"

"If you think so, then you don't know him as well as you think you do." I swiped a set of keys off the hook and glanced at the number. "I'm taking car thirty-two."

"That's not your assigned car."

"It is now," I said airily, and walked out.

"Bitch!" she yelled after me.

I chuckled softly. No doubt she'd run to Jack and have a whine, which meant I'd get in trouble when I got back, but hey, if it pissed her off, then the pain of listening to Jack rant was worth it.

Though why I felt the need to be such a bitch around that woman, I couldn't honestly say. She just rubbed me the wrong way—and that was never a good thing to do to a werewolf. Especially one armed with a mouth that tended to run out of control at the worst possible moments.

I found the car and headed out of the underground parking lot. Liam Barry lived in a Middle Park apartment that sat on busy Beaconsfield Parade, right opposite the beach. It was, I discovered when I got there, tiny—boasting one bedroom and a minute kitchen and living area—but the views were incredible.

I walked over to the mess of men's magazines and discarded clothes, and stared out at the sea and sand for several moments, wishing I could throw open the windows and let the cool salty breeze in. Let it wash away the stale and unused feel of the apartment.

Forcing myself to turn away, I let my gaze sweep the

tiny, dusty interior, looking for something that jumped out. Nothing did. The magazines and mess were pretty much what I expected from a high-flying bachelor—which, until he actually married Callie, was what he'd been. An attached bachelor, granted, but a bachelor all the same.

I toed through the magazines, then moved into the kitchen. His fridge had a sour smell, and the milk looked to be forming into butter. I shut the door quickly, wrinkling my nose at the odor. On the side of the fridge were several bills—electricity and gas. The only thing unusual about them was the fact they were overdue. For some of us, overdue bills were a fact of life—especially when we had a brother who loved shopping sprees—but Liam made a ton of money. Still, maybe he was just one of those people who tended to forget them.

I blew out a breath, then turned and walked into the bedroom. It was barely big enough to hold the king-sized bed. And the rumpled, stale-smelling sheets suggested they hadn't been used or changed in quite a while. Obviously, Liam didn't spend a whole lot of time here anymore. After searching through his closets and drawers, I gave it up as a bad joke and headed outside to suck in some air.

Once back in the car, I typed Callie's address into the nav computer, then headed there. She lived several blocks up the road in Port Melbourne, in an old industrial area that was rapidly gaining popularity with young trendies who liked being close to both the city and the beach, but weren't willing to foot the million-dollar price tags some of the other beachside suburbs were now commanding. Her apartment was one of those converted warehouses, with views over the bay and port.

Again, the apartment wasn't big, but it had two bedrooms and a larger living space than Liam's. He'd obviously been living here for a while, because his clothes were scattered haphazardly about. I searched through the rooms from top to bottom, but couldn't find anything odd. There were lots of pictures of them together, and some of those had other people in them. They looked like a couple very much in love, which made what had happened all the more puzzling.

I pocketed a photo of the two of them and left. I'd barely reached the pavement when my cell phone rang, the sound seeming shrill and uneasy against the cool calm of the sea air.

Trepidation ran through me, and with some reluctance, I pulled the phone out of my pocket and answered.

"We've got another one," Jack said bluntly.

Chapter 5

I closed my eyes and took a deep breath. It didn't do too much to ease the tension running through me. I didn't want to face the destruction I'd faced yesterday. Didn't want to face the horror and pain of another soul. Didn't want to feel her in me or around me. Two in as many days was at least one too many.

"Exactly the same?" I asked, after a moment.

"Apparently so."

"Where?"

"Essendon."

Which was a northern suburb, and nowhere near Richmond. Which meant whatever the hell was going on wasn't being restricted to the one area. "Cole on his way?"

"Yep. Should be there in five."

"It'll take me twenty or so." I paused. "Were there any witnesses?"

"No neighbors reported anything. The woman's sister found her this morning. She's currently in the hospital under sedation."

As she would be, if this morning's murder was anything like yesterday's. "Did she say anything to the cops beforehand?"

"No. And the cops have tried contacting the woman's husband, but there's no response. Apparently he didn't turn up for work this morning."

Her husband. Good Lord. I briefly closed my eyes and blew out a breath. "I'll get there ASAP."

"Keep me updated."

"Will do." I hung up and climbed into the car. The journey over wasn't a pleasant one, my mind more on the images of bloodshed than the road. It was a wonder I didn't crash.

Cole and his team were already in place and investigating by the time I pulled up. I ducked under the police tape and walked up the steps. The smell hit me almost immediately and I stopped, unwilling to face what I knew waited.

Because not only did death wait, but that thick sense of gloating evil, as well. It wanted a reaction. *Needed* a reaction.

And if my turning stomach was anything to go by, it might just get it.

Though I made no sound, footsteps began to echo through the house, heading in my direction. Cole was a wolf, even if he was a shifter rather than a were, and he must have scented me. He appeared out of the gloom of the hallway, stripping off bloody gloves and tossing them in the special waste unit that had been set up to one side of the door.

"It's as bad as the first one," he said, stopping in the doorway and filling my senses with his warm, masculine scent. It was a nice distraction, but one I knew couldn't last.

"Same deal as before?"

"Yeah, pretty much." His gaze swept me, but it was more clinical than interested. "You ready to face it?"

"Her," I snapped. "Her soul is a *her,* same as she was."

He raised an eyebrow, but didn't say anything. Just reached to one side and handed me another pair of those paper-thin shoe-covers. "Use these. It's pretty messy in there."

I slipped the things on yet again, then asked, "Has the husband been found yet?"

"Nope. But he's looking a likely suspect."

"Except if this murder is like yesterday's. Then something else is going down." I stood up and blew out a breath. "Okay, let's get this over with."

He stood to one side and waved me ahead of him. The stink hit harder the moment I stepped into the small hallway, filling every breath with the scent of death. I shuddered, and tried to ignore it.

Which was a hard thing to do when it seemed to permeate not only the air, but the walls themselves.

"Through the living room and into the kitchen," Cole said, his warm voice almost jarring against the cold stillness of the house.

I walked through the living room, avoiding the bloody splashes and bits of gore. The bird-shifter glanced up and gave me a nod as I passed him, then got back to examining the bloody handprint on the wall.

There were more bloody prints on the doorframe. I flexed my fingers, trying to ease the tension rolling through me.

I knew what to expect. Knew it would be bad. And

yet my stomach still recoiled when I saw the utter destruction of what once had been a human body. No
mere man could have done this. Hell, even with the
strength of a vampire and a werewolf behind me, I had
serious doubts as to whether I could have done this.

My gaze stopped on her torso, hunkered down in a
far corner under a table. Like yesterday's victim, a
knife had been plunged deep into this woman's right
eye, pinning her head to the wall behind.

And she'd died with a scream on her lips and terror
locked in her remaining eye.

My stomach rebelled. I turned and ran for the front
door, barely getting outside before I lost the contents of
my breakfast into the shrubbery. I stayed there, bent
over the mint bush, sucking in the scent as I tried to
calm the trembling in both body and spirit.

I couldn't go back in there. I just couldn't.

I didn't care if her spirit was there. It wouldn't tell
me anything I didn't already know—and I certainly
didn't want to feel any more of her pain than what I'd
already seen.

"Here, drink this."

Cole's soft voice came from behind me. I looked
around, then accepted the glass of water he was offering. After rinsing my mouth several times, I sipped the
remaining water, not wanting to stir my fragile stomach any more than necessary but needing to get some
moisture back into my body. It felt like that house had
drained me in more ways than one.

"I'm sorry," I said after a moment. "That was very
unprofessional of me."

"Yeah," he agreed. "But it's nice to know some of
our killers still have a soft side."

"Oh, there's lots of soft things about me," I said,

trying to force some lightness into my voice and not succeeding very well. "And if you play your cards right, I might just let you uncover them one day."

"A day I can wait for," he said, amusement mingling with concern in his bright eyes. "Did you get any sense of a soul in there?"

I shook my head. There was nothing in there but death that was bloody and raw. That, and the sense of evil that hovered gloating above it. Whether it was a soul or merely a lingering emotion I was somehow sensing, I had no idea. But I had no intention of opening myself up to it to find out.

I shuddered, and took another hasty sip of water. "She had no hair, just like the first victim."

"Yeah. Seems the hair fetish is a part of this, whatever this is."

"Did you find any hair at yesterday's scene?"

"No. Why?"

"Because the fiancé had some hair in his hand when I found him, but not enough, and I didn't see it dumped anywhere along the way. So what happened to it?"

"Anyone's guess right now."

Yeah, I guess it was. "Has anyone tried scenting out the husband?"

"No. I'm the only one here with a nose strong enough to do it, and I can't leave the scene until the investigation is done."

Which may well be too late to uncover anything useful. "You want to get me something with the husband's scent on it?"

He nodded, and moved back inside the house. My gaze swept the surrounding houses, seeing neat, cared-for lawns and dwellings. Why had death come calling in this happy little neighborhood? What had this couple done to bring such destruction down upon themselves?

Cole came back out carrying a crumpled white business shirt. I took it from him and sniffed deeply, drawing in the musky scent of human male. Then I stripped off my jacket and sweater, and handed them to him, along with my purse.

"Keep these safe for me, will you?"

He nodded, then stepped back as I began to shift shape. In wolf form, Cole's scent leapt into focus—a delicious aroma that had my tail wagging and my hormones jumping. I studiously put my nose to the ground and tried to ignore it. After scuffing around for several minutes, I caught the husband's scent and followed it out onto the pavement.

I followed the trail down Kernan Street and onto Robinson, trotting past a mix of houses and apartments, all filled with life if not laughter. It made me feel warmer, somehow.

But dread began to fill me again as I crossed another road and entered another park. I suddenly had no doubt what I would find at the end of this trail, and find him I did. In a stand of trees near the lake.

Like Liam Barry yesterday, this man lay on his back. He'd died with a look of shock and agony on his face and the smell of terror lingering on his skin. The part not covered by blood and gore, that was.

I shifted to human shape, then called it in. Ten minutes before a cleanup team arrived. I swore softly, then set the phone to record, placed it in the branch of a nearby tree, and began my report.

And noticed there were only a few strands of dark hair clutched in his bloody fingers.

Where the hell was all the hair going?

I didn't know, but I had a feeling it was some sort of clue.

The cleanup team arrived precisely on time. I left them to it and walked back to the house. I didn't see any hair floating about on the breeze or caught in trees. Maybe it had already been swept down the street drains. Or maybe the answer was far more sinister.

Perhaps what I needed to do was check out past murders, and see if this pattern had been set elsewhere.

Cole was nowhere to be seen when I arrived back at the house, but his scent was drifting out from inside. I donned my sweater, then grabbed my jacket and purse and headed back to my car. There was nothing more I could do here at the moment—or rather, nothing more that I *wanted* to do.

It was time to go talk to Adrienne's lover.

*J*odie Carr lay wrapped in white hospital sheets, looking more than a little sorry for herself. Her blue eyes—a blue so pale they were almost gray—fixed on me briefly as I walked in, then her gaze skipped away to the window, staring as if there was something more interesting out there than just the brick wall of another building. She couldn't even see sky through that window. For a werewolf, that would have been hard to take, but I guess humans had higher tolerances.

"Jodie Carr?" I asked, stopping beside her bed and digging out my badge.

"Yeah. What's it to you?"

I held my badge in front of her. "I'm here about Adrienne."

She finally looked at me again. "Why? What is she to you?"

The slight edge in her voice had my eyebrows rising, if only because it oddly seemed to hint at jealousy. "Her alpha has asked me to investigate her disappearance."

She snorted. "That bastard didn't give a damn about her, not as long as she obeyed his edicts and behaved like a girl should."

"So he had a suspicion you and Adrienne were lovers?"

She blinked, and for an instant, fear slithered across her face. Not that I blamed her. I'd spent many years afraid of Blake and his get.

"Why the fuck would you think something like that?"

"Because it's true? Few people would try to kill themselves just because they believed a friend was dead."

She looked away and didn't say anything.

"Look, her father thinks she's in serious trouble, so any information you can provide might just help bring her back."

"She won't ever come back."

"And why would you think that?"

"Because she's dead."

I blinked. "Her father doesn't seem to think so."

"Her father is a goddamn moron. He doesn't know Adrienne. He never has."

"He's a clairvoyant. That would give him—"

"Nothing," she spat. "Nothing compared to what I have."

"And that is?"

"Love." She closed her eyes. "She's dead. I can feel it."

The pain in her voice had me wanting to reach out and comfort her, but I had a strong feeling any such move would be rejected. "What story was Adrienne working on before she disappeared?"

"I'm not really sure. It was something to do with the club—something she saw there." Jodie shrugged. "She never really talked about her work much at home. That was our rule."

"What club are we talking about?" Even though I'd already guessed the answer, I asked the question all the same. Better to get a sure answer than to be proved wrong later. "Mirror Image?"

She nodded.

"So they *do* allow humans and werewolves to intermingle sexually there?"

"Yeah. There's a no-claws-or-violence rule, though. Anyone seen getting a little too heavy with a human gets thrown out." She looked at me coldly. "Don't tell me you're one of those wolves who believes a no-mingling-with-the-humans rule is safer for everyone?"

"I've seen what a werewolf in a sexual frenzy can do to another wolf. A human wouldn't last."

She snorted. "You misjudge the strength of humans."

"Or you're overestimating it."

If there was one inescapable fact in this world, it was that werewolves were stronger than humans. We might not be able to rip someone apart limb by limb, but we could rent and tear and brutalize. And if we were in the midst of moon fever, we might not even realize we were doing it until it was all too late.

Given that one inescapable fact, I was betting the humans who went into Mirror Image signed some type of waiver before they were allowed to enter. Letting humans and wolves intermingle in a sexually charged environment *had* to be asking for trouble. Especially during a moonrise.

Jodie didn't argue the point. Just looked away again.

I studied her for a moment, wondering just what Adrienne had seen in a woman who wasn't only human but who was all delicate angles and bones, then asked, "Is the club monitored?"

"Heavily. Cameras and nonhuman bouncers everywhere."

With nonhuman bouncers, they didn't really need that many cameras. Most of us could scent trouble long before it started. But maybe the owners were just being cautious. Or maybe they got off on watching others have sex.

"Did you and Adrienne go there often?"

She sniffed. "It was one of the few places we could go and not be worried about who was watching. There's not many choices for those with human partners."

And for damn good reasons. "And you didn't notice anything odd or out of place during your time there?"

"No."

"When was the last time you saw Adrienne?"

"At the airport. She was going to Monitor Island to chase a lead."

"Don't suppose she mentioned what sort of lead?"

"No, but she was excited. She said it could make her career."

Or break it, as the case may be. "Did she contact you at all while she was away?"

"Every night. The last time she was a little deflated. I gathered she couldn't find anything good for her story." She paused, and took a shuddery breath. "I was supposed to pick her up from the airport, but I got held up in traffic. She wasn't there when I finally arrived, and I thought she'd gotten tired of waiting and caught a cab."

"But she never arrived home?"

She shook her head. "I reported her missing two days later."

"Why two days?"

"Because she's disappeared before, but only for a day or two. She usually comes home after she's blown off some steam."

I wouldn't have been surprised if Adrienne's past disappearances coincided with her more aggressive tendencies. A careful wolf might be able to curb her instincts most of the time, but violence was a part of our soul, and sometimes it just needed to come out.

"I don't suppose you remember what were you doing when Adrienne first started investigating the club?"

"You know she did a newspaper piece on it, don't you?"

"Yes."

"She hated doing that, you know. She preferred crime stuff, investigative reporting. She was good at it, too."

"Then why did she do the entertainment piece?"

"She had no choice. Her old boss retired, a new guy came in. He decided she was more suited to reporting entertainment than crime."

"I'm surprised she didn't quit if she felt that strongly about it."

"Oh, she was intending to, but she wanted to be sure she had another job to walk into first."

Then she was more sensible than me. There were

times in the past I'd quit over jerk bosses, and had been left for weeks scrimping for a dollar to buy my next coffee. Of course, this was well before I joined the Directorate.

"So in the process of researching for the article, she discovered something that teased her instincts?"

"No. It actually happened after the article was published. The owners were pleased with what she wrote and gave her an invitation into the Executive Room—which is a private dance area for special guests. We were coming out of there when we ran into someone coming out of the private room opposite." She paused, and blinked away the sudden spark of moisture in her eyes. "Adrienne had a talent that went beyond the pack's clairvoyance. She could sense things about people. Catch glimpses of their thoughts or their actions through touch. When she bumped into that man, she uncovered something that had her excited."

"You didn't ask what she discovered?"

She snorted softly. "Of course I did. Wouldn't you? She just said that she'd hit the story jackpot, and would tell me more when she was certain."

"She obviously never did?"

"No."

"And you have no idea why Adrienne went to Monitor Island?"

"No."

"Did it involve the person she ran into at the club?"

"I told you, I don't *know*. Why do you keep asking me stupid questions when I've already told you I can't help you?"

Because I'm trying to find out what happened to her. Trying to prevent it from happening to anyone else. But I kept the words inside. It wasn't hard to guess that Jodie was speaking out of anguish more than any desire to be unhelpful.

"What plane was Adrienne supposed to arrive home on?" I'd need to check if she ever actually boarded it.

"A five P.M. Qantas flight."

"And there's nothing else you can tell me? Nothing she said or did that seemed odd to you?"

"Nothing at all." She looked at me then, eyes red rimmed and brimming with tears. "Just go away, and leave me alone."

I hesitated, wanting to ask more, but also not wanting to alienate her completely. I might need to question her again later. So I simply said, "Thanks for your help, Jodie."

She didn't answer, just went back to looking out the window. I headed out of the hospital and into the fresh air as quickly as I could. After sucking in several deep breaths to wash away the lingering aroma of antiseptic, pain, and hopelessness that always seemed to haunt hospitals, I began the long walk back to where I'd parked my car. As I walked, I took my phone out, hit the vid-button, and dialed the cow.

She was as happy as ever to see my smiling face.

"Now what the hell are you after?" she said, voice flat and annoyed.

I restrained my grin. I really *did* like this woman's flat-out bitchiness. "Want you to check out a club for me. I need background and trouble reports."

"What club?"

"Mirror Image."

She raised perfectly plucked eyebrows. "That's the weird one that allows humans and nonhumans to mix, isn't it?"

"Yep."

"Is it connected to the murders?"

"I don't know."

"I'm not going to pull reports on a club just because you're curious about it," she said, in that snotty way of hers.

"It may be connected to a missing-persons case I'm investigating. I'm just covering all the bases."

"Oh, I'm sure you're doing more than that, wolf girl." She sniffed. "I'll send whatever I can find."

"You're such a darling, Sal."

She all but snarled at me. I chuckled and hung up. In that instant, I felt it again. The cold chill of evil. An evil that hungered to kill, and rent, and tear, not talk.

I swung around, and saw it. Not the thing I was sensing, but the car. It had veered across several lanes of traffic and was coming straight at me. I had a brief glimpse of dark hair, thin features, and a grin of sheer delight before I was diving out of the way. I hit the concrete hard, rolled to my feet, and ran for the nearest street pole, my heart racing quicker than my feet. The roar of the car engine didn't get any closer. Instead, the car bounced off another and continued on, scattering pedestrians as it continued down the footpath before swerving back out into the traffic. I didn't bother chasing it. I might have vampire speed, but that car was moving way faster than I ever could, the driver weaving in and out of traffic like a madman.

I dusted the dirt off my hands and knees, then got out my phone again.

"This really has to stop," Sal said. "You might enjoy hearing my dulcet tones, but I have better things—"

"Fucking shut up and put me through to Jack," I said.

"He's in a meeting—"

"I don't care. Put me through."

She muttered something under her breath, then the phone made odd noises as she patched me through.

"This had better be important, Riley," Jack said. "I was in a meeting with the director—"

"Someone just tried to run me over," I snapped. "And I think whatever is killing these people might be following me."

I heard a chair slide back, then footsteps as Jack walked out of whatever room he was in. "Okay, explain."

"Remember the truck yesterday? Well, today it was a car. I caught a glimpse of the driver and I didn't recognize him. It wasn't accidental—he was aiming for me. I got the plate number."

"Give me it, and I'll do a check."

I gave him the number, then said, "It'll probably be stolen."

"No doubt. Now tell me about this thing following you."

I blew out a breath, and leaned against the street pole. "When I went to the first murder yesterday, there was a sense of evil lingering there. A gloating sort of evil, if that makes sense. It faded, so I figured maybe it was either my imagination or some leftover emotion I was sensing. But I felt it today at the second murder, and again now, just before that car tried to mash me between its wheels."

"Do you think we're dealing with a vampire?"

I hesitated. "I don't know. In some ways, it feels like I'm sensing emotions rather than anything real or solid."

"And you felt it before the car came at you?"

"But not before the truck. I don't think whatever it

is I'm sensing is connected to the run-over attempts, if that's what you're thinking."

"Can you feel it now?"

I hesitated, and looked around. The air was rich with exhaust fumes, gas, humans, and eucalyptus—not my favorite scents, but better than death any day.

"No."

"So you can't positively say it's not connected, then."

"Other than the feeling that it's not, no I can't."

He grunted. "I'll talk to Cole, see if he noticed anything unusual that didn't make his report. In the meantime, you be careful."

"Don't worry," I said dryly, "I have no intention of damaging the Directorate's investment."

"Good," he said, and hung up.

So much for concern over said investment. I shoved my phone back into my pocket and continued on to my car.

It took me half an hour to drive over to Callie Harris's parents' place, only to discover they weren't actually there. But Callie's sister, Jenny, was.

"So how can I help you?" she said, tucking a long strand of brown hair behind her ear with fingers that shook.

I sat down on the chair opposite hers and said, as gently as I could, "I need to question you about Liam and Callie's relationship."

"There's nothing to know. They were in love and getting married."

"So they had no problems? Never fought?"

Tears glittered briefly in her eyes. She blinked them away furiously. "Everyone argues. Even people in love."

"Do you know if they argued over anything recently?"

She looked away. "No."

"If you know anything," I said quietly, "even something small, it may just help track down their killers."

She didn't say anything for a moment, looking down at her clenched hands. "How could something they fought about help track down her killer? It didn't mean anything. They'd worked through it, and the wedding was going ahead."

I raised my eyebrows. "It didn't mean anything" was usually a metaphor for "I made a mistake of the sexual kind." "So Callie had a one-night stand?"

"At her bachelorette party." She hesitated, then said in a rush, "She was drunk, it really didn't mean anything, and she was so ashamed of herself afterward."

"When was the party?"

"Two days before . . . before—" She stopped, gulping down air.

I waited a moment, then asked, "And she told Liam about it?"

"She had to. I mean, how could she not? There were ten of us there. Someone would have told him eventually, and that would have been even worse."

Worse than being torn apart by a cuckolded fiancé? I didn't think so. "You didn't try to stop her straying?"

She blushed and looked away. "I didn't know. Not until later."

Because she was too busy getting laid herself, I bet. "Where did this all happen?"

For some odd reason, I was expecting her to say Mirror Image, but she didn't. "At a friend's. She owns a house down Fairhaven way, right near the beach."

Then the friend had some money. Fairhaven had a million-dollar-plus price tag. "Who was the man she slept with?"

She shrugged. "One of the strippers."

"There was more than one?"

She looked away again. "There were ten."

One for each of them, then. Which meant it was not your typical bachelorette party—not if they catered to everyone's sexual needs. "Do you know the name of the company?"

"Nonpareil."

Not one I'd heard of, but then, I really didn't have a whole lot to do with humans and their sexuality. "Did you arrange it?"

"No, Cheryl, the other bridesmaid, did." She hesitated. "You don't think the strippers had anything to do with her murder, do you?"

"Probably not." If only because I doubted strippers would have been a link to the Essendon case. But then, who knew? Maybe the wife had needed to recharge her sexual batteries, or had been to a party that had employed a stripper recently.

"And there's nothing else you can tell me? About the strippers, that night, or their relationship? Nothing that you think might help, however inconsequential?"

She shook her head. "Liam wouldn't do this to her. It wasn't him. He worshipped her."

Maybe, but it wouldn't be the first time someone who worshipped their partner went off the deep end and killed them, for whatever reason. I'd watched enough of the news over my short life to realize that.

I pushed to my feet. "If you do think of anything—however small—give me a call." I gave her a card with my Directorate number on it.

She took it without comment. I headed out, and left her to her tears. But I hoped like hell I never had to confront that sort of pain again, either through work or in my private life.

Once back in the car, I typed "Nonpareil" into the onboard computer and did a search. The stripper business was located in the old section of North Melbourne, and there were no reports or complaints about it.

I started the car and headed over. To be honest, it probably would have been easier to ring, because I really didn't think these men were connected to the murders, but it was too easy to avoid truths on the phone. And if the strippers *had* seen anything out of place that night, I wanted to know about it.

Nonpareil was situated on the first floor of a nondescript brick building. It was surrounded by factories that looked to be carrying the grime of centuries on their facades, and the air was thick with the scent of oil, metal, and humans.

Not the prettiest of places to visit, that was for sure.

I pushed open the glass door and stepped inside. There was no sign of the grime here, just plush red carpets, gold handrails, and rich-looking paintings filled with apple-cheeked men and women cavorting around naked. Not what I'd call sexy, but then, I'd never been a fan of Old World style.

I took the stairs two at a time and found myself in a lobby that was all gold drapery and overstuffed, lush-looking furniture. The scent of vanilla and cinnamon teased the air, but entwined in that was the heady scent of man. Or rather, wolf.

This wasn't a human stripper business, as I'd presumed.

He was sitting behind a large mahogany desk down the far end of the room. In the half-light of the lamp-lit room, his golden skin seemed to glow a dark amber, and his brown eyes gleamed with interest.

"Well, hello there," he rumbled, voice deep and sexy. "What can we do for you on this fine afternoon?"

Why couldn't the Directorate find secretaries—or liaisons—who looked like this? Damn, he was fine. It was just unfortunate that I wasn't here for fun. I got out my badge and showed it to him. "I need to speak to someone about a booking."

"Past booking, I'm gathering?"

"Yes." I stopped near the desk, my nostrils flaring as his scent teased them. Orange and musk. Nice.

"Then you'll need to speak to the manager, Shadow."

Amusement ran through me. "Shadow? Is that his stage name or his real name?"

"Stage. We don't do real names when we're at work. A job like this tends to attract the loons."

He pressed a button and a door to his right opened. "Just wait in there. Shadow won't be long."

"In there" turned out to a small waiting room equipped with several well-padded leather lounges and a coffee machine that had more choices than I'd seen at many cafés. I helped myself to a peppermint mocha and drew the sweet, rich scent into my lungs. Not hazelnut, but almost as good.

Five minutes later, the door at the other end of the room opened and another wolf stepped in. He was tall and powerfully built, with chiseled features and skin so black it seemed to swallow the warm light whole. And the sheer sexual energy radiating off him had my hormones skipping along in dizzy pleasure.

"Guardian Jenson, I presume," he said, his voice a low vibration that rumbled pleasantly across my senses.

I stood so suddenly my coffee splashed over my

hand. It said a lot about my state of arousal that I barely even noticed it. "Yes. Sorry to be bothering you at work, but I need to ask you some questions about a past booking."

"The Callie Harris one, I presume?"

I raised an eyebrow. "Good guess."

"I saw the report of her murder in the *Herald Sun*, and presumed we'd be getting a visit sooner rather than later." His bright blue gaze flicked down my length, and the heat of it echoed through the fibers of my being. "I didn't expect our interrogator to be so pleasant on the eye, however."

I resisted the urge to fan myself, and said, "What can you tell me about that night?"

He waved a hand toward the seat behind me. "Please, sit."

I did, and had the pleasure of watching him walk across the room. He was a big man, but each step was a move of grace and a sense of power restrained. He sat on the chair several feet away, his gaze sliding casually down my body again before rising to meet mine. Lust surged between us, heating the air, sending little beads of perspiration skating across my skin.

He smiled. "It is a definite pleasure to be dealing with a werewolf for a change. No blushes or uncomfortable exclamations."

No, just a whole lot of desire that couldn't go anywhere. I was working, not playing. And if I said that often enough, I just might convince my giddy hormones. "So humans are the base of your business?"

"Of course. Human sexuality may seem outwardly repressed, but their hungers are as strong as any werewolf's."

I sipped at the coffee, then said, "But *they* are not. Isn't it dangerous? Especially during a full moon?"

"Yes, which is why we also employ vamps and shifters. Werewolves are never booked for the moon phase."

"Sensible." Though I'd imagine employing vampires could be just as dangerous. It would only take one to sip more than he needed, and there'd be a whole heap of trouble. Still, I wasn't here to lecture him on his business practices.

"So . . . Callie Harris's party?"

"Ten strippers, and a two-hour contract for sexual services afterward. A good earner."

"Who studded Callie?"

"Ramjet."

I couldn't help grinning. "Are you serious?"

"He's a big boy, you understand." His voice was solemn, but the twinkle in his eyes belied his seriousness. "And he has little finesse, but some like it that way. Ms. Harris apparently was one of them."

"And he hasn't seen her since?"

"There is a no-philandering-with-the-customers rule here, Ms. Jenson. It is strictly adhered to." He hesitated, and I felt the heat of his desire roll over me again. "You, however, are not a customer."

"No, I'm a guardian on duty. Did any of the men present on the night see or hear anything unusual that you know of?"

The scent and heat of his lust increased, swirling around me, filling my senses with his rich spicy aroma, making the low-down ache even fiercer. Part of me wanted to take what he was offering, enjoy the moment and this big strong wolf, but things weren't that simple anymore. Not with Kellen in my life.

"One of the vamps reported a brief mind touch, but it was gone before he could trace the source. Unfortunately," he added, before I could say anything, "he's on vacation for the next two weeks, and isn't available for questioning."

Conveniently? Or was I just being overly suspicious? Certainly there was nothing in Shadow's words or manner to suggest lies. "Did he say if it felt more feminine or masculine?"

"Masculine. I did wonder if it was a husband—or husband-to-be—especially after Ms. Harris's murder."

"So the source of the probe was external?"

"He wasn't entirely sure. As I said, the touch was apparently very brief."

Which didn't exactly help me decide whether it was important or not. "Do you know whether Callie Harris was drunk or sober?"

He raised a dark eyebrow. "That's an unusual question, is it not?"

"Not when I'm trying to find out if her encounter was deliberate or alcohol-induced."

He smiled. "It was very deliberate, trust me."

"Ah." So Callie's sister had been finding excuses to explain Callie's behavior. I wondered if Callie had used the same excuse with Liam. And whether he'd believed it.

I gulped down the remainder of my coffee, then rose and gave him a card. "If anyone else remembers anything, please give me a call."

He took the card, then reached down for one of the pens sitting on the coffee table and scrawled a number on the back of it.

"I know how to contact the Directorate," he said, handing the card back. "So I have no need of your number. However, should you wish anything else of me, please ring that number. It's my private, not business, line."

I smiled as I took his card. "I seriously doubt I could afford your rates."

He raised a hand, his fingers brushing my cheek, a featherlight caress that might as well have been a sledgehammer, so strongly did my body react. "Lust burns between us, Ms. Jenson. Should you ever wish to pursue it, it would be my pleasure. I do have a private life beyond managing this club."

"But I'm not sure I have a life beyond that of a guardian." I stepped away, and tried to ignore the frustrated screaming of my hormones. "Thanks for your help, Shadow."

He smiled. "I'll await your call, Ms. Jenson."

I didn't reply, just got out of there while I was still in control of my desires. Once back in the car, I turned the AC onto full cool, and wondered what the hell I should do next. The guardian training I'd undergone tended to concentrate on the other side of a guardian's life—the killing and surviving. The actual hunting bit was, in many ways, left up to individual instincts.

Right now, my instincts were insisting that if I wasn't going to give them sex, then I sure as hell better give them food. And maybe I'd think better on a full stomach.

I started the car and drove around until I found a McDonald's drive-thru, and ordered a couple of burgers, some fries, and a Coke. I munched as I drove, and after a while, found myself heading toward the leafy and money-rich suburb of Toorak and the home of Dia Jones.

Dia was a psychic—and a blind woman who saw far

too much. I'd helped rescue her kid from the clutches of the madman who was her brother and her master— at least in the sense that he could control all those who'd been created in the lab by his father. That madman was dead, but my help had indebted Dia to the Directorate, and she was one of us now—even though she was officially listed as a consultant.

I hadn't seen her a whole lot since the events on Deshon Starr's estate, though I knew Jack had been in contact with her a number of times. Part of me was iffy about seeing her now, simply because, while I liked her, being in her presence made me feel a little uncomfortable. It was like she could see through whatever I said, and glimpse the truth or lies behind it.

But if anyone could clarify—or at least hint at— what was going on, then maybe it was Dia. And any shortcut to solving our murder had to be a good one if it managed to save a life.

I pulled up in front of her house, which was more in the style of the grand old English mansions often shown on TV than the heavily ornate, American South style that seemed so prevalent on the rest of this street. The brickwork had been painted a warm, soft gold, and ivy crawled up the walls and across the roof, giving the impression that the house had been here forever. I climbed out of my car and walked through the ornate, wrought-iron gates. A lush, somewhat overgrown lawn stretched from the side gate to the porch, and pencil pines lined the boundary. I was still in as much awe of the place as I'd been when I first came here so many months ago. It was a pocket of peace in the middle of a thriving, bustling community.

Of course, Dia had been afraid that the government would take this mansion away from her, as it had started confiscating all of Deshon Starr's properties after we'd destroyed his crime syndicate and killed the man himself. Or monster, as he was. But Dia had a good bargaining chip—the Directorate wanted her services, and this house had been part of the price. I didn't know the other. Jack wouldn't tell me and I hadn't yet found the documents on the Directorate's network.

I walked up the steps and pressed the buzzer. There were a few beats of silence, then the intercom cracked and a soft voice said, "Yes?"

"Dia? Riley Jenson from the Directorate. I need to talk to you, if you have the time."

"Riley? Of course I have. Be there in a minute."

Another few seconds passed, then the door opened and Dia was standing there, as ethereal and beautiful as ever. Her hair—a pure whitish-silver—was loose, and shone with an almost unnatural brilliance as it spilled down the back of her long, flowing white dress. The garment scooped in at her waist, hinting at her shape while not emphasizing it. But no matter how stunning she might look in her floaty garb, it was her eyes that always got me. Even if she was blind, the blue of her eyes was magnetic—and yet, in many ways, unforgiving. And once again I was struck by the sensation that this woman saw far more than she was ever likely to admit.

Of course, the blue of her eyes wasn't natural, just like the silver hair. Her true hair color was a mix of silver and brown, and her eyes were also naturally brown, ringed by blue, but she'd once told me silver and blue suited her better. Dia wasn't only a psychic, but a clone with Helki shapeshifting genes who was able to subtly alter her appearance as easily as I could become a wolf.

"It's lovely to see you again, Riley." Her voice was as

warm as her smile. "But I'm gathering this is not a social call?"

"Unfortunately, no." I hesitated. "How's little Risa doing?"

Her smile broke free, stunning in its richness. "She is beautiful, and will be pleased to see you again. Come in."

Last time I'd seen her, Risa had been barely seven months old, and certainly not up to talking. Yet, like her mom, there'd been a tremendous amount of power in her violet eyes. And even at seven months, she'd seemed to hold far more awareness of the world and her surrounds than any normal child.

But then, I guess she wasn't a normal child. She was the daughter of a clone and who knew what father. I'd seen Risa's birth certificate, but the man listed as her father didn't actually exist. It was yet another puzzle I was determined to resolve—for my own curiosity, if nothing more.

I stepped over the threshold and into Dia's huge hallway. A massive chandelier sprayed rainbows across the soft golden walls and carpets, and highlighted the various toys scattered about the place—though none of them, I noted with interest, rested in the middle of the hall, but rather hugged the sides. Either someone had been cautiously tidying up after the daughter so the mom didn't trip, or the child took an unusual amount of care when playing. I was betting on the latter.

A vase of sunflowers sat on a redwood table, lending some spring cheeriness to the hall, and the staircase that spiraled upward was again scattered with toys. I went through the first of the two doors that led off the hall, noting with a smile that the bright, modernistic painting that had once dominated wall-space above the marble fireplace had been replaced by a gorgeous picture of Dia and her daughter.

I sat on one of the large sofas and was just about to ask where Risa was when she came bolting around the corner on a plastic train, white pigtails flying as she made choo-choo noises.

She gave me a grin and a wave as she flew on by and disappeared out the doorway, barely avoiding her mom's legs.

"My God, she's grown," I said, as Dia chuckled softly and stared down the hallway after her fast-disappearing child.

"She decided to skip the whole walking stage at eight months, and got straight into running. I don't believe she's stopped running—or talking—since."

"That must be hard when you can't see."

She shrugged and moved across the room with calm assurance. "I have good hearing, I have my other senses, and I have employed someone to cook and look after the house. We cope. Of course, once outside, I still have the help of the Fravardin."

Who were the guardian spirits her clone brother, Misha—the man who had been my mate for a while—had met and enlisted when he'd been in the Middle East. They might have failed at protecting Misha in the end, but they had died trying. And even after his death, those who had remained had honored his wishes and kept protecting Dia. He'd once said that he would use them to protect me, but I had a feeling he'd never had the chance to put that into action. Certainly I'd been in deadly situations since then, and no invisible entity had popped along to offer assistance.

And mostly, I was glad about that, despite having a few extra scars I didn't really need.

"So what can I do for you?" Dia continued.

I crossed my arms on my knees and said, "I was wondering if you'd heard any rumors about a nightclub called Mirror Image."

She wrinkled her nose. "I have several clients who attend. I do not like the vibe I get from it."

"What do you mean?"

Risa scooted past on the train again, this time making siren noises.

Dia smiled. "She's destined to work with cars when she's older. If it has wheels and it's fast, she loves it."

I raised my eyebrows. "So she's not psychic like you?"

"Oh, she is. I'm just not sure what direction her talent will take, as it is still developing. But it's there and it's strong. More so than mine." She shrugged, then added, "From what I have seen—or felt—from the clients who have gone there, the club is a good place to be. But I have always sensed something predatory behind it."

"Most werewolf clubs have that feel. The hunt is on for sex."

She nodded. "But this is different."

"In what way?"

She hesitated. "It has something to do with the owners. They are predators."

"They?"

"There are two of them, and they are what the club is."

"Which makes a whole lot of sense," I muttered.

She smiled. "What I see through my visions is not always definable. You know that."

I blew out a breath, then said, "Have you heard any recent news reports?"

She studied me for a minute, blind eyes unfocused and yet curiously aware all the same. "You're hunting whoever is tearing apart those poor women, aren't you?"

"Yes." Unfortunately. "But nothing is making sense. We found both killers dead for no apparent reason, and neither should have been capable of tearing someone apart like they did."

"Sometimes humans can do extraordinary things."

And sometimes something else is involved. "At least one of the victims was unfaithful. I know anger can often give a little extra strength, but this goes beyond that. And what I really can't understand is why these men would go to such extremes. I mean, why destroy their own lives as well as their partner's? That doesn't make sense."

"Jealousy often doesn't. And it can be a very destructive emotion."

Yeah, but the cause of these murders was more than that. I was sure of it. "It just doesn't *feel* right."

And if anyone would understand that statement, then it would be Dia.

She continued to study me for several seconds, then said, "If you want me to help, I need to touch you."

My heart accelerated. I knew it was fear of the unknown more than fear of her. Which was odd, really, considering some of the truly depraved men I'd brought down over the last year. "Why?"

She smiled. "We both know you are afraid of what I might or might not see of your future, which is why you are so reluctant to even shake my hand in greeting. But if you want my help on these cases, I need to see what you have seen. And to do that, I must first touch you."

And here I was thinking I'd been so clever about concealing my apprehension about her powers.

She held out a hand, palm up. With some reluctance, I placed my fingers in hers.

"If you see more shit in my future, I do *not* want to know about it. I've been through enough this last year."

Her expression was serious as her blind gaze swept my face. Sometimes it was hard to remember this woman could not see. "I cannot always control the direction of my gifts. If you do not wish to hear where they lead, then it is best we not do this. I will not censure what I see. I never have."

Which is probably why she'd become as renowned as she was. Good or bad, she told it all—and honesty was rare in her field.

I took a deep breath and blew it out slowly. "Let's just do this, then."

She smiled. "It may not be all bad, Riley."

"Which is not saying that it'll all be good."

"No. It rarely is."

She closed her eyes and her fingers clenched around mine. Electricity washed across my skin—a warm tingle of energy that made the hairs on my arms stand on end and my pulse race. Not in excitement or in fear, but from some emotion that resided between the two. The wolf inside had her teeth bared, ready to fight. But this was a force I'd invited in, and I couldn't back away from that now.

So I held myself still as the tingly sensation washed up my arm and swept across my body, until it felt like I was wrapped in a blanket of energy.

Dia shuddered. "I see the deaths. I see the agony of their souls."

I didn't say anything. After all, what was there to

say? Not only had I seen it, I'd felt it, and that was not a place I wanted to revisit, even in memory.

"I see the two cases. Separate cases." She hesitated, frowning lightly. "I see a woman. She is red, like you. Different, like you. She has a gift, a pack gift that is both different and stronger than her father's, and it sometimes aids her work. The club and its owners hold many secrets, one which the wolf you seek uncovered."

Dia paused, and another shudder went through her. "The second case is different. It is shadowed by a malevolence that constantly hungers for vengeance."

"Vengeance for what?" I asked softly, not sure if by speaking I'd break the vision, but needing to ask all the same.

"Betrayal. He has been seeking retribution for many years."

Which would suggest the second victim *had* betrayed her husband somehow.

"He hates," Dia continued. "And he will continue to hunt and kill until he is stopped."

"You can't tell me who? Give me a name or description?"

She either didn't hear or didn't know, because she tilted her head and said, "An emotional decision comes for you."

My heart sunk to the depths of my stomach. This was exactly the sort of thing I *didn't* want her seeing. "I don't want to know, Dia."

Her grip on my fingers seemed to tighten, even though I made no move to pull my hand from hers. Well, I guess she *had* warned me, and now I would have to face up to whatever she was seeing.

Maybe just this once, forewarned would be forearmed.

"You will gain what you have always wanted, but it will not be in the form you have dreamed of."

I blinked. What I'd always wanted was a hubby and a family of my own—how could I gain all that if it wasn't in the form I dreamed of? "And that means?"

"That sometimes what we wish and what life offers are two completely different things."

Like I didn't already know *that*.

She continued softly, "There are many men in your life, but I see three who will become special."

"Three? I don't need three. I need one." Just one. That wasn't asking too much, was it?

"There is always one. But there are others. One will hurt. One will heal. And one will always be there, regardless."

I hesitated, part of me wanting to ask the question, the other fearing it. "Is one of them my soul mate?"

"Can a spirit with two souls have one soul mate? That is a question only time can answer."

"Well, that's a crappy sort of answer, if you ask me."

She blinked, then squeezed my fingers and released them. "I'm sorry I couldn't concentrate more on the murders, but as I warned, sometimes my foresight goes where it wills."

Yeah, and it didn't exactly give us more than what we already had. Still, if these murders weren't new, as Dia had implied, then a trip into the files for a closer look at past murders was obviously in order. The clues might lay in the past. Whether they'd help us solve the present crimes was anyone's guess.

"Be careful with this thing you hunt," Dia said, rubbing her arms lightly. "I do not think it will be easy to stop."

"The things we hunt never are."

"No." She hesitated. "I'm sorry for dipping into your private life. I know you didn't want to hear that, and it wasn't my intention—"

I waved her apology away. "Don't worry. At least it wasn't totally bad. And at least there's some hope of my dreams coming true, even if not in the form I desire."

She smiled. "Which makes no sense when said like that."

"Tell me about it," I said wryly.

She pressed her hands against the sofa and stood up. "Would you like tea? Coffee? My next reading isn't for another hour, and it's so nice to see someone other than clients for a change."

Technically, I could be classed as a client, given she now worked for the Directorate, but I knew what she meant. While I had my doubts that Dia and I could ever be pals, I wasn't about to walk away from a prospective friendship. I had few enough of those, too.

All of which was my fault. I tended to be the prickly, standoffish type—a leftover of my hellish days with the pack, no doubt.

"Coffee would be good," I said with a smile.

"Good." She walked around the sofa and headed to a side door, but stopped as her daughter came *choofing* around the corner again.

"Where does she get the energy?" I asked with a grin.

"Heaven only knows," Dia muttered, then bent and asked, "Risa, would you like a drink? And some cookies?"

The little girl nodded so fast her pigtails were a blur of white. And then she stilled, looked at me, and pointed.

"Death, Mommy. Death."

Chapter 6

I stared at the finger pointed so firmly in my direction, then at the wide, violet eyes. There was no fear in those eyes, only a matter-of-factness that chilled me.

Whatever it was she was seeing, she believed it.

"Where do you see death, Risa?" Dia asked, her voice as matter-of-fact as her daughter's. Like seeing these sort of things was an everyday occurrence. And perhaps for the two of them, it was.

"Here." The little girl patted her left shoulder.

A chill ran through me. I clenched my fingers and resisted the urge to say anything.

"Can you describe him for me?" Dia asked.

The little girl screwed up her nose. "Dark, floaty. He smiles, Mommy."

"Does he reach for Riley?"

She shook her head. "He watches."

"Nothing else?"

"No."

"That's wonderful. Now, would you like a cookie?"

Pigtails went flying again as the little girl nodded enthusiastically.

"Then we'll race you to the kitchen."

The little girl took off. Dia rose to her feet and looked at me.

"'That's wonderful'?" I asked, eyebrow raised.

"I don't want Risa to be afraid of what she sees, nor do I ever wish her to be afraid to talk about it. So, I praise rather than react, no matter what she says she sees."

"And has she ever seen anything bad?"

"She once saw death with his hand on the shoulder of a client. He died the next week, hit by a truck at a pedestrian crossing."

"Oh." Great. Not that death and I hadn't been chummy before. Hell, I'd even faced the god of death himself and was still alive to tell the tale. "So what does it mean when she sees death near me, but not touching?"

"I'd presume it means you're about to do something dangerous, something that puts your life on the line. Be careful when hunting this serial killer."

"I intend to be, trust me." I shivered and rubbed my arms. "I think that coffee you mentioned might be a good idea now."

She smiled and motioned me to follow her. We went through a large, formal dining room and into a kitchen that was as large as my entire apartment. Unlike the other rooms in this house, though, it had a homey feel to it, filled with warmth and the rich scent of baking. Risa was already in a high chair, munching on cookies.

A thin-looking shifter turned around as we entered, her smile rippling across her face, making her rough, aquiline features glow with cheeriness and affection. Obviously a woman who loved her job.

"A guest! How lovely. Will coffee and cake be good, Miss Dia?"

"Elsa, this is Riley. And coffee and cake would be wonderful."

"Good, good. You sit, I serve."

So we sat and we talked, the topics ranging from her work and clients to news, shops, and TV. It was a tentative beginning, but a beginning all the same.

And, oddly enough, despite the fact her visions had confirmed that my future would not be what I'd always imagined, I left Dia's house feeling a lot more enthusiastic about whatever fate had in store.

I climbed into my car and headed back to the Directorate. Given what Dia had seen of the shadow, my next line of inquiry had to be a search through past murder records, both Directorate and police. Which would probably take ages. But while the computer was doing its stuff, I could at least catch up on Cole's latest findings. Not that I thought anything would be a lot different from the first murder.

I drove into the parking lot and was lucky enough to find a spot near the elevators. The car keys I pocketed. While regulations said that all keys had to be returned to the responsible officer on reentry to the Directorate, I'd probably need the car later, so it was easier to simply keep them. And besides, it would piss off Salliane.

I went through all the scanner and ID checks, then headed downstairs. Rhoan wasn't in the squad room when I got back, but Jack was. "Cole's initial report for the second murder," he said, handing me a folder. "He expects to complete investigations this evening."

I tucked the folder under my arm and helped myself to coffee. "He didn't notice anything unusual there?"

"No." Jack hesitated. "Are you sure this thing you're sensing at the crime scenes isn't a vampire?"

I shook my head. "It's not a vamp. A vamp couldn't get close enough to the scene, not without Cole and his team sensing him." Because a shifter's senses were every bit as keen as a werewolf's. "It doesn't even feel like a soul."

"It's not like you've had a whole lot of experience with souls yet."

And if I had my way, that lack would continue. But this was one instance where I was never likely to get my way. "When I feel souls, I feel the chill of death or whatever the hell the afterlife is before they appear. With this other thing, all I feel is evil. It needs to kill, it hungers to kill, and then it hangs about afterward to gloat in the destruction it causes."

"So it could well be a soul—just one so warped in what it has become that's all you're sensing."

"Maybe." I sipped my coffee, then said, "But how the hell does a soul kill?"

"I don't know. I'll ask our magi division and see if they know."

I nodded. A few months ago I hadn't even known the Directorate had a division that dealt with magic, spirits, and whatnot. It often made me wonder what other divisions we had that I knew nothing about.

"I don't suppose anyone else has talked to the sister yet?"

"No. She's still under sedation." He hesitated. "Why?"

I shrugged. "I was just curious as to whether our second victim had recently been unfaithful."

Jack raised his eyebrows. "You think unfaithfulness is the key to both murders?"

"It's certainly a possibility." I told him about my visits to Nonpareil and Dia. "If unfaithfulness is the key, then we have our link. And our murderer. But he's going to be damnably hard to track down."

"Especially if he's a spirit rather than flesh."

Very true. I walked over to my desk and sat down. "I'm going to do a global search for any past murders resembling our current two. Dia suggested these aren't his first kills, so maybe we'll get lucky. Has Cole given any indication of what killed the second husband?"

"It's looking like a heart attack, same as the first guy."

"Which doesn't make sense, you know. Neither man was heart attack material."

"Given the exertion they underwent, and the shock to their bodies, it's not surprising their hearts gave out." He tossed his plastic coffee cup into the trash. "Kade and Iktar should be finished training next week."

I couldn't help a smile. Having Kade at close quarters would make this dreary old conference room that much more exciting. Although Jack's ethics of not mixing work and pleasure could prove problematic. Especially since Kade was too delicious for my own good. "You still planning to use Iktar in the day division?"

"We'll probably float him, depending on situational requirements. They'll both be officially on deck in two weeks."

"So you've given them a whole week off? You're all heart, boss."

"Given our workload," he said grimly, "they're damn

lucky to get that. Tell Rhoan I want to see him as soon as he gets back."

He walked out. I signed into the system, then set about tracking down police reports. As I expected, it was a long, arduous process, and I was still there four hours later when Rhoan finally traipsed in.

I leaned back in my chair and rubbed a hand across my eyes. "Boss wants to see you."

"Jack can wait. I need something to drink." He raised a plastic coffee cup in question. I nodded. And noted that he was covered in dirt and cobwebs, and looking more than a little raw around the edges.

"You catch your vampire?"

"Yeah. Bastard put up a hell of a fight, though."

"I thought he was only a youngster?"

"Even a young vampire can be bloody strong." He poured the coffees, then handed me one. "This one had help. Bitch scratched me."

He twisted his neck and showed me his battle scars—three deep but healing lines gouged into his skin. "Nasty. What happened to the bitch?"

"Her ass is now in jail. Assaulting a guardian and all that."

"Ah. A human."

"A *stupid* human, who will spend several years in jail for said stupidity." He plonked down on the edge of my desk. "How goes the hunt for the bastard's missing daughter?"

"Slowly. I talked to her lover today, and discovered Adrienne had uncovered a possible story at the night-club."

"Nothing to do with the entertainment piece, I gather?"

"Nothing at all. I'm going there to have a look around tonight."

"Liander wants to take me to the premiere of his latest movie tonight."

I raised my eyebrows. "My, my, my."

"Indeed." He screwed up his nose. "Suits and attention are not my style."

"Since when? You love attention *and* dressing up. It's just that by going as his date, you're making it truly official."

"There *is* that."

"And you're still afraid to make it official, despite the fact that you've all but committed to him."

"Only outside working hours."

"That's all he's ever asked, Rhoan."

"I know." He sighed. "But I like the anonymity of what we share now. I don't want to have my picture in all the trade and gossip mags. It would make my job here harder."

"Have you explained this to him?" I held up my hand before he could answer. "Of course you haven't. That would be the sensible thing, and you don't do sensible in relationships."

"Now, there's the pot calling the kettle black."

"I haven't committed to anyone."

"No, but you have a good man who wants to commit and see just where the relationship goes."

"The difference between me and Kellen and you and Liander is the fact I *do* talk to Kellen. Besides, it's only in recent months we could truly be considered mates. You and Liander have been mates forever, *and* you admit you love him."

"None of which excuses the fact that you won't do

the sensible and commit to Kellen—not even for a month or so."

I gave him a look. "This isn't about me. This is about you. Go home and talk to Liander. Be honest with him."

He took a sip of coffee. "I'll talk if you do."

"Deal."

"I'll check with Kellen, you know."

"Ditto, bro."

He grinned and rose. "I foresee busy phone lines in our apartment tomorrow. That is, if you're intending to come home tonight."

"Got to. I need fresh clothes." I hesitated, half thinking about mentioning the car incident, then deciding against it. He'd only get all fussy and protective, and right now I didn't feel up to handling that.

Of course, he'd be a very unhappy little werewolf when he *did* find out—and I had no doubt he would. Eventually. We might not share the telepathy of twins, but we could often sense when the other was in danger. If the bastard behind these attempts had a serious go, Rhoan would know about it.

So I simply added, "Hope we've got hazelnut."

"Yep. I went shopping yesterday."

"You're going to make Liander such a good little housewife one day."

He snorted. "Given your refusal to shop, the same will never be said of you."

I grinned. "When someone else will do it, why bother?"

"Lazy cow."

"Bitch," I corrected. "The cow is down the hall in the liaisons' office."

He shook his head and headed out the door. I sipped

the bitter coffee and got back to the business of reading files.

Another hour, and the search results were through. It turned out there were more than twenty murders in the last ten years that bore similarities to our current ones. I hit print, then drained the cold dregs of coffee from my cup and rose. Once I'd collected the printouts, I dumped them on my desk and headed out. Enough was enough for one day. My eyes already felt dry and gritty. I needed to get some sleep if I was intending to go out tonight.

As I caught the elevator back up to the parking lot, I dragged my cell phone out and rang Kellen.

"Riley," he answered warmly. "Wasn't expecting to hear from you for another couple of hours."

Just hearing his voice had me smiling. "You feel like checking out a new club tonight?"

He paused a beat. "Given your love for the old clubs, I'm gathering this is work related?"

"Yeah. I've got to check out Mirror Image, and thought you'd like to come along."

"If you're intending to fuck others, it's probably better if I don't. I've staked my claim, Riley, even if you haven't yet agreed, and I *will* fight for what is mine."

"The fact that you'd even think I'd do something like that shows how little you really know me."

"Riley, you're the one that keeps telling me you're a free agent."

"Yeah, but—"

"No buts. Free agents go where they please, do whom they please. But I will not stand apart and watch it."

"I'm not asking you to. And I wouldn't do that to

you. I'm just going to look, nothing more." *No need to get all jealous and antsy,* I thought silently.

Even if knowing that he was made my hormones get all dizzy and excited. Not that my hormones ever needed much prompting.

"Fine, then," he said.

"I'll pick you up at eleven."

"Great."

That didn't sound entirely convincing. With a silent shrug at the peculiarities of men, I hung up and went home.

But the peaceful slumber I was hoping for didn't materialize. When I got home, Blake was waiting for me.

"What the fuck have you been doing?" he said, voice filled with an anger that would have cowed the sensible.

I dumped my keys and handbag on the sofa, then continued on to the kitchen. I had a bad feeling I was going to need a beer. "What I've been doing is none of your goddamn business."

Not the wisest comment in the world, as evidenced by the explosion of anger that suddenly filled the room.

"I am your pack leader," he bellowed. "You will show me some respect."

I grabbed a beer, pulled the tab, and took several gulps. Then I said, flatly and softly, "You and the pack can go to hell as far as I'm concerned. I'm helping because you threatened my mother, not because I want to or need to. And if you don't like it, then fuck off and find someone else to help you."

His fists clenched, and part of me was suddenly glad he was neither real nor here. I remembered the feel of those fists. I might be able to defend myself against them now, but part of me still feared them.

"My granddaughter is *dead*." His voice was low and venomous. "And you strut around here drinking beer and throwing attitude. She's *dead*."

Jodie had already told me that, but regret washed through me anyway. Not so much because Adrienne *was,* beyond a doubt, dead, or because this monster and his kin so grieved for her. The regret was for Jodie, who had so obviously built her world around Adrienne and who now had nothing. "And this is my fault because . . . ?"

"Because you were *supposed* to find her."

"Even a guardian can't work miracles." I took another sip of beer, then leaned a hip on the doorframe and added, "Besides, you're the one with the psi-skills. Why haven't you done anything to find her?"

"Because Adrienne's mind-blind, and therefore a dead zone for me."

In life and now in death, I thought grimly. But at least it explained why he was harassing me rather than Rhoan. He might not be able to read my thoughts thanks to the strength of my shields, but he could still sense me. "So if Adrienne was mind-blind, did that mean she didn't have the family trait of clairvoyance?" And why would Dia and Jodie say otherwise?

"Oh, she had it. In fact, she was probably stronger than most of us."

"How, if she was mind-blind?"

He shrugged. "I'm no expert. Her talent wasn't strictly clairvoyance, though. She wasn't intuitive and didn't dream, but she could touch people and see things. Sometimes past, sometimes future, but always about that person."

"I'm surprised you didn't try to harness a talent like that for the pack's benefit."

It was sarcastically said, but for once, Blake didn't seem to notice. "We tried. She wasn't obliging."

Good for her.

"So what are you going to do about Adrienne?" he continued.

"Same thing I'm going to do for the other three who have disappeared—try to find whoever is responsible."

"Trying is not good enough."

"Well, it'll have to be." I paused. "Where did you get that picture of the man that was in the files you sent?"

"Found it on her desk."

"At home?"

"Yes." He frowned. "Why is this important? Have you found out who he was?"

"Not yet. Was there anything else on her desk? Notes or anything?"

"If there were any notes, it'd be on her laptop. Which," he added, "has disappeared along with her."

She'd had the laptop on the island, so her disappearance had to have happened sometime between her stepping off the island boat and getting the plane back to Melbourne.

Was that drawing of the man she'd bumped into at the club, and was he connected to the disappearances? Or something else?

"There were no notes on the drawing itself?"

"Nothing at all."

Then how the hell did he get the name Jim Denton? I doubted that he just plucked it out of thin air. "If there's nothing else, then you and I have nothing more to talk about. So you can just fuck off and leave me alone."

He glowered at me for several seconds, then said, "Patrin and Kye are coming to Melbourne. Patrin wants a full report."

Great. Just what I needed. One arrogant son of a bitch harassing me in person. "Who the hell is Kye?"

"His bodyguard."

"So the great Patrin needs a bodyguard?" The thought cheered me no end.

"Patrin has been helping police with certain inquiries and, as a result, has been receiving threats. Hence Kye's presence."

"And these threats have absolutely nothing to do with Adrienne's disappearance?"

"No."

"You sure?"

"Absolutely. He should be in Melbourne tomorrow. I expect you to be helpful."

"If Patrin comes anywhere near me, I'll break his fucking neck."

"Remember your mother," he said, and disappeared from sight.

Bastard, bastard, *bastard*.

I blew out a breath, then drained the rest of the beer and tossed the can into the trash. The buzz of anger and alcohol running through my system suggested that while I might need to sleep, it wasn't going to happen anytime soon. For several seconds I internally wrestled with the idea of going to the Blue Moon and catching some action, but Kellen's image kept swimming through my mind. If I wanted to explore the depths of our relationship, then I would have to start getting serious. Maybe not commit-to-a-solo-relationship serious—not just yet, anyway—but I would have to start proving to him that he—that we—were important.

Giving up the clubs would be hard. I loved them, loved the feel of them, loved the passion and excitement within them—but if I had to ditch the Blue Moon to prove that I didn't want to lose what I had with Kellen, then I would.

Because there was a whole lot of passion and excitement there, too.

So I settled for the next best thing to the Blue Moon—a hot, scented bath and several bars of chocolate.

*M*irror Image sat in the hub of an industrial estate, far away from any residential area, nullifying any complaints they might otherwise have gotten over the bass-heaving music issuing from the joint.

I slammed the car door shut and let my gaze run over the neon-lit club. It was a typical factory design—metal roof, high concrete walls, and few windows. What glass there was decorated the front, in what would have been an office area in any normal factory. Unlike regular wolf clubs, this one had no line of people waiting to get in, but given the fact this particular club dwarfed most wolf clubs, I guess that wasn't really surprising.

Just for a moment, I felt something . . . odd. There was something here, something dangerous, and it reminded me of the evil I'd sensed at the murder scenes. Only it wasn't coming from the club, but rather from behind me.

I turned around, but couldn't see anything but the smoke from the nearby factories blowing along with the breeze. The sensation faded and I mentally shrugged. Maybe the near misses had made me jumpier than I'd realized.

Kellen looked at me over the roof of the car, his expression bordering on dubious. "You really want to go in there?"

"Doesn't look like much from the outside, does it?"

"No." He took a deep breath, his nostrils flaring widely. "I can smell humans. Lots of them."

"That's because there are."

"And our government thinks this is a good idea because . . . ?"

"Because the government is mostly men, and men tend to think with their little heads more than their big heads."

He laughed, a warm and merry sound that had a smile tugging my lips. "That is such a female thing to say."

"But it's true, isn't it?"

"Only every other minute." He held out his hand. "Shall we go check out the joint?"

"Let's." I walked around the front of the car and clasped his fingers. His touch was warm and chased away the chills skating across my skin. Whether those chills were caused by the cool night and my somewhat scanty clothing, or something else, I wasn't entirely sure.

My heels clicked on the pavement, a sound that seemed to echo across the night, jarring sharply against the heavy music and rumble of voices emanating from the club. The double glass doors opened as we approached, and the noise hit harder, briefly making my ears ache.

A thick-set shifter with cat-green eyes gave us a welcoming grin. "Here to party?"

"Yeah," Kellen said, voice almost getting lost in the thump of music. "Heard it's the place for couples to be."

"That it is." The shifter's gaze skimmed my body appreciatively, and Kellen's grip went from my hand to my waist. "Come on. You folks been here before?"

When we shook our heads, he escorted us to the payment window, then ran us through the rules. Basically, they had much the same regulations that ruled wolf clubs the world over, along with the addition of the "no harm to the humans" rules Jodie had mentioned. The bouncer didn't ask us to sign a waiver, but then as a shifter himself, he would have sensed we weren't human. Still, I could see forms sitting on the cashier's desk, some of them signed, and figured that's what they were. Humans would *have* to sign a waiver against their right to sue, otherwise the club wouldn't be able to operate, simply because no one would insure them. Weres, the moon fever, and humans could never be a good mix in a sexually charged environment, and anyone who thought otherwise was a fool.

Once we'd paid, we entered the club.

Immediately we were hit by the noise, the lights, and the thick heavy air that burned down the throat and smashed into the senses.

There was nothing subtle about this place, no pretense about what it was and what it was catering to. It was in-your-face, no-apologies sex and indulgence, and the richness of it was almost mind-numbing. I took a deep breath, allowing the heated, lusty atmosphere to soak through my body, and felt the familiar ache begin.

The main room was large and long, and there were plenty of people packed inside. Lights scrolled across the vast expanse—flickers of yellow, red, and blue that highlighted the masses moving on the dance floor while leaving large areas in shadow.

Kellen's fingers squeezed mine, and he nodded toward an empty booth on the outskirts of the left side of the dance floor. "Want to grab that, or would you rather dance?"

Given my near miss with Shadow, and the hankering need that had been plaguing me ever since, there was only ever going to be one answer to that question. "Dance."

We made our way down the stairs, my heels slipping slightly on the highly polished white tiles. The whole place was white, in fact. Floor, ceiling, furniture. White on white. It should have felt as cold as hell, but it didn't, thanks to the lights and the sheer mass of people loving, laughing, and generally having a good time.

Kellen led me onto the dance floor. Down here, the grunts of pleasure and the slap of flesh against flesh mingled heavily with the thump of music, and the air was thick with the rich aroma of sweat and wantonness. But it was mixed with a sense of almost guilty recklessness, and I put that down to the kids-in-a-candy-shop mentality. The humans here might be enjoying themselves, but it was almost like they knew that at any minute they'd get caught and the fun would stop.

Still, the heat of their desire was as thick and as strong as any were's, and my breath caught, then quickened. The press of so much flesh—even if it was mostly clothed flesh—made my skin burn and my already erratic heart race that much harder. I wanted—needed—to be loved.

Kellen wrapped his arms around my waist, then pulled me close and began a slow dance that was totally out of sync with the music. Music that was barely audible over the frantic pounding of my pulse. Sweat formed where we touched, and the air was so thick with the heat of our desire I could hardly breathe.

"Everyone is either dressed or half dressed," he murmured, his hands sliding sensually down my back to my butt. "Do you think we should go naked and stir them up?"

"Not when I'm trying to avoid attention." I pressed closer to him, rubbing myself across his erection. "Besides, the important bits of me are naked."

"Hmm," he said, sliding his hands under my skirt and discovering my bare butt. "So they are."

"And now," I murmured, as I slid down his fly and released him from his jeans, "so are yours."

He smiled and kissed me, and oh, what a kiss. From that point on, there was little conversation. We danced, we played, and we teased each other, nipping and caressing until our breathing was harsh and the need that pulsed between us became all-consuming.

And when it finally became too much to stand, his mouth claimed mine again, his kiss fierce as he lifted me up and onto him. Then he was in me, filling me, and it felt so damn good I groaned.

With my legs wrapped tightly around his waist, I began to move, riding him slowly, savoring the feel of him, the power of him, until the waves of pleasure rippling across my skin became a molten force that would not be denied. A howl of pleasure tore up my throat— a sound lost to the overall noise—as the shudders of completion ripped through us both.

"That," I said, when I'd finally caught my breath, "was amazing."

"Yep." He dropped a kiss on my nose. "Seems you and I are not put off by the scent of humans."

"I don't think anything would put us off if we were horny enough." I unlocked my legs from around his waist and stood. "I need a drink, and I need to find the bathroom."

"The bar is to our right. I'll get the drinks and find a table, which means you'll have to find the bathroom by yourself."

"A tough task, but I think I'll manage." I leaned forward, dropping a quick kiss on his lips, then made my way back through the crowd. There was a good amount of space between the dance floor and the booths, so the overheated air seemed a little cooler around the edges. I fanned my dress as I walked, but it didn't do a whole lot to stop the sweating.

One thing I did notice was the fact that there didn't seem to be any vamps here. Shifters and weres of all types, as well as hundreds of humans, but no vampires. Perhaps there was too much temptation for the young ones, and too much noise for the old ones.

I certainly couldn't imagine Quinn liking a place like this. But then, he'd dislike it for reasons that had nothing to do with the noise, and a whole lot to do with my werewolf lifestyle.

And, I thought grumpily, I really should stop thinking about him. He was out of my life, and I was better for it—no matter what my somewhat treacherous heart might think.

I continued on, skimming the edges of the dance floor, looking for the bathroom and anything out of place. But there was nothing more than sex and a whole lot of enjoyment happening. Which in itself was amazing. Who'd have thought humans could be so sexually free after all the years of giving us crap?

The air near the rear of the room began to get hot again, the air-conditioning obviously struggling to cope with the sheer mass of people down at this end. I went to the bathroom, then stopped under one of the vents just outside the door, sucking in the cool air and letting it caress my sweat-beaded skin. It felt like a tiny spot of heaven in this oven-like environment.

And that's when I felt it—an odd tingling buzz around the edges of my thoughts. Someone—or something—was trying to read me. I scanned the room quickly, but the touch was gone before I could really pinpoint it.

For no good reason, I remembered Shadow's comments about the brief intrusion one of his vamps had felt the night they'd serviced Callie's party. A shiver ran across my skin, and I rubbed my arms lightly.

In a crowd this size, it was a given that there'd be psychically talented people here, whether they were human or nonhuman. There was absolutely no reason to think that that brief touch was, in any way, connected to Callie or the other murders.

But I was oddly certain that it was.

I walked on, my gaze scanning the seething crowd on the dance floor, but I'd barely taken two steps forward when my other talents kicked in, and I felt it.

The thick sense of evil.

It was here.

Here because it had followed me here. I *had* sensed it in the parking lot earlier. Why it was following me I had no idea, and right now, I couldn't afford to worry about it. Because the overwhelming feeling I was getting from the spirit or monster or whatever the hell it was, was excitement. This place was like a newly found candy store to a hungry kid.

Only what this evil hungered for was death. Bloody, brutal, death.

My stomach began to churn. I had to stop this thing, whatever it was. Had to at least *try*.

I stopped, and tried to pinpoint where the main sense of this evil lay. My gaze rested on a petite blonde dancing with a rangy, brown-haired guy. Though they weren't getting all hot and heavy, they had been. Even from where I stood I could smell sex on them, could smell him all over her.

But *he* wasn't the source of the darkness. That was coming from above her, from the shadows that cloaked the ceiling.

My gaze rose. There was nothing to be seen in the rafters—nothing but electrical wiring, cameras, and dusty webs, at any rate. But it was there, somewhere. Hovering. Waiting.

For what?

The woman laughed—a soft, flirtatious sound that drew my attention again. She leaned forward, giving her companion a tender kiss, then turned and walked away.

The shifting feel of evil followed her.

So did I.

I kept close, following the shimmer of her blond hair more than her scent, which kept getting lost in the heated air.

As I walked, I kept scanning for Kellen, trying to catch sight of him. Eventually I spotted him still at the bar. I glanced once more at the blonde, noting her trajectory, then ducked through the crowd, pushing several people out of the way and ignoring the nasty comments thrown my way.

I touched Kellen's arm, and he looked over his shoulder. "Sorry it's taking so long—"

"I have to go," I interrupted sharply, checking to see where my quarry was. As I suspected, she was heading up the steps and toward the door.

"What?" Kellen said, pushing away from the bar. "Why?"

"Work. I'll explain later." I kissed him quickly, then pulled away. His fingers slithered unsuccessfully down my arm as I disappeared between a small gap in the squash of bodies. I ducked through the thick crowd, using my reflexes and vampire speed to get to the doors as fast as possible.

The woman had already disappeared through them. I raced up the steps, heels clattering and sliding on the polished floor, and all but crashed through the doors after her.

"Hey, careful," the bouncer said.

I kicked off my shoes and gave him a tight grin. "Sorry. These heels are the pits on those tiles."

"Yeah, a few ladies have mentioned that. You leaving so soon?"

"Got a call from work." I shrugged, my gaze slipping past him to the windows. The woman was approaching a white Ford parked near the exit.

"That's a shame." The bouncer opened the door and offered me a card. "You'd better take one of these. It'll let you in anytime you please, on the house. Our way of making up for your shortened stay."

"Much appreciated," I said, taking the card as I slipped out the door.

The blonde had gotten into the Ford. I raced to my

car, threw the card on the seat, and started the engine. When the blonde left the parking lot, I was five seconds behind her.

Luckily, it was the middle of the night, and following a white car on empty roads was easy. With one hand still on the wheel, I pressed the com-link in my ear and said, "Hello, hello, anyone listening?"

"Liaison Benson here," a deep voice said. "What can I do for you, Riley?"

Agent Benson had to be new, because I certainly didn't recognize his voice. And I knew most of the liaisons by sound and sight, thanks to the time I'd spent in their ranks.

"I need an immediate trace on the following plate number." I drove a little closer and read it out. "Name and address of the owner would be handy."

"Hang on a sec." Keys tapped in the background while Benson whistled tunelessly. "Okay. That car belongs to one Mary Jamieson. I'm sending full details to your onboard."

I leaned across and flicked on the computer. "I've got a feeling she could be the next victim of our murderer. Any chance of getting guardian help to that location?"

He made a clicking sound. "We're at capacity tonight. I'll check with Jack, see what we can do."

"Let me know ASAP."

"Will do. Oh, and I have a message from Salliane for you."

My eyebrows rose. "What does it say?"

"Give the car keys back, bitch."

I laughed. "Tell her if she wants them, she can come and get them."

"Will do." There was a smile in his warm voice. "I'll contact Jack for you now."

"Thanks, Benson."

"No probs."

The connection went dead, but I left my end open. Who knew, I might need to send an urgent SOS when I got to the blonde's house. And, as Jack often reminded me, I couldn't do that if the voice section of the com-unit was shut down.

The onboard unit beeped to indicate incoming files. I opened them, then alternated between watching the road and my quarry and reading the files.

Mary Jamieson was thirty-four and lived on one of the newer housing estates currently being built over in Derrimutt, on Melbourne's western edge. She was also, according to the file, very married, and the pic we had of her husband bore little resemblance to the man she'd kissed at the club.

So, adultery *was* the connection between all the women. But why would the shadow care? What did it matter to him if these women cheated on their spouses? Even if he'd been betrayed in his own life, why come back from the grave to destroy the lives of complete strangers?

Was he reliving the moment through these other men? Why would even a spirit put himself through that?

"Benson, you still there?"

There was several seconds of silence, then Benson's warm voice caressed my eardrums. "Still here."

"Would you be able to put in an acquisition order for the security tapes at the Mirror Image nightclub? I need the recordings for the main room between"—I hesitated and glanced at the clock—"eleven-thirty and twelve."

Mary and her date had obviously been there longer than that, but I just needed enough of an image to identify him. And the less tape the club had to hand over, the happier they'd be.

"That could take several hours. Private enterprises tend not to be helpful about handing over security tapes."

"Do whatever it takes. I need to know who Mary Jamieson was at that club with tonight."

"I'll see what I can do."

"Thanks again, Benson."

He signed off a second time, and I followed Mary onto the freeway, heading past the city and into the western suburbs. She actually didn't live all that far from me, and part of me ached with the thought of going home and catching some sleep. But that wasn't an option. Not now, and probably not in the near future.

She zigzagged through several streets, entering the Brimbank Gardens Estate and winding through several more streets before she finally stopped. I pulled to a halt several doors down and switched off the lights as she got out of the car. Her house was a pretty little two-story painted in muted pastel colors.

She dug in her bag as she approached the door, but if she was looking for house keys it didn't matter, because the door opened. A solidly built man in his mid-thirties stood there. Even from where I sat, it was easy to see he was far from happy.

She didn't say a word, just pressed a hand to his chest and thrust him back before stepping through the door and slamming it closed.

I grabbed my badge from the secure compartment

under the seat, then climbed out of the car and ran for the house. They were shouting at each other, their words shrill, their voices filled with anger. I leapt over the side gate, heard the skitter of nails on concrete, and swung around to see a big black Lab running at me.

A threatening rumble rolled up my throat. The Lab stopped, his expression one of confusion as he sniffed the air. Then his head and tail dropped, and he hunkered down. Recognition of a superior.

I gave him a pat as I passed, following the voices to the back of the house. Two windows had the shades drawn, but the third didn't. I stopped and peered in.

They were in the kitchen. She was putting on the kettle, and he was yelling and gesticulating wildly behind her. He had some sort of accent, and was talking so damn loud and fast I could only understand half of what he was saying. Not that I needed to when the underlying message was clear.

Hubby knew where she'd been and what she'd been doing—even if not who.

My gaze went back to the woman. The creeping sense of evil no longer seemed to hover over her, but it was here, somewhere. Its darkness stained the night— a floating, nebulous feeling of death and destruction that sent chills skating across my body.

If this thing was a soul, then it was a hungry one.

And Mary Jamieson was about to become its next victim.

Chapter 7

I rubbed my arms, and wished I could pin-point the precise location of the dark soul. It seemed near and yet not, outside rather than inside. Which was why I stood here rather than getting that woman out of the house and away. I might be risking her life by remaining still, but I didn't dare do otherwise until the dark soul was near and visible. This might be our only chance to understand what the hell was going on.

The kettle whistled, the sound almost lost in the husband's continuing tirade. Mary reached for two cups, then tipped coffee into both.

That's when I saw it.

Black smoke, seeping into the room through the partially opened window on the opposite side of the room. It was featureless, this soul, bearing no resemblance to a human in any way, shape, or form. Perhaps it had never been human, even in life, though the anger and need to destroy that seemed to be emanating from it were both very human emotions.

It flicked along the baseboards, keeping itself low and long, barely visible against the dark carpet. When it neared the still-gesturing husband, it began to curl upward and around his legs, elongating and stretching, spreading itself ever finer, until it was nothing more than a smoky cloak covering his back. Then it seemed to melt into clothes and skin, and disappear.

Becoming a part of him.

The change, when it came, was quite sudden. The gesturing and shouting ceased, and an unnatural calm filled the void.

The woman didn't even seem to notice the silence, let alone the sudden leap of menace in the air. She just blithely continued to make her coffee.

Time to get in there.

I took several paces backward, then blew out a breath and ran for the window, diving headfirst through the glass. It shattered, shards scattering everywhere as I hit the carpet and rolled to my feet. Mary turned, her mouth dropping into an O of shock, the teaspoon clenched in her right fist like a weapon.

The husband didn't react. Didn't look. Didn't seem to even realize I was there.

Or didn't care.

It was a chilling thought.

"Directorate of Other Races," I said, raising my badge to show her. "Mrs. Jamieson, we've reason to believe you're in danger."

She raised an eyebrow, amusement touching her lips as her gaze skimmed my admittedly somewhat bedraggled and bloody state. "And do Directorate personnel often bust through people's windows wearing torn dresses and party shoes?"

"Only when we need to, ma'am," I said, my gaze on her still-unmoving husband. "If you'd just drop the spoon and move around the bench toward me, we'll get you out of here."

She laughed. "So who am I supposed to be in danger from?"

I hesitated. "Your husband is not—"

She laughed again, the sound this time harsh and cold. "Frank? He's a spineless little turd who's all talk and no action. In the bedroom, and out of it. Hence the little diversions he's currently raving about."

And she was such a loving, understanding wife.

Christ, why did people like this even get married, let alone remain that way? Surely divorce was better than this sort of misery.

"Ma'am, you'll just have to trust me on this one. Please walk around the bench and come here."

She sniffed, but put down the spoon and began to approach me. The minute she did, the husband moved. Or rather, launched. Headfirst across the bench, straight at his wife.

She screamed and backed against the fridge, hands raised to protect her face. I swore and dropped a shield, reaching for her husband mentally.

And hit a wall.

Not a psychic wall, or even an electronic shield, but a wall that felt shadowy and thick with evil. The dark soul wasn't about to let anyone else take over his revenge.

The husband grabbed his wife and forced her to the ground. I couldn't see them thanks to the bench, but I could hear the smack of flesh against flesh and the resultant squeals of pain. I shoved my badge on top of the bench, then ran around it, grabbing the husband by the scruff of the neck and tossing him backward. He hit the kitchen cabinets with a grunt, but almost immediately came back at us, his eyes glazed and bloodshot, his fists swinging.

I ducked both blows, then grabbed him two-handed, lifting him up and tossing him back across the room. Then I grabbed the woman's arm and hauled her to her feet.

"Now do you believe me?"

She nodded, her split lip bleeding and one eye already beginning to close. Fear flicked through her remaining eye, and the smell of it overran the scent of lilies and sex wafting off her.

"Good," I said. "Now listen."

The husband had landed amidst the broken glass, and had sliced his hands in his efforts to scramble to his feet. Blood dripped onto the tiles, the thick red color becoming a match for his eyes. A result of the possession, or the first indication of a body getting ready to die? I shoved my car keys into Mary's hand.

"There's a black Ford with Directorate plates three doors down. Get in there, lock the doors, and don't come out until I tell you to. If you see your husband coming out of this house alone, start the car and get the hell out of here. Don't go anywhere he knows, just drive until we contact you." I looked at her. "Understood?"

She nodded, lips trembling. "But Frank?"

"Is not himself. He's possessed."

"Possessed?"

"Long story, lady, and we ain't got the time." Her

husband was running at us again. "When I give the word, run."

The husband leapt the bench. Whatever—or who-ever—the evil soul had been, one thing was clear. He was no fighter. I sidestepped, grabbed his body, and flung him at the wall.

"Run!" I said to the woman. "Now!"

She did, her heels clattering on the tiles before the sound disappeared into the thick padding of the carpet. The husband made a mewling sound and crawled off the bench on which he'd landed. He didn't even look at me, just started running after his wife. I leapt at him, grabbing his legs and bringing him down onto the cold hard tiles with a smack hard enough to send blood flying. His and mine.

I wrenched my hand from underneath him, sending a thick shard of bloody glass skittering across the tiles, and tried to grab his arm.

You wouldn't have thought it would be so damn hard to grab the arm of a human, but the man was suddenly an octopus—arms and legs everywhere, slippery as a snake. I finally caught his right hand, grabbing it firmly and yanking it behind his back. It didn't seem to make one bit of difference. He was fighting and twisting and mewling, the noise inhuman—a match for his suddenly inhuman strength. I wasn't exactly a light-weight, but I wasn't The Hulk, either. And keeping this man pinned was becoming harder and harder.

He bucked like a bronco. I gripped him tighter, holding on for dear life as I twisted his arm higher up his back. It had to be hurting, but he didn't seem to care.

He bucked again, and somehow twisted in midair,

so that I was on the bottom, hitting the tiles back-first. Air exploded from my lungs, leaving me gasping.

He began hitting me, the blows raining down on face and arms and breasts. The wolf within rose snarling to the surface. I caught a blow, my hand wrapping around his and squeezing. Bones splintered, broke, and pain flicked through his ever-reddening eyes.

A reminder that a human rested behind whatever controlled his body. I backed off, merely gripping rather than crushing, then bucked, flipping him off me.

I scrambled to my feet as he slid across the tiles, then ran over and hit him, hard. The blow landed on his chin and he was out before he really knew what had happened.

Even so, I didn't relax.

The blow might have taken out the body, but the soul that rested within would be unaffected. And who knew how *it* was going to react?

"Riley?"

The voice was Jack's, and harsh with concern. Damn, we *had* to be short-staffed if Jack was coming out on rescue missions.

"Down here," I said, my gaze not leaving the husband's prone form. He began to twitch, the muscles in his legs and arms moving, even though he was still out. The dark soul inside was trying to get up.

The soft thud of boot heels approached. A second later Jack's suddenly dangerous presence filled the room.

"You called for help with a human?" he said, disbelief evident in his tones as he stopped beside me.

"Not just any human, but one possessed by the spirit

who's tearing the women apart." I paused, and looked at him. "How the hell did you get past the threshold?"

"Got Mary to invite me." He studied the man for a minute. "You've beaten him up a bit, haven't you?"

"Had to. The spirit gives inhuman strength, and he almost got the better—" I stopped as the man lurched into a kneeling position.

"It's going to keep that man moving until it kills him." I looked at Jack. "Can you force it out of his mind?"

"I do that and the soul will escape. We have no way of containing it."

"We have no way of containing it in the body, either. At least this way we'll save one life."

"At the cost of others, perhaps." He held up a hand to forestall my protest. "I'll try. At the very least, it may give me some hint of what we're actually dealing with."

Power touched the air, a tingly, spidery flare of electricity that flowed like wildfire through the air. Its touch had the tiny hairs along my arms and the back of my neck standing upright, but its effect was more dramatic on our target.

He screamed, a high, furious sound, and began to fight, throwing himself left and right, as if trying to rid himself of a physical touch.

Black smoke began to pull free of the husband, curling back in on itself, becoming more solid but still resembling nothing human. I shivered.

"What?" Jack said.

"The soul is retreating."

"I can't see it."

"You can't see souls."

"Unfortunately."

I flicked him a glance. "There's nothing unfortunate about it, trust me."

He gave me a wry sort of smile, though his attention was still on the husband. "We've had this argument before."

"Yeah, and your reasons for thinking it's fantastic still suck."

The soul had pulled almost all the way out of the flesh. The feel of him, so thick with evil and the need to destroy, crawled across my senses.

This soul wasn't sane.

Not now, and probably not in life.

If it had ever actually lived, that was.

I rubbed my arms, smearing blood up my forearm from the cut on my palm.

"What is it doing?" Jack asked, as sweat began to bead his bald cranium and forehead.

"Nothing." There seemed to be a slight pulsating through its opaque form, as if a heart beat deep within the darkness. But I felt no sense of energy, no gathering of power that had been so evident in the other souls who'd talked to me.

For that, I could only be grateful. There was nothing this hateful soul could say that I'd really want to hear.

"So it's just sitting there, above the man's body?"

"Yeah."

"Want to try talking to it?"

"I have a feeling opening my shields to this thing could be a very bad idea."

"Bad as in, oops, it's possessed me?"

"Yeah." I paused. "So you really have no idea how to contain a soul?"

"As I said, no fucking idea at all. I came here prepared to save my investment, not to play with spirits."

I grinned. "Your investment thanks you for caring."

The last tendril of smoke pulled itself free of the
husband's flesh. The pulsing within the soul got
stronger, and a sense of power caressed the air. It began
to rotate—slowly at first, then faster, until the sheer
weight of energy caressing the air had the hairs on my
arms standing.

Then it lunged forward, a face forming out of the
darkness, the mouth wide open, teeth bared. It
screamed—no earthly sound, harsh and powerful
enough to set teeth on edge. I yelped and jumped back,
but it didn't follow. Simply hissed then flicked away, its
snakelike form slithering across the floor and out the
window.

"Our dark soul just left the building."

"You might want to check that it's not taking over
the woman."

"It wants revenge, not death," I said. "And I can't
feel its presence anymore."

But even so, I spun on my heels and ran out the front
door. The sense of evil no longer rode the cool night air.
I took a deep breath, washing the foulness of that spirit
from my lungs, then glanced down the street. Mary
Jamieson sat in the driver's side of my car, her hands
clenched around the steering wheel, face pale and
swollen under the harsh street lighting. Jack's car was
parked right behind mine, lights still flashing and
driver's door open. He really *had* hurried.

Smiling slightly, I headed down to collect her. By the
time we got back, the husband was awake, and more
than a little confused. For the next hour we questioned
the two of them while the paramedics tended to them,

but there wasn't really much they could tell us. The woman's only crime was an affair, and the husband's was caring too much. Or perhaps holding back too much anger.

"So," I said, as the paramedics left. "What are we going to do with them? We can't leave them here, and we can't leave them together. And we have no way of knowing if that soul is coming back."

He sighed, and rubbed a hand across his bald head. "Take Mrs. Jamieson to a safe house and make sure she's comfortable. I'll second liaisons onto watch duty for the two of them until we sort out what's happening."

I looked at the woman. "Mrs. Jamieson? Would you like to pack some clothes?"

She nodded, then walked listlessly down the hall. The knowledge that her affair had almost caused her death had taken some of the bravado out of her.

Not that I could muster any sort of pity. Which was probably cold and uncharitable of me, but I couldn't help it. She was the most unlikable piece of womanhood I'd ever met. She just couldn't stop throwing attitude her husband's way, even though we'd explained that the violence was not his doing. I actually think she would have respected him more if it was.

"What about him?" I pointed at the man sitting on the chair nursing a bandaged hand, and giving me a one-eyed and somewhat baleful glare. Maybe the violence *wasn't* all the spirit's.

"As long as the wife is out of the way, I don't think he's going to be a danger to anyone."

Or so he hoped. Me, I wasn't so sure we could be positive about anything right now. Except perhaps that cheating was the key. I stood up. "Have the magi come up with any suggestions about restraining or killing our dark soul?"

"They're still looking into it. He's not a particularly old spirit, by the way."

I raised my eyebrows. "So he's not some ancient evil, then?"

"No. He was human once, I caught that much. And he hates women." He paused, then shrugged. "I want your full report on my desk in the morning."

"Yeah, yeah. But let me get some sleep first."

"You know, some people speak respectfully to their boss when he gives them an order."

I grinned. "If I did that, you'd fall over in shock."

"Ain't that the truth." He glanced past me. ".The wife is on the move. Get her out of here, get her safe, then go home."

I got.

It was a good four hours later by the time I had her tucked safely in one of the Directorate's plusher safe houses and was finally able to go home. The liaison who'd come to take over was a crusty old coot who missed nothing and talked to no one. The perfect choice to mind someone like Mary. She wouldn't sweet-talk or bully Marcus into leaving the apartment, no matter what she needed.

I yawned hugely as I got into the car and started it up. Sleep called, but I'd promised to drop by Kellen's place and explain, so that's exactly what I'd do.

I drove through the deserted streets, reaching his apartment half an hour later. After parking behind his Mercedes, I climbed out and looked up. The lights gleaming from the top-floor windows suggested he was still awake—not that I'd expected anything less.

He buzzed me in and sent the elevator down. The

security door into his apartment was open, but he wasn't waiting. I followed his rich scent through the living room and into the bedroom.

He glanced at me over the top of the book he was reading. "You look a mess."

"It's been a bad night at the office." I stripped off the tattered remains of my dress, then kicked off my shoes and headed for the shower. He didn't follow, didn't join me, and part of me was glad of that. I just needed some quiet time to wash away the feel of evil.

After I'd dried and combed my hair, I walked over to the bed and lay down beside him. He tucked his arm underneath my neck and pulled me closer without ever putting his book down. It was nice, just laying there, snuggled up against him, and I was tempted to let it stretch on. But he deserved the explanation I'd come here to give.

"I'm sorry," I said. "I shouldn't have disappeared like that without explaining. But I couldn't risk losing my quarry."

He sighed, and finally put the book down. "I could smell the fear on you, Riley. Do you know what it was like for me, knowing you feared whatever it was you were chasing, and yet unable to do one single thing about it?"

"It's my job—"

He turned onto his side and pulled me closer, so that his warm length pressed against my cooler flesh. It felt good. Natural and safe and right, somehow.

Right in a totally different way to how Quinn had felt right.

Which didn't really make all that much sense.

"I'm an alpha," he said. "It's an alpha's duty to protect his pack. You, my frustrating, annoying, and somewhat daft woman, are considered part of that pack for as long as we are together."

I smiled and raised a hand, gently touching his cheek. "This evil was something you couldn't protect me from."

"Which doesn't negate my need to try." He took my hand and kissed my fingertips one by one. Warmth shivered up my arm and desire unfurled.

"I have warned you that my being called out on a job might happen at the most inconvenient times." I raised my free hand and lightly traced my fingertips along his side to his hip, then let them drop, lightly caressing the thickness of his erection.

"And I warned you that one day I will ask you to leave said job."

My hand stilled as I raised my gaze to his. "I can't leave yet. Not in the middle of a case, and not until we know the results of the drug I was given."

"I know, and I'm not asking you to do that now. But I do want you to make a decision."

I resumed my caressing, enjoying the way his flesh throbbed and jumped under my touch. "I know. And I promise, I'll make it soon."

He touched a finger to my chin and guided my gaze back to his. "How soon? As I've already warned, I'm an impatient man."

My gaze searched his, seeing the desire deep in those green depths. Seeing the emotion. Part of me ached to say yes, to commit to this big strong wolf and take the time to explore whether or not he truly was the one.

But I just couldn't. Not yet. I didn't believe in breaking promises, and if I committed, I would mean it.

Yet I was in the type of job where commitment and fidelity didn't matter one iota. Where the only thing that *did* matter was getting your man and bringing him down any damn way possible.

And sometimes, that included sex.

I might be a strong psychic, I might be able to make some people believe whatever I wanted them to believe—including the fact that they'd just had incredible sex with me when the only thing I'd been fucking was their minds—but there was no escaping the fact that, sometimes, *real* sex would be involved.

And that I would more than likely enjoy it.

Truth was, I couldn't commit to Kellen and do my job successfully. I might not have wanted this job originally, but I was stuck with it now. Besides, part of me really did enjoy the thrill of it. A hunter hunts, and there was no longer denying I was very much a hunter.

Yet how much longer could I put Kellen off? How much longer did I *want* to put him off? My dreams were right here for the taking, if I had the courage.

But after everything that had happened over the last few years, my courage when it came to emotional matters was extremely low. And part of me didn't want to take that final step just in case fate leapt out and crushed me again.

"Answer me, Riley," he demanded.

Oh God, oh God.

I closed my eyes, took a breath. Found courage where none existed. "Give me a week. I need to concentrate on this case first, then I'll give you an answer."

Okay, so it *wasn't* a whole lot of courage I found. And while it wasn't the answer he wanted, it wasn't a denial, either. A week gave me time to think. Time to panic.

Time to find said courage and commit.

"It had better be the right answer."

I turned onto my side, then leaned forward and kissed him. It was a sweet kiss, a gentle kiss. A kiss that hinted at possibilities. "I think it could be."

"Good." His hand slipped down my back to my rump, his touch sending little flash fires of desire skittering across my flesh. "Now, what do you think we should do to seal this deal?"

I shrugged lightly, a smile teasing my lips. "Break open the champagne?"

"We'll save that for when you finally say you'll go solo with me next week."

"Ah. Well, what about a good quality wine?"

"I'm not into wine right now."

"Then what are you into?"

"You," he said, then claimed my lips again, his kiss a demanding thing, and so damn hot it had me melting.

After a while, his lips moved on, kissing my lobes, my neck, my shoulder, until finally, torturously, his tongue teased first one nipple, then the other, making them ache with a fierceness I'd never thought possible. I closed my eyes and arched my back a little, enjoying the pleasurable sensations pulsing through me. When he sucked one throbbing nub into his mouth, I groaned in sheer delight.

Then his tongue moved on, trailing liquid heat down my stomach as he tasted and teased. Anticipation sung through every fiber, so that when his tongue finally flicked over my clit, it almost undid me. And still he licked, tasted, and tantalized, until my whole body throbbed to the tune of that gentle yet insistent caress, and the tide of enjoyment threatened to overload my senses.

"Oh God, stop. *Stop*," I murmured. "I can't . . . it's too soon."

I wanted to taste him, caress him, build him to fever pitch, until sweat beaded his skin and his body ached with the need for completion. As mine did.

But he didn't hear me, didn't care. Just kept on tasting me with his tongue, flicking and delving and caressing, until the sensations overloaded my senses, and my body bucked in delight. My fists clenched, grabbing the sheet as I shuddered and drowned in a myriad of delicious sensations.

The trembling had barely eased when his lips caught mine again. He tasted of lust. Of love. Of me, and while I just wanted to keep on kissing him, I also wanted—needed—a whole lot more.

So I wrapped my legs around his body and let him slide deep inside. Slowly, gently, he began to rock. The feel of him, so hard and hot, penetrated every fiber and enveloped me in a heat that was basic and yet so very powerful. Gradually, his thrusts became more urgent, the need more intense. Jolts of pleasure ran across my senses, building to a second crescendo.

"I'm going to make you howl, Riley," he whispered against my lips. "I'm going to make you mine, in every way possible."

His powerful body stroked fast and deep, and yet it was his words that drove me insane with desire. I writhed against him, matching his rhythm, matching his urgency. Lust and sweat and desire built and built, the aroma so sweet and thick on the air that every intake of breath only inflamed already raging need.

"Oh God . . ." The rest of the words did become a howl of utter pleasure as my body bucked wildly against his. He came with me, his roar echoing across the silence, his body slamming into mine so hard the whole bed shook. In the midst of all that pleasure, his lips caught mine, kissing me hard as our orgasms ebbed and sanity returned.

I opened my eyes, stared into the green of his. Saw my future there, if only I was brave enough to take the chance.

He rolled onto his side, then gathered me in his arms. "Make me a promise," he said softly.

"What?" I said, sounding more reluctant than was probably wise.

"No sex outside what you have to do for work. Just you and me, for the next week until you give me the answer."

"Okay." I didn't even have to think about that one, which I guess was surprising given my reluctance to fully commit to the man.

Though I guess I was only agreeing to something I'd harassed Rhoan into in his relationship with Liander.

"Thank you," he said, and continued to hold me while he fell asleep.

Me, I didn't sleep, no matter how much I needed to. My mind was too busy mulling over promises, possibilities, and the right thing to do.

*R*hoan had the coffee made and waiting by the time I walked in our apartment door the following morning.

"What, you've suddenly gained sister radar or something?" I said, as I wrapped my hands gratefully around the mug of steaming liquid. Melbourne had pulled another of its weather tricks, and it was as cold as hell outside.

"It sounded like a herd of elephants running up the stairs," he said, amusement twinkling deep in his gray eyes. "Knew it had to be you. Light of foot you are not in the mornings."

"If I wasn't so grateful for the coffee, I'd kick your kneecaps." I took a sip and sighed happily. Hazelnut might not be "in" when it came to coffee these days, but it had always been my favorite. There was just something about the sweet, nutty aroma that made my taste buds do happy little handsprings. "So, did you talk to Liander last night?"

He nodded. "I actually sat him down *before* sex and talked to him. He understands. He's not happy, but he does understand. You?"

I screwed up my nose. "We talked. I said I'd give him an answer in a week."

"Coward."

"Totally."

He grabbed my arm and tugged me into a hug. "Just don't lose this one through fear, sis. He's a good man. And rich, which is always a bonus."

I snorted softly and pulled away. "Money isn't everything."

"Maybe not, but it sure as hell can make things a whole lot more pleasant."

"So why are you still here rather than living the high life at Liander's?"

"Because I value freedom more than money. And he's clingy enough. Can you imagine what it would be like if I lived with him?"

Actually, I could, and there was no way it would be as bad as my brother was imagining. I drank some more coffee, then said, "You heading into the Directorate this morning?"

He shook his head. "I'm doing the legwork for a

case the night boys are having trouble with. Seems we may have a day-walker on our hands."

I raised my eyebrows. "Day-walker?"

"A nonhuman with vampire tendencies."

"But not actually a vampire?"

"No. They tend to be psychos who like the taste of blood. We've had to track down one or two of them during my years as a guardian." He shrugged, like it was no big deal. "How about you?"

"Gotta go in and write up a report, then I might head over to that club and see if I can track down the man matching the picture Adrienne drew."

"You think he might be involved in Adrienne's disappearance?"

"Probably not, but right now, he's my only lead."

"You *could* wash your hands of the whole thing, you know."

"And leave Mom hanging? Sorry, not going to happen." I hesitated, remembering yesterday's events. "And besides, we now have the joy of Patrin and his bodyguard coming down for more regular reports of our progress."

Rhoan's fingers flexed. "Good. I believe there is some unfinished business between the two of us."

"As I mentioned, he has a bodyguard."

"So?"

"So knowing Patrin, he's probably the type to shoot first and ask questions later. And I don't want a dead brother."

He snorted softly. "Thanks for the vote of confidence."

"Only Superman can run faster than a speeding bullet, bro."

"So I'll disarm the bodyguard before I beat the crap out of Patrin."

"Good." I drained the rest of my coffee in several scalding gulps, then dumped the mug into the sink. "Be sure to let me know when it happens. I'd like to watch."

"I heard that about you."

I slapped his arm as I walked out. His laughter followed me into the bathroom. By the time I'd showered and dressed, he'd gone. I scooped up my keys, wallet, and ID, but left my gun tucked safely in the security box. Jack would have a pink fit if he realized I didn't actually carry, but I hated the feel of it on my body. Hated the weight of it, however slight that might be.

Once back at the Directorate, I plonked down on my chair and began typing up the report of last night's events. Technically, I could have handed it over to the liaisons, but Salliane was down there. And as much as I loved teasing the cow, I just wasn't in the mood for any of it right now.

With that done, I picked up the files I'd printed out yesterday and began reading through them. Wading through files of death and destruction was never an easy thing, and some of these murders were so gruesome—so cold—they made my heart ache.

In the end, I found three possibilities. I went back into the database and requested complete details on all three, then logged off the computer and got the hell out of there.

It was just after one when I arrived at Mirror Image. In daylight, the place really did look like a massive factory, the unadorned concrete walls reaching toward an inhospitable sky. There had to be at least two hundred cars sitting in the parking lot. This place was certainly pulling in the customers.

The heady smell of sex and lust stirred the air as I grabbed my pass and headed in, and my pulse quickened. I might have had an amazing night of sex, but the wolf within was always ready for more.

The bouncer, a big white wolf, gave me a wicked smile of greeting as I handed him the card. He swiped it through the reader, then handed it back. "You've access to all areas. The boss upgraded it this morning."

I raised my eyebrows. "And why would he do that?"

He shrugged. "The boss likes pretty girls." He paused, his gaze running down my body suggestively. "And you are certainly that."

Despite it being an obvious line, I smiled. Hey, a woman has to take compliments when she can get them. "And is your boss around?"

"No, he was called away on some emergency business." He shrugged again. "They don't tell the plebs anything."

The wryness in his tone made my smile widen. There was something almost cunning in this big wolf's eyes, something that suggested he didn't actually miss much at all. And that could come in very handy.

"Do the plebs get lunch breaks?"

The interest in his eyes flared deeper. "They do. In half an hour."

I touched his arm lightly, leaning forward conspiratorially, in the process giving him a nice view of my breasts. There was nothing in my agreement with Kellen that excluded flirting. "And are they allowed to . . . talk . . . to the customers? Accept a drink or two?"

"They certainly can talk." Amusement teased his

lips as his gaze flicked down, then up. "And as long as the drink is nonalcoholic, that will be fine."

I ran my fingertips lightly down to his hand. "I might see you inside, then."

"I think you just might."

I walked away, feeling his gaze on my butt as I headed in. And I have to say, I worked it. Nothing like the interest of a man to make the wolf flirt outrageously.

The main room was hot, suggesting the air-conditioning still wasn't working properly. There weren't as many people pressed onto the dance floor this afternoon, but most of the booths were full. I flared my nostrils, sucking in the scents, allowing the lust and the scent of sex to flood through my body. My pulse, already racing, stepped up another level.

It was a shame I couldn't actually do anything, thanks to the promise I'd made to Kellen. This might be a scouting trip, but if I had sex here, it would be because I wanted to, not because I had to. And that wasn't in the spirit of our agreement.

I walked down the steps and did a circuit of the room, then stopped and got a drink from the almost empty bar. "So," I said, showing my pass as the bartender slid a beer across the counter. "Where's a girl to find some real action in this joint?"

"The Executive Room? That'll be the doors to the left of the bar, ma'am." He pointed out the silvery doors wrapped in shadows. "Just slide your pass through the slot. The Executive is on the left."

I raised an eyebrow, feigning interest when I already knew the answer thanks to Jodie. "So what's the room on the right?"

"It's for guests of the owners, and by invitation only."

"Thanks." I collected my beer and headed for the doors.

I swiped the card through the appropriate slot. The little red light flashed for several seconds, then flicked to green. The door clicked, then opened, revealing a short, shadowed corridor. Better and better.

I stepped through the door, and almost immediately saw the sturdy-looking guard to my right. Bang went my plans for a little easy breaking and entering.

"The Executive Room?" I asked, my gaze skimming the shadows, looking for cameras and infrareds. There were three of the former—one covering each door, and one near what looked to be an elevator—but none of the latter.

"Door to your left, ma'am," he said politely.

"Thanks." I lowered a shield and carefully felt for his mind, my psychic probe little more than a barely-there caress.

The guard wasn't shielded, and his mind was wide open for invasion. Which suggested they either had nothing to hide, or that they didn't think they were ripe for trouble in the safety of their back rooms. It was mighty tempting to do a full mind-raid, but the cameras were on me and I couldn't afford to stand still. Not even for the short amount of time it would take to read his mind.

I turned on my heel and headed for the lushly padded doors to my left. While the cameras weren't infrared, disappearing into shadows in the middle of the corridor was likely to gain more than a little attention from whatever security forces were watching the screens.

The velvety doors slid open as I approached, and the soft purr of music spun out. Like the main room, the dance floor here dominated the space, but there were fewer tables and more sofas and beanbags spread out along the walls. The room itself was warmer in tone, the walls a rich gold and the furnishings a mix of leather and plush materials. The sensual and erotic melodies of the music mingled with the scent of lust and sex in the air, creating an ambience that was relaxing yet sexy. I breathed deep, allowing the atmosphere to soak deep inside. An answering tremor of excitement coursed through every fiber. Now, *this* room was more my style. I guess it was the more intimate atmosphere I found sexier—the main room was just too large for someone used to smaller venues.

I walked down the steps and around the dance floor, looking for anyone resembling Adrienne's drawing. The sights and sighs of mating were all around, and my own lust rose, sweetening the air. A shifter gravitated toward me, drawn like a bee to honey by the scent of a willing wolf in heat. I gave him a smile and shook my head. I'd made a promise, and I intended to keep it.

I claimed a booth toward the rear of the room, placing my drink on the table before tugging off my shirt and dumping it beside the drink. If anyone happened to come looking for me—and there was no reason why they should—they'd think I was on the dance floor. After a quick look around to be sure there were no eyes or cameras pointed my way, I faded into shadow.

It was easy enough to slip through the darkness hugging the dance floor. The tricky bit was timing the sweep of muted lights with someone going through the main door. I missed several chances thanks to the timing of the lights, but finally followed a panting and naked couple out of the door. They went right, to the bathroom. I stepped left, into the deeper darkness.

The guard sniffed, his nose rising a little as he tasted the air. Scenting me, even if he couldn't see me. I gave him no time to place the aroma or hit the alarm, just lowered several layers of shields and stormed into his mind. He was mine in an instant.

I rifled quickly through his thoughts and memories, finding nothing when it came to Adrienne or Jodie, and very little else that was useful—mainly because he did little more than follow orders handed down from his shift supervisor.

I made him open the door and peer inside, as if investigating a noise, then I slipped past him, into the shadows of the smaller room. When he closed the door again, I released him, keeping only the barest psychic hold on him so I'd know if he heard or suspected anything unusual.

This room was all dark paneling and thick comfortable seating. The air was warm and sweet smelling, the aroma a mix of leather, alcohol, and sex. Interestingly, there were no security cams and no dance floor, but there was a large well-stocked bar.

There didn't seem to be anything of interest in this room, and yet instinct prickled.

Frowning, I walked around, inspecting the walls, looking for anything odd. There didn't seem to be anything out of place, and certainly nothing that would explain my growing certainty that this room held secrets.

I flicked to the infrared of my vampire vision, and looked around again. That's when I discovered the other room. It was behind the wall to the right of the entrance, and there didn't appear to be a door into it. Not from this room, anyway.

I walked over, then flicked off the infrared. The wall looked totally solid, but maybe there was a hidden entrance. I mean, it looked like a storage room, so why wouldn't there be a door somewhere? It made no sense, otherwise. I raised a hand, expecting to meet wood paneling. Instead, my fingers met nothing, disappearing into the wall.

What appeared to be solid concrete and wood paneling was, in fact, a fake barrier that divided the room into two.

After a moment's hesitation, I stepped through. Energy caressed my body, making my skin tingle and my hair stand on end. I'd felt a sensation like that before, in the den of the dark god. Someone had set up magical barriers on this door, meaning there was obviously something worth protecting in the room beyond.

But if the barrier had been set to protect, why was I able to step through?

From this side the barrier looked almost nonexistent. There was only a slight shimmer of energy to suggest there was any division between the two rooms. This half of the room beyond was much smaller, with only half a dozen steps between the false wall and the real back wall. Air flowed gently from the thick darkness to my right, but it was the setup on my left that caught my interest.

Someone had set themselves up a recording room, complete with several expensive-looking video cameras that sat on desks facing the false wall. It seemed the owners were filming events in the other room. Maybe they had a sideline of blackmail going on. Which, while illegal, wasn't exactly what I was here to uncover. And given Adrienne hadn't even made it in here, it wasn't what she'd discovered, either. Unless, of course, she'd seen it when she'd brushed against the stranger in the hall.

So why would she then go on to the island? Why not expose the blackmailing scheme, if that was what was going on? Was there any connection at all to the three missing women, or was it pure chance she'd disappeared the same way as those others?

I'd barely stepped away from the cameras when there was a sharp sound from the shadows, then a door opened and light suddenly swept across the darkness, just missing my toes.

Two men were framed in the light, one human, one not. Both armed.

If I didn't get my ass out of there, I was one caught puppy.

Chapter 8

I spun and ran for the shadows behind the last desk. It was a tight squeeze between the wall and the desktop, but I flattened my breasts with my hands and forced my body into the gap.

And not a moment too soon. Light swept across the wall where I'd been only moments before, the bright beam flinging the table legs into sharp relief against the shadows and almost highlighting my fingers. I crunched up into a tight ball and waited.

"Nothing, as I suspected," one man said, his voice low and deep, and somehow familiar. But I wasn't about to risk peering out to take a better look at the speaker. Not with the bright beam of the flashlight still skirting the room. "Told you those damn barriers were faulty."

"They may be faulty, but the scent of a female lingers in the room, boss."

Boss? I thought the man at the front door had said the owner had gone away?

"It's probably left over from last night." Even so, he stepped forward and sniffed the air. I could only hope he was one human who *didn't* have a good sense of smell.

Light pierced my corner. I shrunk back as far as I could, biting my lip and hoping like hell the desk's modesty screen threw enough shadows to keep me hidden. But the vampire veil of darkness that kept me safe could be destroyed so easily. It would only take one flicker of brightness to tear the shadows apart and reveal me.

"Has anyone talked to Mike?"

"No. I alerted you the minute the alarm went off."

The first man grunted, then said, "Mike, get in here."

There was a scuffle of noise, then the guard appeared at the door. I still had my finger on his mental pulse, so to speak, and felt his surprise. For an instant, I thought about letting my psychic touch go deeper, to see what this man saw, but that might be a bad idea. These men seemed sharp enough to sense anything amiss, and I didn't have the time I needed to take full control of the guard's sensory and speech functions.

"Yes, boss?" the guard said, voice sharp and respectful.

"Have you allowed anyone in here? Heard anything odd?"

"No, sir."

"Security is saying you opened the door not ten minutes ago. Why was that?"

Security was obviously tight here. The point was, why? Or was that a stupid question, given the cameras in this room? The owner obviously had a whole lot more going on than just a nightclub where humans could get their inhibited rocks off.

"Don't know. Thought I heard a sound."

"No one came past you into the front room at any time?"

"No, sir. Everyone who came into the hall just headed to the Executive Room."

"Thanks, Mike." Silence fell as the guard retreated. Once the door had closed behind him again, the deep-voiced man said, "You'd better check the stairs and the basement. If we have got an intruder, then that's where they've come from. Call me if you find anything. And get that magi back in here tomorrow to check these barriers."

"Will do."

Footsteps retreated. The holder of the light remained, sweeping the corners before moving into the other room. I rose and squeezed out from behind the desk to catch a glimpse of the man, thankful that the barrier was one-way.

He was built big, and his pale skin seemed to glow with an almost luminous light against the shadows. He wasn't anyone I recognized, and he certainly wasn't the man Adrienne had drawn.

He walked toward the main door, flung it open, then stepped through. Giving me my one and only chance to leave this room. I ran forward. Again the tingling swept my skin, and part of me wondered if there were DNA sensors involved that could warn if someone other than approved personnel went through it. It would certainly explain the quick appearance of the two men.

The door was closing. I ducked through fast, trying

to avoid the guard but not entirely succeeding. One breast brushed his arm. I cursed inwardly but dived toward the deeper shadows, away from the door and the guard.

"What the . . ." the guard said, before my mind rushed into his and stopped the words.

"What?" the other man asked immediately, as he turned around.

It was then that his scent actually registered. Spicy, warm, and human. But also very familiar.

Because it was the scent that belonged to Jared Donovan, Monitor Island's boat driver and serial flirt. Only it couldn't be. This man looked *nothing* like Jared—practically their only similar feature was their eyes.

I *had* to be mistaken. Humans didn't have similar scents—they might all share a strange preference for covering their base scent with all sorts of man-made fragrances, but anyone with a keen nose could always smell past that. My nose was as keen as anyone's, and it had never been wrong.

Until now.

"Mike?"

The sharp question made me jump. I tightened my mental grip on the guard and made him shrug. "Sorry. A goddamn bug bit my neck."

The big man snorted softly, then spun on his heel and walked into the Executive Room. I followed fast before the doors could close, then scooted down the steps and along the dance floor, keeping the shadows close and stripping as I ran.

I had no idea what was going on, and no idea if he'd come in here to play or to hunt my scent, but I wasn't about to make it easy for him. I tossed my clothes onto the seat of my booth, then, still wrapped in shadow, slipped onto the dance floor, releasing the shadows only when the bodies began to press close.

I pushed deeper into the crowd, until the smell of lust was so powerful it was almost liquid and space was at such a premium that it felt like a hundred different people were touching, pressing, and caressing my flesh. That was what I wanted, what I needed. My scent, mixed with many others, creating a confused riot of aromas that no mere human—keen nose or not—would be able to sort out.

It just might be enough to allay suspicion.

So I danced and teased, enjoying the heat of so many bodies pressed against mine, touching them and teasing them even as I enjoyed their caresses, their kisses. And while desire burned, while I ached to give in to the need that burned through my body, I didn't. I had that promise to Kellen to keep, and I would do so, even if it hurt.

It was a good ten minutes before I spotted him again, moving up the stairs and back out the doors. Relief swam through me. But though the temptation to leave was high, I knew it would be dangerous to do so just yet. I had to let the alarm die down. Had to give that man time to forget my scent.

So I continued to dance. And after a while, I spotted the white wolf I'd flirted with at the club's entrance walk into the room. God, had only half an hour passed? It seemed a whole lot longer than that.

Thing was, dancing with him probably wasn't a great idea. The less attention I brought to myself the better. So when he approached with eager lust in his eyes, I touched his mind lightly, sending him into the arms of a more than willing blonde. With him occupied, I got the hell off the dance floor, re-dressed, then left.

No one stopped me. No one even noticed my departure. Even the guard at the front door was too busy chatting up the woman in the payment booth to do anything more than give me a fake smile.

The brightness of the day made me blink. I let my eyes adjust for a moment, then walked over to my car. A scent lingered near the door, the sharp smell of a male, and I frowned, looking around. No one and nothing was near. Shrugging, I got into the car and headed back to the Directorate.

Only I didn't get that far, because Jack called with the news of another murder.

I pulled to a stop at the address he'd given me, and felt the sickness rise. It was one street over from Mary's, and almost directly behind.

The evil soul hadn't left, as I'd presumed. He'd simply found himself another victim.

I closed my eyes and took a deep breath, but it didn't do much to ease the queasiness running through me. I didn't want to go near the place, I really didn't. But I forced my feet toward the house. Whatever had happened in there was my fault, and the least I could do was face the woman's soul and apologize.

Cole appeared as I neared the front door, his features as grim as I'd ever seen them. "This one is nasty."

I shoved my hands in the pockets of my coat to hide their trembling. "Every one of these murders has been nasty."

"This one reaches a whole new level." He handed me a pair of slip-on foot-covers, and my stomach began to churn even harder. "There's only one person involved in this."

"What?"

"No husband," he said grimly. "No boyfriend, no lover, no significant other. Just her."

"But how is—"

He held up a finger, stopping my words. "Come and see."

I slipped the covers onto my shoes, then grabbed a pair of gloves, pulling them on as I stepped into the house. Like Mary's house, this one had a long hallway, and the bedrooms were all directly off it. The kitchen and living spaces were down at the far end of the house.

Our footsteps echoed on the gleaming floorboards as we walked. The smell of blood and fear stung the air, but mixed within those scents was the reek of anger. It was dark, that anger, dark and deep.

Our avenging soul hadn't gotten what he'd wanted, so he'd unleashed his fury on someone else. Someone who hadn't deserved it.

I stepped into the living room, then stopped. The bird-shifter knelt near one of the walls, taking samples from the smears of blood that rained across the room. Cole's other assistant was carefully bagging the blonde hair that was scattered like pale snow all over the floor and furniture.

I gulped back bile and looked to my left. The woman lay in a crumpled heap at the base of the bloody, smashed-in pantry. Her arms, her legs, her body— everything had been wildly slashed, and the offending knife was still clenched in her left hand. It was hard to say if her face had borne the same sort of self-mutilation, because there was nothing left of her face to see. It was smashed beyond recognition, broken into so many pieces it resembled pulverized meat. There weren't even eyes. Somewhere along the line, they'd been gouged out.

My gaze went to the wall opposite, then back to the pantry door. Based on the blood pattern, he'd run her face first into one, then the other, back and forth.

I briefly closed my eyes and took a shuddery breath.

My fault.

All my fault.

This bastard *had* to be stopped before he could kill again.

"Death happened just after one last night, didn't it?"

Cole looked at me. "Yeah. How'd you guess?"

"Because I stopped the thing that caused this from taking the life of the woman who lives behind this house."

He frowned. "What thing?"

"It's a spirit." I hesitated. "A very dark and angry spirit."

He studied me for a moment, bright eyes perhaps seeing more than I wanted him to. "You can hardly be blamed for *not* stopping a murderous spirit. That's hardly a guardian's field of expertise."

"But I could have guessed he'd do something like this." His need for blood and revenge had simply been too great. I should have known that—after all, I'd felt the force of it. Felt the fury in him.

Cole snorted. "You can't be held accountable for the bloody intentions of those you track. Get that thought well and truly out of your head, or you won't last long in this job."

I smiled grimly. "That could be a good thing, you know."

"Not if the little men with white coats come calling."
He nodded toward the stains on the wall. "Whatever
this thing is, it's got a mean temper. I'm not exactly psychic, and even I can feel the anger lingering on the air.
I've called in one of the magi."

I raised my eyebrows. "Really? How could they help
with your investigations?"

"They can't. But by being here, they might be able to
get some sense of what this thing really is, and how it
might be stopped."

"It's worth a shot."

Hell, anything that could generate answers was
worth a shot. I rubbed my arms. The chill in the room
was growing stronger, and I wasn't sure if the cause
was the fading day or a soul getting ready to appear. I
hoped it was the former, not the latter. Part of me just
didn't want to face the soul of the woman. Didn't want
to face her fury and confusion.

How could a simple apology ever be enough?

"There is, perhaps, one tangible clue here." Cole
bent and picked several strands of golden hair. "The
soul or spirit or whatever it is seems to have a fetish for
cutting off women's hair. He's even forced this woman
to cut off her own hair. There can't have been many serial killers in our past with that sort of obsession."

"He might not have been a serial killer in life. He
may have just killed an unfaithful lover, then sui-
cided." And maybe that meant it *was* true that such
souls roamed the earth, unable to enter heaven or hell
or wherever else it was that regular souls went.
Though it didn't explain how he'd gained the power to
enter others and make them commit such atrocities. To
others, and to themselves. "But you're right, it's definitely a clue."

Hopefully, I'd find similarities and answers in one of the three files I'd requested.

The chill in the air was getting fiercer, and I rubbed my arms again.

"It's not that cold," Cole commented.

"It is when you're feeling the chill of afterlife," I muttered. "Have we got an ID yet?"

"Veronica Ward."

The cold sharpened abruptly, and energy ran like ice across my skin. I looked past him and saw her. A wisp of fragile cotton that hovered over the body, rapidly finding form. Finding voice.

Why, it said. *Why?*

I closed my eyes against the pain and confusion in that voice. *Because I couldn't stop it. I'm sorry, Veronica. So very sorry.*

Which sounded as inadequate as I'd feared, but there was little else I could do or say.

It rotated, that soul, its movements more controlled, less frenetic, than the others I'd seen. Considering her options, taking stock before she made any move. I had a feeling she'd been like that in life, too.

But you must stop it, she said eventually. *Before the cycle stops for another year.*

Cycle? So this *had* happened before? *We're trying.*

Fawkner. He lives in Fawkner. It is there you must stop him.

With that statement, the cold energy fell away, and her soul disintegrated, fleeing to whatever region of afterlife she was bound for.

I took a deep, shuddering breath. "Well, that was interesting."

"The soul spoke?"

I nodded. "She said we had to stop him before the

cycle halts for another year. She also said he lived in Fawkner."

"See, I told you we had a serial killer on our hands."

"Yeah, but does she mean now, or when he was alive?"

"Does it even matter?"

"I guess not." I forced myself to study the room. "There is nothing else here that provides a clue in any way?"

"Nothing so far."

"You'll let me know if you find anything? Or if the magi finds anything?"

"First thing."

"Thanks, Cole."

His sudden smile crinkled the corners of his eyes and lent his features a warmth that was stunningly attractive. Needless to say, my hormones did excited little cartwheels. But then, my hormones were feeling more than a little frustrated after all that playing at the club.

"Two thanks in two days," he said, the twinkle in his blue eyes matching the killer smile. "That has to be a record for a guardian, doesn't it?"

"I'm not your average guardian."

"I think that's one point we can both agree on."

I smiled. "Finally. Does this mean we can go on a date, and have sex?" I asked, only half-kidding.

"No."

"Damn."

He laughed, a merry sound that had my smile widening. "You may be a killer, but you're a fun one to be around."

"Thanks. I think."

"No probs." He turned away to continue his investigation, and I headed for the car. Once outside, I sucked in the fresh air, trying to sweep away the remnants of death and destruction. It didn't help much. Both still clung to my skin.

I looked at my watch. It was nearing four. I could go home, if I wanted to. Perhaps find Kellen and ease some aches. But the mere thought had guilt stirring. Someone had died because I didn't know enough. Surely I owed it to the dead to remedy that.

I climbed into my car and headed back to the Directorate. The roads into the city were all grid-locked, however, and I amused myself by checking out the other drivers, trying to guess what they did for a living by the make of their car. To see if I was right, I lightly touched their minds. I was right a good forty percent of the time, which wasn't a bad effort.

When I finally made it into the Directorate, I peeked into the liaisons' office to see if my caramel-haired nemesis was there. Luckily, she wasn't, but the scrawny-looking vamp I'd worked with off and on during my years as a liaison, was. "Hey, David, can you sign my car out for another night?"

"I have a note here—"

"Screw the note. I need the car."

"Salliane will not be pleased."

"Good." I pushed away and headed for our squad room. David's amusement followed me down the hall. No one was around when I walked in, so I helped my-self to coffee then sat at my desk. After going through the security checks, I pulled up the three requested files and started reading them. It took a while, but eventu-ally I hit pay dirt.

"You're looking mighty pleased with yourself," Jack said, as he walked into the room. He dumped a file on Rhoan's desk, then walked over to the coffeemaker.

"I found our killer."

"And?"

"He went by the name of Harvey Wilson, an itinerant handyman who apparently got fixated on one Erma McDonald. Followed her around like a dog in heat, and apparently got violent if she went out with other men."

Jack leaned his butt against the counter and took a sip of his coffee. "They weren't married or anything?"

"No, but Harvey treated her like they were. She took out a restraining order on him, but he seemed to have a sixth sense about the cops and could never be caught violating the order."

"Which he obviously did, if he murdered her."

"Yeah." I glanced briefly at the all-too-familiar images of bloodshed and destruction. "He discovered Erma was engaged to be married. Accused her of having an affair and swore that she would remain true to him, and only him, forever."

"So he tore her up?"

I nodded. "Psychically, not physically. They had a witness—a neighbor whose kitchen window looked into Erma's and who heard everything. Apparently, once Erma was dead, he chopped off her hair and shoved it into his pocket."

"So the cops caught him?"

"Not really. He waited until they arrived and had seen what he'd done, then shot himself." Which certainly fit what was happening now—the gloating sense of evil I kept sensing when we first walked in.

Jack snorted. "Undoubtedly thinking they could be together in the afterlife. Psychos never seem to learn things aren't that easy."

"Well, I wish it was, because then he wouldn't still

be here on this plane of existence, destroying lives." I glanced at the file again. "According to the report, he's been at it for five years now."

Jack frowned. "If his spirit has been killing for five years, why haven't there been more murders?"

"Because he only hunts and kills for one week of every year." And few of the cases actually got reported to us, because by the time the various departments realized they had a serial killer, the killings stopped.

"Unusual for a tormented soul to be so restrained," Jack commented.

"Not if his sprees only happen during the anniversary week of his death."

"Which was?"

"October 31. Halloween itself."

Jack snorted. "Explains a lot."

I leaned back in my chair. "I know Halloween tends to bring out the weirdness in both humans and nonhumans, but I didn't realize it had a similar effect on the spiritual world."

"That's the problem with the world today—no one knows the real meanings of anything anymore."

"I know it used to be an old pagan festival that celebrated the end of summer and the beginning of winter."

He smiled. It was one of those "pleased with a student" smiles that really annoyed me. "That's right. But the Celts—and many other cultures—also believed that during Samhain, the boundary between the living and the dead blurred, and spirits could roam the earth."

"Which explains why he was able to rise on the day of his death, but not how he was able to continue his killing spree for the next five days."

"The days between Samhain and November 5 have been times of feasting, celebrations, and remembrances of the dead down through many centuries."

"Giving him—and spirits like him—the chance to do their evil bidding?"

"Unfortunately, yes."

"How come the guardian division hasn't had more ghostly disturbances to take care of, then?"

"Because our magi division usually takes care of these sorts of problems, not our guardians."

I guess that made sense. I mean, our regular hunter-killers wouldn't even be able to sense a spirit. "So have we discovered yet how to stop a soul intent on murder?"

"Marg and her team are still going through their texts to find out."

Marg was the spindly magi who'd helped us contain a spirit intending to let a dark god loose on the world. A spirit who had turned out to be Quinn's sister—and the reason he'd actually become a vampire.

"Tell her we haven't a whole lot of time to work with. It's been three days already. We only have two more before he's off in hibernation for the next year."

He nodded. "I've asked her to get back with ideas before sunset. In the meantime, I suggest you uncover where he was buried."

I frowned. "Why?"

"Because sometimes a soul sullied by suicide cannot be sent on. They can only be restrained."

And I guess I was going to find out how that was done soon enough. "You seem to know an awful lot about this sort of stuff, boss."

"I'm a vampire," he said. "And you'd know a lot of

stuff if you'd been around for eight hundred years, too."

"Not me. I've got a memory like a sieve."

"Especially when it comes to leaving the com-link on," he said, voice dry as he pushed away from the desk and headed for the door. "You'd better catch some rest once you find out where Wilson is buried, just in case Marg needs your help with the ceremony."

"My help?" I all but yelped. Hell, the last thing I wanted to be doing tonight was wandering about a cemetery helping to restrain a spirit. "Why the hell would she need my help?"

"Because you're the only guardian that can see or talk to souls."

"Marg's a *magi*. Surely she's got ways and means to communicate with the dead?"

"Your way is more direct. Besides, Wilson may get nasty," he said, as he disappeared out the door.

I muttered obscenities under my breath, then started tracking down Harvey Wilson's final resting place. And really, it wasn't all that hard, because Veronica Ward had given me the clue. She'd said he'd lived in Fawkner. Given Wilson had been an itinerant in life, she could only mean that was where he lived now. In the Fawkner cemetery.

Which is exactly where I found him. I scribbled down the plot number and street address, then signed off the computer and went home. Jack was right. I needed sleep. A look in the mirror only confirmed that. My eyeballs were bloodshot, and there were huge bags under my eyes. Which was never a good look when combined with pale skin and red hair.

The last remnants of the sunset were fading as I pulled to a halt outside our apartment. I climbed out of the car and breathed deep. The air was crisp and filled with the sharpness of oncoming rain. With my luck, it'd be absolutely bucketing down come cemetery time tonight.

Then another scent caught my interest—that of a wolf. A *male* wolf. It was a sour, almost unpleasant aroma, and certainly didn't belong to anyone I was familiar with. I scanned the pavement, looking for the origin of the scent. A woman struggled along with bags of shopping clenched in each hand, her very human scent tangy and not unpleasant. Farther down, a somewhat disheveled-looking man sat on the front steps of a building and smoked something that looked hand-rolled. A joint, probably.

No sour-smelling wolves in sight.

I raised my nose, tasting the slight breeze again. The aroma of rotting rubbish, perfume, and the thick scent of humans rode the air. Underneath all that, the vaguest hint of death and decay—a vampire had passed this way recently, and his unwashed scent still stained the breeze. The sour smell seemed to be coming from my building. Maybe the old biddy who owned it had decided Rhoan and I had been such good tenants, she'd let another wolf in.

The thought stopped abruptly as a sharp sound snagged my interest and got my pulse racing.

The air seemed to scream, as if something fast and deadly was tearing through the dusk toward me.

Fear hit like a punch to the gut. I knew that sound. I'd heard it far too often now to mistake it. I threw myself sideways, but wasn't fast enough by half. The bullet tore into my arm, right through the flesh of my underarm, then continued, smashing into the windshield and shattering it into a thousand different pieces.

Glass flew, the glittering fragments raining around me as I hit the roadside. My chin struck hard, smashing my teeth into my lip, cutting flesh.

As the metallic taste of blood filled my mouth, another bullet tore through the air, punching a hole through the still-open car door and pinging off the road inches from my hip.

I swore softly. The bastard had to be up high. He had too good a sight on me to be anywhere near ground level. I scooted forward, my arm burning and bullets pinging around me. And they were all silver, because while ordinary bullet wounds hurt like blazes, they didn't burn like this one was.

Which meant this bastard, whoever he was, knew I was a werewolf. Meaning it was no damn accident I was being shot at.

Could Blake be so angry about me not saving Adrienne he'd sent out a hit?

Probably, but all the same I doubted he was behind the shots. Torment was more his style.

I stopped behind the rear tire and scanned the surrounding rooftops. I couldn't see a goddamn thing . . . until a shadow moved on the top of the apartment building next to ours. It was moving, half-crouched, along the roof, probably searching for a better angle. But I'd be damned if I was going to let him get it. I scooted around the back of the car, and felt another bullet nip at my toes.

The bastard *had* found a better angle.

God, if only I'd had a weapon on me, I could have taken the shooter out when he'd moved. But I'd left my damn laser locked securely in the apartment safe this morning, just like I always did. Stupid, stupid, stupid.

I'd have to risk running. I blew out a breath, then

scrambled to my feet and ran like hell for the building. Bullets pinged against the pavement behind me, but their presence no longer burned. Perhaps he'd run out of silver ones.

But the mere fact that he was still sighting me when I was running as fast as I was physically able meant he had to be something other than human. To human— even wolf—eyes, I'd be nothing more than a blur. But a vamp could track me through infrared vision.

If it *was* a vamp up there, it'd have to be an older one, otherwise he couldn't be out in the dusk. I slammed through the building's front doors and ran up the stairs. This apartment block was almost identical to ours—a neglected old warehouse that had been converted to apartments and rented cheap to those who didn't mind living near the freeway. Though this building, being on a corner and facing suburbia, had less inspiring scenery than ours. At least we could see the city and the bridges at night from our apartment.

And obviously there were no werewolves living here, either, because the high-pitched squeal of rats was evident as the little bastards went scampering at my approach. Like I was going to stop and eat one of them.

I continued to pound up the stairs. Six flights left me winded. The rooftop fire escape door was padlocked— which was totally against the rules, but often done in old buildings like these to stop the jumpers. We'd had a few jump from our roof, and it was never a pretty sight. Even a cat-shifter didn't have much luck against that sort of drop.

After wiping the sweat from my forehead with a bloody hand, I stepped back and kicked open the door. It rebounded against the wall loud enough to wake the dead, but no welcoming bullet pinged into the opening.

I blew out a breath, then dove through the opening, my back hitting the concrete hard before I was rolling to my feet and running for the nearest ventilation shaft. Again, no bullets.

Maybe he'd gone.

Maybe he was waiting for a clearer shot.

I sniffed the air, trying to get some hint of who and what my adversary was. The air ran sharp with many aromas—including the metallic scent of my own blood—but there was no hint of vampire on the breeze.

I switched to infrared and scanned the rooftop. There was no one here. I was totally alone. I swore softly and rose. No bullets smashed through the air to greet my sudden appearance. My quarry was truly gone.

Cursing softly, I walked over to the corner of the building, going near, but not too near, the edge. At least a dozen shell casings littered the ground. Someone had wanted me very dead. Question was, who? And had they moved up from using cars and trucks to using bullets?

I suspected they had. But why? Certainly there was nothing happening in my private life that warranted such actions, so it had to be connected to a case.

Problem was, I only had two on my plate at the moment, and neither of those was a likely prospect. I mean, it wouldn't be our evil soul, because he preferred more direct methods of destruction. I also doubted it would have anything to do with Adrienne's case, because that was getting nowhere fast. And while Blake might be annoyed at my lack of results, I didn't think he'd send hits out on me. Though I had no doubt he *could* have done so if he'd wanted to. He'd know the right people, if only because he was that type himself.

I left the casings lying where they were—not only because I didn't have gloves but because I knew squat about guns and wouldn't have been able to tell one casing from another—and followed the building's edge, looking for a clue as to where my would-be assassin had gone. I wasn't close enough to see the pavement directly below, and technically six flights shouldn't have had my phobia rising, but the breeze whistling up and over the edge gave a feeling of greater height and my stomach twisted.

I reached the other end of the building. There was a small jump over an alleyway to the rooftop of my building, and someone had not only taken it at speed but had misjudged their landing. Several of the aerials were either bent out of shape or broken. The old cow of an owner would have a pink fit—she loved her TV above everything else.

After a quick glance down at the gap between the two buildings, I backed away from the edge and pressed the com-link button in my ear.

"Anyone home?"

"Oh joy, it's the bitch," a familiar voice said.

I smiled. "Hey, Sal, welcome back. I missed you."

She snorted. "Yeah, I'm gone a whole twenty-four hours and you're pining for me. Right. What can I do for you, wolf girl?"

"Someone's just taken a potshot at me. With silver bullets."

"So who'd you piss off this time?"

"No one that I know of."

"I find that *extremely* hard to believe."

So did I, actually. "He didn't manage to kill me."

"You do like stating the fucking obvious, don't you?"

I grinned. "He did manage to put a whole heap of holes in your car."

"Well, fuck him."

"Yeah." I took a breath then, with my heart racing a million miles an hour, ran at the edge, and leapt over. It wasn't really a wide gap, no matter what my stupid fears were saying, and I landed on the other side without a problem. "The shooter was on the roof of the apartment next to mine. I'm currently on my rooftop and heading down."

"Any evidence?"

"Shell casings. There might be prints."

"I'll send a team out."

"Thanks, Sal."

"You won't be thanking me when you get the repair bill, wolf girl."

I chuckled softly, clicked off the com-link, and walked around to the fire exit. The stair door was hanging off one hinge and swaying softly in the breeze. And what looked to be a footprint was neatly etched into the metal. My attacker was on the small side, if this print was any indication.

I stood to one side of the doorway, studying the shadows and listening for anything out of place. The normal sounds and scents of living drifted up from the apartments below, but the air also held the slightest hint of staleness—the type of staleness I'd long associated with vampires. Though this wasn't as bad as some.

My shooter had definitely been past here, but I doubted he was still hanging around. His scent was fading, and I couldn't "feel" any other nonhuman in the immediate vicinity.

Still, if he knew I lived here, there was no saying he wasn't waiting in the shadows near my apartment.

I ducked around the corner of the broken door, feeling a little foolish but knowing it was better than feeling a little dead. Hell, Rhoan would never forgive me if I got myself killed this easily after everything we'd been through this last year or so.

None of the shadows moved, though, and the darkness hid nothing but dust. Even so, I edged down each step carefully, every sense tuned. No one jumped out at me. Nothing but darkness hid on the fire escape.

When I neared the hallway of my own floor, I hesitated, switching to infrared and scanning the area. Again, nothing.

But the heat of two bodies flared to life in my apartment, and neither the shapes nor the murmuring voices were familiar.

Infrared couldn't actually tell me what race the two people in my apartment were. All it could do was tell me that blood pumped through their veins—perhaps a little faster than what was normal for a vampire, but that was no guarantee one or both of them weren't bloodsuckers.

I studied their images a little longer, fixing their positions in my mind, then padded softly down the hall until I was near my door.

After taking another deep breath and releasing it slowly, I stepped forward, hitting the lock in the sweet spot and springing it open.

Two men spun around, one of them reaching for a gun. He was fast, real fast.

But I was faster.

I blurred, running at him at full speed, snatching the gun from him with one hand and punching his jaw with the other, sending him back and down.

Then I turned and leapt for the second man, who

was already running. I hit him in the back, the weight of my body dragging him down. He slammed into the floorboards with a grunt, but twisted and punched. The blow caught my cut lip, sending my head snapping backward and blood flying. I cursed, smashed an elbow into his face, then wedged the tip of my stolen weapon under the point of his chin. His sour scent told me he was the wolf I'd smelled earlier.

"Try something like that again, and I'll blow your frigging head off," I growled.

"Okay, okay," he rasped, voice showing more anger than fear.

For the first time, I got a good look at him. Saw the flat, nondescript features, beady gray eyes, and harsh, uncompromising mouth.

It wasn't a stranger I'd beaten up and threatened.

It was Patrin.

Chapter 9

I have to say, my first reaction was one of intense satisfaction. I'd spent a good portion of my younger years afraid of this bastard and his siblings, unable to retaliate for fear of reprisals from their father. To be sitting here on top of him, sucking in the scent of his anger and fear—to see the blood gushing from his smashed nose and split lip—was an undeniably sweet turnaround.

But in the heat of battle I'd forgotten he wasn't alone, and that was a very stupid thing to do.

As the sharp snap of a gun being cocked confirmed.

"Put the weapon down and step away from him." The voice was soft, almost without threat, and that, in my books, suggested that the wolf with Patrin was very dangerous indeed.

I didn't move, didn't look at him, even though just about every sense I had was tuned for the faintest whisper of movement. I continued to stare at Patrin, letting him see the hatred in my eyes, letting him wonder if I really would pull the trigger.

"You willing to bet the life of your employer on the fact you're faster with a gun than I am?"

"Yes."

"Then you're a fool. And Patrin obviously hasn't told you what I am."

"You're a fucking useless half-breed who needs to be taken down a peg or two, that's what you are," Patrin snarled.

I smiled grimly and wedged the gun barrel into his neck a little harder. Sweat popped out across his forehead and the scent of his fear increased.

God, it felt good. Damned good.

"And who's going to do that, Patrin? You? Or will you run to Daddy for help like you always do?"

"Bitch, I don't need my father's help to take the likes of you. I never have."

"Which is why you're now on your back with a gun shoved into your throat, isn't it?" I said pleasantly.

He snarled and bucked, trying to throw me off. I gripped harder with my thighs, using more force than necessary. Indeed, more force than a wolf should have had. But then, I wasn't just wolf—and he, of all people, should have remembered that.

He swore at me, viciously and fluently. I ignored him, and glanced at the second wolf. He, too, was a red wolf, but from a different pack. His hair was so dark it almost looked black in the fast-disappearing light, and his eyes were golden.

"Please tell your employer if he doesn't remain still, I'm going to be forced to shoot something vital."

"I'm afraid I won't be able to let you do that." He was still using calm tones, and though there was tension to be seen in his lean body, the vibes he was throwing off were all cool confidence.

"And I'm afraid you won't stop me." I hesitated, glancing back at Patrin. "He *didn't* tell you, did he?"

"Tell me what?"

"That I'm a guardian." I glanced at the second wolf again. "I'm trained to track, fight, and kill vampires. Many of my kills have been several hundred years old, and far faster and stronger than you two ever could be."

Which was more than a slight fabrication of the truth, but neither of them would know that. Besides, I hardly think they'd believe me if I said I'd helped bring down a dark god, and that *was* nothing but the truth.

"No, he didn't tell me that. But I still can't let you shoot him. I have to try and stop you. You understand."

What I understood was that his calm demeanor suggested he was well trained, and probably a deadly shot. Patrin would only hire the best, after all. And as much as I would have loved to prove a point to these men, I'd really been shot at enough today.

So I eased the gun away from Patrin's neck, emptied the chamber, then pushed the weapon across the floor to the second man. "I actually have no plans to kill him today. Unless, of course, he refuses to answer my questions."

"Fair enough." The flick of movement had me tensing—and suddenly wondering if I'd misjudged him—but he was merely bending to retrieve his weapon. "I'm Kye, by the way."

"I gathered that." I looked down at Patrin again. "If I get off you, are you going to behave?"

"You're the one that attacked *me*," he all but spat.

"Nice change, huh?"

I climbed off him and stepped back. He got to his feet, rubbing his neck and glaring at Kye.

"So tell me, did that fucker you call Father arrange a hit on me?"

"No, though it's a damn good idea." He dug a handkerchief out of his suit pocket and dabbed rather uselessly at his bloody nose. "Why?"

"Because someone set up an ambush outside, complete with silver bullets."

"Hence your rather dramatic entrance," Kye said, as he walked across to the window.

"Well, finding strangers sitting in my living room after a close brush with silver does make me a little wary." I looked at Patrin again. "And if you don't tell me why you're here, I might get violent again."

"A letter arrived for me yesterday," he said. "From Adrienne."

I raised my eyebrows. "I thought she was dead."

"She is." His voice was flat, devoid of emotion. Yet the emotion lacking in his voice was all too evident in his eyes. Patrin wasn't only angry, he wanted revenge.

That was why he was here—to hunt down and kill his daughter's murderer. Not an unexpected sentiment, even from a wolf as cold and as uncaring as Patrin.

But the fact that Adrienne had sent a letter meant she'd known whatever she was investigating was dangerous. Perhaps she'd even seen her own death.

I wondered if she'd sent a letter to Jodie. I hoped so. "What did she say in the letter?"

"That something was going on at some club."

"Did she say what?" I walked across to the ironing basket and got a clean towel out. My arm was still bleeding, but I didn't want to shift shape with these two men in the room. They might not be out to get me, but I still wasn't about to trust them. And shifting to wolf form would put me at a disadvantage—one the past had proved Patrin would use.

"She said the owners of the club were using one of the rooms to tape politicians and corporate personnel in compromising positions and blackmail them."

So that *was* why she'd disappeared? Because she'd been sticking her nose in where it didn't belong and had discovered too much? But what, then, was the connection between the club and the island? Why go up there at all if she was investigating the blackmailing?

"We are aware of the blackmail angle." Though we weren't following it up, because I'd forgotten to tell Jack about it. "Did she say who the owners were? Give a description?"

He shook his head. "But if the club's under investigation, you should already know that."

"What's on paper, and what the reality is, are often two different things. As you should know." Hell, thanks to the hours I'd spent listening to conversations I shouldn't have as a kid, I knew that Patrin and his bastard father owned several manufacturing firms. But for tax purposes, their names were hidden by a long paper trail. I glanced at my watch. "If that's all, I need you to leave. I have stuff to do before I go to work tonight."

He took a step toward me. Part of me wanted to step back. The other part, the part wanting revenge for old hurts, bristled. It was all I could do not to step forward and challenge.

"I want the name of the club." His voice was low, dangerous.

I clenched my fists, but resisted the impulse to lash out. To thump the cold arrogance from his already bloody face. "It's guardian business, and you will keep your stinking little nose out of it."

"Adrienne is my *daughter*. Her death *will* be avenged."

"Not on my shift, it won't. Not by you, anyway."

He looked me up and down, the cold arrogance giving way to familiar disdain. "And you're going to stop me?"

I gave him a cool, hard smile, then snapped the shadows around my body and ran forward. Before either of them could even react, I'd snatched Kye's weapon and had it shoved hard under Patrin's neck.

For the first time there was fear, true fear, in his expression. Maybe he'd finally realized the pup he'd kicked for so long was no longer easy bait.

I shook the shadows free, then said softly, "Yes, I *will* stop you. And it won't matter how good Kye is, or how many like him you hire. I've learned to use all the skills of my heritage, Patrin, and I'm more dangerous than you could ever know."

Nothing like blowing your own horn, but hey, after years of putting up with his shit, it was the least I deserved. I shoved him, sending him flailing backward toward the sofa, then turned and handed the weapon back to Kye. He didn't say anything, just sheathed the weapon before nodding toward the window. "If your car is the Ford with the shot-out door, there's a couple of people down there looking at it."

I walked across to the window and looked down. I didn't recognize the faces, but the car parked behind mine was Directorate issue.

"It's a Directorate forensic team," I said, and turned around. "Now, is that all Adrienne had to say in that letter?"

"Yes. But this conversation isn't over. I want—"

"I don't give a fuck what you want. Leave, or I'll throw you out." I looked across at Kye. "If I see you or your boss anywhere near the nightclub Adrienne no doubt mentions in her letter, your asses will rot in jail for the next month."

"You can't—" Patrin began.

"Oh, trust me. I *can*."

He muttered something I didn't even try to hear, then pushed off the sofa and stomped toward the door. Kye gave me a polite nod and followed.

I slammed the door behind them, then headed for the bathroom and a long, hot soak in the tub. It wasn't just the blood that needed to be washed away—there was also the dirt and anger from the past.

*M*arg rang at eleven. By midnight, I was standing at Wilson's graveside in the Fawkner cemetery, shivering inside my coat as the wind howled around me and slivers of the dead teased my peripheral vision.

"Here," Marg said, her pale skin giving her an almost ghostlike appearance under the flashlight's not-too-bright light. "Wear this."

"This" was a little sack attached to a looped string. The aromas coming from the sack were a wild mix that had my nose quivering—the sweet, licorice scent of fennel, the reek of garlic, a soft flowery scent I didn't recognize, and something woody. At least it was a better smell than freshly dug earth and old death that was coming from Wilson's gravesite.

A gravesite that had a whole lot of hair scattered around it. At least we finally knew where it had all gone.

I held the little bag from one finger and studied it dubiously. "What is it?"

"Protection. It'll help ward off evil."

Given that I'd seen what Wilson could do, I wasn't betting my life on this little bag. Still, I wasn't about to refuse anything that just might help, either. Wilson wasn't going to be confined without a fight.

I shoved the string around my neck, then tucked the little bag inside my jacket. That way, it was out of the way if I had to move fast.

Marg leaned forward and sprinkled something white into my hair.

"Now what?" I said, resisting the urge to shake my head.

"Pure salt. Works as a ward because evil hates it."

"This is a vengeful soul we're dealing with here, not evil."

She shrugged. "Same basics."

"And how many times have you done something like this?"

"It's not the experience that matters," she said calmly. "It's the knowledge."

Yeah, right. Believing *that* totally. I crossed my arms and scanned the night. Gravesites loomed out of shadows and wisps of white drifted about almost aimlessly. Part of me wondered what held them here, but I had no intention of opening myself up to them and finding out.

I returned my gaze to Marg. She and her assistant had begun to surround the opened grave with incense sticks while murmuring under their breaths.

"What do you want me to do?" I asked, once they'd finished.

"We're going to start the summoning," she said. "Let us know if you feel his presence."

"Right."

I rubbed my arms and tried to ignore the growing sense of trepidation. None of the other women seemed concerned, but then, I'd seen what Wilson could do to people. They hadn't.

Marg and one of her assistants joined hands at the base of the grave and began to chant. Their words were so soft they were snatched away by the wind long before they reached my ears, but the power of them lingered, a sharpening spike of electricity that ran across the night and had the hairs on the back of my neck rising.

I scanned the darkness, my senses—psychic *and* regular—on high alert for anything out of the ordinary. The branches of the nearby trees tossed in the breeze, and in the distance, traffic rumbled. It might have been after midnight, but Sydney Road was never empty of life. And that worried me—especially when we were dealing with a soul who had the ability to control others.

The chanting continued. The feel of electricity in the air remained at the same sharp level, but something else ran under that power now. A throbbing, whispering demand that rode the wind.

Uneasiness swirled through me. I rubbed my leather-clad arms—an action that oddly sent little sparks skittering into the darkness—and scanned the graves again.

The wispy souls had disappeared. Only gravestones, tossing tree branches, and thorny roses were to be seen now. I wondered if the magic had chased the souls off, or whether it was something else.

Like Wilson being forcibly returned from his nightly hunting trip.

My gaze went back to Marg. She seemed to be putting more power into her chant now, her lips moving quickly and forcefully. I still couldn't hear the words, and I was beginning to think the wind had little to do with that.

I shivered. Tension wound through my body, and my nerves felt stretched to the limit. I flexed my fingers, trying to relax, but it didn't really do a whole lot of good. The sense of power and demand was growing, and the night seemed to hold its collective breath.

The third woman began lighting the incense sticks. They spluttered, the faint smells of rosemary and sandalwood touching the air before being spun away by the wind. She only lit half the sticks, leaving one side unlit and open. Then she repeated the process using the salt.

Were they leaving a gate so the spirit could reenter his coffin? If so, they were being overly hopeful. Somehow I didn't think getting Wilson back to his deathbed was going to be so straightforward.

In the distance, a horn blared, the sound cutting across the night. A car engine roared then shot away.

Youths, I thought. Or drunks. Or maybe even both.

Yet the tension in my limbs intensified, and sweat began to trickle down my back. I drew my weapon, feeling suddenly safer with the weight of it against my palm, even if a laser couldn't actually hurt a soul.

Was it only recently that I'd left my weapon locked up, refusing to carry its weight, feeling safer without it?

But now was not the time to worry about such things, because something was coming.

Awareness skittered along the outer reaches of my psychic senses, a darkness that was all power, all hate.

Wilson.

And he was approaching fast.

I scanned the night, trying to pinpoint his position, wondering what he was doing. What he was planning. Marg and her crew might have succeeded in summoning him, but he was fighting all the way.

Brightness speared the trees, twin spotlights that momentarily blinded. I blinked, saw the sweep of them move on as the car followed the road. But how had it gotten in here? We'd acquired the code to the main gates and had locked up after ourselves. The cemetery itself wasn't open to the public at this hour. No vehicles besides our own should have been in here.

As the car drew closer, the roar of the engine became clearer. It was being revved hard, the driver gunning it as he sped around corners. No sane person drove like that in a cemetery. He had to be under the influence— and I didn't think that influence was alcohol.

"I think we've got a problem." I flexed the fingers of my free hand and shifted my stance a little.

"Wilson is here?" the third magi asked softly.

"I think he might be."

"Think? That's not good enough."

Annoyance rose through the tension. "Hey, you're the people doing the summoning. Why the hell haven't you got some means of knowing if he is or isn't in the area?"

"Because that takes more energy, and given the apparent strength of this soul, we need all the power we can get for containment. Which is why you're here."

Another reason to wish I couldn't communicate with the dead. I'd avoid situations like this.

The lights cut through the trees again, closer and sharper than before. I squinted against their brightness and raised the laser. "I think it highly likely that the driver of the car coming toward us is controlled by Wilson."

"Then stop the car."

"Easier said than done, lady," I muttered. Especially when there was a human life in that car. I didn't want to kill him if it was at all possible.

The car broke free of the trees. The front was smashed in, the hood scrunched up, and the windshield shattered. Bits of roses and other plants hung off what remained of the grille, and metal bits trailed along the ground, raising sparks. He'd obviously driven right through the gates rather than opening them.

The driver gunned the engine again and the car lurched sharply toward us, crashing over the curb and onto the grass. I switched to infrared, sighted on the front tire, and pressed the laser's trigger. Blue light slashed across the night, hitting the tire and slicing straight through. The sharp smell of burned rubber filled the air as the car slewed sideways, crashing over a gravestone before it ploughed nose-first into a tree. The engine gave a final splutter then died, and the hiss of steam began to fill the air.

There was no movement from the driver, and I hoped like hell the crash hadn't killed him. The sense of evil—of anger and fury—was very much alive, however, and it sharpened abruptly even as I stood there.

"He's here," I said, and wished it didn't sound like we were all in the middle of some B-grade horror movie.

"Where, precisely?" the third magi said.

"If I knew for sure, I'd tell you."

"I thought you could see souls?"

"I can. This one is just hiding." I stepped sideways, trying to get a better view of the car and the driver.

He was alive, thankfully, because he was breathing. But whether he was knocked out, or merely waiting for the unwary to step into his web was something I couldn't tell from where I stood.

Which meant I'd have to move again.

And I *so* didn't want to get any closer to that thick scent of anger and death.

I edged sideways a little more. The driver was big, hairy, and, even from this distance, smelled human. Meaning he was a threat only in the way all men with big fists were a threat.

I blew out a breath, then walked closer. A dark stream of fluid poured down the driver's rough features, then leapt off his chin to join the ever-widening stain on the front of his crisp white shirt. It didn't take a wolf's nose to realize it was blood. Maybe he *was* out cold. The wound had to be pretty bad to be bleeding that hard, and humans weren't as thick-skinned or as tolerant to pain as us wolves.

He needed help and he needed it fast, but there was little I could do for him until Wilson was under control. Until then, paramedics just meant more bodies for Wilson to use.

"Sir?" I said loudly, my voice seeming to jar against the darkness. "Sir? Can you hear me? Are you all right?"

For several seconds, there was no response. Then the driver's head turned and he looked at me. His eyes were brown and staring, and there was absolutely nothing remotely resembling life or humanity in them.

He might be unconscious, he might be close to death, but none of that mattered because, right now, it was the dead who controlled him.

"He's in the driver," I said to the magi. "Can you guys amp up your summoning strength or something?"

"It's not like there's a dial we can turn," she replied crossly.

"Well, you'd better do something, because this bad boy doesn't seem inclined to move."

Of course, the minute the words were out of my mouth, the driver *did* move, thrusting the car door open and lunging toward me. I leapt back from his grasping fingertips then swung around, lashing out with a booted foot. The blow hit the already-bloody side of his face and sent him flying. His head smacked against the corner of the door. Bone cracked and more blood appeared as he slumped to the ground.

I hoped to God I hadn't killed him, but I had a bad feeling that might not be the case. I'd been reacting to Wilson, and had totally forgotten the body was human.

The thing inside the stranger screamed—a haunting, unearthly, and violent sound—then wisps of smoke began to unravel from the stranger, rolling down the outside of his body before exiting via his shiny shoes.

The snakelike apparition sat there for several seconds, pulsating in time to the ebb and flow of sharpening energy in the air. Then it lunged straight at me.

I yelped and leapt back, and almost without thought, pressed the laser's trigger. The blue beams shot through the smoky form, scattering it briefly but not permanently.

Then, with almost light speed it was on me, wrapping itself around my legs and slithering upward, the cold chill of death, destruction, and hate eating into my senses. I swatted at it, trying to get it off me, my heart racing nine to the dozen as Wilson's wispy form climbed higher and the thick scent of hell seemed to encase me. Then the bag on my chest began to burn, and the sweet scent of fennel and flowers flooded the air.

Wilson screamed again, and the wisps of him were torn from my clothing. Relief flooded me, though I knew the danger was far from over.

But one thing was certain. I was never, ever going to mock anything a magi handed to me for protection again. The weird-looking bag had not only saved me, but probably them, too. Under Wilson's control, I would have been a very deadly weapon.

The bits of his soul were condensing, solidifying again. Once whole, he began to slither away. But his progress was sideways more than forward, because part of him was being dragged ever closer to the gravesite and the open casket.

"He's about six feet away," I told the third magi, "but he seems to be heading for the trees more than the grave."

"He's a strong one," she said, seemingly unconcerned.

I glanced across at Marg and the other magi. Sweat dotted their faces now, and the veins along their necks were beginning to stand out against their pale skin. Marg in particular looked ready for a seizure.

But the sense of command and energy was stronger, the sparks of it crawling across my skin and making my hair float out from my scalp.

Slowly but surely, Wilson was being drawn closer to his grave.

He still wasn't going easily, twisting and rolling and snapping against the leash of magic.

Then another power joined the energy in the night, one that contained the chill of death.

Wilson, not the magi.

Trees moaned and splintered, then there was a huge cracking sound. A massive tree branch broke free and went hurtling through the night. Not at me, but at the magi.

I cursed and raised the laser, quickly incinerating as much of it as I could. Ash, splinters, and leaf rained around the three women. There was another crack, then another, and suddenly the air was filled with flying debris. I kept the trigger depressed, the laser growing hotter in my hand. Branches, leaves, and gravestones filled the air—deadly missiles that crashed toward the women. I was never going to get all of them and I didn't even try, merely slicing through the biggest of them, the ones that could do the most damage.

Through it all, and no matter how many times they were hit, Marg and the other magi continued their chanting. The power they were raising grew so sharp it felt like thousands of ants were clawing and nipping at my skin and the air was so thick it burned my lungs.

Then there was another high-pitched scream, and the wisp that was Wilson's soul shot toward the open grave. The wood and rubbish in the air fell to the ground, and the night was suddenly quiet except for the thick and edgy sense of power.

The third magi quickly lit the remaining incense, then completed the salt circle.

"He can't leave now," she said, with a glance at me.

Her eyes were cat-bright in the night, and filled with a sense of power.

"He can still attack us, though."

"Trust me, he'll soon have something else to worry about."

She walked past the two women and reached into the small carryall that was sitting several yards behind them. What she drew back out looked an awful lot like a nail gun.

"What's that?"

"A nail gun."

Which explained why it looked like one, I suppose. "What do you intend to do with it?"

"Shoot specially made iron nails into his chest and his skull."

"*What?*"

She glanced at me. "The iron nails will pin his spirit to his remains and prevent him from leaving."

"Really?"

She nodded. "Iron has been used throughout history as a preventative or warding measure against demons and ghosts."

"But . . . how? Why would something like iron—a real material from this world—affect a spirit, who is very definitely *not* of this world?"

"No one is really sure. There are some theories that the slow fire of the oxidation process has something to do with it, but no one has ever truly tested it. We just know it works."

She sighted the nail gun and let off two quick shots. Almost immediately a scream ripped through the air, a sound filled with anguish and fury combined. A sound that went on and on, sawing at my nerves and making my ears ache.

I had no sympathy for the spirit that was Wilson, however. He deserved the pain he was in. Deserved the eternity of it he was now locked into.

The magi with the cat's eyes looked at me. "You'd better call an ambulance for that poor fellow in the car, then you can go."

I raised an eyebrow. "Really? You sure?"

She nodded. "He's pinned now. We'll just finish the binding, then add some extra protection around his coffin before we get it backfilled."

"What happens if he gets handy with his psychokinetic skills again?"

"He won't. We have him totally contained with the salt, the incense, and the magic. This is one bad soul whose nights of destruction are over."

Thank God for that. I walked over to the man from the car, checking that he was breathing, and that he wasn't likely to choke in his own blood. Then I called in the medics as ordered. At least I hadn't killed him outright. For that, I was grateful.

With that done, I got the hell out of there. Wilson was no longer my problem, but that didn't mean I'd finished dealing with the dead.

After all, I still had Adrienne to find.

Chapter 10

$\mathcal{O}$nce beyond the cemetery gates, the tension that had been so much a part of the last few hours slithered from my body, and I was suddenly able to breathe easier. It wasn't just Wilson—and the knowledge of what he could have done—that had wound me up so tight. It was the awareness of all those other souls. The feeling that I only needed to open myself up a little and all their hopes, their dreams, and their anguish would be mine. That the sum of their beings could easily overrun me, until I was nothing more than a conduit for their pain.

I shivered. I mightn't be able to entirely avoid dead people given my job, but cemeteries were definitely off my list of places to visit in the future.

I slipped back into the flow of traffic and glanced at the dashboard clock as my stomach rumbled a reminder that it actually hadn't been supplied with sustenance in a while. It was nearly one, so most of the fast-food joints would be closed by now, but the restaurants near the Blue Moon would still be open. In fact, most of them ran twenty-four hours a day, just to make the most of the constant flow of patrons coming to and from both the Blue Moon and the Rocker. And the close proximity of the clubs meant I'd be able to ease a deeper ache after filling my belly.

Except that I'd made a promise.

With a sigh that was only slightly filled with frustration, I dug my cell phone out of my pocket and dialed Kellen's number.

"Hey," I said when he answered. "You feel like something to eat?"

"Riley, it's nearly one in the morning."

"So?" I glanced in the mirror to check there wasn't a cop car behind me. It wasn't exactly legal to be talking on a cell while driving—not without using hands-free, anyway—and while as a guardian I could probably get out of the fine, it would create a whole lot of paperwork. And that would only make me *and* Jack grumpy.

"So some of us do actually eat at regular hours." Amusement lurked in Kellen's rich tones. "Hell, some of us even keep regular sleeping hours."

Which explained the sexy, just-woken-up tone I was hearing under the amusement. "So you're not interested in coming out for a snack?"

"That depends on what else is on the menu."

"Now, there's a typical male response," I said dryly. "Won't come out for food, but will make the effort if there's sex involved."

"Absolutely right," he said. "When and where?"

"I'll be at Eddie's in ten minutes," I said. "I'm feeling like a burger, and he makes the best."

"Order me a coffee," he said. "And add lots of sugar. I've got a feeling I'm going to need the energy."

"You surely will."

He chuckled softly and hung up. After a glance at the road to see what the traffic was doing, I pressed another button and dialed the Directorate. Naturally, Sal answered.

"What an unmitigated pleasure to speak to you again so soon," she cooed.

Right. "So Jack's in the room, huh? Why don't you just shag the man?"

"Because I, unlike some, have a little class, and I prefer to build up to a relationship rather than take the wham-bam approach."

She might be a few hundred years old, but it seems her human prejudices had survived the crossover well. "If class means remaining a frustrated old cow, then give me crassness any day."

"Oh, you can be sure you have that market covered." Her tone was still so very pleasant, even if her words held the familiar hint of snark. It had to be killing her.

"And with the sort of charm you're currently oozing, it's a wonder Jack isn't just falling at your feet in lust."

"Oh, he surely will."

"You want to bet on that?"

"No." She paused, then added, "And we can cut the crap now—what do you want, bitch?"

Her voice was back to its unpleasant best. Jack had obviously left.

"Did the forensic team checking the rooftop come back with anything?"

"The bullet casings indicated a high-powered rifle.

There were no prints on either the casings or at the site. They suspect a professional hit."

"Which doesn't make any sense, because I haven't pissed anyone off lately."

"As I said before, I find that very hard to believe."

I ignored the jibe, but mainly because I couldn't think of a good retort. "Did you manage to do the background check on Mirror Image?"

"Yes. There's nothing untoward. It was legitimately set up, and has been running without problems for six months. There have been no complaints at all."

Which in itself was more than a little unusual. Hell, most clubs got complaints, whether they deserved them or not. "No rumors or reports that suggest something less than savory happening there?"

"Nothing at all. Why?"

"Because I suspect there's a blackmail scam being run out of the club. Who's the registered owner?"

"Owners," she corrected. "Jorn and Yohan Duerr. They're twin brothers who apparently settled here from England two years ago."

They are what the club is, Dia had said. Meaning they were not only twins, but also mirror images of each other.

"Were they English born?"

"No. German. They went to England when they were twenty."

"Any chance of doing a history check in both countries?"

"If there were any convictions, they wouldn't have been allowed into the country."

"Yeah, but a lack of convictions doesn't mean they weren't involved in anything nefarious."

"Is there any particular reason we're digging this deep?"

"I've just got a feeling about them."

"You and your damn feelings cause us more work than anyone else." She sniffed. "I'll see what I can do."

"Thanks." I hit the brake as the light ahead changed to red. "What about bank accounts—any unusual activity in any of those?"

"I didn't go that deep."

"Could you?"

"Possibly."

"Can you send the info as soon as you get it?"

"I'll try."

"You're such a sweetheart."

"Swivel on it, wolf girl."

"Oh, I intend to."

She made a growling noise and hung up. I grinned and tossed the phone on the seat beside me. The light flashed back to green and I zoomed off.

I parked in a side street not far down from Eddie's, and walked back. Despite the late hour, Lygon Street was alive with people, music, and the delicious, multi-layered scents of cooking and food. I breathed deep, allowing the scents to roll through me, savoring every tasty moment even as my stomach grumbled to hurry up.

"Hey, gorgeous," a familiar voice said.

I turned around and saw Kellen approaching. He was dressed in jeans and a somewhat crinkled black shirt that fitted his lean body to perfection and showed off his arms and shoulders.

My hormones did a happy dance. I stepped forward and kissed him long and hard. It was a good kiss, a hungry kiss, a kiss filled with all the desire that had been pent up inside me.

When we finally parted, he said, "Are you *sure* you want to get a burger first?"

His green eyes were shining with amusement and caring, and something inside sighed with happiness. I slipped my arm through his and tugged him toward Eddie's. Thankfully, it was only half-full, and there were plenty of tables. "I haven't eaten in hours. I need the sustenance."

"A wolf can survive days without food, you know."

"Not this wolf. Besides, I need coffee."

"Ah well, that's different. I've seen your coffee-deprived state, and it isn't pleasant."

I lightly punched his arm. "You're supposed to be charming until you get your wicked way with me."

He guided me across to a table in the back corner, and held the chair out for me. "But I'm going to get my wicked way with you regardless of whether I'm charming, so why not be honest?"

"I might change my mind."

"After the heat in that kiss?" He gave me a sexy grin and shook his head. "I doubt it."

"Have you always been so arrogantly confident?"

"When it comes to my woman? Yes."

My woman. Just hearing those words made me feel warm and fuzzy inside.

Still, I couldn't help saying, "I'm not your woman yet."

"But you will be."

"There's that arrogance again."

"It's confidence, my dear, not arrogance." He reached across the table and took my hand. His fingers were warm against mine, his skin slightly roughed. "We are good together."

"I've never denied that."

A waiter approached the table at that point, and we ordered. Kellen stuck with coffee, but I ordered a burger, fries, and the biggest mug of coffee they had.

Once the waiter had gone, I said, "I want this, Kellen. I just need a little more time to finish these cases."

"And next week it'll be another case, then another."

"I made a promise, and I intend to keep it." I squeezed his fingers lightly. "In the scheme of things, a week isn't all that long."

And I wasn't entirely sure who I was trying to convince with that statement—myself or him.

He studied me for a moment, then said, "So, how is the kidnap case going?"

I shrugged. "Pretty damn slowly. I think the club is running a blackmail scheme, and I'm pretty sure Adrienne guessed her life was in danger."

He untwined his fingers from mine, and leaned back. "So her disappearance has to do with the blackmailing scheme, not the disappearances of the women?"

"I really can't say for sure, yet." I just wished I could get hold of that letter. There had to be more in it than Patrin was saying, because he sure as hell wouldn't have left the safety of pack lands otherwise.

"So where does that leave the investigation?"

"Right now? At goddamn nowhere."

The waiter arrived with our coffees and my food. I took all the lettuce off the burger, then grabbed it two-handed and bit into it. Meat juices flooded my mouth and I couldn't help the rumble of pleasure that rolled up my throat.

Kellen shook his head, a smile touching his lips. "I can see the chance of any sort of sensible talk has gone out the window."

"Too right," I said, around the mouthful of burger. "This is *good*."

"They usually are." He picked up his coffee and sipped it while I continued to chow down, alternating between the burger and fries, and splashing them both down with coffee.

"Feeling better?" he asked when I finally finished, his voice dry and his eyes twinkling merrily.

"Totally." I wiped my mouth with the napkin, then tossed it back onto the table. "However, now there are deeper hungers that need to be fed. You feel like heading to the Blue Moon?"

"It's closer than home or my car."

It wasn't closer than my car, but getting lusty in a government vehicle would probably attract more attention than either of us would want.

I stood up and dug out my credit card. "My turn," I said. "You paid for the last coffee."

"I do have a little more money than you."

"Like I care. And fair is fair."

He leaned forward and kissed my forehead. "I do love the fact that my money isn't a factor to you."

"Hey, don't get me wrong, it's nice that you have money." I hesitated, then gave him a cheeky grin. "It means you can get me bigger and better presents come Christmas and birthdays."

"Ah, so there is a mercenary soul deep down inside."

"There's lots of things deep down inside." I paid the waiter, adding a generous tip, then slipped my arm through Kellen's again. "And maybe one day I'll allow

you to plumb those depths and uncover all my little secrets."

"Oh, a moment to anticipate, to be sure."

We stepped out onto the street. It was nearly two-
thirty, and the crowds had thinned out a little. But music still pulsed from the Blue Moon and the scent of lust
and arousal ran on the air, as delicious as the aroma of
food.

I breathed deep, then gave a contented smile. "I love
this place."

He raised an eyebrow, amusement still playing on
his lips. "Lygon Street?"

I nodded as we walked toward the club. "I love the
scents and the sounds. It always feels so alive, so vibrant, no matter what time of day or night."

"I guess." He looked around, as if taking it all in for
the first time. "The only place we have in Sydney that
compares to this is the Oxford Street area."

"That's mainly for gays, isn't it?"

"Used to be, before the wolf clubs moved in. Now
it's a mix—and a huge tourist attraction, believe it or
not."

"Oh, I'd—" I stopped mid-sentence as the ghostly
tingle of awareness ran across my skin.

A vampire was near.

A vampire whose stench I'd smelled before, just before he'd taken a potshot at me.

The sensation of danger hit so hard that it left me
gasping for air. Something fast and deadly was tearing
through the night toward us.

Another goddamn bullet.

I threw myself sideways, knocking Kellen out of the
way in the process.

"What the hell—?" Instinctively, his arms went

around me, cushioning my body with his own as we hit the pavement, hard.

Something burned past us, then a woman screamed. It was a high-pitched, wailing sound of horror and utter disbelief.

Gut churning, I broke free of Kellen's grip and twisted around. The bullet intended for me had found the head of the man behind me. And by found, I meant smashed into, and basically obliterated. Blood and bone and bits of God knows what else covered the woman who'd been walking beside him. She didn't even seem to notice, just stood there screaming and staring at the shattered remains of the man at her feet.

"Oh fuck," Kellen said.

Oh fuck, indeed. I pulled free of his arms and scrambled to my feet. After freeing my gun, I shoved my bag at him. "Grab my phone and call the Directorate. Tell them someone's had another potshot at me and taken out a civilian. Tell them I'm hunting the shooter."

"*Another* potshot?" He made a grab for my arm, his fingers slipping down the leather of my jacket before he gripped my wrist. "What the hell is going on?"

"I don't have time to explain." I stepped back and pulled free of his grip. Saw the surprise flicker in his eyes. Despite knowing what I was, he hadn't really realized the strength that it gave me. "Just ring the Directorate and look after that woman. I'll be back."

"But—"

I didn't hear the rest of his sentence. I simply turned and ran, following the faint scent of death and decay. The shot had come from behind and above, and that was where his scent was still coming from. I scanned the rooftops as I ran, and saw a shadow flicker on one.

This time the bastard *wasn't* going to get away from me.

I ran into the restaurant. Waiters and patrons were already lining the windows, ogling the carnage. Only a few of them turned to look at me.

"Rooftop stairs?" I said to the nearest waiter.

He pointed to the corner. "But it's locked."

"Not for long." I ripped my badge from the pocket of my jeans and showed him. "Directorate. You have a shooter on your roof. Keep everyone here and calm."

He nodded. I ran between the tables and up the back stairs. Luckily, this building was only three stories high, so I wasn't even puffing by the time I crashed through the fire door up top. There was no time for finesse because that would only give the bastard more time to escape.

Bits of wood went flying and the thick scent of unwashed vampire stung the night. I swung around, following the scent. Had a brief glimpse of metal gleaming softly in moonlight before there was an explosion of air and something the size of a Mack truck smashed into my leg, sending me spinning.

I hit the ground with a grunt. Pain bloomed, flooding my body until it felt like every inch of me was burning.

Silver. The bastard was *still* using silver. And this time the bullet was lodged in my leg.

Meaning I couldn't shift shape, couldn't run. With nothing else to do—besides crawl, and that was *never* a fast means of escape—I lay still and played dead. Given the shooter was a vamp, he'd know I wasn't, of course, but he couldn't be entirely sure I wasn't unconscious. And given the stairwell walls were giving me cover, he'd actually have to come within sighting distance if he wanted to finish me off.

His undead aroma stained the night, neither retreating nor moving closer. My fingers twitched against the laser's trigger and the scent of blood—my blood—filled the night. It had to be calling to him, and there were few vamps in this world who could resist such a tempting little treat.

For several heartbeats, nothing happened. Neither of us moved. I tried to keep my breathing steady, tried to ignore the burning in my leg, tried not to acknowledge the fact that the bullet would soon begin to numb and deaden my flesh. Sweat broke out across my forehead, running down my cheeks and stinging my eyes. Sweat caused by the heat of silver in my body, by fear of the consequences if I didn't remove it.

Then the vampire moved. I blinked, switching to infrared, and the dark heat of his body leapt into focus. He was walking oh so carefully toward the stairwell, his gun up and ready to fire. The minute I twitched, he'd shoot. Of that I had no doubt. And I really didn't want another piece of silver in my body.

Better by far not to give him the chance.

I carefully cranked the laser up to full strength. Rhoan had once told me that these lasers had the power to blast a hole through several brick walls and still kill someone on the far side. I hoped to God he hadn't been bullshitting. My life might very well depend on what happened next.

I sighted the laser on the vampire's dark form and pressed the trigger. The bright beam shot across the night, powering through the walls with as little effort as it powered through flesh. Only he moved, so instead of slicing off his head, I cut off a leg and a part of one arm.

His limbs plopped to the ground and he screamed—a high, inhuman sound. He fell, and flopped around like a fish out of water. I couldn't feel sorry for him. Not when his silver bullet was burning inside me.

And not when he was dragging himself toward me, the thick scent of burned flesh mingling with the reek of his anger, filling the night with his need for revenge.

I took a deep breath, then rolled sideways. Pain unlike anything I've ever felt ripped through my body, followed by a white-hot burning sensation. Dizziness swept through me, leaving me weak and ready to throw up.

I hissed, sucking in air, furiously blinking away the sweat dripping into my eyes as I tried to sight my would-be assassin. He was heading to the right of the stairwell, so I now had a better angle at his neck.

I pulled the trigger without hesitation. The bright beam flashed out, once more slicing through concrete and flesh and bone with equal ease.

The vampire's head rolled to one side, and his body stopped moving.

I was safe but not out of danger. I blew out a breath and pushed into a sitting position. The entire length of my left leg was a mess. Thankfully, the bullet had smashed through the fleshy section, not bone. Blood still pulsed from the wound, and with my jeans already saturated, there was nowhere else for the blood to go but on the ground. And the pool was spreading fast.

I had to get the bullet out. Had to get help. Fast.

I pressed the com-link button and said, "I hope to God someone is listening, because I need help."

"We got Kellen's call," Jack said, in a voice that

hinted at annoyance. Probably because I had the com-link off once again. "Rhoan's already on his way, as well as a med team. What's the situation?"

"I've been shot with silver. The vampire is down and out. And I need to get the bullet out."

"Rhoan's two minutes away."

"I'm on the roof above Tivoli's." I sucked in a breath, gathering courage, trying to ease the sick sensation of fear. "And I need this bullet out *now*."

Already the numbness was beginning. I'd been shot too often with silver in the past, and as a result, I'd de-veloped a hypersensitivity to its presence. For most wolves, there was at least some breathing space before the effects truly started to roll in. But for me, the minute silver lodged in my flesh, my body started re-acting. I couldn't afford to wait for help. The numb-ness, and the creeping death, might have already taken hold by then.

"Riley—" Jack said, concern suddenly overriding the anger.

"Boss, give me five. I need to remove this bullet."

I took another deep breath, and released it slowly. My whole body was shaking with the knowledge of what I was about to do. What I had to do if I wanted to survive. I ripped the sodden jeans away from the wound, to get a clearer view. God, the wound seemed positively huge . . .

Probably just as well. It gave me plenty of room to maneuver.

Giving myself no more time to think, I stiffened two fingers then drove them into the wound's opening. Deep into my own flesh. Heat flashed white-hot through my entire body and a scream tore through me, only to lodge somewhere in my throat. Sweat became a torrent pouring down my face and suddenly I couldn't breathe, couldn't see, could only feel. And it *hurt*. Oh God, how it hurt.

I hissed, panting for air, as I forced my fingers deeper, feeling past muscles and sinew, searching for the bullet lodged deep in my leg. Again heat flashed through me and black oblivion threatened. I fought the tears and the pain, trying to stay awake and aware. Then I touched the bullet, shifted it, and I screamed again. But somehow, I got my fingers around it. Somehow, I pulled it free of flesh. With the little strength I had left, I opened my hand and let the bullet roll away, then called to the wolf within. Shifting shape would at least stop the bleeding, even if it didn't immediately heal the wound. With the bullet gone, the bleeding and fierce burning stopped. All that remained were nausea and weakness.

And then, finally, the utterly peaceful bliss of unconsciousness.

R iley?"

The voice invaded the black peace of unconsciousness, and recognition stirred. *Rhoan*. If he was here, I was safe from whoever else might come after me.

I mumbled something unintelligent then turned away from him, not ready to surface just yet. Not ready to face the pain and nausea that undoubtedly awaited.

"Riley? We're taking you to the hospital. Even though the bleeding has stopped, you've lost too much blood."

"No hospital," I murmured, but the words didn't seem to reach my lips.

"The medics are here now. I'll come with you."

"No hospital," I said again, and wasn't sure if the words hit my lips that time or not.

Because everything faded again.

*W*hen I finally woke, it was to the smell of antiseptic. Never a pleasant aroma at the best of times, but when it's accompanied by an underlying note of sickness and disease, it just became a gut-churning stench.

I hated hospitals. Always had. But it wasn't just the smells that got to me—it was the death. The feeling that the dead awaited. Even when I couldn't speak to the dead, the awareness of them in places like this had haunted me.

But thankfully, there was another scent overpowering those hospital smells, and it was all warm spice and leather. A scent I could concentrate on, depend on. A scent I'd recognize anywhere.

"Bastard," I muttered, opening my eyes to look at my brother. There were dark rings under his eyes and his lips had that bloodless look vampires tended to get when they hadn't been eating properly. He mightn't be wholly vampire, but he sure as hell looked like one right now. Thankfully, he was never likely to smell like one—even on his sweatiest days. "You took me to the hospital. I told you not to."

"You," Rhoan said tartly, voice sounding a whole lot fresher than he looked, "were muttering all sorts of things, and not one of them made sense."

"You could have guessed. You know I detest hospitals."

"I also knew you needed one. There was blood everywhere."

"Speaking of which—have you eaten recently?"

He gave me the look. Meaning he hadn't. "Don't you start lecturing me, or I'll get the doctors to hold you here longer."

"Bitch." I pushed up into a sitting position, but the sudden movement made my head spin. So, obviously not fully over that whole blood-loss thing yet. "What happened to the vampire?"

"You shot him dead."

"So? Dead is not always dead with a vampire. Didn't Jack mention something about their consciousness taking longer to fade than their body?"

"Yep." He shifted his feet from the bed and reached down into the bag on the floor. I smelled the chocolates before he pulled them out. "I brought you these. Thought you'd appreciate something decent to eat."

"If you think offering me a chocolaty bribe will make me forgive you for dragging me into a hospital . . . you could be right." I accepted the purple box with a grin, and quickly opened them up. The rich, chocolaty scent drifted up, and I sucked it in with a happy sigh. Not hazelnut coffee, but damn near as good. I picked out a strawberry cream and a caramel, then offered the box to Rhoan. "So did Jack actually get anything out of the shooter before his consciousness left?"

"He was a gun for hire. His calls came in on his business phone and part payment had to be deposited into his account before he'd start tracking down the target."

"He doesn't have caller ID or anything on his phone?"

"Nope. Guaranteed anonymity is part of the deal."

I bit into the chocolate, felt the gooey strawberry filling spill into my mouth. Bliss itself. "Bank transfers aren't anonymous."

"No. But the money for this one came through an overseas account."

"Which are harder to track down?"

"They are when they're opened under false names."

While I had no doubt that the Directorate, with all their resources, would eventually pin down the actual owners, it would take time. And if there was someone wanting to get rid of me, we didn't exactly have a whole lot of time. "So how did he track me down?"

"Bug underneath your car." He picked out several chocolates, then handed me back the box.

"Did he put it there?"

"Nope. He was just sent the receiver."

"So someone got close enough to bug my car." Which I suppose, considering I parked either in the street or in public parking lots most of the time, wasn't a hard thing to do. "But I can't think of one person that I've annoyed enough to go to the extreme of hiring a hit man."

"What about Blake? Or Patrin?"

I shook my head. "Granted, they're both angry that I didn't manage to save Adrienne, but they still want me to track down her killer. If they *were* going to do anything, they wouldn't do anything until after that happened."

And personally, I didn't think they'd do anything afterward. Patrin was a bully-boy like his father, but I'd proved that I could well and truly defend myself against him. And bully-boys tended to back away from situations they knew they couldn't win.

"I'm afraid I tend to agree with you."

The dry note in his voice had my eyebrows rising. "And you've changed your mind because . . . ?"

"Because Patrin and I had a little chat after I saw you

safely into the hospital." He shrugged, not looking in the least bit repentant. Not that I really expected him to. He'd been at the receiving end of as many of Patrin's taunts and blows as I had. "He swears he wouldn't waste a bullet on useless half-breeds like us, let alone pay someone else to waste said bullets."

That was the truth if ever I'd heard it. "What about Kye?"

He frowned. "What about him?"

"How many arms and legs did you break before you convinced him you weren't intending to harm his boss?"

"None. He saw the family resemblance, apparently, and refused to intervene." He hesitated. "I have to say, he's fast for a werewolf."

"He's in the protection business, so he'd have to be."

"Yeah, but this more than that. I was moving with vampire speed, and he tracked me. Had his gun on me all the time. That's *not* normal."

I shrugged and popped another chocolate into my mouth. This one was nutty. Nice. "No, but he's the best for a reason. Maybe he has some sort of psychic gift that allows him to 'feel' where vamps and such are."

"Possibly." He sniffed and reached for another chocolate. "I intend to do a bit more investigation into his past. I've got a feeling we need to know more about him."

"Ah, the family trait of clairvoyance is hitting you, too, huh?"

"No, it's just my nose for trouble. And trust me, that one is." He paused to munch on his chocolate. "So, if it wasn't Patrin or Blake, then who?"

"I don't know. As I said, the only case I'm dealing with now is Adrienne, and that's sort of stalled."

Stalled because I needed to talk to the owners of the club, and hadn't gotten around to it yet. But now that Wilson was contained, I'd have the chance.

But I didn't really think it could be them. I mean, why would they want me dead? They didn't know I'd sprung their little blackmailing operation, and even if they *had* noticed me at the club, why would they think I was a danger? They couldn't possibly know who I was, and if they had tried to do an identity search on me, it would have come up on the Directorate computers.

Yet that man at the club—the man who had smelled the same as Jared—had appeared to be hunting me after he'd almost sprung me in the camera room. I frowned, and asked, "In your experience, have you ever met two humans who smell the same?"

Rhoan raised an eyebrow. "That's an odd question."

"It's an odd problem." I explained what had happened at the club. "It was the same scent. The *exact* same scent. But he wasn't Jared."

"Easily explained if he was a shapeshifter."

"Jared and the man in the club were both human, not Helki."

"There's no saying Helkis are the only ones who can shift into other human forms. I'm sure there's other nonhumans out there totally capable of shapeshifting. We just don't know about them yet."

"The operative word there is nonhuman. We're talking about humans."

"There's no reason why humans couldn't shift, either."

"They're humans. Humans don't do that sort of thing. It's what makes them human, and us nonhuman."

"No, that's DNA. Humans are quite capable of all sorts of psychic skills."

"Shifting isn't a skill. It's part of our DNA pattern."

Rhoan popped another chocolate into his mouth, then said around it, "Were the body shapes similar?"

I hesitated, then nodded. "Why would that make a difference?"

"What if it's not shifting as we know it? What if it's more a gentle remolding? They can alter minor feature characteristics—nose, chin, ears, perhaps even hair—but major things like facial shape and eyes stay the same. It'd be enough to fool others, but it isn't actually a full shift. Not in the way we shift, anyway."

"Possible." Jared and the man in the club certainly had the same color eyes. "If that's true, then we perhaps have our first link between the club and the island."

"But still no link between Adrienne, the other murdered women, and the club. After all, Jared wasn't involved with any of the women, was he?"

"Well, if he's some sort of face-shifter, how would we know? He could have appeared as anyone to them. Besides, Adrienne didn't sleep with anyone up there."

"Have you spoken to the partners or parents of the other women who have disappeared?" Rhoan asked. "Asked them if their daughters mentioned meeting anyone on the island?"

I shook my head. "Haven't really had the time to follow that up."

"I might do it, then. See if a clue shakes loose."

"Ta." I downed another chocolate, then asked, "So, how is Kellen holding up after last night?"

"I was wondering when you'd get around to asking."

My eyebrows went up again at the censure in his voice. "What is that supposed to mean?"

"That means, you claim to care about the man, you say you want a long-term relationship with him, and yet he's never first in your thoughts." He tilted his head and studied me for a minute. "Tell me, if it had been Quinn with you last night, would you have taken so long to ask?"

If it had been Quinn with me, I wouldn't have been alone on that roof and probably wouldn't have been shot. But Quinn and I were history, no matter how much my heart ached at the thought of him.

But then, how much of what I felt for Quinn was real, and how much of it was vampire-implanted suggestion? I never would know, and in the end, that was a relationship killer more than anything else he had done.

"Kellen and I haven't known each other that long."

"You've known him about the same length of time as you've known Quinn."

"But Quinn was actively discouraging my interest in Kellen. It's only these past few weeks that we've really played it basically one-on-one."

"Basically is not wholly."

"There speaks the man who has spent half his life avoiding a commitment to the man he professes to love."

"And you've spent half your life nagging me about. It's payback time, sister dearest."

I grinned and shoved another chocolate into my mouth. "So," I said, around the gooey peppermint mess, "when do I get out of this joint?"

He glanced at his watch. "The doctor was supposed

to be here an hour ago to give you a checkup. If you pass that, you can leave."

Meaning I'd better not mention the lingering light-headedness, or I'd be stuck here another night with the antiseptic reek and the ghosts.

"Why don't you go see what's keeping him? Otherwise, I'm just going to check myself out."

"You can try." He rose and gave me a somewhat cheeky grin. "I am, however, bigger than you and I will drag you back to this bed if I have to."

"Yeah, right." I waved a hand at the doorway. "Just go find that doctor."

He headed out. Five seconds later, Kellen came in, bearing the biggest bunch of flowers I'd ever seen. Pleasure shot through me.

"Hey," I said, by way of greeting. "No one's ever brought me flowers in the hospital before."

"You almost didn't get them now," he said, with a sexy grin that had my hormones hopping in delight. "Except the flower seller practically accosted me and accused me of not caring."

"Guerrilla tactics for flower sellers? Man, things must be tough in that business."

"Well, there weren't many men getting by her without buying some flowers, let me tell you."

He placed the flowers on the bedside table, then sat down on the edge of the bed and caught my hand in his. His fingers were as warm as his smile, and yet he seemed tense. Maybe he hated hospitals just as much as I did.

"So," he said, "how are you feeling?"

"Fine." I shrugged. "Better when I get out of this place."

"So no aftereffects of being shot by silver?"

"No." I hesitated. "But it wasn't the first time I've been shot with silver, and probably won't be the last."

"No, I guess not."

I frowned at the edge in his voice. "What's wrong?"

His gaze searched mine for a minute, his green eyes curiously flat. "You don't know?"

"Know what?"

He snorted softly. "Guess I had that coming."

"What?" God, I felt like I was watching a foreign movie, with the main character speaking a language I just didn't understand.

"It doesn't matter."

"It obviously *does,* so explain what the hell you're talking about."

"I shouldn't have to explain, Riley."

"So consider me thick and do." And then, suddenly, realization hit me. "You think you should have been able to protect me?"

My voice was incredulous, and annoyance shot through his eyes.

"I'm an alpha. It's part of my job to protect those I care about."

"But that's ridiculous. A, because I can generally protect myself, and B, because the shooter was a vampire and regular werewolves haven't the speed to go up against one."

"You did. Have."

"But I'm not your regular, everyday werewolf."

"Something I'm seeing more and more."

I raised my eyebrows at the deepening edge in his voice. "It's not like I've ever hidden what I was from you." Not when we started going out for real, anyway.

"No, but hearing it and seeing it are two entirely different things." He shuddered. "You didn't even react when you saw that man's brains splattered all over the sidewalk. Not emotionally, anyway."

"Because I was too busy trying not to get shot."

"People trying not to get shot don't get up and race toward their attacker. That's not normal, everyday behavior."

But I wasn't a normal, everyday person. I hadn't been when I was born, and was even further from that now.

"So what, exactly, are you saying?" The question came out a little hoarse, because fear suddenly had my heart lodged somewhere in my throat.

"I don't know." He squeezed my fingers lightly, though if the gesture was meant to reassure me, it failed miserably. "I can't help my innate need to protect you."

"But I'm not asking you to stop it, so what's the problem?"

"The problem is, I obviously can't. It's in my nature to *try*, but there are things—people—in your life that I will never be able to protect you from."

"I can't help what I do, Kellen. And the one thing I don't expect from you is protection." Caring, comfort, and understanding, yes. And definitely love. But protection? I had Rhoan for that. It had been just the two of us from the beginning of our lives, and it would be the two of us until the very end. I needed no one else when it came to that.

"I know you don't," he said, "and that's probably part of the problem right now."

I stared at him for a moment, then rubbed my eyes wearily. "So what does this mean for you and me?"

Because it sounded like the shit was going to hit the fan again—emotionally rather than figuratively—and

I really wasn't ready for another kick in the gut. Not after I was starting to pull it all together again.

"Right at this particular moment, it means nothing." He hesitated. "It's just that, like you, I have things I need to think about."

"What's the point of me coming to a decision if you're in the process of backing away?"

"I never said I was backing away, Riley. I just said I needed to think a few more things through. You're not getting away from me that easily. Not after I've fought so long to pin you down."

And yet, despite his words, despite the warmth flaring across his lips and the tenderness in his bright eyes, part of me wasn't reassured.

He glanced at his watch, then said, "What time are you getting out of here?"

"I'm not sure yet. Rhoan's gone to find the doctor."

"Would you like me to come back and pick you up? Take you home?"

By home, he meant his place, not mine. And I wasn't sure I was ready for that after everything he'd just said. So I shook my head.

"There's a heap of stuff I have to do at home, and I haven't even unpacked from the holiday yet."

"So when do I get to see you again?"

"That depends on your definition of 'see.'"

"You know what my definition is." He kissed my fingers, his lips so warm on my skin. A tremor ran through me. I wanted to feel his lips all over me, kissing and teasing and exploring. I ached for his touch with a suddenness that surprised me, and yet reluctance—or was it fear?—held back the words that would have had him in my arms tonight.

It was stupid, I *knew* it was stupid, but I couldn't get

rid of this fear. What if I gave more of myself to this man, and he had more second thoughts?

Tuesday, I thought. I had until Tuesday to give him the answer. Which gave him until Tuesday to settle his thoughts and decide whatever it was he had to decide.

He glanced at his watch again. "I have to leave for a meeting. Promise you'll ring me if you get out of here tonight?"

"I'll ring."

"Good." He rose and kissed me good-bye. It was a light kiss, a gentle kiss. Like I was a porcelain doll that was so very fragile.

Only I had never been—and never would be—fragile. And if Kellen wanted that in a relationship—wanted someone he could protect—then he was chasing the wrong woman. Not that I didn't want someone to love and protect me. I just needed someone who could love me as I was. And that included the part of me that was a trained hunter. A trained—if somewhat reluctant—killer.

I might have told Kellen what I was, but until tonight it hadn't really connected on any deeper level. And I could only hope that the realization of who and what I was didn't spell the end for us.

Because I didn't want to lose him.

Chapter 11

It was another three hours before the doctor managed to drag his overworked butt into my room. After a quick check—during which he marveled over the pink scar on my leg and healing capacity of were-wolves in general—he declared me fit enough to go home. To say I limped out of there in record time would be the understatement of the year.

Once in the car, I rang Kellen to let him know I was out. He invited me to lunch the next day, and I accepted happily. No matter what he might have said, he still wanted to be with me. Right now, that was all that mattered.

When Rhoan and I got home, I had a shower and something decent to eat. With body and belly happy, I went into Rhoan's room, grabbed his laptop, then hobbled over to the sofa.

Rhoan plopped a coffee on the table next to my feet, the heat of the cup warming the side of my foot even though it wasn't actually touching, then sat down on the sofa opposite.

"What are you looking for?"

"I asked the cow to do a full background search on Jorn and Yohan Duerr, the owners of Mirror Image."

"Do you think the man you smelled at the club was Jorn or Yohan in disguise?"

"Possibly. And if he was also the man Adrienne ran into at the club, then it would certainly explain her rushing off to the island."

He frowned. "How?"

"Apparently she has a psychic gift that allows her to see images of the past or future when she touches people."

"Oh, that would not be a fun one to have."

"No worse than having ghosts wanting to sit around and chat." I rubbed my leg gently, wondering how long it was going to take for the ache to go away. "Jorn and Yohan apparently shipped over here a couple of years ago from England. I just wanted to know why they came here—whether they were running to better weather, or simply running from trouble."

"If they were running from trouble, they wouldn't have gotten into the country."

"Convictions keep people out, not suspicions."

"True. And new identities are easy enough to get."

"I'd like to think DNA scanning will put an end to all that." I reached past the laptop and picked up the coffee, taking a sip before placing it back down again.

"DNA scanning technology is expensive *and* still being trialed," Rhoan said. "It won't get into airports or docks for years."

I grunted, looked into the eye scanner, and waited

for the laptop to connect into the Directorate's computer system.

"I guess even if they are finally installed, the bad guys will have worked out a way to get past them."

"Always. Cops playing catch-up with criminals is the way of the world."

The laptop beeped, an indicator my file had been retrieved. "Well, well, well," I said, after scanning the first page. "It seems that Jorn and Yohan owned a nightclub in London that was linked to over a dozen disappearances. All of the missing women were blondes, and all of them were from well-off werewolf families."

Rhoan raised an eyebrow. "Linked how?"

"Seems they were all last seen on the nightclub's premises." I scrolled past the full details of the victims. "The report says that the owners were very cooperative with the police, and handed over all available security tapes. Apparently Jorn and Yohan were never under serious suspicion, and the tapes showed each of the women dancing with a different man on the night of their disappearance. The disappearances were never solved, and the file remains open. Interestingly, the disappearances stopped once they sold the club."

He took a sip of his coffee, then said, "Odd coincidence that they've started up again here, and not long after opening another club."

"Neither you nor I believe in coincidences like that." I scrolled to the next page. "Oh, and it gets better."

"More murders?"

"One more. In Germany." I read the report quickly. "The twins were born in Germany. Their mom died young, and their daddy had a habit of bringing home new moms weekly."

"Whores?"

"Nope. Daddy was a doctor, and tended to float his boat amongst the well-off and comfortably rich. Wasn't too concerned about whether his conquests were married or not."

"Don't tell me, he slept with one married woman too many?"

"Even better. He slept with a rich young werewolf very close to the full moon."

"And she tore him apart in the heat of the moment." Rhoan shook his head. "Humans never seem to learn."

"You can't just blame humans. Us wolves have a responsibility of care, too, you know." After all, we knew how violent we could get.

"So what happened to the wolf?"

I hesitated, reading on quickly. "Nothing. The mating act was consensual, and the death itself was deemed accidental. She did minimum time."

"I take it the twins didn't take this too well?"

"They were witnesses to the mauling, and apparently neither of them said a word before or after the trial. Doctors said it was shock."

"And the wolf? How long did she survive after serving her time?"

"Two days. She was found by her sister shot with silver and beheaded in her apartment." I hesitated. "Her head was never found."

"Wonder what they did with it?"

"I don't think I want to know, thanks."

He grinned. "No sense of adventure, that's your problem."

"Too right. The boys were suspects but apparently had watertight alibis. They were both at a nightclub, and plenty of people saw them."

"An easy thing to arrange if you're a face-shifter."

"Yep." I moved on to the next file. I had to hand it to Sal—when she went digging, she really dug far and wide. Next were two passport photo shots, and I frowned. Neither of the men looked anything like the man I'd seen in the club. The man who'd been called boss.

Of course, it was always possible that he was head of security rather than one of the twins, as I'd been presuming, and therefore it was totally possible for him to be called boss without actually being the owner.

"What?" Rhoan said.

"Wait." I went into the system and did a photo search through the motor registration and licensing departments. Once I had my photos, I split the screen and put them both up.

"This," I said, turning the laptop around and pointing to the passport photos, "is the Jorn and Yohan who came into Australia fifteen months ago. And this"—I pointed to the license photos—"is the Jorn and Yohan who own the club. And he," I added, pointing at the license photo of Jorn, the paler of the twins, "is the man who smelled like Jared."

"Jorn Duerr, Jared Donovan, and what was the other guy's name? Jim Denton? Same initials, same man?"

"Good possibility. So does that mean it was Jorn who chatted up all the women on the island?"

"The only way you're going to know that is by asking the women themselves."

"Sorry, I've had my quota of speaking to the dead for this week. But we could try talking to the parents."

He glanced at his watch. "It's not too late now to make some calls."

"You'll help?"

He nodded. I placed the laptop on the coffee table, took a quick sip of my coffee, then rose to get my cell phone. He took two numbers, I took one. But it took longer than I thought it would to get information, simply because talking to anyone who has suffered a loss was hard—especially when the mere act of talking to them again raised their hopes of possible leads. A possible ending.

"Okay," Rhoan said, when he hung up from the last of them. "According to the parents of my two ladies, neither of their daughters slept with anyone up there. They did, however, mention meeting a human who was trying to chat them up. One lot can't remember a name, the other thought it was something like Yuri."

I leaned back in the sofa with the remains of my cold coffee. My leg was aching and I couldn't be bothered getting up to refill my cup. I sipped it, and tried to bluff my taste buds into thinking it was iced coffee. "Mine think it was John. Which means both twins are working the island. What I don't get is, why would they wait until the women are back home before they abduct them? Why not do it while they're away from normal surroundings?"

"I think you need to ask our two suspects that. But," he added hastily, as I made motions to get up. Never an easy thing to do when you had a sore leg, I might add. "Not tonight. Tonight you need to sleep and rest. Tomorrow we'll head over to the club together and suss out the place."

"Jack might not be happy about that. They are, after all, human."

"I said suss the place out, not beat them up. We can do that *after* we get some evidence. Right now, we have nothing but theories."

"And a background that points to a long history of kidnapping crimes."

"They weren't convicted of anything in either England or Germany. If we move too soon, we'll lose them here, too." He paused. "Do you think they could be behind the truck and the shooting attempts on your life?"

I frowned. "Why would they even suspect I was onto them?"

"We share the same surname as Adrienne. She disappears, you appear. A suspicious mind wouldn't think that was an accident."

"But how would they track me? I mean, no one but you and Kellen knew where I was going from the airport."

"They put trackers on your car. It wouldn't be hard to slip one into your purse." He rose. "Where is it?"

"Over near the door."

He walked over, picked up the purse, and started fishing through it. After about five minutes, he dropped the purse and walked back. "There you go."

The thing in his hand was about the size of a dime. Which was rather large for trackers, these days. Hell, I'd had ones the size of a pinhead embedded into my foot. And then there was the ones in my ear. "Jared helped carry my bags the day I left the island. I wonder if he slipped it in then?"

"Could be." He dropped it on the ground and stomped on it. "Might be worth you going in disguise tomorrow."

"Good idea. I still have those wigs Liander gave me."

He nodded. "Then go get some rest. You look beat."

"If I tried telling you to go rest, you'd have a tantrum."

He gave me a grin. "Too right. I'm a boy. Boys can look after themselves. You're a girl. You need to be loved and protected."

I tossed my empty cup at him. "And you said you hadn't been listening in on my conversation with Kellen."

He laughed and caught my cup one-handed. "So I lied. Now go get some rest."

I did.

*R*hoan pulled into one of the many vacant spaces in the parking lot and stopped the car. He leaned forward, crossing his arms over the steering wheel as he stared at the building that housed Mirror Image.

His look was one of amusement. "God-awful-looking place in daylight."

I pulled at the black wig irritably, then said, "Doesn't seem to stop anyone from coming, though."

Indeed, the lot was half full, which wasn't bad considering it was barely eight in the morning. Even the Blue Moon would be ecstatic to have this sort of crowd at this hour, and *that* place was doing the best of all the wolf clubs.

"They've got an awful lot of security lining the building."

"Cameras and infrareds are pretty much the norm nowadays, aren't they?"

"They've also got motion sensors."

"So?"

"So, why have motion sensors and infrareds on a building that supposedly houses twenty-four-hour action for human and nonhumans?"

"Given they're apparently getting into a little

blackmail action with some of their 'special' guests, it's not entirely surprising they're security conscious. They wouldn't want the police wandering in and uncovering their covert operations, now, would they?"

"No, I guess not." He glanced at me. "You ready?"

I nodded and opened the car door. Even though it was still early in the day, the sun held the promise of heat. Melbourne weather had apparently decided that we needed some of the warmer stuff after the series of chilly days, and the forecasters were predicting a hot one. Hence the jeans and the bright yellow tank top. I needed to get some sun on my arms.

We walked across to the front doors. The bouncer, a big man with shoulders the size of a tank, cheerfully waved us through to the payment area, then opened the main doors.

Music blasted out. Rhoan looked at me. "Techno. I hate techno."

So did I, but I shoved a hand into his back and lightly pushed. "Stop whining and get inside."

Bright light hit us the minute we entered, momentarily blinding me and forcing me to a halt. It rolled on quickly enough, leaving dots of red and yellow dancing before my eyes, dots that seemed to get lost in the myriad of colors so evident on the packed dance floor. The scent of sex and lust swam around us, its sweet aroma stirring my hormones to life yet again.

I touched my brother's shoulder and pointed to an empty booth halfway along the wall to our left. He nodded, and we made our way down the stairs, my heels once again slipping on the polished white tiles. It was a wonder they didn't do something about that, because they were leaving themselves wide open for lawsuits in the sue-happy environment of modern Melbourne.

"Fuck," Rhoan said, once we were seated. "This place is *huge*. It's got a good feel, though. Even with all the humans."

I raised an eyebrow. "So you've changed your mind about the 'no humans in wolf clubs' rule?"

"Not in the least."

I grinned and nodded toward the double doors at the end of the bar. "The private rooms are in there, but the doors are security-key coded."

"Good thing about security-keyed doors is the fact that a loss of electricity fucks them up." His gaze scanned the room. "What's down near the back?"

"Bathrooms and fire exits."

"What about an electrical switchboard?"

I shrugged. "It's not something I tend to notice. Why?"

"Because we need to cut the power." He rose. "When the lights go out, get through those doors. I'll meet you there."

"The room we want is on the right."

He nodded and walked away. I crossed my arms and watched the dancers on the floor for a while. Desire stirred, but I ignored it. Not only because I'd made a promise to Kellen, but because it would be stupid to risk it even if I wasn't here to work. Besides, most of those out on the dance floor this morning were human. Maybe all the nonhuamns had gone into the private area.

Of course, my reluctance to dance with humans didn't actually stop them from coming over and asking. After the tenth such refusal, I began to hope Rhoan hurried himself up. Coping with hurt male sensibilities wasn't high on my list this morning.

After another five minutes, I had my wish and the nightclub plunged into darkness. I switched to infrared, slipped off my heels, then rose. Given that everyone else was basically staying still—except for those caught in the middle of sex—I didn't want the sound of my heels clicking giving me away or attracting attention. I pulled the shadows around me, just to be doubly sure I wasn't seen, then headed for the security door.

It was unlocked, as Rhoan had said it would be. Knowing the guard would be at—or near—the door I opened it quickly, and stepped inside. He was fast, I had to give him that, one hand going for his gun while the other reached for the alarm button on the wall. He never completed either move, simply because I stormed into his mind and stopped both.

The alarm, I discovered, *wasn't* affected by the power cut, because it was on the backup system. I shuffled through his thoughts and discovered that the downstairs area—the area we needed to get into if we wanted to sniff out more of what was going on in this place—was also connected to the backup generators.

The one good bit of news was the fact that the room behind us wasn't being used. Though it would be tonight. Some ripe for the picking—or should that be right for the taping?—minor politician had been invited in for a drink and a game.

Which I found truly amazing. Granted, being caught in compromising positions wasn't something new when it came to politicians of *any* caliber—but with technology getting ever smaller, and ever cleverer, you'd think they'd learn to keep their pants zipped. Or, at the very least, learn to keep themselves away from compromising situations.

The door behind me opened again, and a familiar shadow moved stealthily inside.

"How'd you cut the power?" I asked.

"Found a screwdriver behind the bar and shoved it into a couple of power sockets."

I stared at Rhoan. "You're kidding, right?"

"No."

"You could have been killed doing something like that!"

"I'm not stupid. The handle was insulated."

I shook my head, unable to believe he'd taken such a risk. "Next time you feel the urge to do something that dumb, let me know. I'll hit you over the head and maybe knock some sense back into it."

"Look," he said, a touch impatiently, "it was the only way to blow the system without making them suspicious. And if they have power-surge cutoffs installed, we haven't got a whole lot of time to waste arguing before the system is back up again."

"I think the fact *everything* went off means they haven't got surge cutoffs installed."

"Riley, just shut the fuck up and concentrate on the matter at hand."

"Forgive me for not wanting a dead brother," I muttered, and rifled through the guard's thoughts again. "Seems they've got a largish contingent of guards on standby downstairs."

"How large is large?"

"Ten on standby, fourteen altogether." I hesitated. "They're all nonhumans. Weres, shifters, and vamps."

He raised his eyebrows. "That's a rather big force to have considering they've had no trouble here, isn't it?"

"Maybe they have no trouble because they *do* have so many guards. Given the crowds they get, it'd certainly be worth having a decent security force ready to go when needed."

"I guess that's true. You want to get us inside the room?"

I mentally ordered the guard to open the door into the smaller room. Once we were safely inside, I carefully erased my tracks and all but released him—though like before, I kept a mental eye on him, just in case he heard us and went to sound the alarm again.

"Okay," I said softly, after scanning the room. "The wall to our right is a false one, and we should be able to step right through it. But they've set some sort of magical barrier that raises the alarm. And if it's electrically enhanced, it's probably going to be one of the systems connected to the backup generators."

"Do we need to go through it?"

"The basement, storage areas, and probably the main offices are accessible through the stairs in that half of the room." I paused, and reached into the guard's mind again, trying to get some idea of the floor plan. Unfortunately, he couldn't tell me much. Guards like him—employed to guard certain rooms, nothing more—rarely ventured beyond the staff rooms on the lower levels. "There are probably other stairs down, but we'd waste too much time trying to find them."

And this particular guard always took the elevator I'd seen in the hall earlier.

Rhoan flexed his fingers, his knuckles cracking lightly, then waved his hand at the wall. "So lead the way."

I did. Energy caressed my body as I went through the wall, once again making my skin tingle and my hair stand on end. The room beyond was unchanged, the cameras still on the tables, still pointed at the false wall. Ready for the action being planned for tonight, no doubt.

I headed right, following the faint breeze that stirred the air. The door was hidden in the shadows, but light seeped out from underneath it. It wasn't bright, but any light was a pain. It made our ability to shadow virtually useless.

"Emergency lighting," Rhoan commented. "That's unfortunate."

"And that's an understatement if I've ever heard one."

He walked past me and pressed an ear to the door. "I can't hear any noise close by, but we'd better be ready for trouble anyway." He glanced at me. "You did bring your gun, didn't you?"

"Yes, I brought it. I'd be stupid not to carry after the near miss with the silver-bullet–bearing rooftop assassin." Of course, I was also still carrying my shoes, which made better weapons for close-in fighting than a laser did—in my opinion at least.

I could—and would—use the laser if I had to, but only if it was absolutely necessary. I might feel safer with the weight of it in my hand, but I wasn't so blindly down the guardian track that I'd shoot on instinct. Not yet, anyway.

"You've been shot at before and it hasn't prompted any great need to carry a weapon," he said mildly. "Just thought I'd check."

I didn't bother responding. He turned the handle and cautiously opened the door. Pale yellow light splashed across his feet and seeped into the room. Definitely emergency lighting—it wasn't bright enough to be anything else.

The air stirring past my nose carried the warmth of the morning, along with hints of diesel and oil. Perhaps the stair went down to some sort of maintenance area.

Rhoan slipped through the door and began to ease his way down the concrete steps. After ensuring the door closed quietly, I followed. Our journey downward was slow and filled with tension. We were far too visible on this stairwell, and that made for easy targets.

Though why I thought they'd risk shooting us I didn't even want to think about. And I just hoped it was fear of the unknown rather than pesky clairvoyance stepping in with some cheerful news.

Thankfully, we made it all the way down the stairs without discovery. The door at the bottom was unlocked, and there seemed to be nothing but silence beyond it.

Rhoan opened it carefully. A warm wind rushed in to greet us, and the scents of oil and diesel were heavier on the air. But underneath them ran the tangy scent of males. Human males.

The scents weren't sharp, weren't defined, meaning there was some distance between us and them, but it was a warning that we had to proceed carefully.

"Loading bay," he said softly. "The main door is only half down."

I slipped through the doorway and stopped beside him. Sunlight filtered through the gap between the floor and the top of the roller door, highlighting the oil stains splattered all over the concrete. The loading bay itself was empty of vehicles, but not of boxes. Most of them were alcohol filled, if the writing on the side was anything to go by.

Rhoan glanced at me and nodded toward the right. He headed left. The bright sunlight streaming in through the half-open doorway left little in the way of shadows, and I could only hope that whoever was doing the talking didn't suddenly decide to come out into the loading bay. We'd be sitting ducks. Or dogs, as the case may be.

I ran lightly up the stairs and walked along the wall, stepping past the boxes before edging my way to the door. Rhoan, pressed against the wall on the other side, raised three fingers and began counting down. When there were no fingers left, I reached out, grabbed the door handle, and pulled it open. Rhoan was little more than a deadly blur that flowed inside. I could barely see him, so the humans inside had little hope. The talking stopped abruptly, but there were other sounds. With Gautier gone, Rhoan was now the top guardian at the Directorate, and what he did better than anyone was killing. Not that he killed the two men—just knocked them out cold.

I stepped over their collapsed forms. The room was small, and filled with various machine parts, though there were tools and oils and other stuff scattered about the shelves.

I looked down at the two men. "We can't leave them here. Someone will trip over them coming through the door."

He raised an eyebrow, amusement glinting in his gray eyes. "Safety concerns for possible assassins? How sweet."

I slapped his arm. "No, asshole. I'm worried about them being tripped over and *found*. Let's not make it too easy."

"I wasn't intending to." He motioned to the door on

the other side of the room. "Go check that. I'll move these two into the shadows."

I walked across the room and pressed an ear against the door. The mechanical sounds we'd been hearing seemed to come from here. Certainly they were stronger—so much so it was almost impossible to hear anything else over them.

I glanced at Rhoan to make sure he was ready, then gripped the handle and carefully opened the door.

It slammed right back into my face and sent me reeling backward. I barely had time to swear before it was opened again and two wolves in human form were lunging toward me. I hadn't even scented them—but they'd obviously smelled me.

I scrambled backward, trying to collect my wits, trying to keep out of their reach. Out of the corner of my eye I saw Rhoan move, and realized my attackers hadn't grasped the fact I wasn't alone. So I stopped moving, letting them get close, moving just fast enough to avoid their blows, then dropped my shoes and released a quick one-two jab of my own, hitting one in the gut, the other across the chin.

Chin boy reeled backward—straight into Rhoan's waiting arms. I grabbed the other, spun him around, and threw him backward. He hit the concrete wall hard, his head smashing into it with a crunch that made me wince. As he slid unconscious to the ground, I spun to see if my brother needed help. I shouldn't have bothered.

"How's your nose?" he said, not looking at me as he stepped over the body of the man to the still-open door.

"I'll live." The door had squashed my nose back against my face, but it wasn't broken and wasn't even really bleeding. Not much anyway. "What's beyond?"

"Machine room." He paused, cocking his head slightly. "I can hear distant footsteps. I can't tell where exactly they're coming from."

"The office areas won't be near the machine room, I wouldn't think."

"No." He glanced at me. "Ready to move on?"

I nodded. He slipped out the door and, after picking up my shoes, I followed. The room beyond was lit by globes high in the ceiling, but there were enough shadows to provide some cover should we need it.

We walked down a set of metal stairs, the sound of our footsteps seeming to echo across the silence. The room below wasn't actually full of machines. Sure, there were generators and water pumps, but there was also a vast array of switchboards, electrical stuff, computer stuff, metal boxes of various shapes and sizes, and God knows what else. Calling it a junk room would have been more appropriate.

We reached the floor and ran across to the nearest machine, keeping close to the various bits and pieces as we made our way through the room.

The sounds of nearing footsteps were becoming evident, but it was still hard to pinpoint a location. At times, they seemed to be all around us, though if that were the case, we surely would have seen them as we ran from the cover of one machine to the other. Only the dead could move fast enough to confuse a werewolf's sight—and we weren't normal werewolves. And even if we *had* been, we surely would have smelled them. Most vampires tended to be smelly beasts at the best of times.

We were nearing the far end of the machinery room when goose bumps began to scamper across my skin. I scanned the immediate area, then what walls were visible beyond it, seeing nothing out of place. Yet I couldn't escape the sensation we were about to walk into danger.

I stopped.

It was then I smelled him.

A vampire, stepping up behind me.

I spun and lashed out with a stiffened hand. He caught it hard and fast, amusement flashing across his thin lips. Or maybe that was contempt. Hard to tell sometimes with suckers.

I twisted and slashed out with the heel of my shoe. The wooden stiletto scraped across his face, and sparks flickered as the smell of burned flesh bloomed.

The vampire swore and began to crush my fingers, as if hoping to restrict my movements by sheer force of pain alone. At the same time, a tingling began to buzz around the edges of my thoughts. He was trying to get a mind-lock on me. Like *that* was ever going to happen.

"There's more," Rhoan said, his voice harsh as the sound of flesh hitting flesh joined the scent of burning in the air.

I didn't reply, just wrenched my hand away from the vamp. Surprise flickered in his eyes, but I didn't give him enough time to wonder why a mere wolf could free herself so easily from his grip. Just hit him as hard as I could, my fist flattening his nose and sending him flying backward. He hit the side of a generator with a grunt and slid to the floor, blood gushing from his nose and filling the air with its thick scent.

Another guard came at me. I ducked his blow, dropping to the ground and spinning around with an extended leg, sweeping him off his feet. He hit the ground with enough force to bruise his spine, but he didn't even grunt, just sprung back to his feet and leapt toward me.

I whacked out with a shoe, the spiked heel spearing through his hand. Fire flickered as his flesh began to burn, and he made a gargling sound. I ducked his punches, then thrust up, hitting him hard under the chin and sending him flying backward, my shoe still stuck in his paw.

Rhoan suddenly appeared beside me. He hurled away another wolf, then grabbed my arm. "Let's get out of here. The four remaining guards are undoubtedly on the way."

"We can beat four."

I twisted away from the blows of the vampire with the bloody nose, then kicked him in the nuts, as hard as I could. He went down with an oomph and didn't get up.

"Not without killing the other six." Rhoan disappeared from my sight for a moment then reappeared, the smell of blood thick on his skin.

"There are other options to killing. Like, calling in help." Hey, the things in our ears were there for that very purpose.

"Right now, they might think we're just thieves. The minute they know the Directorate is onto them, they'll pack up and leave. That's what happened in England after the seventeen kills there."

I ducked another blow then punched upward, aiming for the vamp's chin. He dodged, the bastard, and lashed out at me with a booted foot. The blow caught me in my still-healing thigh and pain flared. I hissed and whacked him with my remaining shoe. "Seventeen? I thought it was only a dozen or so?"

"There were four other similar kills the police

couldn't connect to the club." He shrugged. "I did a little investigating after you went to bed."

"You didn't tell me that."

"Slipped my mind." He paused, then added, "The
other men just entered the room. We need to get out
now."

"Then go. I'll follow."

"Like hell. Sisters first."

He shoved me forward. I staggered a few steps,
caught my balance, then ran like hell back through the
machine room, heading for the loading bay and the
half-open door. Hoping, of course, that it wasn't now
closed. Although the lasers would soon take care of that.

Rhoan grabbed my arm, his grip tight, bruising.
"Faster."

We pounded through the shadows, ducking and
weaving as the remaining guards came at us, shoving
them out of the way more than fighting them.

We reached the steps and pounded up them. I thrust
open the door and ran inside. We'd gained precious
seconds on our pursuers. Part of me wondered if it was
going to be enough, simply because we had no idea
what waited in the loading bay. I certainly didn't trust
the silence coming from that room, that was for sure.

"Push the shelving unit down," Rhoan said, pointing to the unit on the left while he headed right.

I moved quickly to one side and shoved it with all
my might. The unit made an odd sort of groan then
slowly began to topple. Machinery bits and tools scattered, clanging across the floor and making enough
noise to raise the dead. Or another alarm. Though I
guess that was a pretty pointless worry when they were
obviously more than a little aware of the fact they had
uninvited guests.

Rhoan shoved a heavy-looking desk in front of the shelves. "That'll hold them for a few seconds."

I restrained the impulse to point out we'd actually wasted seconds creating the block, and just headed for the other door. There was still no sound coming from the loading bay, but awareness tingled across my skin as I gripped the door handle.

I glanced at my brother, saw him nod, then thrust the door open. Rhoan flowed through it, a shadow filled with deadly intent. The man on the other side didn't have a chance.

I leapt over his body and followed my brother's fleeing form, my gaze on that bright patch of sunshine and the freedom it represented.

From the corner of my eye I caught the hint of movement. I risked a glance and saw the man with the gun.

"He's armed," I yelled, reaching for my own weapon.

But I was too slow. Far too slow.

Something hit my shoulder and spun me around. Somehow, I retained my balance and kept running. That batch of sunshine was close, so close.

Ahead, Rhoan stumbled, his fingers brushing the concrete as he balanced and went on. Something silver glittered in his shoulder. Fear hit me. I reached back, feeling my own shoulder. Felt something small and metallic sticking out from it. I pulled it free.

A dart.

He'd goddamn darted us.

Oh, fuck . . .

It was my last conscious thought as the concrete rushed up to meet me.

Chapter 12

Waking was a nightmare. My skin felt like it was on fire and everything ached. Everything thumped. My head, my heart, my body. Even whatever it was I was laying on. It was a thick, heavy beat that was both monotonous and relentless, going on and on and on.

It took me a while to realize that it wasn't actually me, that things *were* thumping. It was an engine. Not a very powerful engine, but an engine all the same.

With that realization, my other senses came online. The air was thick with the smell of fish and the tangy saltiness of the ocean, but behind it came the smell of diesel and man.

Jared. Or Jorn. Or whatever his real name was.

And given the fishy smell and that endless, relentless thumping, it was pretty much a given that neither he nor I was anywhere near the club.

I took a deeper breath, trying to find Rhoan.

Wherever he was, it wasn't close. His leathery, spicy scent was absent.

I shifted and realized my hands and feet were tied—and had been for some time if the cramps shooting up my legs were anything to go by—and cautiously opened my eyes. What met my gaze was metal and wood.

A box.

A *cage*.

The bastard had *caged* me. Like an animal.

But this was one animal mere wood and metal would *not* contain—although there was no point in busting out until I knew the whole situation. I might very well step from the frying pan into the fire.

It was something of a habit, after all.

I twisted my legs around so I could look at my feet. My shoes were gone, and the ropes that were binding my ankles were thick and strong. They were also damp, meaning they were tightening as they dried out, digging into my skin. There were blood smears under the ropes already—I must have been struggling against them when I was unconscious. The knot itself didn't look too hard to undo, but with my hands bound behind my back, undoing it was next to impossible.

But maybe I didn't need to undo them. Maybe I just needed to change shape, and the ropes would slip off. I mean, they'd been tied to a human, not a wolf, and therefore I should have plenty of maneuvering room in my wolf shape.

I called to my wolf, felt the power of her sweep right through me, only I didn't expect the pain that came with the change. It burst through my mind—a blinding, hot, bone-breaking pain caused not only by limbs twisted into positions not natural to a wolf, but by the presence of silver. I might not be able to see it, but it was close. Close enough to be affecting my shapeshifting.

I bit back a howl and twisted around, desperate to get my legs free. The ropes fell away, releasing my limbs, allowing my legs to fall into a position more natural to a wolf.

The pain eased into a deeper throbbing ache, but the burning presence of silver didn't go away. It was all around me—under my feet, near my sides, over my head. Yet there wasn't a bit of silver in sight. Only wood and the metal strapping holding the cage together.

I scrambled to my feet. It made the ache worse, my abused and overstretched muscles shaking under the additional pressure of my weight. I ignored both and sniffed out the confines of my cage. If it had been used before, then I couldn't tell for what. There were no odors caught in the wood, no fur or scent markings to hint at what might have been here before me.

I stepped to the corner and pressed my nose against the wood. The familiar burning got stronger, a warning that silver was close. My frown increasing, I shifted back to human form and pressed a hand to the wood. My fingers burned with the same awareness of silver that my nose had. It wasn't *in* the wood, it was *beyond* it. How far was anyone's guess. I was so sensitive to its presence these days, it could be one inch away or it could be one foot.

There was only one way to find out. I clenched my fist, drew it back, and punched at the wooden side of my cage with all the force I could muster.

My fist went through the wood as easily as a hot knife through butter, then was stopped abruptly by something thin and metallic. Something that burned as soon as my hand touched it. I swore and jerked my fist away, shaking it to ease the pain and seeing the red welts already forming across my fingers.

The bastards had covered my box with a mesh of silver. Anything else I could probably break, but this was beyond me. I guess I had to be thankful the silver wasn't touching me. I might be uncomfortable right now, but at least it wasn't killing me. I shifted position and carefully peered out of the hole I'd created.

Little more than darkness and the metal struts of the boat greeted me. If I was in a hold, then it either wasn't a very big one or I'd punched a hole in the wrong end of my cage.

I shifted again, and kicked out with a bare foot, being careful not to get anywhere near the silver mesh. The wood cracked and splintered, falling away in chunks rather than smashing into splinters. The space beyond the mesh wasn't much different. A little bigger, a little less dark, but otherwise, the same. I was alone in this fishy-smelling hold.

I wondered where Rhoan was. Wondered if he was locked up like me. I wasn't getting any sort of sick feeling that he was in trouble or hurt, so wherever he was, he was obviously okay. For the moment, anyway.

So where the hell was the Directorate? Why hadn't they come riding to the rescue? That was the whole idea of the trackers in our ears, wasn't it?

Maybe they just didn't know we were in trouble. Hell, I don't think either of us bothered to tell Jack what we were intending to do this morning. Hard to come riding to the rescue if they didn't know they were needed. I pressed the stud in my ear and said, "Hello, hello? Anyone listening?"

There was no immediate response. Not surprising, I

guess. We were out on the ocean and the com-unit didn't have a huge range. The tracker did, though, so sooner or later they'd realize something was up and come a-hunting. All we had to do was hang on until then.

But just in case they *were* picking me up, I added, "Rhoan and I need help, ASAP. We're on a boat and traveling to God knows where."

I flicked off the send function but left the receive one on, just in case someone tried to contact me. My next step was finding out who was on the damn boat with me. I lowered some shields and carefully reached out, telepathically searching for minds—human or not. There was an odd sort of blankness coming from what I gathered was the front of the ship, given we were moving in that direction, but other than that, I might as well have been alone. Which I wasn't, so either the boat driver was mind-blind, or he was wearing a psychic wire to protect him from telepathic intrusion.

With that avenue of investigation going nowhere, I checked my pockets to see what I had to work with, but they'd been cleaned out. The laser, my wallet, phone, everything was gone. The only thing left was lint and the remains of what had once been a tissue, and neither of those was going to be a whole lot of use for anything. Not even blowing my nose. With nothing else to do, I laid back down and waited.

It was a long wait. The engine droned on and on. Footsteps would stride across the deck above me occasionally, but I couldn't hear voices. Couldn't hear anything to indicate there was another living soul on this boat besides me and the owner of those footsteps.

The day stretched into the evening, a fact I knew

only by the lengthening of the shadows and my own innate awareness of the night and the moon.

Eventually the aroma of earth began to run underneath the scent of fish and ocean. The ship bumped against something hard and the footsteps moved across the deck and then disappeared. A few seconds later, the thumping of the engine stopped. For a while, there was nothing breaking the silence but the creak of the boat and the lapping of the waves.

Then a car—maybe even a truck, given the low note of the engine—approached and came to a halt. Doors opened, footsteps echoed, and then, finally, I heard Rhoan—swearing like a trooper.

I sat up quickly and looked through the hole my fist had made. Nothing. The cover was still well and truly in place over my hold. "Rhoan! Where are you?"

The swearing stopped. "In a goddamn box," he yelled back. "It's silver meshed. You?"

"Same. You know where we are?"

"I think it's safe to assume we're not in Kansas anymore, Toto."

I snorted softly. If Rhoan was making wiseass remarks, he was neither hurt nor worried.

Another engine fired up, this one more spluttery. Rhoan cursed again, then, his voice barely audible over the noise, said, "They're hauling me up from the hold. There's a truck waiting."

So obviously, we had not yet reached our final destination. Part of me wanted to ask what plans he had, what he wanted me to do, but given our captors were close, that would be pretty damn pointless.

"You have any idea what is going on?"

"Nope. Hang on, Riley. I'll get us out of this."

He would, or I would. One or the other of us would

find a way to get free, of that I had no doubt. We'd been through too much together to let a couple of murdering thugs defeat us now.

There was a thump, another curse from Rhoan, then chains rattled and the truck reversed away, the sound of its engine quickly fading into the distance.

I waited in my dark little hold, wondering when my turn would come. I could hear movement and the rattle of chains coming from what had to be the dock, but so far, no other truck had appeared.

An hour passed, my awareness of time sharpened by the rising of a moon that I couldn't actually see. The power of it burned through me, a silvery warmth that flowed through my bloodstream and offered me strength. Offered me comfort. The full moon was some days off yet, but its beauty still filled me.

Not that it would do me much good here in my little wooden prison.

I hoped they didn't plan to keep me penned until the bloom of the moon. I'd felt the fury of a bloodlust once before. I didn't ever want to go through that again.

After another few minutes, the sound of the truck began to bite back into the silence, drawing closer. Obviously, they only had the one to move us.

Above me, doors crashed open and moonlight filtered in. Someone jumped down into the hold, and the thick, musky scent of a human filled the air. I peered through the hole and saw grimy jeans and grimier work boots. He was tall and thin, with hands that were so covered in dirt, grease, and God knows what else, they looked black. Because of the darkness, it was hard to get a definite image of his features, but he wasn't young. His hands were the hands of an older person.

Chains rattled around my prison, then straps were

drawn up over the box and suddenly I was rising into the air. I gripped the floor of the box hard, not liking the way the thing swayed. It felt too much like falling.

Goose bumps trembled across my skin, and bile rose. I bit it back and closed my eyes, trying to remain calm. It was only *old* fears rushing in. It *wasn't* a premonition. I wasn't going to fall. Not here in this crate. Not anywhere.

The crate thumped down on something solid, making me jump. But it didn't ease the crazy fear running through my system, so I continued to breathe slow and deep, trying to keep calm as gears crunched and the truck began to trundle away from the dock.

The scent of eucalyptus gradually replaced the salty scent of the ocean. I shifted, peering out one of the holes, watching trees and thick ferns pass by. Oddly enough, this island looked almost tropical. The plant life was thick and lush, and many of the plants weren't the types to survive in the colder climes of Victoria.

The truck bumped along the track, occasionally bogging down and sending sand spurting into the air as the wheels spun then gripped. The incline got stronger, suggesting we were going up.

After about half an hour, the road flattened out and the crunch of stone under the tires replaced the squeak of sand. Light twinkled tantalizingly in the darkness, and the scent of barbecuing meat touched the air, making my taste buds water and my stomach rumble.

Unfortunately, I didn't think we were going to be the recipients of that barbecuing meat.

And indeed, the truck trundled past the lights and the smell, coming to a halt in an area of darkness. We weren't in the middle of nowhere, though. Through my peephole I could see the shadowy form of a building. It seemed more barnlike in structure than houselike—though if it was a barn, I couldn't smell any of the usual scents that went along with it. Definitely no horses or hay, that was for sure.

Then another engine kicked into gear and the box was on the move again. I gripped on tight as it swung into the air then around to the right, swaying crazily as it was lowered. I let out a relieved breath when the box hit something solid, then I was being wheeled toward the barn. My box was dumped, doors slammed shut, then footsteps retreated.

Alone again.

This was making no sense whatsoever.

"Rhoan?" I said into the silence. "You here?"

I didn't hold much hope that he was, simply because I couldn't smell him.

The continued silence was my only answer. I peered through my hole again, seeing concrete and heavy metal bars. The type even a werewolf would have trouble getting through.

It actually took me a moment to realize that my box was no longer covered by the silver mesh. I kicked out with a bare foot, smashing open the box in an instant.

Even though my cage hadn't been small, the feeling of freedom that hit when I was no longer confined was immense. I sucked in the cool night air, then stood up and looked around.

The barn was a large one, and had at least a dozen pens just like this one. Some had hay, some didn't. Some had the silver mesh nets covering the heavy metal bars, others had nothing but metal and concrete floors. Some, like mine, had bunk beds in them— though given the filthy state of the mattress, it'd be pretty much a given I'd be sharing the bed with more than a few bugs. I shivered. Give me cold concrete any day.

I turned and walked closer to the front bars, giving them a shake to test their strength. They didn't budge. They might not be meshed like some of the other cages, but there wasn't a hope in hell of me breaking out of here. Which made me wonder just what the meshed cages had been designed to hold.

I leaned my arms against the metal and studied what lay beyond the open doors of the barn. A wide road swung away down the hill, lined on either side by thick greenery. The house and lights I'd seen earlier weren't visible through that door, and the one to my left was shut.

I stepped back, my gaze rising to the ceiling. Even that was barred. Which meant a lot of thought had gone into construction of this cell, and that sent a chill skittering down my spine. This wasn't just a one-off, nothing-left-to-lose capture. This was something else entirely.

But until someone popped along with an explanation as to what the hell was going on, I wasn't about to guess. My imaginings would probably be far worse than the reality. After all, I'd been in some pretty shitty situations over the last year or so—and I seriously doubted whether fate could throw anything else at me worse than a god of pain set on world domination.

So I sat on the floor and waited yet again. I *hated* waiting, but there was nothing else to do but pace. And that would get old very quickly.

The moon had passed its zenith and had begun the long track toward dawn before someone finally got motivated enough to visit.

His scent touched the air long before I actually saw

him—musky, spicy human. Jared. Or Jorn, as the case may be.

His footsteps were light, measured. A man who was sure of himself. A man who was used to power and getting his own way. I reached out telepathically but, like on the island, felt nothing except an odd sort of blankness. Only it didn't feel electronically induced, but rather natural. He had shields every bit as strong as mine. Meaning, I wasn't going to be able to read him or control him—not without a lot of time and effort.

And I had a bad feeling time was the one thing I didn't have much of.

Jorn strode through the door, dressed in jungle greens and thick boots, and stopped in front of my cell. His expression was an odd mix of arrogance and excitement. Not sexual excitement, but the sort of excitement that went with a chase.

I looked him up and down, noting the sheathed bowie knife strapped to his left leg, and a pistol holster attached to his hip.

"Shall I call you Jorn? Or do you prefer Jared?"

Amusement played about his lips. "You worked it out."

"Took me a while. I never realized there was a branch of humanity who could alter their features."

"It's a family gift."

"Just like the family trait of madness?" I said sweetly. "Tell me, was it you or Yohan in the truck and the car?"

"That was my brother. He never was a very good driver."

If he had been, I might have been squished meat under the truck's tires. "And the shooter?"

He grimaced. "A misjudgment on our part, because

we were foolish enough to believe his assurance that he was good enough to take you out."

He almost had been, but I wasn't about to mention that.

"Why choose an exclusive island like Monitor to set your trap? Why not choose something more accessible to the masses?"

"Because there is something decidedly delicious in hunting the spoiled wealthy. It's the eyes," he added, expression almost dreamy. "The realization in those final moments that, despite all their wealth and power, there is nothing they can do to stop death. Plus, of course, it was bitches like them who killed our father. None of them deserved to live."

"So did you sleep with said bitches?"

He snorted. "I've seen what you lot can do to human flesh. No thanks. Besides, flirting got me all the information I needed." He hesitated, and grinned. "You women are so careless with your purses."

My missing driver's license, I thought suddenly. *That's* how the shooter had my address, and probably how he knew the addresses of the others. "How did you handle all the other staff at the island?"

"We adjusted the memories of a few. With the rest, it was just a matter of timing. We simply ensured our appearances coincided with the downtime of those we were copying."

These boys might be insane, but they were damn clever as well.

"Why did you attack us at Mirror Image? If you had let us go, you could have made an easy escape."

He raised an eyebrow. "But we already have. It'll take your people a very long time to trace us to this island, and by then, we'll be gone."

"But by kidnapping us, you've only crystallized the Directorate's suspicion and ensured they'll come after you. And trust me, that's never a good thing."

He smiled. "Perhaps. But we've never hunted a guardian before. We thought it worth the risk."

"One you will not live long enough to savor."

He shrugged. "The threat of death is all part of the glory of the hunt. There's no thrill where there is no danger."

I raised an eyebrow. "Only the insane would consider hunting two guardians fun. Most people tend to run from us, given any sort of choice."

"We are not most people. And our last hunt was a disappointment. We need a good challenge before we move on."

I studied him for a moment, wondering why he was so damn confident that he felt no qualms about telling me everything, then said, "So why have you been hunting them? Why not just shoot them, then slice off their heads, like you did your first victim?"

"Because we were young then, and blind to the prospects of the hunt." He paused. "Was Adrienne the reason you appeared on the island and the Directorate began investigating the club?"

"Yes." Better to let him think the Directorate had been wise to their ways, when in fact I'd only been investigating thanks to Blake's blackmailing insistence. God knows how many other women they would have taken before the Directorate had become aware of their activities. The number might even have been as high as the seventeen that went missing in England. "Is that why you left the UK and came here? Because the authorities got wind something was up?"

"The regular authorities we could have handled. It

was only when the Directorate took a serious interest that we had to move on." Annoyance flickered—a brief, black cloud in his otherwise cheerful expression. "We had hoped to source quite a few more hunts here before we were forced to go elsewhere."

"So why Adrienne? She looked nothing like the woman who killed your father."

Something flicked through his eyes. Anger. Or madness. It was hard to tell which. "We had no option when she appeared on the island asking questions. Plus, she had that sketch."

"Which was you, I take it."

He nodded. "Unfortunately, it turned out your pack-mate had an interesting psychic skill that allowed her to read a person's past. She ran into me at the club, and apparently caught glimpses of our murderous little habit."

"She told you this?"

He smiled benignly. "Of course she did. She thought it would help her live."

"So she and the others *are* dead?"

"Yes. Though they do live on in our memories. And through our trophies."

I stared at him for a minute, my stomach turning as I remembered the fact that the head of their first victim had never been found. "You take trophies?"

He chuckled, and it was a cold, inhuman sound. "Of course. All hunters do. The heads of all our prey line the walls of our lodge, so we and others can admire the beauty of their death. Although Adrienne has not yet joined them. Our taxidermist went on holidays."

Oh God, that was just . . . *beyond* sick. These weren't just animals we were talking about, these were people.

Living, breathing human beings. Or rather, nonhuman beings.

And how in hell did they find a taxidermist who'd even *do* such a thing?

"You will pay for those trophies," I said, my voice flat, devoid of the anger that was running through me. Just like Rhoan, when he stepped into his guardian shoes and became the efficient killing machine he'd been trained to be.

A shiver went through me, and deep down something screamed *no*. But I had to wonder how much longer that voice would last if I kept getting thrown up against the psychos of this world.

"That's the whole idea," he said cheerfully. "We hunt. You try to make us pay. Of course, there are rules."

I snorted. "Like I'm actually going to obey any of your rules once I'm out of here?"

Perhaps not the wisest thing to say, but hey, if he knew *anything* about guardians, then he knew rules didn't often figure in our actions.

"You will obey, or your partner pays."

Yeah, like *that* was a surprise. And of course, I would obey their rules because there was no way on this earth I'd risk my brother's life. "The problem you're faced with is the fact that if you *do* manage to kill me, there is nothing left to make my partner obey your rules."

"There is no *if* in the equation." He dug into his pocket and pulled out what looked like one of those keychain garage-door openers. "And we have this as our security on your partner. He has a miniature bomb planted in his armpit. If he disobeys the rules, the top half of his torso will be blown apart. Hard to get revenge when you only have half a body and no brain."

I stared at him, wondering what was worse—his matter-of-fact tone or his obvious delight at his handiwork.

"The first thing any sensible person would do is rip the device out of their body."

"The device's power is sourced from the body's heat. Disconnect that source and it will instantly detonate."

"That's not very friendly."

"We may enjoy our hunt, but we are not fools." He glanced at his watch, then pushed away from the bars. "We will release you at five. Walk down the path and out the red gate. Go anywhere else but out that gate and your partner will lose his life. We will give you a ten-minute head start."

"Gee, thanks," I said dryly.

"Use the time wisely."

He turned around and walked out of the barn. I flicked to infrared vision, watching his body heat push through the thick shrubbery to the left of the path before disappearing from my line of sight.

So the hunter had become the hunted. Nothing new in *that* situation. Question was, why was he so damned confident?

Granted, he and his twin had a good number of kills under their belts, and those kills were either weres or shifters who were traditionally stronger and faster than humans.

But Rhoan and I were guardians. Trained killers. Well, Rhoan was. I was still very much the new kid on the block, and more than happy to stay that way. Yet Jorn had shown no fear of either of us. Had absolutely no doubt that he could track me down and kill me.

Why?

He obviously knew what guardians were capable of—they'd moved out of England to get away from Directorate interest there.

So why the confidence?

Was it just another pointer to their obvious insanity? Or had they done to me what they'd done to Rhoan?

I felt under my armpits, but there didn't seem to be anything foreign there. Which didn't mean there wasn't a bomb somewhere inside me, just that I couldn't feel it. And I couldn't remove something I couldn't feel. Though if what Jorn had said about its power source was true, then removing it wasn't the best option right now anyway.

Which left me with only one thing to do—nothing. Just wait for the hunt to begin.

Another hour went by. I rose and began stretching, readying muscles but trying not to think about the hunt that was coming.

Then, finally, the door clicked open. I remained where I was, nostrils flaring, trying to catch any scent that would indicate that either Jorn or Yohan was close. There was nothing. Just the freshness of dawn.

I stepped out of my cell, the concrete cold under my bare feet as I looked at the ceiling. No cameras. Nothing to tell them I was on the move. What would happen if I waited here? The barn might not be the best fighting arena, but there were plenty of shadows to hide within. How would they know just where I was?

Unless, of course, there was a sensor at the red gate he'd told me to go through.

I blew out a frustrated breath, then walked forward. I couldn't afford to risk Rhoan's life on what-ifs. If Jorn and Yohan wanted a hunt, a hunt they would get. And this hunter fully intended to see the tables turned.

Hints of red and gold touched the predawn sky, and the air was crisp, holding the scents of eucalyptus and sea. I padded along the edge of the path, keeping to the shadows, ears attuned to the growing hum of the day, listening for any sound that was out of tune. There was still nothing to indicate either man was watching. Maybe they were intending a fair hunt.

And maybe tomorrow I'd become human.

Yohan and Jorn might want a good hunt, but in the end, they also wanted—needed—to win. Which meant, if it got down to the nitty-gritty, fairness would go out the window.

The red gate came into view. It was a big, wooden affair that merged into the surrounding ferns and was stained almost black. The gated opened as I neared, meaning someone *was* watching, even if I couldn't see them. Maybe the whole island was dotted with cameras.

I walked through, realizing as I did that the gates weren't actually black, but a very dark, reddish color. A dark red that smelled of death.

Blood stained that wood, not paint.

A shudder went through me, which was probably the precise reaction they were after. It *had* to be a tactic to unnerve their targets, to make them think about what might happen. After all, not everyone was like Rhoan and me, and used to the scent of death.

I headed into the shadows of the nearby forest. The trees and ferns closed in, surrounding me with shadows. I pulled them closer, hiding my form, and followed the rise of the land. I needed to get up higher and see just what was around me. Maybe even get some idea of where the buildings were, and where Rhoan might be.

I ran up the steep slope, trying to slip past the heavy fern fronds without breaking them, keeping to firmer ground so my footsteps weren't as visible—a difficult task when the ground was so covered by leaves and other forest rubbish.

Sweat began to trickle down my spine and my leg started to ache. Too much more and I'd probably begin to limp. Not what I needed right now. I blew out a breath and struggled on, only to slip on a bit of rotten leaf matter and come down hard on my knees.

And noticed then, as I was biting back a yelp of pain, that the cheery songs of the birds had suddenly silenced.

Felt the sting of silver fly over the top of my head and punch a hole in the tree trunk three feet ahead.

Ten-minute head start my *ass*.

Though why I had been stupid enough to believe it was anyone's guess. I mean, it wasn't like I was unfamiliar with bad men making promises they never intended to keep. Swearing softly, I swung around and sucked in the air, trying to scent my pursuers.

Nothing.

No giveaway aromas, no sound. The forest was deathly quiet and very still, yet an odd sort of tension seemed to run through the trees.

Human tension. The sort of tension that came with excitement and danger.

I might not be able to see or smell them, but something within me could *feel* them. Or rather, feel what they were feeling. Which normally would have pissed me off, simply because I shouldn't have been able to feel such a thing. But right now—and for the first time in my life—I was actually thankful that the drugs were producing a talent that was immediately useful.

They were down the hill and to my left. Not close, but obviously close enough to use a rifle sight. Which they were probably using right now to get another fix on me. Maybe the shadows weren't as deep or as thick as I'd presumed, and the gathering light was enough to break my cover.

Either way, I couldn't stay here. I scrambled upright and pushed through the ferns, keeping low as I ran, not worrying about leaving a trail for them to follow. It was better to simply get some distance between us again.

Fronds and branches whipped across my body as I ran, making me wish I had a sweater on. Preferably a dark one. But I was stuck with a bright yellow tank top, which meant that I might as well stand still and wave a target in the middle of all this lush greenery.

Which had me wondering again just where this island was situated. We couldn't be along the coast anywhere near my home state. Victorian islands were more scrubby than lush, and it certainly would have been a whole lot colder at this early hour of the day.

I continued to scramble upward. The smell of my sweat stained the air, and my lungs were beginning to burn, my breath coming in short, sharp gasps that echoed across the silence.

Easy enough to track, if the twins had good hearing.

And they obviously did, because they were still behind me, still chasing. I might have vampire speed, but in this environment it was damn hard to use it. And every now and again I felt the quiver of silver approaching, heard the ping of a bullet off a nearby tree trunk.

The crest of the hill finally came into sight. The trees didn't thin out, however, remaining as thick at the top as they'd been on the slope. I paused, reaching for that sense that allowed me to "feel" them. One was heading to my left, the other to the right. They were still below me but not climbing any farther just yet.

I had time to see where the hell I was.

I quickly scanned the trees until I found one that was ripe for climbing. I scrambled up the trunk then through the gum's leafy branches, my heart going a mile a minute.

I swung out on a thick branch, walking along carefully until the bough dipped and quivered under my weight. The island stretched before me, a small dot of green in the otherwise blue surrounds of the sea. We had to be in Queensland—or at least the top end of New South Wales—somewhere, given that blueness. Victorian waters looked a whole lot darker and colder. There didn't seem to be any rooftops poking out through the trees below me, but there was a sandy-looking road that wound up from the beach. I followed the course of that road, edging around on my branch, and finally spotted a building sitting in a clearing one hill over.

It didn't appear to be a house, or even a barn like the one I'd been taken into. It was small and squat, and very, very strong looking. A cell, I thought, for dangerous quarry. That's where Rhoan would be.

All I had to do now was get rid of my pursuers, then get over there and free him. Easy.

Not.

Another bullet burned through the air, this time slicing past my ear and drawing blood. I yelped softly and dropped to the ground, the shock of the jump reverberating up my spine and sending shooting pain through my healing leg. I brushed my fingers against the ground to regain my balance and sucked in the thick, aromatic air.

This time, I smelled Jorn. He was to my right, and moving fast. I called to my wolf form and shifted shape, then ran left and down, intending to come up underneath him. I ran fast—limping only a little—and kept to the shadows, my wolf form more suited to this sort of landscape, making little noise and leaving nothing in the way of a trail.

He shouldn't have seen me. Shouldn't have heard me.

Yet somehow, he did.

This time I was close enough to hear the muted sound of a gunshot before the bullet even neared me. I threw myself sideways, restraining a yelp as a rock dug painfully into my side, then rose and ran straight for his scent.

Another gunshot.

Another bullet dodged.

Then his scent filled the air and he was before me. I launched straight at him, teeth bared, a growl rumbling up my throat.

He scrambled backward, excitement and fear flashing across his features as he attempted to raise the rifle and use it as a club. I was on him before he succeeded, my teeth slashing past cloth and deep into flesh. Blood filled my mouth, exciting the wolf, sickening the human. I ignored the latter, ripping my teeth sideways, taking a huge chunk of flesh with me.

He screamed and hit me hard in the side. It felt like iron, that blow, and pain rose—a red tide that momentarily blotted out the wolf's eagerness. Winded and aching, I leapt away, spitting out his blood and skin as I twisted around to face him.

His left arm was a torn mess. Blood poured from the wound, soaking his shirt, filling the air with its scent. He was lucky. I'd been aiming for his neck, and I hadn't missed by much.

"For this," he said, moving his bloody left arm, "you will pay."

I bared my teeth and growled, then hunkered down low and launched myself at him again. He swung the rifle around, using the stock like a club, the weapon swishing through the air with enough force to break bones. I twisted away, felt the breeze of it skim past my already bruised side. My claws dug into the soft soil as I hit the ground, the dirt flying free as I jumped at him again.

I was in the air when I felt the burn of approaching silver. Heard the crash of steps through the trees behind us.

Yohan, coming to save his brother.

Rhoan and I might not share the telepathy of twins, but these two sure did.

I twisted awkwardly, making bones crack along my spine as I dropped to the ground. The bullet crashed past the tip of my ear and exploded into a nearby sapling, sending leaf and branch matter flying. I lunged forward, tearing at Jorn's legs, slashing through his skin and drawing blood. He lashed out again, the rifle butt coming down hard on my side. I yelped, and dove for the shadows of the nearby trees.

I might be a guardian, I might be speedy and strong, but a silver bullet could still bring me down. And it was far better for me to tackle them one at a time. Especially when it was becoming increasingly obvious that while these two might be human, they had reflexes and senses as sharp as any nonhuman.

Killing them wasn't going to be as easy as I'd presumed.

I shifted back to human shape, using the change to help ease the ache in my side, then ran on, down the hill, up the next one, trying to get some distance, some maneuvering room, between us. But they remained annoyingly close.

I wasn't making that much noise, not now, nor was I leaving that much of a trail. Running as I was, there was always going to be signs to follow, but they shouldn't have been able to track me this easily while running flat out. And yet they were.

Did they have psychic skills other than telepathy? I was beginning to think that was probably the case. I'd never actually heard of a talent that allowed people to track nonhumans, but as Rhoan was wont to say, there were more strange things on this earth than we would ever know about.

I ran a hand across my forehead, flicking away sweat, my gaze searching the trees ahead. The scent of the sea was growing stronger, and the treetops were beginning to shiver with a sea breeze. The last thing I needed was to find myself out on the sand. I needed the trees as protection from the bullets until I found a way to separate the two of them again.

Awareness of the twins surged again, and a second later the air screamed a warning that several bullets were hurtling toward me. I threw myself down, sending leaf matter and dirt flying as the bullets burned over my right shoulder and pinged into a nearby trunk. Bark exploded into the air, raining down around me. For several seconds I lay there, listening to their light steps, the easy way they seemed to move through the forest. Was it worth confronting them? I could take the two of them, I had no doubt of that. The only problem was the silver bullets. It would only take one to end my fight, and with Rhoan still captive, I dared not risk getting hit. Better to run, to wait for the right moment.

Only patience had never been one of my virtues, and I was getting more than a little pissed off at being shot at so much.

I blew out a breath, then scrambled to my feet and ran on up the steep slope. The thick lushness of the island's interior was giving way to a wilder, scrubbier look, and the wind was stronger, battering its way through the trees and chilling the sweat against my skin. It was an almost pleasant sensation.

The rise in the land sharpened abruptly. The leg that had been shot with silver previously was beginning to not only burn, but feel weak. Like the barely healed muscles just couldn't go on. My limp was certainly getting more pronounced.

Sky came into sight, a pale blueness peeking through the trees, calling me on. To what was anyone's guess, but it had to be better than this goddamn slope and the bastards hunting me.

Another bullet burned through the air. I dropped, winding myself even though I didn't think that was possible, given my current breathless state. The bullet cracked past and disappeared into the inviting blueness. If I could get down the other side of this slope fast enough, I might buy myself enough time to find a way to separate them. And once I did that, the bastards were dead.

I surged to my feet and ran on, my gaze on that blueness and the promise it offered.

But I should have been looking at where I was going. Or rather, where the land was going.

Because I reached the crest and suddenly there was nothing underneath me.

No ground, no leaf matter.

Nothing but air.

And I was falling, tumbling, down into that emptiness.

Chapter 13

I'd only been a pup when Blake had thrown me off the cliff. But even now, I could recall those moments clearly, simply because the world around me had suddenly seemed to slow. Oh, the wind had battered me full force and the ground had rushed toward me, filling my vision, filling my world, forever embedding itself into the worst of my nightmares. It was just time itself that crawled. The falling seemed to go on and on and on. The ground rushed toward me and yet never seemed to get closer. I'd screamed, I'd quaked, I'd fought to grab something, anything, to stop my fall or to at least break it. To no avail.

But never once in any of those long minutes had my life flashed before my eyes.

Maybe it was because I'd been so young, had done so little.

I was older now.

And as I fell toward the sparkling blue of the ocean

and the jagged rocks that lined the cliff's base, images of my past reeled drunkenly before my eyes—the flashes almost too fast for me to even see them. Mostly they were memories of good times. With Rhoan, with other people I'd cared about, and boyfriends of old. And there was Quinn, who could have been something more had he only played it fair.

But with all those memories came something else. Something deeper. Stronger.

Regret.

For all the things I hadn't done, for all the steps I hadn't taken.

And the biggest of those regrets was Kellen.

I *should* have given him the time he wanted. Should have given him commitment.

I should have shoved the fear aside and made a grab for my dreams. He'd been right in saying that I was never going to find what I was looking for if I didn't occasionally *stop* looking and take a damn chance on someone.

Dammit, I didn't want to *die*!

Not now, not when there was finally someone in my life that I loved, someone who showed every sign of being the one. And even if it turned out that he wasn't my soul mate, then at least I could say I gave it a go. At least I'd know the fear of being left broken hadn't stopped me from living life to the full.

I twisted around, grabbing at the cliff as it rushed by. My fingertips scraped stones, finding no purchase on the slick surface. There was nothing here, nothing at all, that would stop my fall. No grasses, no branches, no tree roots sticking out of the sandy soil. Nothing but slick rock.

I swore and continued grabbing at the cliff face,

refusing to give up, refusing to believe that this was the end. But the ocean and the rocks were rushing ever closer, and there was nothing, absolutely nothing, I could do to stop it.

I closed my eyes, not wanting to see the death that was speeding toward me. The best I could do was hope that either fate was kind and made it a quick one, or that by some miracle I missed the worst of the rocks and somehow found the ocean.

God, how I wished I was a bird. Wished I could just shift shape and fly like the seabirds that drifted around the cliffs. Wished I had wings to ride the breeze, skimming the rocks and riding the wave-tops to freedom rather than splattering myself all over them.

Even as the thought crossed my mind, the tingling of shapeshifting ran across my body. Panic surged and I desperately fought to stop my body from shifting shape. My wolf form would have even less chance on the rocks below, her bones more delicate, more easily smashed.

But the shifting would not be denied. It surged on regardless, heedless of the danger, reshaping flesh and bone, until what was falling was something other than human.

Only it wasn't my wolf.

This form felt lighter, freer.

I looked at my arms, saw red-tipped wings—feathers—instead of paws.

A bird. I was a goddamn *bird*.

Oh God, the drug. It was changing me, as it had changed the others who'd taken it.

No, I thought, *no.*

Then I shoved it all aside. Shoved aside the fear. I had no time for it, not if I wanted to live. I frantically pumped my newly formed wings up and down. But having a bird shape didn't exactly mean I knew how to fly. Obviously there was an art to it, because I was flapping for all I was worth and still falling. I didn't even think my speed was slowing.

I cursed fluently, but it came out as a weird croaking cry. A cry that sounded an awful lot like that of a seagull.

Great. I was going to die in the form of a creature considered little more than a winged rat.

The rocks were so close that the salty droplets of sea spray was splashing up from them and hitting me. There was little time—so little time—for a miracle.

And yet, it came.

The sea breeze hit me, battering me sideways, and momentarily lifting me upward. In desperation, I stopped pumping and spread my wings wide. The wind caught underneath, feathers fluttering as I was lifted up, away from the rocks and out into the deeper ocean.

There the wind dumped me. I landed chest-first in an ungainly, unsightly, and very un-birdlike way. It didn't matter a damn.

I was *alive*.

I felt like flapping my arms and dancing for joy on the rolling waves. Against all the odds, I was *alive*.

But it was an exuberance that was short lived.

I might be alive, but the means by which I'd survived had been a dramatic one. The ARC1-23 drug given to me over a year ago had finally stopped making little changes and started making big ones.

I could take on *other* shapes, and that was the one thing I'd been absolutely hoping would never, ever happen. Because it meant that my hopes of escaping the

Directorate and my role as a guardian were ashes. I was Jack's girl now, like it or not. My only other choice was being sent to the military to join the other half-breeds who'd been affected by the drug in the research centers.

There was no way in hell that was going to happen. At least with the Directorate, I could have some semblance of a normal life—even if my job there could in no way ever be considered normal.

But at least not *all* my hopes were dead. When it came to Kellen, the *how* of survival didn't matter. I was alive, and now had the chance to give him—to give us—the commitment we deserved.

Fate had booted me up the rear end with this fall, and I wasn't going to ignore the warning. I was going to make a grab for what I wanted, and hope that it was right.

Movement caught my eye, and I looked up. High atop the cliff top, two figures had appeared. Both men had their rifles slung over their shoulders, but Jorn was looking a little worse for the wear, his arm and leg bloody and hair in disarray.

He'd be easy to track once I got back onto land. The scent of his blood would leave a lovely trail for the keen nose of a wolf to follow.

The two men argued on the top of the cliff for several minutes. I floated on the waves, paddling for all I was worth against the current to remain where I was. It was more tiring than I thought it would be, but maybe that was a combination of the short seagull legs and overall weariness from all the running I'd been doing up until the fall.

Yohan glanced at his watch, but neither of them moved, just stayed there watching the ocean, waiting either for signs of life or confirmation of death. Exhaustion was creeping over me, and the need to resume one of my regular shapes was growing.

And deep inside, the niggle of concern was beginning. What if I couldn't resume my regular shape? That had been one of the main problems facing the others who'd been shafted into the military—the inability to resume human shape.

But then, they'd apparently gone through multiple shapes, exploring the width and breadth of their new skills, until the cells in their bodies could no longer remember original forms.

I had no intention of being that stupid.

I might explore this new ability, but it would be under controlled conditions, with Rhoan by my side.

Though the form of a red-winged gull was not exactly an enticing one. Why a damn gull? Why couldn't I have chosen something more exotic? Sexy? Dangerous, even? Like a hawk, or an eagle. Hell, even a cockatoo had more appeal than a damn seagull.

Still, the wings of this gull had saved my life. And maybe, just maybe, it might ease my fear of heights. After all, if I learned to fly, I'd never again have to worry about getting pushed off a cliff.

The two men finally moved away. I waited for another five minutes, watching the cliff top, searching for any sign that they were merely in hiding rather than having left, but there was nothing.

I paddled sideways across the waves, riding the surges and letting the current pull me ever so slowly toward the cliff base. To the right of where I'd fallen, the steepness of the cliff eased and the rocks weren't as fierce looking. I paddled closer and let a wave surge drop me on top of one. My webbed red feet gripped the wet stone securely, and I waddled away from the waves, shaking my body and fluffing my feathers to get rid of some of the water.

Once I was far enough away from the foamy fingers of water, I took a deep breath, then reached down, deep down inside, to where the shapeshifting magic resided, and called for my human shape.

For a moment, there was no response, and panic surged. I closed my eyes, fighting for calm, picturing my human shape in my mind, remembering my body shape, my scars. The funny shape of my toes.

My skin began to tingle, then the shapeshifting magic surged, sweeping across my body, remolding flesh and muscle and bone, until what was sitting on the rock was once again human.

A human shaking with relief and fear.

I hugged my knees close to my chest. Every inch of my body trembled, my chest felt tight, and my wounded leg felt like jelly. But I was alive, I was whole, and I was human again. I sucked in great gulps of air, and tried not to think about what I would have done if my body hadn't responded, if the part of my soul that made the shifting so easy had suddenly forgotten the patterns of my humanity.

It was a good five minutes before the shaking stopped enough for me to concentrate on what I had to do rather than what might have been. What still *could* be if I wasn't very careful.

I rose and looked up, studying the cliffs. God, it was a *long* fall. My stomach rose and my body began to shake. I gulped down air, fighting the rise of terror. I was here, I was alive, and I had a brother to save. There was no time for fear or panic right now.

Thinking about Rhoan helped. As the panic began to ease, I switched my gaze to the lower regions of the cliff, looking for some way up. There wasn't even a track a goat could climb.

Not that I was intending to become a goat anytime soon.

I shifted, my gaze following the cliff top, seeing the gradual fall before the island dipped around to the right and disappeared from sight. Hopefully, there was a bay or something around that corner.

I made my way forward, leaping from rock to rock, carefully picking my way through the sharp rocks and shells but cutting my feet nevertheless. I ignored the wounds, trusting the sea would wash away any blood I left behind.

Right now, I just needed to get to solid ground, away from the cliffs and the sea.

When I finally rounded the corner, and saw that the cliff tops did indeed sweep down into a shallow sandy bay, relief flooded me. I jumped into the sea and paddled toward the shore. I wasn't the world's greatest swimmer, but I think I would have broken world records right then. I dragged myself up onto the sandy beach, then on into the trees. There I threw my hands wide and dropped down onto the ground.

Land. Solid and real. Not sand, not sea, not rocks. *Land*.

I would have hugged it if I could.

After wasting several seconds simply enjoying the solidness under my body, I rose to my knees and shifted to my wolf shape. I needed her nose to hunt my quarry, and to do that, I needed to go back to the cliff top. Just the thought of it had my knees shaking.

But there was no other choice. While freeing Rhoan was a priority, getting the bomb control was even more so. Until *that* was destroyed, there was no point in pulling Rhoan out of his cell. And I doubted the twins would be hunting him today, given the injuries I'd inflicted on Jorn.

I turned and padded through the trees, my limp not quite as bad in my wolf form. I followed the coastline, keeping well away from the cliff edges as the land began to rise again.

Finding the area where I'd gone over wasn't hard. Footprints marred the sandy soil and the undergrowth where I'd fallen and they'd stood was all broken and flattened. The scent of Jorn's blood lingered on the air, a sweet aroma that stirred the hunter to life. I nosed around the ground until I caught a slightly sour, foresty scent. Yohan, undoubtedly. At least if I lost Jorn's trail, I might be able to follow Yohan's.

Nose to ground, I made my way through the trees, slipping easily through the underbrush, avoiding the sunlight so that my red coat wouldn't gleam, melding with the deeper shadows of the forest. Hopefully making it harder for anyone to spot me.

Not that I thought they'd be looking for me, but I'd learned a long time ago never to underestimate the bad guys. They just didn't think in the same linear patterns as sane people.

Jorn's scent sharpened abruptly. I stopped, sniffing the wind, tasting the flavors that ran underneath it. He was still bleeding heavily, the blood smell thick and rich on the air. Twined around it was the reek of sweat and the musk of man.

He was close. I twitched my ears, trying to hear him. His scent was coming from my left, but given the way the wind swirled through the undergrowth, I wasn't relying on it to give me position.

If he was making any noise, I couldn't hear it—and

as a wolf my hearing was pretty keen. So he was either unconscious, sitting quietly, or it was a trap.

I laid on my belly and crawled forward. It wasn't exactly easy, given the undergrowth and the fact my wolf form was designed more to run than creep.

I ducked my nose through some thick greenery and discovered a small clearing. Jorn sat on a log on the far side, leaning back against a tree trunk. Blood caked his left arm and leg, his shirt was caked with sweat, and there was a decided look of pain on his face.

Couldn't say I was sorry about that.

Though his eyes were closed, I doubted he was unconscious. The pain, the way in which he sat, the tension in his clenched hands—it all spoke of awareness.

I looked beyond him, my nose raised slightly, tasting the air for Yohan's sour scent. It lingered—a memory more than a reality. He'd definitely been here, but not recently.

Which gave me my chance at Jorn.

Despite the rush of eagerness that had my toes twitching, I didn't move. The clearing might be a small one, but there was still open space between me and him, and he had his rifle within easy reach. I wasn't about to bet my speed against his, even if I *should* be faster. Not when there were silver bullets involved.

Which meant I had to try and provide a distraction, and hopefully give myself extra time to attack before he reacted. I carefully backed through the undergrowth, then rose and padded through the trees, making a wide, looping arc around the small clearing before coming up on his right side.

When I was close enough to smell the stink of his sweat and blood, I shifted to my human shape and reached down to pick up a nice big rock. With my fingers clenched around it securely, I crept forward until I was within throwing range.

This close, I could hear his breathing, see the blood still running from the wounds. Maybe Yohan had gone to fetch medical help for his brother, which meant I had to do this fast.

I raised my arm and threw the rock as hard as I could. It tumbled through the air so fast it was little more than a blur and yet, somehow, Jorn sensed it.

I should have known fate wasn't going to let me off so easily.

He twisted around, avoiding the rock and bringing the rifle up in one smooth movement. I laid low and wrapped the shadows around me. Jorn frowned, his gaze sweeping the tree line, moving past my position with barely a twitch or pause.

He couldn't see me. Couldn't sense me.

Maybe Yohan was the one who could sense—track—nonhumans.

But Jorn still had extraordinary hearing, because he'd obviously heard the whir of the rock through the air. It had been warning enough to assume fighting readiness but not enough to fire randomly. For that, I had to be grateful.

Thankfully, the rock had disappeared back into the trees, and he wasn't making any move to discover just what had flown at him. Maybe—hopefully—he thought it was a bird rather than the beginnings of an attack.

I waited until he settled down again—albeit more watchfully—then slowly, carefully, inched my way backward. Given he obviously had good senses, I'd have to do this the old-fashioned way—with speed and power and a whole lot of luck.

Once I had retreated deeper into the forest, I rose

and padded around until I was roughly behind his tree. I could see his elbows to either side of the tree trunk, and underneath one was the butt of the rifle. He was ready for action, so I really would have to be quick.

I took a deep breath and released it slowly, then silently counted to three and moved forward. Fast.

He was going to hear me, but I was counting on my vampire speed and the cover of the shadows to fool his senses long enough. But a good hunter didn't rely on sight alone, and given the thick carpet of debris lining the forest floor, there was no hope of ever remaining silent.

I felt the bullet even before I heard the gunshot. I leapt high in the air, making my body an arrow, flying straight at Jorn. The bullet ripped past my belly and disappeared into the shadowed forest.

And then I was on him, hitting him, knocking him backward. He grunted, the weapon flying from his grip. I hit the ground and tumbled to my feet, racing over to the gun.

I only barely beat Jorn there. I dropped beneath his blow, then swept low with my leg, sweeping him off his feet. He hit the ground back-first. I stepped on his left leg, flipped the gun around, and smashed the barrel down as hard as I could onto his knee. I had a whole lot of strength behind me thanks to my dual heritage, and his knee didn't stand a chance. Bone smashed and splintered under the force of the blow, and he screamed, his body crumbling as he tried to protect himself.

The sound of his pain echoed through the forest, and I had no doubt it would bring Yohan. It would have called me, had it been my brother lying there screaming.

Which meant I didn't have a whole lot of time to do what had to be done.

I hit his chin with the heel of my hand, forcing him backward, then straddled his belly and dropped down onto it, my knees pinning his arms and preventing him from moving. I didn't really have the time—or the strength—to waste cutting through his shields, but my guardian training under Jack had taught me some neat little tricks, and one of those was a means of preventing him from contacting his brother telepathically.

I reached out psychically, skimming his shielded thoughts, wrapping them in a field of power. It wouldn't stop Yohan from knowing something was wrong, but it sure as hell would stop Jorn from telling him the details. My tired state meant I probably wouldn't be able to hold the shield for long, but it would be long enough to do what I had to do.

And Jorn hadn't yet seemed to realize what I'd done. "You will—"

"Yeah, yeah," I cut in. "I know the song, you'll make me pay for your pain, yadda, yadda, yadda. In the meantime, you're going to answer a few little questions."

He spat. Unpleasant fellow.

I wiped the spittle from my face, then hit him. Hard. "You want to do this the hard way, we will."

"My brother will fucking kill you."

"Your brother isn't here yet."

"He's coming."

Of that I had no doubt. Once I'd cut the telepathic link between them, Yohan would have immediately turned back to see what was going on. I would have, had it been Rhoan sitting here. I hit Jorn again, smashing his nose and sending blood flying.

He swore and bucked hard, trying to dislodge me. "Your partner is *so* dead."

"You haven't got the controls, Jorn. Yohan has." It was a guess, nothing more. It was too dangerous to release him and pat him down.

"Yeah, and it's only going to take one little press—" As power surged across the shield I'd raised around his thoughts, he stopped and frowned.

The realization that he had no telepathic link to his brother had hit. His gaze jumped back to mine. "What the fuck have you done?"

I smiled benignly. "Never underestimate the powers of a guardian. And if you want to live, you'd better tell me how to disconnect that bomb."

"It won't help you. You're dead, whether you kill me or not. Yohan will get you."

"So humor me anyway. What have you got to lose?"

He smiled. It was still an arrogant and confident thing. Not believing he would die, even now. And, for the moment, he was right. I couldn't kill him just yet— not until I'd ensured the bomb unit was out of Yohan's way and my brother was safe.

"The unit is only dangerous when it's activated. Turn it off and it's as safe as can be."

"And Yohan has it?"

"Of course."

I saw the flick in his eyes. Tasted the lie.

Yohan wasn't running toward us as I'd presumed. He was running back to activate the unit.

I thrust a hand against his neck and began to squeeze, my fingers digging deep into his flesh, cutting off his breathing. Cutting off his blood supply.

"Where is the unit kept?"

"House. Safe," he gasped.

"Where in the house?"

"Trophy room," he said, voice little more than a wheeze as his face began turning an interesting shade of purple. "Far end."

I hit him then, knocking him out cold. It would have been good to kill the bastard, but I just couldn't risk Yohan getting to the controls first and taking revenge on my brother.

I rose and ran. Down the hill, through the forest, ignoring the pain in my leg and the pain in my body, my feet flying as I ducked and weaved through the trees and undergrowth. Yohan might have had a head start, but I had a vampire's speed and I was using every bit of it.

Still, the house was on the other side of the island, and even the fittest vampire can run out of breath occasionally. And I wasn't even full vampire, so I was blowing hard and dripping sweat by the time I ran down the last slope and onto the main driveway that led to what they quaintly called their lodge—a massive, sprawling series of connected buildings that was undoubtedly built from their blackmailing activities.

Something pinged near my toes before skittering away into the nearby trees. I looked up, and saw the gates and the armed guard in the security box next to it.

That bullet hadn't felt like silver, meaning they wouldn't be deadly unless they hit something vital. Not that I was intending to get shot if I could help it. Without breaking stride, I bent and scooped up a largish stone with my free hand. Bullets ripped through the air—several so close I could feel the burn of them as they passed by my arms and legs. If that guard wanted to kill me—or at least bring me down permanently— he would have been trying for torso shots. Yohan must have wanted me alive and wriggling, and that was just fine by me.

I threw the stone hard. It whirled through the air, little more than a deadly blur. If the guard had any awareness of it, he certainly didn't show it. The stone smacked into his face and blood spurted. He barely had time to howl before I was on him. I ripped the weapon free from his grip, then hit him with the barrel of Jorn's rifle. He slumped to the floor, out cold before he'd even hit it. I tugged him onto his side so that he didn't drown in his own blood, then looked around the small box until I found the gate switch, and threw it.

I bet the gates of hell itself didn't open so quietly or quickly.

I grabbed the guard's rifle, broke it open to grab the bullets, and shoved them into my pocket. It never hurt to have spares. The weapon I tossed into the forest—at least it was one less that I had to worry about.

I raised my nose and tasted the air. The tang of eucalyptus was strong, combining sharply with the salty freshness of the ocean. I couldn't hear the crash of waves, but if that scent was anything to go by, we were close to a beach. The island wasn't that big, after all, and I'd just run through the heart of it.

But Yohan's scent was absent, as was the hint of any other male's. I didn't trust that information one bit—they were here somewhere. I could "feel" them, feel their growing sense of anticipation.

They were probably setting a trap, waiting for me to walk right up to it. I might still be considered green when it came to guardian skills, but I wasn't stupid.

That anticipatory feeling was coming from directly ahead, which was where the house was. So therefore I went left, through the trees, avoiding the paths and the occasional infrared sensor. Once around the back of the house, I stopped. All the windows were closed, and I was betting the doors were locked.

I studied the walls and eaves, looking for cameras and infrareds. There were several, and I had no doubt they were active. The roof had more than a couple of loose tiles and presented a definite opportunity if I could get up there unseen. My gaze went to the trees, and I smiled. Several had long branches that overhung the roof, and I could get to them without being spotted by the cameras. Lovely.

I backed into the forest and walked back to my chosen tree. I scrambled up the trunk and then out onto the limb. It was only a short drop to the tiled roof. After that, I padded quickly and quietly to the nearest batch of loose tiles. It was easy enough to slide them aside and slip quietly into the roof cavity. From there, it was simply a matter of crawling over the ducting and wiring until I found a manhole.

What I dropped down into was a workshop that looked bigger than my whole damned apartment. There were all sorts of machines and tools here—some I could name, many I couldn't. The smell of metal and oil and stale, sweaty man was thick in the air, and my nose twitched in distaste. Obviously, whoever worked in here didn't believe in deodorant.

I padded forward, following the wall until I found a door. Pressing my ear against it revealed little. I blinked and switched to infrared. No telltale signs of body heat, either. I gripped the handle and slowly opened the door.

A wide corridor filled with shadows lay before me. The long layout of the building suggested this corridor was probably a main one. The house itself was deathly quiet. No surprise given it housed a trophy room filled with stuffed nonhumans. I just had to hope no ghosts haunted the corridor. I mightn't be able to converse with "older" spirits, but I could see them and I could feel them. And I didn't need to deal with their fury on top of everything else.

I moved forward quickly, my feet making little sound on the wood flooring. I glanced at the rooms that I passed but found nothing resembling a trophy room.

I was almost at the top end of the house—and surely near the trophy room—when I heard the footsteps. The scent of man sharpened abruptly. They were coming my way fast.

I broke into a run, moving quickly through the shadows, scanning the rooms as they flashed by. Nothing. Down the far end of the hall, a red light winked. They had sensors in this end of the house.

Damn.

The body heat of six men suddenly leapt into focus through the walls, all of them bearing weapons. I wrapped the shadows around me but kept on running. I had to find that room before they found me.

Two men rounded the corner. I raised my stolen rifle and fired without sighting. The men scattered and the shot ripped through a window, sending glass flying.

More men appeared, low and fast. I fired another shot, heard an answering retort. Felt a sting of pain as the bullet burned across my forearm and pinged away. Then, finally, I found the trophy room.

I dove for the doorway, hitting the floor chest-first, and slid several feet forward on the smooth flooring, crashing headfirst into an armchair. Behind me, the door slammed shut, and the sour scent of man spun around me.

I'd dived right into the middle of a trap.

I gripped the rifle and spun around. Yohan was standing at the door, a rifle aimed at my head in his left hand and a little silver box clenched in his right hand.

Well, *fuck*.

"I wouldn't attempt to fire that weapon," he said softly, his thumb poised over the button, "because I'd hate to kill either of you before it was absolutely necessary."

"If you had any sense," I replied, wishing I sounded less winded and a whole lot more threatening, "you'd kill me anyway. A guardian is not someone you want to be playing with. We tend to get nasty."

He smiled. It was a rather amused little smile—one that suggested little understanding and an overwhelming sense of superiority.

"My brother has felt some of your nastiness. You should be glad you didn't kill him, or else your partner would now be smeared against the walls of his cell."

Part of me wanted to snarl right back, to bare my teeth against the threats and go after him, regardless of the consequences to me. Rhoan's safety was what held me back. I wouldn't risk his life, no matter how confident I was of beating the cocky bastard in front of me.

"I didn't kill him because I intend to drag his sorry ass back to the mainland. Yours, too."

"Oh, you can try, little girl," he said, as his finger moved away from the button. "You can try."

"Okay, then." The words had barely left my lips when I raised the rifle, pressed the trigger, then flung myself forward.

My bullet hit him, smashing into his arm, flinging it backward and spraying blood and bone everywhere.

The control went flying and a shot fired out, the bullet burning past my left side.

I caught the control one-handed mid-dive, hit the floor hard, and rolled to my feet. Another shot echoed. I threw myself sideways, sliding behind a large leather sofa. It offered little protection, leather and stuffing flying as the bullet blazed through and barely missed my belly.

Yet I stayed behind the sofa, all senses straining for any hint of movement, and looked at the control.

It was a simple affair, with just an on/off button and a second red button. I switched it to off, then gripped the unit and smashed it against the floor as hard as I could. It probably wasn't the best way to get rid of a firing mechanism, but it was all I could do right then. I couldn't risk Yohan getting his hands back on it if I went down. At least Rhoan was safe. As safe as he could be until I took out Jorn and Yohan, anyway.

Another shot echoed. Stuffing and leather went flying as the bullet streaked past my nose and disappeared into the nearby wall.

I twisted around, and scrambled to the far end.

"Give it up, little guardian. You're trapped in this room. The windows are shatterproof and there are guards waiting in the hall."

"Go fuck yourself, Yohan." I rose, shot out the light with the last of my bullets, then tossed the gun to one side and dove toward the window, hitting the auto-close button.

Another shot rang out. I twisted away, but not fast enough. The bullet ripped through the fleshy part of my calf, missing bone and tendon, but tearing flesh and muscle. Pain exploded and I fell, my leg momentarily unable to support my weight.

Darkness swept into the room as the curtains closed. I pushed to my knees, barely restraining a hiss of pain as sweat popped out across my forehead.

Yohan laughed. *Laughed.*

What was it about bad guys that made them feel so superior in moments like this? Just because a quarry was down didn't mean it was out. Besides, Yohan and his psycho brother had enough respect for the capabilities of guardians to leave the UK when the Directorate started investigating their activities, so why the laughter now?

Or was it just me he didn't respect?

"Do not think the shadows will protect you, little guardian. I can smell your fear. Smell your blood."

"Humans haven't got senses that sharp," I said, wrapping the shadows around me and moving as soon as the words were out of my mouth.

It hurt—hurt bad—but nowhere near as bad as the bullet that smashed into the spot I'd just vacated would have.

"Ah, but we are the pinnacle of human development. We are what you animals strive to be."

"What's with the animals comments?" I moved position as soon as I spoke. Again he fired the rifle at the spot where I'd been. The noise was beginning to hurt my ears. "Does it make your slaughter more palatable or something?"

I moved position again, scooting around behind a desk. Despite his earlier claims, he obviously *wasn't* smelling my blood or my fear, because he was only shooting *after* I spoke.

"It was an animal that killed our father, and such animals will continue to pay for that as long as either of us live."

And if he thought he was going to live for too much longer, he was more insane than I figured. "That's a warped way of justifying murder, you know."

He took another shot, then said, "It's not murder. It's ridding the world of dangerous pests. Besides, there's nothing more magical than seeing the realization of death spark in your prey's eyes."

Definitely, certifiably crazy.

He continued, "Give this game up, guardian, and you'll get your chance in the forest. If you don't give up, I'll simply shoot you dead in whichever hole you've crawled into."

Great options. Dead now, or dead later. How generous of him. I took off my sodden tank top and wrapped it around my bleeding leg. As tourniquets went, it wasn't great, but at least it would provide a little support when I had to stand.

I reached up onto the desk and felt around. My fingers brushed against papers and pens, then finally hit something more solid. A stapler. I gripped it lightly, then carefully rose to my feet.

Pain bloomed, roaring up my leg. I gritted my teeth against the urge to scream, and forced myself to breathe deeply and softly. Sweat rolled down my cheeks and my back, and my stomach rolled threateningly.

I tried to ignore it all, and threw the stapler across the room. It hit the wall and fell to the floor with a clatter. Almost instantly, Yohan fired, the flash of the gun a flame in my infrared vision.

I ran at him, as hard and as fast as I could. He heard my steps, but he barely had time to react before I was on him, grabbing the weapon with one hand and breaking his arm with my other, making it impossible for him to hold a weapon, let alone fire one.

He went down, screaming for help.

Whiny, little coward . . .

The door opened. I flipped up the rifle and fired without sighting. One man went down, his gut exploding. Two of his colleagues leapt over him, coming at me. I fired again, hitting one and missing the other.

That one ducked to one side and raised his gun. But despite the light seeping in from the hallway, the shadows still covered me, and he hesitated, confusion on his face.

"Shoot her, shoot her," Yohan screamed. "She's here somewhere. Just bloody shoot."

Other men were coming into the room now, preventing the first man from simply firing at random. I pivoted on my wounded leg, hissing in pain as I hit the nearest guard in the chest, pushing him backward into another. They both went sprawling.

I shifted position, this time moving as silently as I could, and came up behind the door. With the benefit of infrared, I could see two more men entering. They were the last of the reinforcements—at least for the moment.

I gripped the door handle, waiting until they were closer, then slammed the door closed hard, sending them reeling backward. Then I was diving away as the sound of several gunshots roared, echoing in my ears.

I hit the ground and rolled to my feet, only to go down on one knee as my leg gave way yet again. I gritted my teeth against the scream rolling up my throat, my fists clenched, my nails digging into the heel of my hand in an effort to deflect the pain. It was tempting to shift shape and begin the healing process, but shifting wasn't instantaneous, nor was it discreet. And I wasn't entirely sure the shadows would cover the change.

I scrambled away and heard the footsteps behind me. I'd taken two men out, but there were still two guards left in the room and two men out of it. Time to get serious.

I pushed to my feet, spun, and lashed out with a still-clenched fist at the nearest man. He went down like a ton of bricks. I dove forward, grabbed his gun, and twisted, firing at the other man. He, too, went down.

"If you want to live," I shouted to the two remaining men in the hall, "I suggest you get the fuck away from this place."

There was a moment's silence, then the sound of footsteps retreating. Wise men.

I rose, hobbled over to the nearest window, and hit the nearby button. The curtains swept open, tearing the shadows from my side and revealing the contents of the room in all its grisly glory. Not just the bloody remains of the men I'd downed or killed, but the remains on the walls.

Jorn and Yohan's trophies.

I'd been expecting to see the three missing Australians, as well as the seventeen from the UK, but there were more here than that. Dozens more. All mounted on wood like animal trophies of old. All posed smiling and happy. All so lifelike, as if at any moment they would tear themselves free and step from the wall, whole in body and soul.

And all with a hint of terror and fear lingering in their glassy eyes, as if their souls still abided nearby, waiting for help that never came.

My stomach roiled, and it was all I could do not to throw up. I'd seen some pretty damn gruesome things in my time, but somehow, this seemed far worse than anything else. These two had been taking their revenge for their father's death for years and years. And in the process, had killed well over fifty women.

I turned and looked at Yohan. I don't know what he saw in my eyes, but his face twisted in fear and he pushed backward with his legs, as if trying to get away from me. He slid on the flooring, but not very far.

"I'm human. I demand my time in court," he screamed, spittle spraying from his lips. "You can't shoot me."

"That would work if I actually cared. But I don't."

I raised the gun and shot him, splattering his brains out the back of his head and across the floor.

It was easy. So easy.

Seemed I was more of a guardian—more like my brother—than I'd ever wanted to believe.

And right now, looking at their trophies on the wall, I didn't damn well care.

I shifted shape to start healing my wounds, then threw the gun on Yohan's remains and walked out of the room to find Rhoan before Jorn could.

Chapter 14

Rhoan took care of Jorn while I rang Jack from one of the phones in the house. He'd actually had a team out looking for us, having realized something was wrong when both of us failed to report in. It might be normal for me not to, but Rhoan always did. He was the good twin when it came to that sort of stuff.

It took a good six hours for Jack's cleanup team to get to the island, because, as I'd suspected, we'd been shipped up to the twin's privately owned island off the Brisbane coast. The blackmailing business was obviously a well-paying one.

While Rhoan waited down near the dock for the boat, I went searching for our IDs and wallets. I not only found them, but Adrienne's soul as well. She was waiting in the back of the house, close to a huge walk-in freezer where her body undoubtedly was. I didn't go check. I had no need to see her flesh when her spirit was standing right in front of me.

You seem familiar, she said, her words running through my mind, as ethereal as her body, which merely hinted at red hair and gray eyes, and little else.

And yet there was a strength in her, a surety in her words, that I'd not found with other spirits. Especially other spirits who'd been dead for a while. Generally when I saw the older spirits, they were little more than wisps who had no shape and who could form no words. I wondered if it had anything to do with the psychic gifts she had in life, or perhaps even the fact that she'd known her death was coming, and had been prepared for it.

We share the same pack. I'm Riley.

My reply was somewhat reluctant. There was nothing to be gained by talking to her now, because there was nothing that I could do to help her. We'd stopped her killers and found her remains, so that she'd be scattered on home soil and her soul could rest in peace.

So why was she still here? What was keeping her bound to this earth?

Ah. I remember. My grandfather disliked you.

To put it mildly. *Yes.*

He sent you to rescue me?

He did. I didn't make it in time, though. I'm sorry.

She smiled, though it was a warmth that washed across the air more than any real facial movement in the mist that was her body. *Sometimes fate will not be derailed.*

Very true. I hesitated. *Is there something you would like me to do for you?*

Tell Jodie I'm sorry. Tell her that I loved her, no matter how often it seemed that work was more important. She hesitated. *And tell her not to join me too soon. She has a long, good life yet to lead.*

If Jodie had her way, she'd be joining Adrienne in the afterlife as soon as possible. But perhaps Adrienne's words would give her the courage to go on in this life. *Can do.*

And make sure my father obeys my will. Jodie is to have what is mine. Promise me you'll make him give her what she's due.

The grin that split my lips was decidedly nasty. I wondered if she would understand why. Wondered if she could even see it. *I promise they won't cheat Jodie out of a cent.*

She sighed, and it was a sound filled with relief. *Thank you.*

Her words hung on the air as her image began to fade. Obviously, that had been the reason she'd been clinging to this existence. She'd wanted to take care of her lover.

Nice to know that love lingered even in the afterlife.

"Be happy, wherever you're going, Adrienne," I said, oddly wishing that I'd known her better. I had a feeling that she and I would have gotten along just fine.

Which was odd really, considering my overall hatred for her whole damn family. But then, I guess she'd been an outsider, just like me. Only her fault was her sexuality, not her parentage.

I left the room and the fading warmth of her presence, and went down to the dock to wait for the team with my brother.

It was another six hours before we finally stepped out of the terminal at Tullamarine. As Rhoan waved down a cab, I sucked in the cool evening air and felt an odd sense of peace run through me. Cold or not, this was home, and it felt good to be here.

It would feel even better once I had Kellen's arms

around me. But before I could go to him, I had a promise to fulfill. To do that, I needed to go back to the Directorate and start investigating. Threats wouldn't bring Blake to heel. He'd lived with violence all his life, and it held no fear for him. Blackmail was a different story. And the pup who had listened unnoticed at too many doors knew more than a few pack secrets. Now that my grandfather was dead, I had no reason not to use them.

The long shadows of night were creeping in as I walked up Miller Street, heading toward Brighton Beach. Houses worth more than I could ever imagine loomed around me, but my gaze barely left the main prize—a modern brick-and-glass house at the far end of the street.

Blake was inside. So were Patrin and Kye. The pack didn't actually own the house. According to the records we'd found, it belonged to a judge who just happened to be one of Blake's buddies. He was currently overseas on holidays, and had given Blake the run of his "beach hut." I was betting he was also the reason Blake had gotten his hands on all the police files he'd sent to me.

"Okay, we're set," Rhoan said into my ear. "Liander's wired into the security systems, and he'll switch off all alarms and sensors at seven forty-five."

I glanced at my watch. Five minutes to go. Perfect. "And positioning?"

"According to the infrared, we have two people on the ground floor, and two in the first-floor living area."

Meaning the first-floor bedroom was free—exactly what I needed. I shifted my arm and let the thin white rope slide from my shoulder to my hand. The claw-

hook was hanging out of my back pocket. I got it and
began attaching it to the end of the rope. "So Kye and
an unknown are keeping watch downstairs, and Blake
and Patrin are upstairs."

"I do so like it when a plan comes together."

I smiled. "Have fun inside, brother."

"You can bet on it."

I stopped in the shadows of a wattle tree one house
down from Blake's, and scanned the area. No one was
around, and none of the four men were visible through
the windows of their house. Not that they'd see me once
I wrapped the night around me.

I glanced at my watch again. Two minutes to go. I
waited in the shadows, excitement and the bitter need
to get revenge pulsing through me. When the minute
hand finally clicked onto seven forty-five, I pulled the
shadows around me, then leapt the fence and raced
across the well-manicured garden, around to the bedroom balcony. One neat toss had the rope and hook
over the balcony wall. I tested that it had snagged properly, then quickly climbed.

The balcony doors weren't locked. Kye and his friend
were obviously relying on the no-longer-working sensors and alarms to warn of intruders. I slipped through
the doors and padded across the huge white-on-white
bedroom. According to the floor plans we'd found, there
was a parent retreat beyond the main bedroom, with
the main living areas beyond that. I carefully opened the
bedroom door and peered out. The retreat room was
shadowed, but the door at the end was open, allowing a
good glimpse of the main rooms beyond it. Patrin was
sitting in a lounge chair, reading the *Age*. Blake wasn't
immediately in sight, but infrared told me he was sitting
at the dining table, doing paperwork.

I slipped out the door and raced across the room. The lights tore the shadows away from me the minute I entered the living room, but I was moving so fast they never had a chance to see me anyway. I grabbed Patrin by the scruff of the neck and hauled him upright. He barely had time to yelp a warning before I'd grabbed Blake, yanked him off his chair, and threw him across the room. As he bounced off a wall and slithered awkwardly to the floor, I switched my grip on Patrin, thrusting upward by the neck until his feet were off the floor. He was a big man and it took a lot of effort, but the sheer look of terror on his face made it all worthwhile.

"Consider this my final progress report, as well as a little warning," I said, as Blake picked himself up off the ground. "We've found Adrienne's body, and we've taken care of the men who killed her. Now I want you out of my life forever."

"There's no need for—"

I cut him off. "Oh, there's every fucking need."

I dropped Patrin a little, then heaved him with all my strength, throwing him across the dining table. He didn't quite clear it, his butt and legs getting entangled in the chairs, sending both him and the chairs crashing to the floor. He yelped but didn't move, and the scent of his fear was a wonderful thing.

I stalked forward to Blake. He didn't back away, didn't move, and the look of contempt hadn't shifted from his face. "The threat of violence doesn't worry me."

"Good," I said, stopping several feet away from him. "Because I have no intention of hitting you. I will, however, destroy you and your whole family if you do not leave my mother alone, or if you contest, in any way, Adrienne's will."

He blinked, surprise briefly moving the contempt. "Why would you care about Adrienne's will?"

"Because she asked me to care."

"What?"

I smiled coldly. "The pack trait of clairvoyance didn't only go strange in Adrienne. I can speak to the dead. I spoke to her."

"Even if I choose to believe that, what I or my family choose to do in regard to Adrienne's will is none of your business."

"Adrienne made it my business." I stepped forward, until I was all but standing on his toes. This close, I could feel his body vibrating with the force of his anger, and part of me wished he'd just let it go. Give me an excuse to hit him. "I've done a little investigating of my own, Blake. Does the name Petri Constructions ring any bells inside that thick head of yours?"

Wariness flickered through his eyes. "Of course. It is a building firm the pack owns and runs."

Sound whispered behind me. "Take one more step, Patrin, and I'll throw you off the balcony." He stopped. I smiled benignly at Blake and said, "Petri Constructions was a successful business concern that belonged to one Shawn Davis, a friend of yours from way back. When he died—of apparently natural causes— his will surprisingly left the construction company to you rather than his pack and family."

"So?"

"So, as I said, I've done a little digging. I found his grave and talked to his soul." Which was my first lie, but Blake was never going to know that. "Seems things surrounding Davis's death and will aren't quite as straightforward as they appeared. It also seems that it took the disappearance of one Michael Davis from the Davis red pack to stop them contesting the will." I grabbed his collar and dragged his face down to mine. "I will destroy you, Blake, if you do not leave my mother alone, or if you contest Adrienne's will. Destroy you, and ensure you and your whole damn get live in poverty and disgrace for the rest of your lives. And I will love every single fucking minute of it."

I threw him back, suddenly needing to rid his scent from my nostrils. He hit the wall with a grunt, and flung out an arm to brace himself.

"Do you believe me?" I said softly.

"Yes," he replied, his voice filled with murderous fury. Fury he knew he couldn't unleash. And that was such a delicious sensation.

I glanced at Patrin, then said, "Rhoan, all finished up here. Meet you out front." I looked back at Blake. "And don't think about enlisting your cop or judge buddies to help you out of this situation. They're going to have enough problems of their own."

He didn't say anything. Didn't do anything. He couldn't, and he knew it. It was sweeter, so much sweeter, than using my fists as I had so often dreamed of doing.

I gave him a smile, then turned and walked across to the balcony. The leap down to the ground jarred my leg, but I refused to limp as Rhoan joined me and we walked away.

As soon as I got home, I rang Kellen. I desperately wanted to see him now that everything else had been sorted out. I wanted to tell him my news, my decision. Get my new life—*our* new life—under way.

My fingers were shaking as I pressed his number. It rang several times, and then a voice said, "Yes?"

For several beats I wasn't entirely sure it was him. His voice sounded rough, tired almost beyond recognition.

"Kellen? It's Riley."

"You're home?"

"Yes. Do you want to meet somewhere, or would you rather I come over to your place?"

"I'll come to you," he said, then hung up.

I frowned down at the phone for several seconds, not quite believing that he'd hung up on me. He wasn't usually so abrupt, but maybe it was just the tiredness. He'd sounded like hell, so maybe work had been a pain in the ass again.

"Everything okay?" Rhoan asked, one eyebrow raised.

"Yeah." He was coming to see me, and that was all I had to worry about for the moment. "What are your plans for the evening?"

"I'll shower, change, then head over to Liander's. He'll be wanting to kiss my war wounds better."

I snorted. "You hardly have a damn scratch on you."

"I have a bump on the head."

"Hardly worth sympathy."

"You're just jealous of my beautiful, unmarred skin."

This from the man who had almost as many scars as I did. "Totally," I said dryly.

He grinned and gave me a hug. "Being a guardian is so much more fun now that you're one of us."

"Being a guardian is many things, but I wouldn't say a fun time was one of them."

"Depends on your definition of fun, doesn't it?"

"Well, getting shot and blowing away bad guys is not mine." I paused, feeling the lie in my words but still not wanting to acknowledge it. Dammit, I *wasn't* my brother. I wouldn't enjoy my job. I *wouldn't*. "The only guys I want to blow are sexy *good* guys, and only in a sexual sense."

Not that *that* was a thrill I'd be pursuing anytime soon with anyone *other* than Kellen. And while there was a part of me that was sad over that, mostly I was just happy to be pursuing a long-held dream with someone I cared about, and who cared for me.

It might not work out in the end, I knew that, but at least I was here, taking the chance instead of skipping away from it.

The cab finally pulled up at the front of our apartment building. Rhoan paid the driver with his credit card while I raced upstairs to get first dibs on the shower and the hot water.

Once clean, and with coffee and chocolate in hand, I sat down on the sofa to wait for Kellen. My brother showered and then headed out, leaving me alone to a silence that seemed filled with expectations. Thankfully, it wasn't all that long before Kellen's footsteps echoed in the hall and his rich, warm scent drifted on the air.

I walked over to the door and opened it. He looked good, despite the tiredness etched deep in his face, and my heart did this happy little dance.

"Hey," I said, a smile splitting my lips. "Nice to see you again."

"And it's a damn relief to see you." He stepped

through the door and wrapped his arms around me, holding me so tight it was difficult to breathe.

And I didn't care one little bit. It felt so good, so safe, so right. Like all my troubles, all my worries, just faded away under the warm security of his touch.

"Would you like a coffee?" I said into his shoulder, not wanting to move and yet knowing we couldn't stay in the doorway forever. "And I'll tell you what happened."

He pulled away slightly, and there was something in his eyes, an intensity that I'd never seen before, that made me oddly nervous.

"The coffee can wait. And I know what happened."

I arched an eyebrow at the edge in his voice. "Jack contacted you?"

"Jack or the Directorate didn't tell me squat."

Confusion swirled, and right in amongst it, apprehension stirred. "Then how do you know what happened?"

"Because it's what always happens. Your job got messy and you totally forgot about the other people in your life while you were dealing with it."

Ouch.

But at least his comment explained the reason for the edge in his voice and the anger in his eyes. "I was supposed to meet you for lunch, wasn't I?"

"Yeah." He gripped my arm and led me over to the sofa. "But as usual, I wasn't first in your thoughts."

"That's not true—"

"It's been true from the word go," he said grimly. "I've just done my best to ignore the fact until now."

He sat me down, then sat down on the sofa opposite. "We need to talk. Here and now."

"I agree."

He raised an eyebrow. "You do?"

"Yes. Because I've come to a decision."

"And what might that be?"

He said it in an angry, resigned sort of way that made my heart ache. He was expecting the worst, and that was my fault, because I'd never really given him anything more of myself than a few weeks away together. Every time he'd asked me for more, I'd asked for more time. I kept saying I wanted a relationship, but every time he tried to pin me down, I'd made up excuses or reasons as to why I couldn't.

Well, not anymore.

"I want to make the commitment and go solo with you. I want to see if this thing between us is real or not."

He stared at me for a moment, the intensity in his eyes sharpening. And suddenly there were butterflies in my stomach and my heart was doing a crazy sick dance.

Because something was *wrong*.

He wasn't reacting in the way I'd expected at all. There was no joy, no relief, nothing. No damn reaction at all. He just sat there, looking at me, with that odd intensity in his eyes and a tautness around his mouth.

"Say something," I said softly. Pleadingly.

"That's great."

But it was mechanically said, with no warmth or feeling behind it. And yet the air was sharp with tension, and his green eyes fairly burned with emotion. What exactly that emotion was I couldn't say, because it seemed a mess of anger, desire, determination, and God knows what else.

It frightened me, as his response to my words was frightening me.

What was going on?

Why was he doing this, reacting like this, when he'd finally heard the words he'd been pressing me to say for weeks?

I didn't understand it, but I feared it.

God how I feared it.

I crossed my arms and leaned forward on my knees, my hands clenched out of his sight. "What's wrong?"

"Nothing," he said abruptly, then sighed and ran a hand through his thick, dark hair. "And everything."

"That doesn't tell me a whole lot," I said, and this time there was a touch of anger in my voice. But its source was the fear. The concern over the way he was reacting.

He looked at me for a moment, then shook his head. "You really *don't* see the problem, do you?"

"If I did, I wouldn't be sitting here feeling so sick to my stomach. I'd be trying to fix whatever it is."

He leaned forward and pulled a hand free from under my arm, wrapping his fingers around mine. His skin was warm compared to mine, his touch strong and steady. "Why didn't you ring me when you couldn't make lunch?"

Exasperation ran through me. An exasperation wrapped in anger, and it made my voice sharp. Or maybe that was the fear twisting deep inside. "Because a psycho knocked me out and kidnapped me."

"So why didn't you ring me when you were free?"

"Because there was still stuff to do, things that needed cleaning up."

"So they were all more important than making a simple phone call?"

"I just wanted it all over so I could concentrate on you." *You and me.* I bit my lip and blinked.

Dammit, I would *not* cry.

I wouldn't.

Not until I was sure there was something to cry about.

He caressed my wrist with a gentle finger. As warm and as good as his touch was, it only succeeded in stirring the butterflies in my stomach to an even greater frenzy.

"As I said before, I'm never first in your thoughts, Riley. I'm never the one you turn to, never the one you share hurt, or pain, or dreams with. I care for you—care for you a lot—but I'm beginning to doubt the feeling is returned."

"Which is why we go solo—to discover if this is the real, soul mate deal, or just another good thing not meant to last."

"But I can't go solo as things stand. The last few days have proven that."

Maybe I was dense. Maybe the last few days had been tougher than I'd thought, because he was confusing the hell out me. And yet I had a feeling that *he* thought it should have been all so perfectly clear. "What do you mean?"

He smiled, and it was a tired smile, a smile filled with sadness. "I'm an alpha, remember? As I keep reminding you, it is in my nature to want to protect all that is mine. But there can never be any protecting you. Not with your job."

"I'm not expecting—"

"I know, and that's not my point." He hesitated, then added more softly, "Do you know what it is like, being left behind? Knowing that you're in danger, that at any second you could be killed, and that there's nothing, absolutely nothing, I can do to help you?"

I touched his cheek lightly. He didn't lean into it,

didn't react in any way. It seemed he was holding more than the emotion in his words in check.

"But I'm here, I'm safe," I said, after a moment.

"And one day, you might not be here, might not be safe." He squeezed my hand, then released me and sat back. Moving away from my touch. And I felt sick, so sick, that bile rose up my throat and I had to swallow heavily.

"I can't live like that, Riley. It's just not in my nature."

"But—"

"The only way we could work is if you give up your job. Otherwise, there's just no way we could last."

"I can't—" The words came out an agonized cry. Of all the things I wanted in this world, that had to be second in line, right after a family of my own. I'd *love* to give up my job as a guardian, and just be another wolf working for the Directorate. Like I had been, before Talon and Misha and their psycho brother had come into my life.

But with the drug in my system starting to make huge changes, I dared not walk away, even if I could. Who knew what was yet to come?

I couldn't handle it alone. Couldn't rely on Rhoan. We simply didn't have the resources to monitor what was going on in my body.

"Can't, or won't?" he said, harshly.

"Dammit, Kellen, this is unfair!" I thrust to my feet and began pacing. "You've asked for a commitment, and now that I'm ready for that, you're backing away and saying we can't work. Where is the justice in that?"

"There's no justice, just honesty, which in this case is more important."

He stood and walked up behind me. But I stepped away from his touch, unwilling to feel the familiar warmth of his arms. Control was tenuous enough as it was. I might just lose it if he held me tenderly while in the middle of breaking up with me.

He dropped his hands to his side, then added, "I can't help what I am any more than you can. I don't want to make this decision, Riley, honestly I don't. But I can't spend a lifetime waiting at home for you. Wondering if this time will be the time that you *don't* come home. I believe we could be good together, but I want the whole white picket fence ideal, and that just doesn't include a soul mate who risks her life and our happiness on a daily basis."

I wrapped my arms around my body and just looked at him. I was shaking, shivering, because suddenly there was no warmth in the room. Or maybe it was because my future suddenly seemed as bleak and as lonely as it had in the worst of my dreams.

Why do this now? I wanted to scream. *You knew what I was, you knew about my job. Why do this when I'd finally decided to take that step, to take a chance?*

But I kept the rage and frustration and hurt inside, and didn't do or say anything.

Because deep down I understood.

I mightn't like his words, might hate his actions, but the truth was, I understood them. I wouldn't want to be committed to someone whose job was so dangerous that I knew one day he simply wouldn't come home. That one day, I'd feel his death and know my life and my heart had just turned to ashes.

It was a big thing to ask of anyone.

Cops and firemen knew all about it. They had the

highest percentages of divorce and relationship breakdowns for good reason.

Even so, I couldn't help saying, "Don't do this." *Please don't do this.*

He sighed. "I'm sorry, Riley, I really am. But the last few days have really brought home just what life with you will be like if you don't give up work. And I'd rather live without you than live with that."

My eyes were stinging, my body shaking, and my heart seemed to be just aching deep in my chest. And I couldn't think of anything to say, because there *was* nothing to say. His mind was made up, and nothing short of me quitting my job was going to change that.

I should have let myself smash down on the rocks. It would have hurt a whole lot less.

I took a deep, shuddering breath, then said, "Go. Just go."

"Riley—"

"No," I said. Forcefully, flatly. "No more. There's nothing else you can say or do to make this any better."

He stared at me for several seconds, an aching, angry heat I could feel more than see, then turned on his heels and walked out.

As the door clicked shut, the tears came. Great, sobbing gasps of pain that came from deep within, from the place that had held so many dreams.

Dreams that now lay shattered and broken on the ground.

Just like my heart.

About the Author

KERI ARTHUR received a "Perfect 10" from *Romance Reviews Today* and was nominated for Best Shape-shifter in *PNR*'s PEARL Awards and in the Best Contemporary Paranormal category of the Romantic Times Reviewers' Choice Awards. She lives with her husband and daughter in Melbourne, Australia.

Destiny Kills

On sale February 2008

Some things I remember.

Some things I can't.

Like who I am.

Or how come I'm sitting here naked on a beach next to a dead man.

And yet I know *why* I'm here. I'm waiting for the dawn, to give him a final kiss good-bye before she guides his soul onto its next life.

The breeze that curls around me is cold, as cold as the surrounding sand is harsh. And yet these sensations are a fleeting thing. Goose bumps might tremble across my skin, and sand might grate against my buttocks and thighs, but both fail to register on anything more than a flesh level. I feel no cold, no pain, no sorrow.

Nothing.

It's as if I'm dead inside. As dead as the man lying beside me. Yet, for some reason, I'm still breathing and he isn't.

Why?

It's a question that haunts me, teasing the frozen edges of my thoughts and memories.

Why him and not me?

I don't know, I just don't know, and yet I know it's a question that's important. I know my life might well depend on the answer.

I drew my knees close to my chest and studied the distant horizon. Though dawn was yet to stain night's cover, it was coming. Already its warm power vibrated across the air, an eager humming that was both familiar and alien. I didn't understand the sensation, didn't know the reason behind it, and yet the mere fact I could feel it had relief sweeping through me.

It was frustrating, this not knowing. Not remembering.

I let my gaze move across the ocean, watching the waves roll lazily toward the sand, seeing nothing out there in that vast expanse of white-capped blueness. No ship. No boat. No pursuit.

But I didn't bother questioning why I was expecting any of those things because the past remained locked under a blanket that was almost absolute.

Almost.

I rubbed a hand across eyes that felt like they'd cried a thousand tears, then glanced down at the body of my friend. I might not remember my own name, but I knew his. Egan Jamieson. Not only my friend, but also my guardian, my lover, and a man to whom I owed a debt more important than life itself.

He'd saved me.

He'd given me freedom at the cost of his own.

The need for revenge welled deep and fast and furious, until I was all but shaking with it. They would pay for this. Whoever they were, they would pay.

For Egan.

For all of us.

A vow that was useless unless I could damn well remember who, exactly, I needed to take revenge upon.

I grimaced and returned my gaze to Egan. In the fading moonlight, his skin seemed to glow with a rich warmth, as if the sun itself still burned beneath his flesh. A birthmark marred his back, a snakelike stain that seemed to dive into his skin and out again, until it almost coiled around his spine. In the night, it took on a reddish-gold appearance and contained a sheen oddly reminiscent of scales.

I shifted, and ran a gentle finger down the mark. It was cool and leathery compared to his skin, as if it were indeed scales. In life, he'd never let me touch the mark he hated. It was a mark that had cost him dearly, he'd once said, but had never explained why or how.

Oddly enough, I'd never felt anything but pride about my own mark, which was similar to his in every way except color. Mine was all blues and greens and silvers, as if the brightness of a sunlit sea danced upon the surface of my skin. An inheritance from my mother, not my father.

I blinked at the thought, then grabbed it hard and tried to follow it back. But the fog of forgetfulness snapped in place, and all that was left were questions.

Yet more fucking questions.

I blew out a breath, then stretched out my left leg as the throb of pain finally began to impinge on my senses. There were scrapes across my kneecaps, and deeper cuts down my shins, cuts accompanied by darkening patches that indicated bruising. But none of the wounds were currently bleeding, and there was no blood dried against my skin.

I glanced at the sea. No footprints marred the pristine sands. Not for as far as I could see. Nor were there vehicle tracks of any kind. Though I guess with the tide coming in, none of that was really surprising.

But still, I had a feeling we'd come from the sea, that my skin bore no stain of blood because it had long since been washed away. That the wounds themselves were clean rather than festering, because of the saltwater.

I let my gaze follow the gentle curve of the beach until it reached the distance point. No lighthouse, no buildings, no indication of movement or life. Nothing to say where we were.

Maybe we were both dead. Maybe this was nothing more than the dream of waiting that came before the soul moved on to the next life.

I again glanced down at Egan. I knew if I rolled him off his stomach, I'd see the bloody stain in the sand. See what remained of his chest after those bastards had shot him.

I closed my eyes and pushed the resulting images away. There were some things I didn't *want* to remember, and the bloody mess of his chest—the way he'd struggled to survive, to remain free—was one of them.

And yet, while he might have fought them to the very end, he'd done it for my sake. He'd once said that for all intents and purposes, he was dead to the outside world, so why did anything matter? That had made no sense to me at the time, and even less so now, when he'd given his life for it.

The hum in the air intensified. Energy danced across my skin, a crazy tingling that warmed the chill from my soul. I watched the horizon, waiting, as the hum of power reached a crescendo and slivers of red and gold suddenly broke across the sky. Warmth began to flood through my body, as if the rising of the dawn was also a rebirth of my emotional and sensory centers. A stupid thought, really, when I was just at home in deep, dark waters that had never seen the sun, never known warmth.

God, it was so damn *frustrating* getting little snippets and hints here and there, but never any real, definitive answers or memories.

I drew my knees close again, ignoring the slivers of pain and the blood that began to trickle down one leg, watching as the sunlight spread, smothering the stars and warming the night from the sky.

Watching as the growing light gradually flushed across Egan's unmoving body.

The warmth still radiating under his skin seemed to stir as the daylight caressed him, growing brighter as the day did, until the intensity made my eyes water and forced me to look away.

Still the heat and the brightness grew, until my own skin glowed under its radiance. But flesh was not designed to contain such heated iridescence for long, especially when that skin no longer belonged to a living, breathing soul. As the light broke free, reaching skyward with exuberant fingers, tears began to trickle down my cheeks.

"May the Gods of sun and sea and lake guide you on your journey, my friend," I whispered, my voice croaky, hinting at long disuse. "And may you find in the next life what you could not in this."

Then the radiance caressing my skin began to die, taking with it the underlying hum of energy. Day had broken. It was only those in-between times—first light or twilight—that held the great moments of power.

There was nothing left of Egan. Nothing except the stain of blood on the sand and an odd glint of silver. His ring.

I reached out and carefully plucked it free from its resting place. In the growing sunlight, the rubies glinting in the coiled serpent's eyes glowed like fire. It had always sent a shiver down my spine, this ring, despite the obvious workmanship and beauty.

When I'd asked him about it, Egan's golden eyes had grown somber. "It belongs to a path that was mine, one taken forcibly from me," he'd said, and in his normally calm tone there'd been an undercurrent that was an odd mix of anger and resignation. "But one day, maybe you could help me return this ring to the man to whom it truly belongs."

I'd always gotten the feeling that the task would not be a pleasant one.

I closed my fingers around the serpent, pressing the cold metal into my palm. I might not be able to do anything else for Egan, but I could do this. Find the ring's owner and return it. And perhaps along the way, discover its history and the reasons why Egan had had murder on his mind.

Because it was an odd desire for a man who claimed nothing mattered anymore.

I pushed upright. A dozen different aches came to life, and weakness trembled through my limbs. The sort of weakness that came from long hours of constant activity. My gaze went to the ocean, leaping across the waves to the distant horizon.

Somewhere out there laid the answers.

Somewhere out there laid my home.

But until the fog encasing my memories cleared, I could not blindly walk out into the sea and just start swimming. The ocean was a vast and often angry being, and I could not tempt her waters without a destination in mind.

It was a thought that raised my eyebrows. I might not be dead, but madness was surely a possibility. I mean, what sane rational mind contemplated swimming *oceans*?

I did.

Because I could. Because I had.

I rubbed my forehead wearily, aware for the first time of the slight ache behind my eyes. Maybe when it passed, my memories would fully return. Maybe then I'd know what sort of creature contemplated swimming the oceans as easily as a bird might fly.

Because whatever I was, it wasn't human. That was a certainty I felt deep in my bones, deep in my soul.

But until memory resurfaced, one thing was certain. I couldn't stand here naked and exposed on a beach. The mere fact that someone had blown a hole through Egan's chest suggested someone would rather see us dead than free. And that, in turn, meant they'd surely be looking for me.

I turned around. Rugged cliffs ranged high above the pristine sands, lining and isolating the long sweep of beach. There were tracks—paths made by the passage of feet over time, meaning this place, wherever it was, was at least reachable. Which meant there surely had to be some sort of city or town, or at least a dwelling, nearby.

The first thing I needed was clothing, simply because the last thing I needed was to attract attention.

I glanced over my shoulder, studying the rolling waves for a moment, then resolutely made my way to the cliffs and the nearest track.

No one but goddamn goats had been using *that* particular track, let me tell you.

I was sweating, shaking, and wheezing by the time I finally got to the top. I leaned my hands on my aching knees, sucking in great gulps of air as I studied the surrounding countryside.

The slope rolled down to a small cottage. The area around the cottage wasn't fenced, and a blue car sat out in front, indicating someone was home. Beyond the house, the slope rose again, and the tops of pine trees were evident beyond it.

I glanced back at the house. The cottage didn't look big enough to be a permanent residence, so maybe it was one of those places vacationers rented out short term. I hoped so, because vacationers were more likely to go out for the day, leaving their possessions—or, more particularly, their clothes—unprotected.

Of course, to steal their clothes, I first had to get there. Right now, collapsing in a heap seemed a much better option.

I blew out a breath and forced my feet down the grassy slope. My legs protested the activity, and warmth began to trickle not only down my shin, but the side of my face as well. I swiped at it with a hand, and it came away bloody.

Maybe Egan wasn't the only one who'd sustained serious injury. And a decent blow to the head would certainly explain the gaps in my memory.

I rubbed my hand down my thigh and kept on walking. What else could I do? I was in the middle of goddamn nowhere, with no idea who I was or how I'd gotten here. And no idea who I could trust. *If* I could trust.

As the slope flattened out, the grass became long enough to brush my butt, which in turn made me wonder if the grass was actually long, or I was short. I *felt* long—long and rangy—but self-perception is an odd thing when the memory can give no references. I held my hands out and studied them critically.

Dirt-covered as they were from scrambling up the goat track, they were still somewhat elegant—all long and slender. Neither my fingers nor my palms had calluses of any kind, so I obviously didn't do anything too strenuous for a living. A fact backed up by the length of my nails—or at least what remained of them after the climb.

I glanced down at my feet. There was nothing elegant about *those*. Given their length and width, they could only be described as paddles. Getting shoes would be hell.

The thought intrigued me for some reason and I stopped to lift a foot. Thick, hardened soles. Obviously, I didn't wear shoes all that often, if *that* foot was anything to go by.

A door slammed, and laughter ran across the meadow. I dropped to my knees, my bruised left leg hitting a rock and making me wince. Two people emerged from the cottage, the woman still laughing and touching her companion. Newlyweds, I thought for no particular reason.

They climbed into the blue car sitting in the driveway, the man opening and closing the door for the woman before getting into the driver's side and driving off.

On the right-hand side of the road. And though three-quarters of the world drove on the right-hand side of the road, I was suddenly sure that I was in America. Which in itself wasn't much help, because America was a damn big country, but at least it was a starting point.

Thanking the fact that luck seemed to be on my side this morning, I waited until they were out of sight before rising and making my way quickly toward the house.

The front door was locked, as was the back. But a window along the side was open enough to slide a hand in and push off the screen. After that, it was a simple matter of pushing up the window and sliding in.

Which I did. I hit the floor with an awkward thump

and sat there listening, waiting to see if anyone else was in the house. Which is something I should have done *before* I started breaking in.

Obviously, I could cross "thief" off my list of possible past professions. Unless, of course, I was a very bad thief.

The only sound to be heard was the soft ticking of a clock. The air was still, and smelled faintly of age and lavender. This particular room had been made up as a bedroom, but the bed was single and obviously unused. Which probably meant I wouldn't find anything in the wardrobe or small dresser. I checked them anyway. Nothing but mothballs.

I walked to the door, my footsteps echoing noisily on the polished floorboards. The room directly opposite was a bathroom, complete with an old claw-foot bath and a shower big enough for two. The main bedroom sat to my right, and the kitchen to my left down the end of the hall.

I glanced back at the bathroom, eyeing the shower and wondering how much time I had. Surely enough to get cleaned up? I could no more run around looking like something the sea had coughed up than I could run around naked. Not if I wanted to avoid detection.

Besides, I might not have noticed the bite of the sand when I was sitting on it, but I sure as hell did now, and it was *nasty*.

"Stop with the excuses," I muttered, even as I wondered if dithering was a habit of mine.

I marched into the bathroom. After a quick hot shower that seemed to uncover a dozen more cuts and bruises, I toweled myself dry, then moved across to the mirror.

It was an odd feeling, seeing a face I knew was mine, and yet having no memories to correlate to the fact.

My face was lean and angular, with a nose that was almost too big and a mouth that looked prone to dimples. My eyes were the green of a deep ocean, framed by long lashes that were as black as my hair. Under the bright bathroom light, highlights of dark green and blue seemed to play through the black, as if the sea itself had kissed it.

My gaze moved to the massive black-and-purple bruise smeared from my temple to my cheek. Someone had hit me *really* hard. Hard enough to split my skull open. The bruise, and the healing three-inch gash on my head, proved that. It could also explain why my memory was working in fits and starts.

That explained the memory loss. But still . . . What on earth had I done to deserve such treatment?

For the first time since waking on the beach beside Egan, I felt scared. Scared of the past I couldn't remember, scared of where the future might lead.

Scared of the fury that lay waiting deep inside me.

I rubbed my arms. In the mirror, Egan's ring gleamed, the rubies afire with life as my hands moved up and down. A shiver ran down my spine. I didn't like this ring, didn't like its touch against my skin. It never seemed to warm up, as if its metal soul was as cold and as unforgiving as the waters underneath the Arctic ice.

I frowned at the thought, pushing it away as I headed into the main bedroom. A quick search through the woman's clothes revealed an inclination toward skimpy and revealing. She was also several inches shorter than I was, and the skirts that would have been miniscule on her were positively indecent on me.

I eventually found a pair of black track pants that fit me more like three-quarter-length shorts, and a blue sweatshirt that showed off plenty of midriff, and I left my thieving at that. Anything else, she might miss.

I padded down the hall to the kitchen, which turned out to be a kitchen and living area combined. After peering through a curtained window to see if I was still safe and alone, I flicked on the TV, changing the channel until I found the news, then walked across to the fridge. Opening the door revealed a nice selection of drinks, including Coke with lime. Very cool. I grabbed a bottle of that, as well as enough stuff to make a hefty sandwich, then dumped it all on the kitchen counter and began putting it together. I might be able to live for several weeks without food, but I'd grown used to eating every day . . .

The thought trailed off into nothingness, and I swore softly. With a little more force than necessary, I thumped the top slice of bread onto the sandwich, then squashed it down and cut it. After finding a plate, I grabbed my Coke and walked across to a chair to watch the news. Hell, maybe I'd get lucky and find out what part of the damn country I was in.

"And in scientific news this week," the newsreader said, his tone one of false charm that newsreaders the world over seemed trained to use, "scientists in Scotland today are claiming to have found several genes that can accelerate human healing, and perhaps even extend human life beyond what is currently considered the norm. Professor James Marsten, of the Loch Ness Research Foundation, had this to say—"

The picture flicked to a craggy-faced, gray-haired man, and something within me stirred. It was something more than recognition. Something stronger.

Hate.

The type of hate built on a foundation of fear. Years and years of fear.

"While our findings are still in their infancy," he said, "we do believe it will lead to major changes in the way we deal with human health. Indeed, current investigations lead us to believe that the regenerative capabilities of these genes could eventually give humans much longer life spans."

The newsreader came back but I didn't hear anything he said because I was too busy staring at the picture of the scientist frozen on the screen behind him. Fury rose, until my hand was shaking so hard I had to put the bottle of Coke down. *He* was the cause of this all. And I wished he were dead so badly I could practically taste it.

The sheer depth of what I was feeling was scary, but at least it gave me some sort of starting point. You had to know someone pretty well to hate *and* fear them this badly, and that meant Marsten was someone I had better find out more about.

Other news reports came on, and the anger began to fade. I munched on my sandwich, watching but not learning anything more than the fact that I was definitely in America.

I sighed and took a final swig of Coke to empty the bottle. Watching the news for information had been a long shot, at best, but at least it *had* given me someplace to start. Though how I was going to find more information about Marsten without him finding me again . . .

The thought faded. Frustration swirled through me as I picked up my plate and headed back to the kitchen.

Outside, a door slammed, and my heart just about crashed through my chest. I dumped the plate and Coke bottle in the sink, then ran to the nearest window and peered out.

The newlyweds were home.

And a cop had come back with them.